Beyond the Darkness

Avra Blake

ISBN: 979-8-9919774-2-5 (paperback)
ISBN: 979-8-9919774-1-8 (hardback)

Cover design by GetCovers
Illustrations and cover art by Yang: @yanghinataboke

For anyone who feels they're not enough.

Part One

Moonlit Shadows

Moonlight pours around me as
Shadows hold my limbs and
I search.
What beyond the darkness waits?
Light or night or choices I must make?

Slowly slipping through the shadows,
Mist and whispers brush my skin.
Solid milky white and thick it
Swirls and dances, blocking
Sight of night and light alike.

Heavy. Weary. Searching endless.
Hopeless struggle through this
Sea of white and gloom.
Falling, I surrender.
Slowly sinking into silver-white caresses of
Endless empty loss and loneliness.

The sun is gone and won't return.
The night is long and dark, but holds
Me close as gentle breezes pull
Me from the mist and starlight soothes
my dreams.

Chapter One

Thea hated Market Day.

Her hair stuck to her face, hot and sweaty, as she tugged the deep folds of her dark hood further over her face. Her skin itched with the heat and the urge to run as every muscle in her body coiled tight, ready to spring at the first sign of danger. Every face seemed to hold hidden motives—from the lively faces of the merchants, to those of the men and women who eagerly swarmed from stall to stall, making purchases. How many soldiers, Syndicate members, or bounty hunters were there lurking in the crowd?

She tried to push the anxiety from her mind. She hated Market Day, but coming here was something she had to do. She and Kai needed the supplies, and her brother's knee injury hadn't healed enough for him to make the trip. She wouldn't want him to, even if he could. It was too dangerous.

So even though it scared her to be around so many strangers, she told herself she would be fine. She could outrun just about anyone if she had to.

She took a deep breath and scanned the crowd, forcing herself to see the woman buying vegetables as just that, and the man exiting the clinic as just an ordinary man.

Still, the itching in her legs and the twisting in her stomach wouldn't go away as her eyes slid across the square toward the fuel merchant. The line was long, as usual. Few villages in the Wilds were connected to the power grid, so recharged fuel cells were something almost everyone needed. The only way to get them was from the merchant who traveled to Karza from the capital each Market Day.

Thea's shoulders ached and her stomach rumbled as the smell of spices and grilled meat drifted from a nearby food stall. She sighed. She couldn't afford to waste money on street food, but she could afford a few minutes to sit down and rest until the lines thinned down. The trip home would be long and tiring. Resting when she could was the smart thing to do.

Her gaze wandered toward the tavern. A woman in a crisp uniform stood at the top of the steps. Even though soldiers were a common sight on Market Day, Thea's breath still caught at the sight of her. She was probably only here to meet an acquaintance, perhaps the dark-haired man she was currently speaking with.

Still, her presence was a reminder to Thea that she didn't have time to rest. She needed to exchange her fuel cells as quickly as possible and get out of town.

Thea wound her way through the crowd toward the fuel merchant, staying as far from the tavern as possible. She kept her eyes on the soldier. The man she'd been talking with entered the tavern, but she remained on the steps, looking out over the crowd, like she was searching for someone.

She could be looking for me.

Thea felt her channeling jump inside her at the thought. She took a deep breath and tried to force herself to stay calm. Letting herself lose control would only draw attention to herself. She couldn't let her fears get the best of her. Even if the woman was looking for her, she wouldn't be easy to find. There were so many people, even Kai would have a hard time pinpointing her energy. She didn't have to worry. They wouldn't be able to find her. They wouldn't be able to take her back.

The line in front of her crawled forward until at last Thea reached the front. She exchanged her empty fuel cells and secured the new ones in her pack. As she moved through the crowd away from the merchant, she glanced back toward the tavern again. The woman was gone, but several other soldiers had taken her place. One of them pointed toward the fuel merchant and then in her direction.

They knew she was there.

Even in the crowded square, under the burning sun, she could easily remember the chill of the research labs. The bitter taste of medicine rose in her throat and her channeling scratched at her insides, trying to tear free. She wrapped her arms around herself as though she could forcibly keep the energy inside. She ran, pushing her way blindly through the crowd, not seeing the offended looks of those around her as she bumped and jostled her way past them.

At last, she broke free from the press of the crowd and turned into a dark alley. She threw a final look over her shoulder but couldn't tell if the soldiers were following her. There were too many people between her and them.

It didn't matter. She could run now, escape. She didn't have to go back.

Thea heard the cry of surprise before she felt the jolt as she crashed into something solid. She lost her balance and fell backward to a seated position on the ground. The impact knocked back her hood, leaving her pale hair clinging to her face from the combination of static and sweat. She looked up to see who she'd bumped into.

A large man smiled down at her and stretched out a hand to help her up.

"Hey, sorry about that. You alright . . .?"

Thea's own apology caught in her throat, and she froze as the man's question trailed off unsubtly. She could tell by his expression. He recognized her.

Fresh panic froze her in place.

The man wasn't wearing a uniform, but the handgun fitted into a well-supplied belt at his hip told her he was no ordinary villager.

"I'm alright," she mumbled as she slid her heavy pack from her shoulders. It wouldn't be easy to escape while wearing it, but it could be a useful tool to help her create an opening. She focused her channeling into her arms and legs, the muscles bulging with a dull ache as they expanded.

She struggled to her feet without taking the man's hand, then took a step back before reaching down for her pack. Using her enhanced strength, she flung the pack toward him. She didn't wait to see if it hit. Instead, she sprang upward explosively, using the energy she channeled into her leg muscles to increase her jump enough to reach the rooftop above.

Instead of soaring upward she felt a painful jerk on her arm before landing hard on the ground. Her head rang as it smacked against the paving stones beneath her, making her vision blur with pain and tears. She blinked, trying to focus on the second figure looming over her.

The second man's black hair and clothes almost seemed to blend into the surrounding shadows, making him difficult to see. He took a step back, like he was hesitating. Thea took advantage of that hesitation and quickly channeled as much energy as she could into her limbs before pushing herself up and away from the ground. The sudden burst of wild energy ripped through her body as she shot into the air, higher than she'd intended. Her legs nearly buckled as she landed on the roof above with a crash.

A soft groan escaped her lips, but she pushed more energy into her legs. She had to get away. She couldn't let them catch her.

She couldn't go back.

Trying to keep her breathing steady, she ignored the pain and forced herself to sprint across the flat rooftops before the men could follow her from below. After hurdling the outer wall, she finally allowed her pace to slow, but she didn't stop to catch her breath until Karza had become a smudge behind her.

Her legs wobbled and her stomach heaved with dry retches as she crumbled to her knees. Sharp pain shot through her head as she channeled her energy to enhance her vision and hearing, scanning the open landscape for any sign of pursuers. There was nothing.

Still, there was no doubt now. They knew she was here. It was only a matter of time before they found the village. She needed to get home to Kai.

She only let herself rest for a few minutes before enhancing her legs again. Her muscles burned in protest as she stood and forced herself forward. Keeping her senses alert, she pushed herself into a brisk walk. She had to force herself not to run. It was still a long way home and there was no telling what danger awaited her. She needed to save as much energy and strength as she could.

The small village was quiet as Thea made her way through the dusty streets toward the house she shared with her brother. The stillness only made her more tense. What if something had happened to Kai? What if the soldiers had come? What if they were waiting for her?

She let out a sigh of relief as her house came into view. Kai stood outside, leaning on his cane with a worried expression on his face. She quickened her pace when she saw him, ignoring the sharp pain that accompanied each step.

"Thea!" he called out as he hobbled forward to meet her. He reached one arm behind her back, trying to support her. "Are you okay?"

"I'm okay," she insisted, trying to step out of his reach. She didn't want him to aggravate his injury while trying to support her. She wobbled, and Kai grabbed her arm to steady her anyway.

"What happened?" he asked as he led her toward the front door.

"There were bounty hunters in town," she said with an anxious glance over her shoulder, like she expected an assailant to spring up behind her. "They attacked me, but I got away."

Kai released her arm as they entered the tiny house. He prodded her gently toward the couch, but remained in the doorway, looking outside, his gaze unfocused.

"Were you followed?" he asked.

"I don't think so."

Kai frowned. Thea didn't sit. Instead, she waited, holding her breath and looking up at Kai as the square line of his jaw tensed. At last, he shook his head and turned back to her with a reassuring smile.

"I don't sense anyone," he said.

Thea sank down to the couch with a relieved sigh.

"Where's your pack?" he asked, looking back outside in confusion.

"I left it," she admitted as she covered her face with her hands. "I'm sorry."

"We really needed those supplies," he said. His voice sounded tired.

Thea hunched her shoulders as she peeked through her fingers to see him pinch the bridge of his nose. She covered her face again and let her pale hair curtain around her face, as though hiding her embarrassment could somehow make up for her mistake.

She heard Kai's shuffling gait, but didn't look up. He sat down on the low table in front of her and pulled one hand away from her face with another sigh.

"Hey, I'm sorry. I'm not upset."

His voice was soft and soothing, which only made her feel worse. Once again, he was burying his own worries to prioritize hers. She had to stop making him do that.

"The only thing that matters to me is that you're safe," he continued. "I mean it."

"We can't afford to buy new fuel cells," Thea murmured as her hands dropped to her lap, fingers fidgeting together. Her voice wobbled as she tried to keep the lump in her throat from turning to a sob. "The money Dad gave us is almost gone. I should have been more careful. I shouldn't have left the pack. I was just so scared."

Once the tears started, she couldn't stop them. Her pent-up anxiety spilled out like a breaking dam. No matter how much she wanted to bury her emotions, to help Kai focus on solving their predicament, all she could feel was that twisting worry in her stomach as she remembered her encounter in town.

"You're safe, and that's what matters," Kai said as he placed one hand on her shoulder. "We'll figure the rest out."

When she didn't respond, Kai began to rub soothing circles into her shoulder.

"It'll be okay. I promise. We're together and you're safe. It's going to be okay."

She gave a small nod and finally met his eyes.

"Good," he said with a warm smile. "Now tell me what happened in town."

Before she could speak, a hiss followed by a burning smell drew their attention.

"Oh no! My stew!"

Kai jumped up, groaned, and sat back down, his hand over his knee.

"Stupid thing," he mumbled before standing more carefully.

"Maybe I should—" Thea started to say, but Kai waved her off.

"You rest," he said. "I could tell before you even got home that you used too much energy today. Your legs are hurting, I bet. I'll want to put something on them later."

Thea wiped her eyes and leaned back into the couch.

"What did you make?" she asked, too tired to argue with him.

"Mom's stew."

Thea tried to smile, but the expression felt more like a grimace.

For as long as she could remember, their mom had been too weak to cook. Their father was better at cooking anyway, but the vegetable stew she'd often made when Kai was younger was his favorite meal. Their dad had tried to replicate the dish, but Kai always insisted that it wasn't the same.

Mom's stew was something Thea had never tasted. Now that their mom was gone, she would never get the chance.

"I hope you didn't add anything weird to it this time," she said, trying to hide the emotion in her voice with a forced chuckle.

Kai's own laugh mingled with the scrape of ceramic and the clang of utensils as he scooped a lumpy, gray-brown paste into two bowls.

When Thea saw it, she added, "I don't think that's stew."

"Just for that, I'm giving you an extra scoop," Kai retorted with a dramatic flourish of his ladle.

"Wait! I'm sorry! I meant to say it looks delicious and I can't wait to eat it."

Thea had spent more time learning to cook from their father than Kai had. She enjoyed the process, and the time spent with him. Kai had always been more interested in meeting new people or listening to stories from travelers at the inn where their father worked. He'd only started cooking by necessity after the two of them went into hiding. Even though Thea had tried to teach him some basics, his cooking hadn't improved much. He never measured anything, and always added the ingredients all at once, regardless of how long they would each take to cook. The only aspect of cooking he did seem to enjoy was adding different medicinal herbs to their food, a practice that was rarely a benefit to the food's flavor.

"Too bad," he sighed as he sat down next to her, a bowl in each hand. "If I hadn't burned it, this one might not have been half bad."

Thea eyed the food warily, though she knew she would eat all of it regardless of how unappetizing it looked or smelled. This was what they had, and she couldn't afford to waste it.

"You're right," she said, as she took the first bite. "If it weren't for the texture, the smell, or the burnt aftertaste, I would say this was actually pretty good. Probably the best you've ever made."

Kai tapped his bowl against hers with a grin.

"Well, thank you. I'll just ignore the fact that you were actually insulting my cooking, because the secret ingredient is love."

She snorted and choked on the food in her mouth. Kai set his own bowl down and stood to get her a drink of water. After taking a drink and wiping her eyes, she saw him still standing, staring at nothing with a serious expression.

"Kai?"

He shook his head and smiled, but didn't look at her as he sat down, like he was distracted.

"Do you sense something?" she asked, her good mood immediately turning to worry.

He shook his head again and turned his attention back to her.

"Why don't you tell me what happened in town? Sorry, dinner kind of distracted me."

Thea swallowed and set her food aside, her anxiety returning.

"There were soldiers in Karza," she said.

"That's not unusual."

She nodded. "At first I thought the same thing, and just tried to get my shopping done without drawing attention to myself. I think they sensed me though. They pointed in my direction and started moving toward me."

Kai frowned. "You said they attacked you?"

"No, I don't think the ones who attacked me were soldiers, but I could tell they recognized me. I think they might have been bounty hunters."

She scrunched her face as she tried to remember details. It had happened so fast, and she'd been so panicked.

The man she'd run into wasn't just big, he was muscular and intimidating. The second man had seemed short by comparison, but she hadn't been able to get a good look at him.

"One of them was definitely a Macro," she said, remembering how the second man had seemed to come out of nowhere. "He was really fast. Before I'd even realized he was there, he'd grabbed me."

Her tone turned to grumbling as she described him. She wasn't used to losing when it came to speed, and she didn't like it.

"The other man didn't do much," she continued, "so I don't know. He had a gun, though."

Kai interlaced his fingers under his chin, his expression serious.

"It's strange that the soldiers would act just from sensing your energy," he said. "It's not like you were the only Macro in Karza, or even the only Manipulator. That's worrying. It's like they expected you to be there."

If Kai was worried too, that meant her fears were justified.

"We can't stay here, can we?"

Tears burned her eyes, and the words came out in a choked whisper.

Kai wrapped one arm around her shoulder.

"I don't know," he said, his voice cracking with the same hopelessness she felt. "Right now, you should just rest. Focus on recovering your energy. I promise I won't let anything happen to you."

He squeezed her against him as though his tight hold alone were enough to keep her safe, but the firm weight of his arm around her wasn't enough to stop her trembling or the fresh tears that slipped down her cheeks.

What could she and Kai do on their own against the whole Military?

What would happen to Kai if he tried to protect her?

Running had only brought them more danger.

Hiding hadn't worked.

So long as the Military wanted her, she couldn't see how things could ever be okay.

Weapon
Fighter
Killer

All they ever see in me
All I can ever be
I can't break free
From this longing, this need
So I let them use me

Failure
Danger
Monster

All they ever see in me
All I can ever be
I can't break free
From this regret, this pain
So I let it gnaw away inside me

Outcast
Traitor
Villain

All they ever see in me
All I can ever be
I can't break free
From this darkness, this history
So I let it define me

Chapter Two

"The rumors are true. He's a monster."

Nix looked up toward the roof as he wiped a smear of blood from his cheek with the back of his hand. He wasn't worried about the gun pointed at him. He'd dodged plenty of shots from someone with far better aim than the trembling man pointing his barrel at him now.

The man fired and missed. He was already running before the bullet hit the opposite building. He scrambled down the pile of rubble on the other side of the roof and disappeared into the streets beyond.

Nix let him go. Unlike his partners, who had bounties of their own, he wasn't worth it. Maybe his story would discourage anyone stupid enough to come after Nix for his bounty in the future. He would take any reprieve he could get, even if it didn't last long.

Nix was used to being a target. He had been his whole life. Beating up assholes was as second nature to him as breathing. It didn't matter if they were Military, Syndicate, or just random idiots who didn't know better. These weren't the first bounty hunters to come after him, and they wouldn't be the last.

Nix sighed and rubbed his forehead as he glanced longingly toward the nearby outer wall. It would be so much easier to slip away and return to base than make his way to the crowded town center.

I hate Market Day.

He let out a quiet chuckle in spite of the discomfort that accompanied the unusually distinct thought. Unlike the other thoughts in town, these refused to meld into the rumble of noise that he could almost ignore. They were so clear he could feel the person's anxiety as though it were his own.

It made his head throb even more than normal.

I hate Market Day, the thoughts continued, but it's something I have to do. I may as well get it over with.

Nix rubbed his head again and let out a resigned sigh. He supposed he should follow the same logic. He'd much rather leave town now, and head back to the base, but he wasn't particularly in the mood for a lecture from

Gram. Besides, the tavern had good sandwiches, and he was hungry. He might as well get this over with.

A crowd of people bustled from stall to stall in the town's central square. Their chatter mingled with their thoughts, creating a cacophony of noise that Nix couldn't shut out, but that one stream of internal narrative continued to rise above the noise.

I don't stand out. No one will notice me. No one is looking for me. All these people are just ordinary people, too. I just have to get fuel and then I can leave. I just have to stay calm.

Distracted, Nix bumped into someone as he passed by, causing them to drop one of their packages.

"Sorry," he mumbled with a frown, his voice harsher and more impatient than he intended. He reached to pick up the package, but the other person's eyes widened, and they scrambled to retrieve it themself before hurrying away. Nix caught only fragments of their thoughts.

Scary. Dangerous.

He sighed and rubbed his cheek, wondering if there was still blood smeared on his face, or maybe the person had simply been frightened by his expression and his dark clothes.

As he turned back toward the tavern, he caught sight of Mel standing on the steps that led up to the entrance. She scanned the crowd with a serious expression, but her eyes lit up when they landed on him. She bounced down the stairs toward him, her buoyant enthusiasm clashing with the stiff neatness of her uniform.

"There you are!" she called. "Where have you been?"

Nix just shrugged in response.

"Gram and the Commander are already inside," Mel informed him with a wink. "Gram said you'd probably try to sneak off and hide somewhere, but he also ordered that sandwich you like, so I think he knew you'd come."

"He knows damn well my telepathy range is limited on Market Day," Nix grumbled. "If he wants me to get any information from the soldiers, of course I'd have to come."

A lot of good it was going to do with those thoughts drowning out nearly everything else. Even standing next to her, Nix couldn't pick up a damn thing from Mel, only murky impressions. The only thing he was sure of was that Mel hadn't been scanning the crowd for him.

She let out a laugh but stopped as Nix hissed and rubbed his forehead.

"Hey, are you okay? What's wrong?" Mel laid a hand on his arm, her face full of concern.

Those thoughts spiked even louder as their owner spotted Mel near the tavern. Whoever it was, did not want the Military to find them. He raised his channeling slightly, the way he did when he tried to focus his telepathy. He thought maybe he could filter out the thoughts that way. Instead, the pressure in his head only increased, making his ears ring.

"I'm fine," he said as he turned away and moved toward the tavern door. The sooner he got this over with, the sooner he could leave.

"Hey there handsome, good to see you again." Kay, the tavern's owner, stepped closer to him—too close as was their habit. "We're real crowded today but for you I always have room."

Nix shot them a glare and stepped away uncomfortably, bumping into a server crossing behind him.

"Gram's already here," he growled.

Kay grinned, confirming that they had been teasing him as usual.

"The upper floor is full of soldiers," Kay said. "If you start a fight and break stuff, don't think I'll let you off easy just 'cause I like you."

"I'm pretty sure they're more likely to start a fight than I am."

Kay laughed as a server handed them a large tray of drinks. Before moving away they said, "Gram ordered that sandwich you like. I just took it up. Better hurry before it gets cold."

Nix and Gram always sat on the upper floor where it was usually less crowded, and they could watch the room below for signs of trouble. As Kay had said, nearly every table, on the upper floor was full. Most of the occupants were soldiers, glaring at him as he passed.

Gram sat at their usual table near the railing. Nix couldn't pinpoint his thoughts, but he didn't need to. The teasing grin on Gram's face was one he was all too familiar with.

Looks like those punks gave you a hard time, he was sure Gram was thinking.

A slightly older man in a crisp Military suit sat at the table with Gram. Commander Astley of the Military Police. Though the Military had little actual authority in the Wilds, the Commander's responsibilities also extended to overseeing peacekeeping efforts there. A bounty system was used to keep criminals in the Wilds in check, making peacekeepers like Gram little more than government sanctioned bounty hunters, though the Military didn't like to admit it.

Besides being Gram's superior officer, he had also once been Gram's mentor and close friend.

He'd also been one of the officers most vocally in favor of Nix's execution.

He jumped to his feet as Nix approached, his usually calm face red with fury.

"What's he doing here?"

Nix fished two black cards from his pocket and threw them on the table before sitting down in front of his waiting sandwich.

"You'll find them by the east wall," he said gesturing to the bounty cards. "There was a third man with them. He didn't have a bounty, so I let him go."

The Commander glared at him, making no move to pick up the cards. The nearest soldiers fidgeted in anticipation, but Nix ignored them. He knew the Commander wouldn't actually start a fight that could risk hurting the civilian patrons of the tavern. Whatever else, he was a man with a moral code.

As he expected, the Commander smoothed the graying sides of his already neat hair before running his hands down the front of his dark jacket. He sat down with a disgruntled huff before picking up the cards and handing them to a wiry looking soldier at the nearest table.

"Barton, take some men to go check it out." Turning back to Gram he said, "Don't you think you're being too careless, openly associating with this criminal. I can't protect you if someone like Ethan Zane decides to arrest you both."

Gram let out a long, loud laugh, earning surprised and annoyed looks from the soldiers and patrons at other tables.

"You know, I'd actually love for Zane to try. I owe him some cracked ribs after all."

The Commander frowned.

"I'm serious Gram. Andrea Stewart isn't someone to take lightly, and Zane is serving under her new command. Even without a grudge against you both, you know he would jump at the chance to boost his career."

"Don't they have more important things to worry about than old grudges?" Gram argued. "Nix isn't with the Syndicate anymore. Why can't they just let it go?"

The Commander shot Nix a look of disgust.

"You know Commander Stewart was opposed to allowing you to become a peacekeeper in the first place, Gram," the Commander said with a shake of his head. "Now she has enough authority to cause problems. I'd rather you stop giving her more reasons to have you tried for treason."

"Nice to see the Military hasn't changed at all," Gram grumbled with an eye roll. "Still wasting time arguing about the things that don't matter."

"And you haven't changed either," the Commander snapped. "I've already done everything I can for you. I can't keep protecting you if you insist on keeping him around."

Gram set his drink down on the table with a loud clang before running one large hand through his brown hair.

"That's not really why you're here, though, is it?" Gram asked, changing the subject with an accusatory glare. "Iris's kids. You're still looking for them."

The Commander looked away, his face turning pale.

"You know I don't like it either, Gram. The last thing I want is for Research to make more monsters like him. If I'd had my way, we would have gotten rid of him and been done with all of this."

"You know that wouldn't stop them. Now that they know telepathy exists, they won't stop until they can create the ability themselves," Gram said coldly. "The last thing they care about is who gets hurt in the process. But this is about more than just Research, Nolan. I don't understand how you can keep doing this. You know that boy is your—"

"He's not," Nolan cut him off, then sighed. He seemed to shrink in his chair as he continued. "Iris made that clear."

"I know you don't really believe that," Gram countered. "Either way, it doesn't change the fact that this is wrong, and you know it."

The Commander shook his head.

"What do you want me to do, Gram? Throw away my career like you? What good will that do? Besides, there's no question, that girl is unstable. She could hurt someone. Reports suggest that she already has. Do you really think it's better to leave her out there on her own? If we find her, bring her in, maybe we can get her the help that she needs."

"And then what?" Gram's voice rose angrily, "Are you going to push for her execution too, like you did with Nix? Or turn her over to the researchers until she's so sick she dies anyway?"

"We've been through this before, Gram," the Commander said. "This has nothing to do with Iris or Alyssa. You know it's not my decision to make. I'm just following orders."

Even with the other thoughts pounding in his head, Gram's flash of pain was strong and unmistakable. The Commander had gone too far. Nix pushed his plate away angrily and balled his other hand into a fist. Chairs squeaked as the Micros sensed his energy rise and jumped to their feet.

Gram shook his head slightly toward Nix before leaning back into his chair in a sulk, his arms crossed over his chest.

Nix exhaled and relaxed his hand. The Commander stood and waved off the soldiers without looking at Nix.

"Like I told you before, we haven't seen them," Gram snapped.

"I know you don't like it Gram, but it'll be better if we find them before Commander Stewart or some bounty hunter." The Commander almost sounded regretful, whether for upsetting Gram or because he didn't like the assignment he was given, Nix wasn't sure. "If you really want to help them, this is the best way to do it."

Gram snorted and the Commander sighed again.

"Think about my offer. The Military needs you. I need you."

Gram glanced up with a frown.

"Do those idiots in charge really want to start another war?" he asked.

"The war never ended, Gram. You're naive if you think otherwise."

Nix didn't like the Commander any more than the Commander liked him, but he was right about this at least. The two sides had reached a stalemate long before any of them were even alive, but the fighting had never stopped entirely. Each side would do just about anything to undermine the other; and if the right opportunity presented itself, neither would stop short of ripping the territories to shreds if it meant claiming a decisive victory.

"We'll be returning to the city in a few days. Let me know your answer."

The Commander threw another disgusted look toward Nix before turning on his heel and marching off. Most of the soldiers rose from their seats at nearby tables to follow after him.

"What did he want?" Nix asked.

"He wants me to come back," Gram said with a sigh. "He's being put in charge of an operation to root out Syndicate presence in the Eastern Territory."

Nix scowled and Gram broke into a grin.

"Don't worry, just because he wants me to go back, doesn't mean I plan to accept."

"Why not?" Nix asked, looking away with a snort. "It's not like you left the Military by choice. If you have the chance to go back, why not take it?"

Gram let out a sigh. "You really are a dumbass, you know that?"

With that Gram was back to sulking. Nix ignored him. It wasn't difficult with the pounding in his head and all the thoughts forcibly taking his attention. He dropped his head into his hands with a sigh and squeezed his eyes shut as he rubbed his temples with his fingers.

"Guess those punks gave you a tough time," Gram teased.

Nix snorted. "Don't be ridiculous. They were nothing. My headache is just worse than usual today."

"You get anything from Nolan?" Gram asked tentatively, a note of worry in his tone.

Nix shook his head.

Gram stayed silent. Nix didn't look up, not wanting to see the surprise or worry on his face. Market Day made it harder for him to read specific thoughts, but usually he was still able to get something.

"Maybe you should head back to base," Gram said softly.

"I'm fine," Nix snapped. He wanted to return to base, of course, but he didn't like when Gram treated him like a kid. He didn't need someone to take care of him or tell him what to do.

Gram stood with a sigh and Nix followed him down the steps and out of the tavern, glares and whispers following them as they went.

Nix squinted and sucked in his breath as he stepped out into the bright sunlight. He held up his hand to shield his eyes as he scanned the crowd with a frown. They were out there in the square somewhere, the owner of those thoughts.

"Let's get out of the sun," Gram said, wiping his forehead as he walked toward the shade of a nearby alley. In spite of the heat, Nix hesitated before following him into the dark, narrow space. He ignored the prickling of his skin and took a deep breath as he leaned against the cool stone wall.

"You're staying in town?" he asked.

"Well, one of us has to do some work," Gram shot him a mischievous look. Nix just rolled his eyes.

"Normally I'd stay in town until the merchants leave either way, but I want to talk to Mel again and do some asking around, see if I can get any information on those kids."

Nix shook his head as Gram pulled a bounty card from his pocket and tapped it, bringing up the projection of two faces—a boy and a girl in their late teens who were obviously related. The pictures were several years old, but sufficient to help bounty hunters recognize the siblings. The girl had round brown eyes, a square face, and light blond hair to her shoulders. Her bounty information stated that she was nineteen, an escapee from the Northwarden Research Facility, a Macro and a Manipulator. Her brother, a twenty-four-year-old Micro, had similar features, though his hair was so light it was almost white. As much as he looked like his sister, his resemblance to the Commander, was also obvious. They had the same gray eyes and the same sharp nose.

Nix had recognized her the first time Gram had shown him the bounty information. It hadn't been his intention to rescue anyone when he'd broken into the Northwarden facility. He'd only wanted to steal the research data. Of course, deactivating the security at the facility meant most of the test subjects were able to break out without further aid from him.

Except her. He'd found that girl unconscious in the hallway and carried her out.

He'd had no idea at the time she would end up being someone Gram would try so hard to find.

"Do you really think they'd come to Karza?" Nix asked, looking away from the image. "If they want to avoid the Military, wouldn't they go West?"

Gram shook his head and put the card back in his pocket. "Sounds like they tried that. Rumor is they caused some trouble in Senari."

"Where'd you hear that?"

Nix did his best to keep track of Syndicate activity, but he hadn't heard or read anything about trouble in Senari outside of the usual clan squabbles.

Gram didn't answer. He seemed to be concentrating, trying to pick out the Macros in the square. He let out a groan and shook his head.

"You have too much damn energy, you know that?" he grumbled as he ran a hand through his hair. "I can hardly pick up anything else."

"Or maybe you just suck at sensing," Nix said with a smirk.

"Well, it definitely doesn't help that you're here. And neither does that scary face of yours," Gram taunted. "I can't get any work done if you keep starting fights I have to pretend to ignore."

Gram chuckled at his own joke, but Nix ignored him.

"There's definitely someone out there who doesn't want to be found," he said, steering the conversation back to the siblings. "They're afraid. Doesn't mean it's her. Plenty of people want to avoid the Military."

"They're in the square now?"

They know I'm here.

Nix couldn't answer. His breath stuck in his lungs as the alley seemed to disappear around him, replaced with the memory of the research lab. His stomach churned with a sudden wave of nausea. The panic felt so real, so immediate, like the bodies in the square were actually pressing around him, trapping him, keeping him from running.

The thoughts entered the alley, and he nearly lost his own balance from the sudden jolt of surprise as someone crashed into Gram. The choking fear cleared somewhat, but the thoughts remained just as loud. He looked down at their source, a woman who'd fallen to the ground in front of them.

The dark hood of her jacket had been knocked back, and her pale hair clung to her face. Her small frame and fear-filled eyes made her look younger than she actually was, but she still looked older than the picture Gram had been looking at only moments before.

It was her. The girl the soldiers were looking for.

Gram's expression made it obvious that he recognized her too. He did a poor job of not showing it as he held out a hand to help her up.

He knows who I am.

She didn't miss Gram's size or the gun hanging at his side. The word bounty hunter flashed through her thoughts along with a fresh wave of panic.

I can't go back.

She didn't take Gram's hand, but repositioned herself as though she was going to stand up on her own. She quickly made a plan to throw her heavy pack at him, hoping to knock him off balance so she could escape. She still hadn't noticed Nix standing in the shadows deeper in the alley.

Nix moved at the same time she did, rushing toward her with a burst of speed. If she fled to the rooftop, she'd only make it easier for the soldiers to find her.

She was fast and he almost missed her, but he was faster. He grabbed her by the arm as she took off from the ground. She fell hard, the air knocked from her lungs. His own head rang with the impact and he staggered back. His vision blurred and it was all he could do to stay on his feet. She didn't miss his moment of hesitation. Without waiting for her own dizziness to pass, she pushed herself off the ground explosively. Pain ripped through her body, and he thought he might pass out.

He shook his head, swore, and jumped after her.

"Wait dumbass!" Gram shouted after him.

Nix didn't wait. She was moving fast. If he didn't go now, he would lose her.

Following the girl was easy. Her thoughts invaded his. He could feel her weariness and the dull pain building in her head as she forced herself to take each step.

She reached a small village southwest of Karza and Nix positioned himself on a small hill outside of the town to wait and observe. He knew where the siblings were now, so he could easily leave and report back to Gram, but he couldn't be sure that no one had followed them. Gram was probably pissed enough that Nix had run off on his own. If he had led the Military right to the girl and then left her undefended, Gram would only be more upset.

The village, like most in the Wilds, bore heavy scars from the war. The outer wall was little more than a pile of rubble, only standing intact in intermittent patches. The most livable houses had cracked walls and missing windowpanes.

The girl met her brother outside of one such house, with a crooked door sitting askew in a cracked frame. In spite of the derelict condition of the house, the surrounding yard was kept neat. Welcoming patches of green sprouted from a variety of boxes and pots, forming a colorful walkway.

The brother was waiting for her outside the house and the girl's worry for herself quickly turned to worry for him as he hobbled toward her, leaning heavily on a cane. He'd injured his knee, it seemed, in a way that hadn't healed even after some time. She stepped away as he tried to steady her, which only made her wobble on her aching legs.

The man was tall, much taller than her, and she had to crane her neck to look up at him as she explained, inaccurately, what had happened in town. Nix let out a snort as she called him and Gram bounty hunters. She hadn't even considered the possibility that their encounter had been pure coincidence, or that they had done nothing to lead her to assume they were after her.

Nix stiffened as the girl waited with bated breath for her brother to sense their surroundings for anyone suspicious. It didn't take a lot of talent for Micros to sense his large channeling pool. There was no way the brother would miss him.

To his surprise, relief flooded her thoughts as her brother shook his head.

He hadn't sensed anyone.

Nix tried to focus his telepathy on the man, but the girl's thoughts only grew louder with the attempt, crashing through his head like a mallet.

He pulled back and rubbed his head, confused and frustrated.

Why were her thoughts so loud, and why hadn't her brother been able to sense him? Was there something wrong with his abilities?

There was no way for him to know what was going on. Maybe he could ask Lucan later, but at the moment all he could do was observe. He slumped to the ground against a small scrub tree as the girl admitted to leaving her pack behind. Another careless decision. Surviving in the Wilds without adequate resources was only something one could do if they were willing to take what they needed from others. He doubted that was something these siblings were willing to do.

The girl's thoughts turned to her parents as the brother served her a bowl of sludgy looking stew. Nix recognized the sad ache mixed with warm nostalgia—a longing for a time that would never come again. Nix had felt similar thoughts from Gram whenever he thought back on the past.

Nix had never understood it. Remembering the past only made him want to forget.

Thoughts of any imminent danger seemed to be forgotten as the siblings ate their meal. They laughed and made jokes about the brother's cooking and the girl settled into a comfortable contentment. Her brother's presence had a calming influence on her. Maybe it was his easy and relaxed demeanor, or maybe she simply trusted his abilities enough to believe no one had followed her.

After they'd finished their meal, the brother became quiet and distant, something that must have been unusual for him as his behavior triggered the girl's anxiety again. Nix tensed along with her as she wondered if he did sense someone after all. Once again, he simply shook his head.

After that, the girl recounted the events in town. Nix huffed at the sense of wounded pride she felt that he'd managed to match her speed when no one else had before. He was the one who should feel disgraced. She was fast, but nowhere near as fast as him. There was no reason she should have gotten away from him in the first place. He should have been able to stop her.

It seemed likely the siblings would decide to leave their village in order to avoid being discovered by the Military, who now knew for certain they were in the area. Where would they go? Neither one seemed capable of traveling far. The girl was exhausted and hurting after her trip home. The brother's old injury seemed to limit his ability to travel.

Nix wanted to return to base, but he was still wary about leaving them undefended. He decided to wait out the night. If the soldiers hadn't made a move by morning, they were unlikely to do so before he or Gram could return.

He reached into his jacket and pulled out an old radio and screwdriver, something he'd shoved into his pocket that morning so he could keep his hands busy while waiting in town. He loosened the screws and pulled off the back of the radio, trying to distract himself from the girl's thoughts pouring through his head.

A shadow, a wraith, a ghost
Reality a blur as dark descends
A cage of loneliness and endless wanting
Solitude's embrace the only touch I feel

Injection of rejection
Their animosity becoming my addiction
A burning need, an aching hole
I crave their hate while longing for redemption

Chapter Three

Nix woke feeling the disorientation of having fallen asleep unintentionally in an unfamiliar place. Why was he outside? Why did it feel like he was still dreaming? Why did his head hurt so much?

His breath caught as he realized the dream filling his thoughts wasn't his, but the girl's. The familiarity of it was chilling, so similar to the dream he'd only just woken from, a swirl of memories he'd rather keep buried.

Maybe the experiments done to her had been successful in creating some kind of pseudo-telepathy? It was the only explanation that made sense to him. Maybe that was the reason her thoughts were so clear. Maybe she was transmitting them without realizing it.

Nix took a deep breath and let it out slowly, trying to clear his head.

He needed to get back to base.

His stomach rumbled.

Maybe Gram would at least let him eat before shooting at him.

He didn't.

Gram fired from around the opening of the gate as Nix neared the walls. Nix dodged the first two shots, but the third caught him in the shoulder. Once Gram started firing multiple rapid shots, it was hard to tell where they would go. There was almost no avoiding taking at least one hit, especially with the dull ache in his head and the heavy exhaustion in his body making him feel slow and sluggish.

The bullets were blanks, of course, and therefore not dangerous, but even through the heavy fabric of his jacket, they still stung. Nix let out a frustrated grunt as Gram fired the next series of shots. His foot slipped on the loose gravel as he tried to move in close. Gram closed the short remaining distance himself and knocked Nix off his feet. Nix landed hard on the ground, the jolt sending spikes of pain through his already throbbing head. He didn't bother to get up. He was too tired and Gram was too angry. One shot usually meant he was joking. Three meant he was annoyed. More than that? He was definitely pissed off.

"You look like hell," Gram said with a frown as he stood over him.

"Being shot at and knocked on your ass will do that to a person."

"Don't tell me you don't deserve it, running off like a dumbass." Gram's face broke into its usual grin, and he reached down to help Nix up. "But I guess I'll call us even for now. Let's get some food."

Gram usually heated food as soon as he sensed Nix returning. It never saved Nix from whatever lecture Gram had on his mind, though. That day was no exception. He'd run off on his own, again, with no plan and no backup. Half the Wilds were trying to get their hands on him, not to mention the soldiers.

The usual.

Nix finished two trays of food before Gram finally leaned back in his chair with a sigh. Fortunately, Gram was pretty quick to let things go, once he'd picked a fight and had his say.

"Well, you learn anything last night?"

Nix reached for a third meal and answered Gram's question telepathically so he could continue eating.

"It's possible the telepathy experiments were at least partially successful."

"What makes you say that?"

"Her thoughts are...distinct. Maybe she's projecting them without knowing it?"

He met Gram's narrowed eyes, then shrugged uncomfortably before returning to his food.

"Is that what was going on with you yesterday?" Gram grumbled.

Nix shrugged again. *"It's nothing I can't handle."*

Gram suspected Nix wasn't telling him everything, but he didn't push it. He shook his head and rubbed his hand over his face.

"I better let Luc know. You, sleep."

"Tell me what happened after I left," Nix said, pushing his last empty food tray away. "No one followed us, but I'm sure the soldiers noticed."

"It can wait. You look like you could pass out any minute, and I'm not about to carry your sorry ass to bed."

Gram was right. He was exhausted. Lack of sleep was something he was used to. Staying awake for most of the night was normal for him. It shouldn't have been a big deal, but the intensity of the girl's thoughts, and his futile attempts to dampen them, had left him drained.

Nix made his way down the hall to the sparsely furnished bedroom that was supposed to be his. He spent little time in the main house, preferring the openness of the rear vehicle bay he used as a workshop. Today he was too tired to drag himself all the way there.

He slung his jacket over the empty chair in the corner and pulled off his boots before flopping onto the bed.

He didn't know how long he slept, but he woke gasping for air, his heart racing. Beads of sweat ran down his face and neck. His shirt clung to him, hot and sticky.

The room was hot, too hot, too stagnant.

Air.

He hadn't opened the window and he couldn't breathe.

His legs wobbled as he stumbled to the window and fumbled to open the shutters.

They wouldn't open.

His fingers scrambled frantically until finally, the latch released. Bright light filled the room as he threw the shutters back, but he hardly paused to cringe at the sudden brightness. He slid open the windowpane and sucked in several breaths of fresh air, relief filling his lungs until his breathing began to slow.

He moved away from the window and sank to the bed, his head dropping into his trembling hands. It had been his second nightmare in less than a day, and he knew the trigger. It was the girl and her suffocating thoughts. Her fear, her memories—they stirred up too many things that he'd rather forget but never could. The black nothingness, the faces that haunted him, the deaths, the labs. He rubbed his face and concentrated on keeping his breathing steady, on the light shining on the floor, on the rough calluses on his hands from a decade of sword training.

Once his breathing returned to normal, he peeled off his sweaty shirt and turned his neck stiffly from side to side. He rolled his shoulders with a sudden longing for a hot shower.

Nix had been living at the base with Gram for years now, but it still felt new to him. Even after all this time he still ate every meal like he didn't know when the next would come. He relished regular showers like a luxury. He expected it to end at any moment, for Gram to realize, like everyone else, that Nix really was just a monster.

Until then, it was nice to be able to take advantage of the comforts he wouldn't have on his own.

After showering and putting on fresh clothes, Nix made his way to the kitchen. Gram entered as he was heating up a meal.

"Didn't expect you to be up already," Gram said.

Nix shrugged. "I need to get back out there."

"I don't like the idea of you going out there alone again. Not with the Military on the move," Gram said with a sigh.

"That's exactly why I need to go. Unless you want the Military to find them."

"Yeah, and what about when they find you?" Gram countered. "I don't know what was up with you yesterday. You said the girl's thoughts are clearer than others? Seems like that was throwing you off quite a bit."

"I said I can handle it," Nix spat. "It just surprised me yesterday. That's all. Anyway, I thought you were planning to stay in town. Why did you even come back?"

"How else was I supposed to find out if you were still alive, dumbass?" He sighed and shook his head before continuing. "I talked to Mel after you ran off like an idiot. They got a tip that the girl's been seen in town on Market Day, figured she might show up again. Their Micro sensed someone besides you with a lot of energy, but when she ran into us in that alley, they lost her. Nolan thinks we had a hand in helping her escape, so they'll be searching in the direction you both went. Which means it's only a matter of time until they find her."

"So what's your plan?" Nix asked, though he already knew. "Bring them here?"

Gram frowned and gave a slight nod. "Sounds like the Military is serious. I'd rather we not leave them to fend for themselves anymore."

Nix didn't know why that confirmation bothered him. He tried to push the feeling away as he pulled his phone from his pocket and moved his empty food tray to one side so he could project a map onto the table in front of them.

"Their village is here," he pointed out the location on the map. "They talked like they were planning to leave, but I doubt they'll do anything for a day or two at least."

"Any idea where they plan to go?"

Nix shook his head.

"They didn't talk about it while I was there. I doubt they would travel back towards Karza. And they probably wouldn't go east either."

Gram nodded. "There isn't much that's habitable further south. It's hard to imagine they'd go that way. There aren't even any roads. That just leaves the west."

"Didn't you say they caused some kind of trouble in Senari?"

Gram nodded. "Mel says the Syndicate has been looking for them, too. Word is the girl got into it with some guys in Senari. Injured two of them. Seems a little far-fetched to me. What do you think?"

Nix shrugged. She was no fighter, that much was obvious from her movements and poor decision making, but he hadn't been able to stop her in the alley. He could claim he had been distracted by her thoughts, but he knew that wasn't the only reason. She was fast, and she had a lot of channeling, but she lacked control. That could be a dangerous combination.

"The Commander said she's unstable. I don't know if it's because of the experiments or just because she doesn't know how to control her abilities. Maybe it's both. Either way, I think she could hurt someone. More likely, she'll just get herself hurt if something doesn't change."

Gram's frown deepened.

"So what's your plan?" Nix asked again, his tone reflecting the irritation he felt at the thought of the siblings coming to the base.

"I don't want to raise a ruckus around their village. The less attention we draw the better," Gram mused, mentally noting Nix's irritation but choosing to ignore it. He figured Nix was usually irritated about something, and he'd been around him long enough to know that prodding would only make it worse. He continued, "I don't want to scare them either, but it seems there's no avoiding that. The girl, Thea, seems pretty high-strung."

Nix scoffed. That was putting it mildly.

"She thinks we're bounty hunters," he said. "No matter what we do, she's going to think we're trying to turn her in."

"Either way, we ought to bring Luc in on this. If something is wrong with Thea because of the experiments, then he'll be the best person to help her. Besides, he'll want to meet them too."

Gram was already referring to the siblings by name as if he'd known them for years.

"Then I should get back out there," Nix grumbled, as he stood and returned his phone to his pocket. If Gram was right and they were going south, having it wouldn't do much good. He wouldn't have a signal. "I'll take a radio and contact you with any changes."

"I still don't like the thought of you going alone," Gram insisted. "Besides, Kai's a Micro, isn't he? Won't he sense you?"

Nix shrugged.

"He didn't last night. In any case, I can track them easier than you can if they decide to leave."

"Your energy sensing sucks," he added mentally.

"Asshole," Gram thought before speaking out loud. "Fine. You keep an eye on them. I'll contact Luc and we'll join you once he's able to get away from the clinic. Maybe my energy sensing sucks, but it's enough to track your crazy ass channeling all over the Wilds."

Nix scowled as he turned to leave.

"Be careful out there," Gram told him. "I've gotten kind of used to having your dumb ass around so try not to do anything too stupid."

Nix rolled his eyes, but his mouth pulled up into a crooked smirk.

"No promises, but I'll see what I can do."

I see the world
through my own eyes but
only hear my voice
inside my head
like someone else
is speaking.

My body does
not feel like
it belongs to me
but instead
like something far away.

It feels like
being watched.

Chapter Four

Thea and Kai had left their village early that morning. They traveled south at first, hoping to avoid any typical routes, but they planned to loop back toward another village to the west. Thea didn't like the idea of traveling west again, but they didn't have much choice. Traveling east or north would only put them in danger of having the Military find them. She only hoped they would be far enough south to be beyond the notice of the Syndicate. Her encounter with them in Senari had only proved to her that everything she'd been taught as a child was true. They were dangerous.

It had been during her first trip to Karza for Market Day that she had learned the Syndicate was looking for her. She'd made the mistake of entering the tavern to rest. The room itself had seemed ready to pounce on her, but fortunately one of the servers had ushered her out a side door. They'd told her then that it wasn't just the Military who were looking for her, but the Syndicate, too.

It had surprised her. Whether they simply wanted revenge for their injured men, or if they had another purpose in mind, Thea didn't know. She didn't want to find out. She did everything she could to avoid being recognized after that, including wearing a hood as well as avoiding the tavern.

One of the two bounty hunters she'd run into had been dressed in black, the way many of the Syndicate dressed. Was it possible they were more than mere bounty hunters? It didn't matter. The Syndicate was just as bad. The only option was to make sure neither group found her. That was why she and Kai had to leave.

Their pace was slow as they travelled. Thea worried about Kai's knee. She knew that walking long distances was still difficult for him. That was why she always made the trip to Karza alone.

"How's your leg?" she asked. "Maybe we should stop soon?"

It hadn't been that long since their last break, but Thea had noticed a change in his walk. He was favoring his injured knee more.

Kai tried to smile, but the expression looked more like a grimace.

"I was hoping to make it to those rocks," he said. "We should be able to find a more secluded place to make camp."

The rock formation Kai pointed to was still pretty far away. Thea looked around, hoping to find some other shelter where they could make camp, but the surrounding area was too flat and open.

"We should at least take a short break," Thea insisted.

Kai shook his head.

"I'm okay, I promise. I'd like to keep going."

Thea shifted the heavy pack on her back and tried to focus on the weariness in her legs and the aching in her shoulders. Kai always knew what she was feeling, but it didn't mean she couldn't still trick him.

"Actually, I think I could use a break," she said, trying to sound guilty.

"Ok, let's take a short break, then." Kai gave her a half-hearted smile that told her he wasn't fooled by her act.

Thea smiled in relief anyway.

Take care of your sister.

She'd heard their parents tell Kai the same phrase for as long as she could remember, but she was an adult now and their parents weren't there. It was time she started taking care of herself, and maybe sometimes, she could take care of Kai, too.

The rock formation turned out to be much larger than Thea had guessed while viewing it from a distance. It rose from the ground taller than a city tower and covered as much ground—if not more—than the entire town of Karza. One side was sheer rock, another was jagged spires. Boulders taller than Kai littered the ground around the base of the rock formation, creating an eerie maze of stone. They set up their camp in a smooth recess that had been worn away by wind and rain. Between the boulders and the surrounding scrub trees, they were well hidden from view. Even a fire wouldn't be easily noticeable by any observers.

Of course, no one would try to track them using their physical senses alone.

Thea shivered. Worrying about Kai had been a decent distraction while they'd been traveling, but now that they had set up camp, she felt jittery.

Little noises made her jump, and she found herself straining to listen for sounds that weren't there.

She was so distracted the pot she'd been stirring boiled over, its liquid sizzling in the fire below, sending up a puff of smoke. She coughed and fanned the smoke away from her face.

"That isn't like you," Kai said as he ground herbs into a bowl, his voice muffled by the mask he wore over his mouth and nose.

"I was just distracted, I guess," she said. "What are you making?"

Kai only wore a mask while grinding herbs if he was worried about breathing them in.

Thea froze.

"Are you making those herb bombs?"

He'd been quiet all day. She'd thought his leg had been bothering him, but she realized now it was more than that. He hadn't just been quiet. He'd been distracted and tense.

"Kai, what aren't you telling me?"

Kai sighed and set down the bowl. Instead of answering her, he turned toward the darkness beyond their small camp, his brow furrowed in concentration, his eyes unfocused.

He sensed someone.

"We're being followed," he told her at last, turning back to face her.

The words felt like a blow to her chest, stealing her breath away.

"Why didn't you tell me sooner?" she asked quietly.

"I didn't want to say anything to make you worry until I was sure. Whoever it is has kept their distance, but they never get too close or too far away. They stopped whenever we did. I don't think that's a coincidence."

Thea felt her cheeks burn. She'd thought she'd been taking care of him, but all along he'd been protecting her from the truth, keeping her from doing something reckless. She felt foolish for not realizing what was going on sooner.

"How many are there?"

"I..." Kai paused, doubt clouding his expression. "I'm not sure. There's a Macro with a lot of energy, of that I'm certain. Sometimes I think I'm picking up others, but it could just be my nervousness playing tricks on me."

"It's probably that bounty hunter from Karza," Thea squeaked. "Which means his partner must be a Micro after all. How else could he track us?"

"Maybe." Kai sounded uncertain. "You should eat while I finish this."

Kai picked up his bowl again. Thea's stomach felt heavy. After only a few bites of food, it began to ache. She set aside a bowl for Kai and began cleaning up. After packing up what she could, she began levitating small rocks and shooting them at the nearby wall, trying to hit the same spot with each rock.

"That's not resting," Kai said without looking up.

"How can I rest?" Thea asked in frustration. "We could be attacked at any moment. I can't just sit here."

"That's exactly why you shouldn't be wasting your energy," he countered patiently.

He'd begun scooping the crushed herbs into small envelopes of waxed paper. The envelopes were made for storing herbs, to keep them fresh, but Kai had realized the thin paper was also fragile enough to break easily when thrown or manipulated, making an ideal container for his invention. Once the paper was broken the powder would fill the air like dust, spreading its disorienting effect to potential attackers. As a Manipulator, Thea could launch the packages at an enemy while maintaining a safe distance.

Not that they'd ever tested them against real opponents.

"I'll know if anyone gets close enough to attack. That Macro is still keeping their distance."

"What if it's a trick?" she asked. "What if that Macro is trying to confuse your senses? You said it was hard to tell if anyone else was following us. Maybe his job is to let someone else sneak in closer."

Kai frowned as he thought about her words, then shrugged. She thought the movement seemed stiff, like he was trying too hard to appear unconcerned.

"That's good thinking," he said. "I would still sense anyone close enough to make an attack though. That Macro has a lot of energy, but like I said, they're keeping their distance. If anyone were closer I would know it. After all, I can still sense people when you're around."

In spite of his assurances, Kai seemed more on edge after that. It made Thea feel more anxious every time his hands stopped working. He was right, though. She shouldn't waste her channeling on throwing rocks. Instead, she paced back and forth until he'd finally sealed the last envelope and pulled the mask away from his face.

"What now?" she asked as she moved to his side.

"Why don't you hide some of these around the outside of the camp so you can use them on anyone who gets close," he told her, holding up one of the herb-filled envelopes. "We can keep a few with us just in case, but it would be better not to use them here where it's enclosed. We'd end up breathing in the herbs too."

Thea nodded and gathered up the envelopes, careful not to rip the fragile paper. She shivered as she moved away from the warm glow of the fire toward the darkness that lay beyond their camp.

The surrounding boulders cast long dark shadows in the moonlight. The vision was eerie. The deepness of the shadows tugged at the back of her mind—something like a memory she couldn't quite recall. Her heart pounded with more than just anxiety for their current situation. She froze, clinging the envelopes too tight in her arms. She wanted to turn back, stay close to the warmth of the fire and the comfort of Kai's presence. She wanted him to put one arm around her and tell her everything was going to be okay.

But it wasn't. Someone was after her and she needed to do whatever she could to keep herself and Kai safe. She wasn't a child anymore. She didn't need Kai to lie to her.

She took a deep breath and stepped into the shadows, enhancing her vision and hearing to scan the darkness for the slightest movement.

As she placed the envelopes, she infused a small amount of her own energy into each one. It would make them easier to control later, so long as that energy didn't dissipate before she needed it.

Once she'd finished, she returned to sit close to Kai as he ate the dinner she'd left out for him. She felt a lonely ache she couldn't explain, like he would disappear if she looked away from him. She leaned her head against his shoulder, appreciating his warmth and the reassuring comfort of being near him.

Kai stiffened.

"Someone's coming. It's not the Macro. You were right. There are others. They're close. I couldn't sense them before."

Thea stood, her adrenaline already pounding in her ears. She moved toward the rocks, but Kai grabbed her arm.

"Thea, wait."

"I'll hide among the rocks," she told him. "And use the envelopes on anyone who gets close."

Kai hesitated, but after a moment, he let go.

"Try to stay hidden," he said. "If the envelopes don't work, come back here and we'll think of something else."

Thea looked around, wishing there was some place Kai could hide.

"What about you?"

"They aren't here for me," he said sadly, then held up one of the envelopes he'd kept for himself. "And I have these."

Thea turned back toward the cold darkness beyond their camp. The best way to keep him safe was to stop anyone from getting to their camp in the first place.

"You know I should be happy that you listened to me for a change," Gram said as he and Lucan climbed off his bike, "but I did bet Luc you'd do something stupid, so I'm honestly a little disappointed."

Nix rolled his eyes and pointed toward the rock formation.

"They're camped on the far side of those rocks."

"I know I said to keep your distance, but aren't you a little far away?" Gram asked as he adjusted his night-vision eyepiece.

"I didn't want the brother to sense me," Nix said, not wanting to voice the real reason he kept his distance.

Before Gram could reply, the girl's thoughts changed from a distant whisper to a drumming rumble. Something had made her channeling spike.

"Wait." Nix held up his hand to cut off Gram's response.

Someone was approaching their camp.

Nix swore under his breath and started to run.

"Wait, dumbass!" Gram called, but Nix didn't stop.

"*Someone else is there,*" he transmitted. They didn't have time to sit around hatching plans. They had to act now.

Running closer to the siblings' camp meant Nix couldn't use his telepathy to locate the intruders. Instead, he enhanced his other senses. He knew it would only make his growing headache worse, but he didn't have a choice.

He heard movement in the scrub trees to one side of the rocks and turned toward the sound. Maybe it was stupid to rush ahead on his own, when he didn't know who was waiting or how many there were. Gram wouldn't be far behind, though. In the unlikely event that he couldn't handle things on his own, he could count on Gram and Lucan to back him up.

Shadows moved among the trees. He counted at least five, but there could be more that he couldn't see. He approached warily, weaving between the trees while listening for any signs of an attack. As the trees opened up into a small clearing, a familiar figure stepped out from the shadows.

"Well, well, long time no see, Ghost."

Nix swore silently. He'd let his guard down and walked right into a trap.

Since he couldn't rely on his telepathy, Nix stepped forward into the clearing in order to give himself as clear a view as possible. He moved casually, as though the Syndicate members were just his old comrades instead of a group of people who hated him and wanted him dead.

The nearest figure stepped back as Nix moved forward. At least his reputation was still intact. That alone might be enough to stall their attack until Gram arrived.

"What are you doing here, Kuda?"

"What does it matter to a traitor like you?" Kuda spat.

Nix let out a snort.

"Drop the act, Kuda," he growled. "You aren't any more loyal to the Syndicate than I am. You're just too much of a coward to leave it behind."

"At least I'm not some peacekeeper's pet," Kuda snarled, drawing his sword.

Ah. At least one thing made sense.

"Kaori sent you," he said. It wasn't a question. Though why she'd have sent Kuda here, Nix couldn't begin to guess. "I know she didn't send you to capture me. So, what does she want with those two?"

Nix gestured toward the rock formation where the siblings had set up their camp. He shook his head. He didn't really expect an answer.

"It doesn't matter," he continued as he shifted his stance and drew his sword. The nearest figures shrank back a step. "Because the result will end up the same. You're going back empty-handed."

Kuda laughed.

"I guess you haven't changed, Ghost. You still like to talk big, but there are ten of us and only one of you."

Nix snorted again, though he scanned the clearing in surprise. He still couldn't see them all. He was definitely at a disadvantage without his telepathy. Where the hell was Gram?

"Then I guess you haven't changed either if you still think you have even the slightest chance against me. If you were smart, and let's be honest, we both know that's not the case. If you were smart, you'd take your squad and go."

Nix didn't wait for the others to make the first move. He pushed more channeling into his senses while trying to ignore the pounding in his head. The girl had heard them and was foolishly running toward them. He had to end this. He rushed toward the nearest fighter, hurling them into a tree. He heard the scrape of footsteps behind him and the sound of metal slicing through the air. He pivoted to the side, just barely avoiding the attacker's blade. He swung his own sword in a low arc, slicing the other man across the chest before he could parry.

"You idiots!" Kuda whined angrily. "What are you doing? I told you, you all need to attack him at once!"

"Go ahead," Nix said mockingly. "Come at me if you want to end up like your friend here."

He let the word *friend* drip from his lips with all the disdain he could muster. There were no friends in the Syndicate. No one would come to the fallen man's rescue. The only question was whether their hatred would outweigh their fear. He had to do whatever he could to make them feel the latter. With a tinge of regret, he stabbed his sword down into the man's abdomen. Gram wouldn't approve, but at the moment he didn't have much choice. Nix knew the other man would have gladly killed him if he had the chance.

No one moved to challenge him. No one wanted to die.

Nix rushed toward Kuda, whose enhancement was only mediocre. He could hardly even react against Nix's superior speed. Nix grabbed his sword hand, crunching it painfully with his own enhanced strength until Kuda was forced to drop his sword. Nix let go and grabbed him by the collar, holding his sword against the other man's neck.

"Tell Kaori the girl is mine," Nix growled. If he let them think he was simply after the bounty, they'd be less eager to come after her again. "The next time anyone interferes, they won't be lucky enough to leave alive."

❖

Thea clutched the small envelope in her hand as she slunk carefully through the shadows, straining her hearing to pick up any sounds. The sound of voices rose from a small copse of scrub trees. She knew she should stay near the camp and the hidden envelopes, but she had to know who had come for them. She had to see how many there were. After that, she would return to Kai. He would know what to do.

A shout filled the quiet night, and she started to run, her channeling scratching beneath the surface, clawing to get out. Her muscles felt stretched to bursting as they struggled to contain the flowing energy, propelling her faster. She was breathless when she skidded to a noisy halt at the edge of the scraggly trees. She ducked low behind a large bush, peering into the shadows.

A group of people stood in a ring just inside the clearing, dressed in black, with swords in hand. Some wore jackets, but several wore short-sleeved shirts, revealing the distinctive tattoo on their arm. They were from the Syndicate.

Thea recoiled. How had they found her?

There, in the center, stood one of her attackers from Karza, the Macro. He was holding another man by the collar, a sword to his throat.

"Tell Kaori the girl is mine," he snarled. "The next time anyone interferes, they won't be lucky enough to leave alive."

Her skin burned as her energy rose and overflowed from her body. Dust swirled around her as her out-of-control channeling pulled at anything it could latch onto. The fabric of her cloak ruffled as though caught in a breeze. Two of the figures turned in her direction.

They sensed her.

She wouldn't be able to sneak quietly back to Kai now.

She infused the envelope she was holding with energy and let it hover above her hands momentarily before using her energy to launch it toward the center of the clearing. The paper ripped as it shot from her hand, leaving a trail of powder as it flew. Thea jumped away, her eyes stinging. Two of the men were already running toward her when she landed, seemingly unaffected by the herbs. Because the envelope had broken too soon, it's trail had been easy to avoid.

She reached into her pocket for another envelope, strengthening it with a slight amount of her own energy. This time she threw it toward her attackers, then used her ability to rip the paper.

Too much energy made the packet explode in a larger cloud than she'd anticipated. This time, she couldn't avoid it. She could feel the powder burning in her nose and throat as she tried to stumble away.

Her head swam as she ran from a third attacker. She had to get back to the rocks where she'd hidden the rest of the envelopes. She heard a grunt behind her and turned back. The Macro from Karza was there. He'd knocked her pursuer to the ground.

The girl is mine, he'd said.

He was removing the competition so he could take her bounty for himself. She pushed herself faster, trying not to stumble as the needle pricks of energy in her legs turned to searing pain.

The sound of his footsteps was getting closer. He was gaining on her. She ground her teeth and pushed more energy into her speed, sure she could outrun him. He'd surprised her in Karza, but she'd managed to get away from him then and she would again.

She channeled her energy toward the ground, pulling at the rocks and dust beneath her. She launched the swirl of dust and stone back toward him. She heard the scrape of his footsteps as he moved to dodge, followed by a slight hiss. Had she hit him?

Her vision blurred. The dizzying effect of the herbs was sinking in, and she could no longer ignore it. His hand caught her arm, and she swung her free elbow back on a wild instinct. Her elbow tingled from the impact of connecting with his cheekbone. He let go with a grunt and she stumbled forward, her feet scrambling for purchase.

She was close enough. She reached out her hands, the movement helping her focus, and pulled down. Three of the hidden envelopes shot toward them, along with another spray of rocks and dust. Thea tried to jump out of the way, but instead fell awkwardly, her head smacking against the sharp corner of a boulder. The envelopes exploded above them. She heard the soft thud and could just make out the man's shape falling to his knees behind her.

It wasn't enough. She had to get back to Kai.

She'd failed to keep him safe. She'd failed to protect herself. They were going to take her. She couldn't go back.

She tried to pull herself up, but her limbs had no strength. Tears stung her burning eyes as she collapsed again, before darkness filled her vision and she sank into unconsciousness.

Surrounded everywhere I turn by bark
        and shadow
The looming trunks and grasping branches block
        my searching
And depths of night reveal no sight or sign
        for hoping
You are here

My fear becomes a weight on every step
        and stumble
Though dread that hammers loud inside my chest
        compels me
The time for rest will come when once again
        I know that
You are found

A beaming ring of light comes into view
        ahead now
And with it hope of end to labyrinth's grasp
        and worry
Instead of open sky and sweet relief
        despair waits
You are lost

My anguish from my lips escapes with tears
        of sorrow
Your broken form lies still upon the ground
        unmoving
I cannot stop this tide of red from wounds
        uncounted
You are fading

A splash of sticky fluid drips around
        our bodies
The droplets red as blood and hot as fire
        are falling
And streaming down from every branch and trunk
        to drown me
I am burning

A gaping wound with raging tide of red
       consuming
A fire that spreads and tears its way throughout
       my body
I scream until my sight is gone and breath
       has faded
You are gone

Chapter Five

"Thea! Thea!"

Kai's voice.

She blinked to clear away the blurriness from her vision and reached out for him in the dim light. Her fingers dug into his sleeve, desperate to find the comforting solidity of his arm beneath the thin fabric.

It had only been a dream. It wasn't real. Kai was here. He wasn't hurt. They were both okay.

Her stomach clenched and she could feel its contents rising into her throat.

"I'm going to be sick," she managed to gasp, her voice hoarse.

She was only vaguely aware of another person dashing to her side. She didn't have time to think about it as she wretched into the small bin. Her head shattered with pain and spots danced before her eyes. Dizzy and shaking, she closed her eyes and leaned her head back into the soft pillow beneath her.

"Here, drink this." Kai pressed a cup against her lips. She lifted her head again without opening her eyes. The warm liquid was sweet with a citrusy tartness. Its warmth was soothing to her throat and seemed to spread into her body as she swallowed.

"Another dream?" Kai asked softly after removing the cup from her lips.

"It was awful," Thea whispered, her voice catching on a sob.

"Here."

She opened her eyes and whipped her head toward the sound of the unfamiliar voice, earning herself another wave of pain and nausea. The surge of panic she felt as she looked around the unfamiliar room only made her discomfort worse. A man stepped closer from beside the low table where Kai sat in front of her. He was carrying another cup in his hands. Thea recoiled against the couch where she lay, knowing she was too weak to do anything to protect herself.

"It's okay Thea," Kai assured her quickly, placing one hand under her shoulders to help her sit. "He's a doctor. He wants to help."

Kai placed another cup in her hands. The outside was so cold it made her fingers ache.

She raised the cup to her lips and took a tentative sip of the cold liquid. It hit her like a jolt, though it wasn't painful. The warm drink had been soothing. This one filled her with a buzz of energy. Her head began to clear, and she found it easier to force her rising channeling back down.

"Who are you?" Thea asked the doctor. "And where are we? The last thing I remember...We were attacked last night."

"My name is Lucan Avery. Like your brother said, I'm a doctor. I have a clinic in Karza that I visit on Market Days." The doctor's voice was crisp, with a slight melodic lilt to it. He wore his sandy colored hair tied back in a low ponytail, a few wispy strands escaping to frame his face. His smile seemed kind, but there was something about the way he studied her with his pale blue eyes that made her shiver.

"I assure you, we mean you no harm," he continued. "My friends have been looking for you—"

"You're with them?" Thea interrupted. She all but dropped the cup onto the table in front of her, the cold liquid stinging her skin as it sloshed over her hand.

"Thea." Kai's tone was placating. "They don't want to hurt us."

She shook her head, ignoring the spike of pain that accompanied the movement.

"They attacked us, Kai! They took us prisoner." Her voice cracked. How could he be so calm?

"You're the one who attacked last night," snapped a deep voice from behind her, making her jump.

She recognized the voice even before she turned around to see her attacker from the night before. Though his dark clothes appeared to be fresh, his jacket remained coated in dust and herbs, traces of their scent filling the air and making her nausea return. His black hair hung over his forehead, adding menacing shadows to his glare. The scratches on his cheek and the bruise forming under one eye might have been gratifying under different circumstances. At the moment it was all she could do to keep herself from trembling.

"Nix—"

The doctor started to speak but before he could continue another man entered and slapped her attacker hard on the shoulder. Thea flinched at the sound.

"Is it really necessary for the first thing out of your mouth to prove what an asshole you are?"

Thea recognized the man she'd run into in the alley. His size was no less intimidating now than it had been then. He was nearly a head taller than the other man, broad-chested and muscular.

"Don't mind him," he chuckled as he turned toward her, "he's just a sore loser."

The shorter man ignored him, his glare deepening to a scowl as he moved toward the window on the other side of the room—as though trying to put as much distance between himself and everyone else as possible.

"How are you both feeling?" the taller man asked.

His tone was friendly and the concern in his brown eyes almost seemed genuine. Rather than making her feel comfortable, his expression and behavior only heightened her confusion—and anxiety.

Kai, it seemed, had no such reservation.

"Thea just needs rest, and time to recover. She'll be fine."

Thea sucked in a surprised breath and her hand reached out to squeeze Kai's forearm. How could he be so calm?

He placed one hand over hers reassuringly.

"I think you'd better explain things to my sister," Kai continued. "There are a few details I'd like more clarification on as well."

Kai moved to sit by her on the couch. Thea swung her legs around to the floor to make room for him. The movement made her dizzy. She closed her eyes and tried to breathe slowly, hating the weakness that must be evident to her captors.

When she opened her eyes again, the large man wasn't looking at them. Instead, he was frowning in the direction of his partner by the window. Thea followed his gaze, but the dark-haired man was simply sitting on the deep sill of the open window with a scowl. The bigger man cleared his throat and turned back toward her.

"My name is Gram," he said in his friendly tone, "Gram Wyman. You've already met Lucan. He's the best doctor I know and an old friend."

"Gram and I knew your mother," the doctor added.

Thea's eyes widened in surprise. She searched her memories, but neither man seemed familiar. She was sure she'd never met them before. Was this some kind of trick to get them to lower their guard?

"When I saw your bounty information, I recognized you right away," Gram said. "You look like her."

"So you are bounty hunters!" Thea's voice came out in a loud squeak of fear.

"If you want an explanation, you should be quiet and listen," the man by the window snapped.

Thea shrank into Kai's side, stunned by the sudden harshness of his voice.

Gram let out an exaggerated sigh.

"And that's Nix. He's got a terrible personality, so you can just ignore him."

"This is a waste of time," Nix grumbled. "I'm leaving."

Gram just nodded. Even after the door banged noisily shut, he continued to look away in the direction the other man had gone. His expression reminded her of the one Kai sometimes had when sensing energy. He tore his hand through his brushed-back brown hair before crossing his arms over his chest and dropping into a chair across from them.

"Dumbass," he muttered. "Like I said, ignore him. He's seriously an asshole. Like if you ranked all the assholes who have ever lived, he'd be at the top. Way above the others."

"Ignore both of them," Lucan cut in. "They can be quite annoying when they are fighting with each other."

He stepped in front of Thea again, this time carrying a small tray containing a steaming bowl and a pile of cloth bandages.

"I'd like to change the bandage on your head, if that's alright. I can continue to explain things as I do. Gram will probably be sulking for a while."

He threw a disapproving glance toward Gram as he set his tray on the table. As he turned back toward her with a smile, Thea reached a hand up to her head, hesitating. Kai squeezed her other hand again.

Now that she had calmed down a little, she realized that the doctor must have already explained everything to Kai. That was why he was so calm. He seemed to trust them, and he was never wrong. She nodded slowly, feeling embarrassed.

"I just want to know what's going on," she said. "You say you want to help us, so why did that guy attack me last night, and in Karza?"

Lucan sighed.

"Unfortunately, Nix can be a little impulsive, and a bit abrasive. I'm sorry that his actions frightened you and caused you injury."

"Dumbass little shit," Gram muttered again.

Lucan sighed. His hands were gentle as he unwound the bandage wrapped around her head. She winced as dried blood and medicine pulled at her wound.

"Gram and I grew up in the same orphanage as your mother. She was like a big sister to us."

Thea glanced at Kai, wondering if she had ever told him more about her childhood. She knew that Kai was only her half-brother, and that their mother had moved to their town from the capital, but she didn't know much else about her mother's life before meeting her father. Her mother didn't like to talk about it.

If it were true that these two men were like brothers to her, why had she never mentioned them? Why had they never met?

"I was adopted by a family in the city," Lucan continued. "My father is a doctor too. Kai has been telling me about some of your health problems. It may require some study, but I'm sure we can find a way to help you."

His voice and expression reminded her of the cold analysis of the researchers as they performed their tests. She pulled away from him with a wince before he could finish securing the fresh bandage on her head. It hung limp against her face, but she hardly noticed it.

More lies to fool her into complacency. More promises to help her when they only wanted to study her, use her.

Bile rose in her throat, and she thought she was going to be sick again.

"I'm sorry," Lucan said, quietly sliding away from her on the table. "I didn't mean for my comments to be insensitive. I truly only want to help."

Kai squeezed her hand, and she gripped the fabric of his sleeve with her free hand, trying to ground herself.

"I should be honest with you," Lucan said, his words careful. "I used to work in ability research."

Thea let out a small squeak of surprise. Kai stiffened. Clearly, he was hearing this confession for the first time.

"The Military had been trying to recruit my father for years. He's a kind man, and a good doctor, so I never understood why he refused. So many people suffer because of their abilities, and there's so much we don't understand about them. I thought that with the Military's resources, we could find ways to solve these problems. My father disagreed, but I joined the researchers anyway."

Kai let out a breath and Thea realized she'd been holding hers as well. She forced herself to exhale slowly, though her heart pounded in her ears, muffling Lucan's voice.

"Sadly, it didn't take much time in the research facility for me to realize he was right. The Military didn't care about helping people. All they wanted was to use people, to use their abilities as weapons. All of this was before they started doing telepathy research. It seems their reckless experiments have only gotten worse. I'm sorry."

Thea relaxed the vice grip she had on Kai's arm. Lucan's disgust with Military research seemed genuine. If he was telling the truth, maybe she could let him help her.

"May I fix your bandage?" he asked.

Thea nodded. "I'm sorry."

"No, I'm sorry to have startled you. I must confess, sometimes I become too eager when there's a medical problem to solve." Lucan met her eyes and smiled. "I want you to know, none of us here have any love for what they are doing in those facilities. The last thing we would ever do is send you back there."

Thea gave him a small, tentative smile. She wanted to believe him. She wanted it desperately. She and Kai had been doing this alone for so long. It was almost too much to hope that someone might actually want to help, but Lucan still hadn't explained why Gram had their bounty information or why the other man, Nix, had attacked her. She opened her mouth to ask but Lucan stood up, half-turning toward Gram.

"Are you done sulking?" he asked, with a frown. "Why don't you explain the rest while I prepare us some food."

Gram shrugged as Lucan picked up the tray.

"Come on Luc, you're making me look bad," Gram said, still sounding childish, though a teasing smile spread across his face.

Lucan sighed and left the room, shaking his head.

"Look, the point is we're trying to help you," Gram said to Thea. "I'm not after the bounty, I just wanted to find you before the Military did. When we ran into you in that alley, we knew it was only a matter of time before the soldiers tracked you down. That's why Nix followed you. That's why we were there last night."

"How did you get my bounty information in the first place?" Thea asked, her skin pricking with apprehension.

Gram looked away from her and rubbed the back of his head with a nervous expression. It was almost comical on a man of his intimidating size.

"Well, actually, I'm a Peacekeeper."

Thea sucked in a breath and Kai squeezed her hand again. Gram chuckled.

"Yeah, I figured you wouldn't like that. Like Luc said, none of us like what those Researchers are doing. I'm not going to let them take you back."

There was a hard finality in his voice that Thea knew could only be sincere.

"What about the others who were there last night? They were from the Syndicate, weren't they? Your friend seemed to know them."

Gram's face darkened and he let out a sigh before rubbing his face with both hands.

"Yeah, they were. I don't know why they were there, or why they would be after you."

Kai shifted and Thea looked up to see uncertainty cross his face. Gram wasn't telling the truth. Or he was keeping something from them.

She noticed Gram didn't deny that Nix knew them. Neither he nor Lucan had offered any information about him.

Was he really their friend? Did the others really trust him? Maybe he was simply a hired mercenary with an agenda of his own. Maybe he was after her bounty. He'd basically said so himself.

"I think we should probably let my sister rest," Kai said with a tight smile on his face. "We can talk more later."

Thea forced a smile of her own and leaned her head back against the couch to show her exhaustion. She didn't have to act. Her body ached and her head spun with pain, worry, and questions.

Gram nodded and slapped his knees before standing up.

"Sorry about sticking you on the couch," he said. "We have plenty of space, it's just not very habitable at the moment. We'll clear out a room for you, but for now just get some rest here. Luc'll bring you some food in a little while."

After Gram closed the door behind him, Thea flopped onto her side on the couch, groaning as the motion sent a spike of pain through her head. She heaved her legs up and draped them across her brother's lap, careful to avoid putting weight too close to his knee.

"Where are we anyway?" she asked, studying the room for the first time. In addition to the couch and chairs, a small sideboard sat in the corner near the window. There were two doors on opposite sides of the room. Nix had left through the door near the window. Since she had seen sunlight through the open doorway, she knew it led outside. Gram and Lucan had left through the door behind. It probably led deeper into the house.

Kai didn't answer her. She raised her head to look at him across the couch. He'd rested his elbows on her legs, his fingers interlaced under his chin. She reached for one of the pillows underneath her and tossed it at him gently.

"Sorry." Kai's frown was replaced with a smile as he reached over to bop her on the head with the pillow. "What did you ask?"

"I asked where we are."

She took the pillow from his hand and hugged it to her chest, rolling her eyes slightly before returning his smile.

"Apparently, it's an old Military base that was abandoned after the war. Most people in the Wilds try to steer clear of peacekeepers and the Military, so it's fairly private. The walls are mostly intact so it's secure too."

"Unless it's the Military you are trying to hide from," Thea pointed out. "This place won't be much of a deterrent to them. So what now?"

"Lucan explained a lot of the same things to me before you woke up. I could sense that he was telling the truth, so it was easy for me to trust him." He hesitated. "They didn't tell me the Syndicate was there last night. When you asked about it, Gram's emotions changed. There's definitely something he's not telling us."

"I thought the same thing. Something didn't seem right, especially about that other guy—Nix. Notice they didn't tell us anything about him. And they didn't answer my question about his connection to the Syndicate."

"I don't know," Kai shrugged noncommittally.

"So what do you think we should do?"

Kai shrugged again.

"Like I said, I trust that they're sincere about wanting to help us, even if they are keeping something from us. For now, I think we are safest staying here. I'll see what I can find out about Nix, and what they know about the Syndicate."

Kai shifted her legs off him so he could stand up.

"Did you sleep enough?" he asked. "If you're still tired, you should try to rest."

Thea shook her head, not wanting to return to sleep, not wanting to have another nightmare. Her body betrayed her with a yawn and Kai chuckled softly.

"Try to rest," he said.

He moved to one of the chairs across the room and Thea rolled onto her back with a grunt of pain. Her headache had worsened, and her empty stomach still felt nauseous. She was tired, but she wasn't sure she would be able to sleep even if she wanted to. The conversation with Gram and Lucan, played over and over in her head, making her anxious.

She heard the sound of footsteps and a soft knock at the door. Lucan poked his head in slowly.

"I hope I didn't wake you," he said in a soft voice. "I wanted to bring you something to eat. I made some broth that should help if your stomach is still feeling upset. There's also medicine that will ease any pain you may be feeling and will help you to sleep."

Thea sat up slowly.

"Thank you."

In spite of her misgivings, she was grateful for the kindness Lucan and Gram had shown her so far.

Lucan placed the tray of food on the table then left, closing the door softly behind him. Kai handed her the steaming bowl of light-colored broth, then took the plate with a heartier looking breakfast for himself.

The broth smelled good, and her stomach rumbled hungrily. Like the warm, herbal tea from earlier, the soup seemed to penetrate her aching muscles and ease the pounding in her head. Even before swallowing the two small capsules resting on the tray, she could feel her eyelids drooping sleepily. She sank down onto the sofa and found that it didn't take long before her mind began to drift hazily toward sleep.

When first we met you looked at me
With your dark eyes full of eager
Curiosity and a hunger for recognition
Something I understood because
I always wanted the same
To belong
To be more than just a nuisance
To be what only you saw in me
But with time that fire burned
And only ashes stayed
Because a hunger like that
Can only bring pain
And neither you nor I could ever find
What we wanted from each other
Or anyone else
And now here we stand on opposite sides
And the blood on your hands is mine
We used up all our chances
I wonder if you found what you were looking for
Without me because we never found it together
Now it's too late for me but maybe you'll do better
I hope you won't forget me
I hope you'll find what I never could

Chapter Six

After storming out of the living room, Nix retreated to his workshop, a three-walled vehicle bay at the opposite end of the base. He spent most of his time there, as it was far enough away from the main house to lessen the constant thrum of Gram's thoughts in his head.

The distance did little to quiet the girl's thoughts, though. He rubbed his forehead as he slung one leg over his bike. He needed to get away. He eased his bike out of the rear gate, then opened the throttle. As he sped across the hard ground, the refreshing coolness of the air whistling past his face and through his hair began to lessen the tension he felt. His head cleared the further he drove from the base, like a weight was being lifted from him.

He didn't have any particular destination in mind, but soon Karza came into view, still just a smudge in the distance. Maybe subconsciously he'd intended to drive toward town, or maybe it was simply habit.

Something was still bothering him, and had been since the previous night. The Syndicate hadn't been there for him, of that he was certain. They'd been there for the girl.

But why?

Nix slowed his bike as the town wall came clearly into view. There was someone waiting there, directly in his path. He reached out his telepathy, but came up with nothing. He let out a sigh and drove forward slowly, keeping his thoughts alert. She was probably alone, but there was always the possibility this was a trap.

Nix skidded to a stop a few feet away from the other bike and reached into his pocket for his knife. He'd been in such a hurry to get away, he hadn't grabbed his sword. He regretted its absence now.

Kaori was sitting on her bike, leaning over the handlebars, her long, dark hair spilling over her shoulder.

"What are you doing here?" he asked, though it was clear she was waiting for him.

Not being able to hear Kaori was normal, and something that had always been a relief to him, until the time came when he wished more than anything else that he knew what she was really thinking. He scanned their surroundings for other thoughts, but only picked up the rumble of thoughts from town. He didn't find it reassuring. He still wasn't entirely convinced that everything was normal with his abilities.

He enhanced his vision and hearing. Not that it would do much good. He knew better than to trust his senses around Kaori.

"Hey Ghost, it's been a while."

Kaori climbed off her bike and tossed her dark hair over her shoulder as she approached. His eyes trailed over her fitted sleeveless shirt, the dark tattoo circling the trim muscles of her arm, the way her pants enhanced the curves of her hips.

He swallowed and looked away.

"What if I said I'd missed you?" she asked, finally answering his question.

"Then I wouldn't believe it."

She laughed, high and mirthless.

"As cold as ever I see. Too bad."

She was close enough now to lean against his bike. Her leg pressed against his and her shoulder brushed his arm. She smiled and he wanted to lean closer. Instead, he leaned away.

"So you aren't going to tell me then," he said with a roll of his eyes. "That's typical I guess."

"Come on, don't be like that." She ducked her head slightly and looked at him through her lashes like she was trying to keep his attention. It worked. "How long has it been since we saw each other?"

She leaned in even closer, close enough that he could smell the familiar scent of perfume in her hair, see the triumphant glint in her eyes as she tallied the score in the game they always seemed to be playing—the one only she knew the rules to.

"Come on, why don't you buy me a drink in town and we can catch up properly? I'll tell you all about my new bike."

Nix's eyes followed her gesture to the bike he hadn't paid attention to before. He let out a low whistle, his fingers brushing her arm absently as he climbed off his own bike.

The thick layer of dust coating the bike was an inevitability of riding in the Wilds. Still, Nix could see the shine of the paint underneath. The tread on the wide tires was still thick and deep. The bike was clearly new, and it certainly wasn't a model one saw around the Wilds. Even the soldiers didn't usually have such nice vehicles. Nix could guess at the machine's power from just a glance at the visible components.

"Where'd you get it?" Nix asked, unable to keep the admiration out of his voice as he circled the bike.

Kaori laughed.

"Well that finally got your attention. You're the same as ever, I see. I was hoping you could give it a tune up, actually. All this dust can't be good for it."

Nix nodded.

"The default filters won't be enough. It has good tires for the terrain though." Nix caught himself and sighed. "Gram would be seriously pissed if you came to the base right now."

Kaori frowned and her voice turned sharp as she said, "You really have been spending too much time with the peacekeeper. You're starting to sound as crude as he is—"

She clipped off the last word, as though unhappy she'd slipped into her old habit of parroting her father. Nix just shrugged and resisted the urge to look away. He didn't have to be who she wanted anymore, and he certainly didn't have to follow the ideology of a man they both hated, a man who'd been dead for five years. They stood for a moment in awkward silence before Kaori sighed and tossed her hair over her shoulder to regain her composure.

"I imagine the peacekeeper would be pretty jumpy with the new friends he's got stashed away at the base," she said in an offhand tone, as though there'd been no break in their conversation.

Nix tensed. She'd distracted him with the bike and her usual head games, making him all but forget the reason he'd come to town in the first place.

"Let me guess," she continued with a casual glance at her fingernails, "he sent you off like a good pet to gather information for him? Or maybe he's finally gotten tired of you now that he has someone new to play with?"

She smiled icily as he frowned.

"And what about you?" he asked as he moved away from the bike. "You still like to make other people do the dirty work for you, I see. Though I don't get why you're interested in those siblings."

"I have no idea what you're talking about, Ghost."

Kaori cocked her head to one side in a look of puzzlement that he could almost believe was genuine.

"Kuda. He doesn't leave Chusan unless it's on your orders. We both know that."

"And your point is?"

She didn't deny it.

"He showed up last night with about nine others. They were after the girl and her brother."

Kaori laughed.

"You think I sent them? Please give me more credit than that. I know Kuda wouldn't stand a chance against you, no matter who was with him. The truth is I haven't seen him in months."

"You're telling me it's just a coincidence that he was there last night and the next day I run into you. Besides, if you didn't send Kuda after the siblings, how did you know they were at the base."

Kaori just shrugged.

Nix didn't like it. He didn't believe in coincidence, and he didn't believe Kaori could know so much if she wasn't involved.

"Word is my brother's been looking for them," Kaori said, surprising him. "And you know Kuda is too stupid to break away from him completely."

"That doesn't sound like Ryu," Nix said hesitantly. "Why would he want the girl?"

"She injured three Syndicate members in Senari. As incompetent as he is, even Ryu can't ignore that. Especially if the Military wants her for research."

Nix scowled. Was Ryu becoming interested in ability research? Or did he simply want to keep the Military from succeeding with their own?

"Enough about my brother," Kaori said, stepping closer to him again. He recognized the edge in her voice even though she tried to keep her tone nonchalant. "Why don't you come back to town with me? We can get that drink, and you can forget about being the peacekeeper's errand boy for a night."

His eyes wandered to her lips as she slid one hand against his chest. She bent her face closer to his. Her hair spilled over her shoulder and the familiar, intoxicating scent of perfume filled his head once more. He was more than tempted. He wanted her. He always had. And the last thing he wanted at the moment was to return to base.

But it wasn't that simple.

He clenched his jaw and stepped away.

"I'm busy," he growled, though they both knew it wasn't true.

She sighed.

"I'll be around," she said as she climbed back onto her bike. "Come find me when the peacekeeper decides he's had enough of you."

She threw a casual wave over her shoulder before turning her bike around and peeling away in a cloud of dust. As she disappeared behind Karza's wall, a part of him regretted not following her. He looked down at his hand and rubbed the long white scar on his palm, the permanent reminder that regardless of anything else, he couldn't trust Kaori. He clenched his hand into a tight fist before climbing onto his own bike and turning away from Karza.

Gram didn't shoot him when he got back to base. That was a good sign that at least he wasn't still angry. When Nix entered the kitchen later that evening, Gram slid a plate across the counter toward him, piled high with food.

"Glad you aren't dead," Gram said gravely, grabbing a second plate for himself.

Nix's mouth watered as he crossed the room. The only thing he'd eaten that day was a meal bar, and even rewarmed, Lucan's cooking was far superior to the prepared meals he and Gram usually ate.

Nix sat down tiredly on one of the stools at the counter, but instead of eating, he dropped his head into his hands and rubbed his temples with his fingers. The relief he'd enjoyed during his time away from the girl's thoughts was already being replaced by tension in his shoulders and a dull ache behind his eyes.

"It really is that bad, huh?" Gram asked. Nix could see the worry creasing his brow, but thankfully none of his petulance from earlier.

Nix shrugged. He didn't want to talk about it.

"I talked to Kaori," he said instead.

"Dammit Nix!"

He realized his mistake too late. Kaori was the wrong subject if he wanted to avoid an argument.

"She found me," Nix interrupted before Gram could start another lecture.

"I'm surprised you came back in one piece." Gram sat down next to him with an annoyed flop. "Well, did you learn anything else?"

"It's Kaori we're talking about. She never gives straight answers," Nix grumbled. "But she said she had nothing to do with the Syndicate being there last night."

Gram scoffed again. "And you believe her?"

Another shrug.

"Kuda's loyal to her but he's too much of a coward to break away from Ryu completely." Nix frowned before continuing, not sure he really believed that argument. "She made it sound like Ryu wants the girl because she was a Military test subject. It's hard to imagine Ryu would ever get involved in research but I don't know. It's been a long time and people change."

Nix took a bite of his food, chewing in contemplative silence. He was surprised when Gram suddenly jabbed his fork in front of his face.

"I know what you're thinking, and the answer is hell no."

Nix's eyes widened before he looked away, annoyed.

"I didn't say I believed her," he grumbled, "but you know how she is. She'd do just about anything to spite her brother. If Ryu really is going after the girl, Kaori would definitely be willing to help us."

"Yeah and stab you in the back in the process. Or did you forget about that? We go through this every time, dumbass."

"I'm just telling you what she told me," Nix snapped.

Gram let out another sigh.

"Look, I get it," Gram's voice grew softer. Clearly he didn't want to start another fight. "You two have a history. It's hard to move on from that. But as far as I see it, that history has never worked out in your favor. Maybe you know a side of her that I don't, but all I've ever seen from Kaori is lies."

Nix never talked about his past, not even with Gram. Gram knew she'd betrayed him and left him behind. He also knew that in spite of that Nix never could seem to cut her out of his life completely.

What Gram didn't understand was that Kaori was more than just a lover he couldn't get over. He'd been following her lead ever since they were kids. Even after all this time he struggled to figure out who he was supposed to be on his own.

"I put Kai and Thea in the barracks." Gram's voice interrupted his thoughts. "It's close to the house and far from the workshop."

Nix nodded his appreciation as Gram stood up and cleared their plates away from the counter, then stretched with a yawn.

"Kay sent me about a dozen messages while you were gone," Gram told him.

Nix let out a snort. "What do they want this time?"

"Sounds like things are pretty rough in town. Most of the merchants have left, but they claim half the Wilds have turned up, looking for Thea. They want me to come keep an eye on things. Maybe I can learn something useful while I'm there."

"I'll come with you," Nix said, standing.

"No, I need you here. I know Luc is capable, but if anything happens, I don't want him to be on his own."

"Then I'll go back to town," Nix argued. "You can stay here."

"Right, that sounds like a great idea. I'll just send you off on your own to a town full of people who either want you dead or captured."

"I can take care of myself," Nix spat.

"Please, Nix, I need you to do this. I have enough to worry about right now. I don't want to have to worry about you too."

The pleading worry in his voice told Nix any argument he made would be futile. Gram rarely insisted Nix do anything. He'd lecture him for doing stupid things, of course, but usually left him to do what he wanted.

"Fine," Nix grumbled. He opened his mouth and closed it again, unsure what else to say. Gram was just as likely to get himself into trouble in Karza as Nix was.

"I'll be careful," Gram said with a grin. "And I'll contact you if anything comes up."

Nix stiffened even before the creaking sound of the back door reached them. The siblings were coming. He turned, ready to dash for the front door before they could reach the kitchen.

Gram stopped him by placing a hand on his elbow.

"You really should do something about that scary face of yours," Gram said with a grin, though his eyes narrowed slightly. "I'd rather you didn't scare Thea any more than you already have."

"Then you should let me go," Nix grumbled, shaking Gram's hand off his arm.

It was too late. The siblings were already rounding the corner into the kitchen. The girl stiffened and let out a squeak of surprise before grabbing her brother's arm in panic. The brother's face broke into a smile, though there was a confused stiffness in his eyes as he glanced toward Nix.

"Hey guys," he said, "we came to see if you have an extra water pitcher or something we could keep in the barracks."

Gram shrugged and gestured toward the cupboards.

"You're welcome to check. Take whatever you need."

"Thanks," Kai said as he moved toward the cupboards. His sister followed close behind him, keeping her head down and her shoulders hunched.

Why is he here? I thought he'd left.

Nix resisted the urge to roll his eyes. Instead, he moved to leave the kitchen, but Gram grabbed his arm again.

"Good timing. I wanted to let you know I need to make a trip back to Karza. Lucan will be here, and so will Nix, so you don't have to worry."

"Why?" the girl blurted out, her voice high and cracking. She wasn't asking why Gram was leaving. She was asking why Nix was staying. Her fingers wrung together in front of her as she hunched her shoulders in embarrassment for having voiced the question.

"I wish I didn't have to," Gram said, "but I need to check on some things. Hopefully I'll be back tomorrow or the day after at the latest."

"I hope everything's okay," the brother said, turning to them with a frown. He glanced between them with that same odd expression. Nix wished he knew what the man was thinking, but the girl's thoughts made it impossible to tell. He balled his hands into fists to keep himself from rubbing his forehead. Why was Gram making him stay here for this? It was only scaring her more.

He's dangerous.

Gram seems okay. Even Lucan.

But I don't want him here.

I don't trust him.

Her thoughts made memories of his own resurface, something that always happened at the worst times.

Monster.

He's done enough harm already.

If it were up to me, we'd leave him in his cell and forget about him.

His palms grew hot and slick. Beads of sweat tickled his neck, and his vision turned hazy. He pulled his arm away from Gram's grip with a rough jerk and took quick strides out of the kitchen without looking back. As soon as he'd rounded the corner out of sight, he broke into a run. It didn't matter that it was only a few feet to the door, he needed to get outside. He needed to get away. He couldn't leave the base, not with Gram leaving, but he could put as much distance between himself and the girl as the outer walls would allow.

That was scary.

Why is he so mad?

I thought he was going to do something.

I wish he wasn't here.

It wouldn't be enough. As long as he was at the base, he wouldn't be able to escape her thoughts.

It was going to be a long few days.

The gray-green
cast of the
light overhead,
dim and sickly,
makes me shiver
though my heart
pounds like a
drum inside my
chest and sweat
drips down my
neck.

The gaping mouth
of the pod
in front of
me waits to
swallow me up,
to sear my
body with its
burning heat,
leaving me nothing
but a husk,
a dry and
broken shell.

Cold blue eyes
peer down at
me, studying
like I'm a
specimen
in a dish,
no trace of
any kind of
sympathy,
only detached
inquiry.

I turn and
try to break
away, to run,
but strong hands
grab me, hold
me down and
force me to
the ground as
a deep growl
rumbles in my
ear.

"The girl is mine."

I break into
a wild run
until I'm far
away from that
prison, from that
nightmare
that haunts me
even when awake.

Branches close in
around me, grasping,
tearing,
scratching,
cutting
off my escape.

A sharp hot
pain burns in
my side and
falling to my
knees in despair
I see you lying
there.

I'm too late.

Darkness closes in
around me, hot
and suffocating.

I can't breathe.

I gasp for
air but can't
cry out.

I'm trapped.

I sink into
the empty black.

Alone.

Chapter Seven

"You're avoiding Lucan," Kai said as he plopped down beside her in the courtyard that connected the barracks to the main house.

Thea cringed. There was no accusation in Kai's tone, but she could tell he didn't approve.

"No I'm not." It was pointless to lie to Kai, but the words slipped out defensively.

Kai just flashed a grin and raised his eyebrows.

"You know, sometimes it's really annoying that you know everything," she grumbled.

He laughed and draped one arm over her shoulders affectionately.

"I know it's hard to trust strangers," he said, keeping his voice light. "And I know he makes you nervous because of his connection to the labs. I'm not trying to push you. I think it's okay to take your time. I just don't want to see you wear yourself out stressing about it so much. Your channeling still hasn't fully recovered."

"Yup, you're definitely annoying," she grumbled, but bumped her shoulder against him affectionately.

"And I'm going to keep being annoying so long as you keep pushing yourself too hard," he told her with another laugh. "So I guess that's indefinitely."

She turned away from him in mock outrage and bumped against him again—this time harder—but she couldn't hold in her laugh.

"For what it's worth," Kai said, his voice softening, "I think they're good guys. They want to help us, and I think we're as safe with them as we were on our own. Safer actually."

"All of them?" Thea asked.

Gram had left them here with Nix. As much as she hated to admit it, her track record against him wasn't good, but she was sure she was the only one who could possibly stand up to him. She shivered at the thought.

Kai frowned and looked away from her, toward the barracks. Thea resisted the urge to whip her head around, expecting Nix to pop up from the direction of Kai's gaze.

"I don't know," he said with a shrug and a forced smile. "I don't think Gram would leave us here with Nix if he thought it would put us in danger. We just have to trust that."

Thea shook her head. She couldn't. She was sure Nix had motives of his own, regardless of what Kai thought. At the very least, he had some kind of connection to the Syndicate that Gram and Lucan avoided talking about.

"If it helps, Lucan is a Macro too."

"Really?" Thea squeaked. It didn't help. She wasn't entirely comfortable with Lucan either, hence the reason she had been avoiding him.

Kai chuckled at her reaction.

"Sorry. I guess not. I trust him though, if that helps. He says he thinks he can help my knee. It'll never be the same as it was, but he thinks I can improve my mobility and get to where I can walk without much pain."

Thea smiled and leaned against his shoulder. If that were true, that Lucan could help Kai, then it would be worth trusting him.

"I think he can help you too," Kai said softly, "when you're ready."

Thea nodded. She didn't know if she would ever be ready, but she couldn't keep waiting for a day that might never come.

"I think I'm ready to try," she said, her voice small and a lot less brave than she would have liked.

"An herbal soak for the micro-tears, I think. And maybe a supplement to even out your channeling."

Lucan's voice was quiet as he wrote on his tablet. It felt more like he was talking to himself than to her. Thea found it unsettling. It reminded her too much of the researchers, who hardly ever looked at her as they performed their experiments.

She wasn't a child, she reminded herself, and she did want to get better. She didn't want to have to rely on everyone else to take care of her. The best way to do that was to take responsibility for her own health, instead of simply being a victim.

She cleared her throat and forced herself to ask, "Micro-tears?"

"In your muscles," Lucan didn't look up as he made more notes. "Your legs are still hurting, correct? There are micro-tears in your muscles from using your enhancement."

Finally, he set the tablet down and met her eyes. His expression was kind and patient, but with a hint of eagerness.

He wasn't a researcher, she reminded herself again.

"There are two problems most Macros tend to have, and they are related. First, it's too easy to use our channeling without giving it much thought. We can end up using much more than we need, rather than regulating it. Most people, outside of the Military, never have the opportunity to learn proper channeling awareness or control."

He grew silent for a moment with a slight frown on his face, as though he were lost deep in thought.

"And the second?" Thea prodded, startling him out of his reverie.

"Right," he continued with an apologetic smile. "The second, like I said, is related. It's too easy to end up using our enhancement like a crutch, to rely almost exclusively on our ability instead of our natural physical strength. That's hard on the body. It's better to strengthen yourself physically and only use the smallest amount of channeling necessary to give your natural abilities an extra boost."

Thea eyed Lucan, noticing for the first time that he did seem very physically fit. He wasn't as broadly built as Gram, but his forearms, visible below his rolled sleeves, were well toned. She suppressed a shudder. She realized it wasn't just his aloof personality or ties to ability research that made him a little frightening. He was powerful. If he wanted to, he could be dangerous.

"You're a Macro too," she stated, though she'd meant it as a question.

Lucan nodded.

"The colloquial term for my ability is Waller, though it's actually a form of enhancement. Have you ever hardened an object using your channeling?"

Thea nodded hesitantly as she thought of the night she'd fought Nix. She'd used her energy to stiffen the paper envelopes, to keep them from breaking open so easily. She'd never thought much about it. It was just something she'd realized she could do.

"Making a wall, or channeling shield, is similar. In terms of channeling parameters, it's similar to manipulation, so not every Enhancer can do it. It's unclear why, but Manipulators also seem to be unable to create channeling shields, even though they should meet the required channeling parameters.

"Sorry," he said, pausing with an apologetic smile. "I'm probably confusing you."

Thea shook her head.

"A little, but only because I don't know all the terms. I wish I understood all this more."

Her face burned as tears stung her eyes. She'd gone to the lab for help but instead they'd used her, broken her. In the end she didn't understand her abilities or herself any more than when she'd gone to them in the first place. Her words tumbled out and she found she couldn't stop herself.

"I have these abilities that I don't even understand. When I manifested, my teachers said I was special, and that I could have a great future. It seems to me that all I've really gotten is pain and worry. And...and people have gotten hurt because of me."

Her last words turned to a sob. She bit the inside of her cheek, trying to stop herself from crying. Why had she told Lucan all that? She was embarrassed for showing how weak and confused she was. She didn't need to cry in front of him, too.

"I'm truly sorry for what you've been through," Lucan said and the kindness in his voice was such a stark contrast to his absent-minded indifference that Thea couldn't hold back her tears anymore. He handed her something to wipe her face, as the tears streamed down her cheeks.

"You should know that you aren't alone," he said. "Unfortunately, most people outside the capital don't understand their own abilities, or how abilities in general work. Education is sorely lacking in that area, even though more than half of the citizenry is expected to manifest with an ability."

Thea gave him an uncertain smile. His words were probably meant to reassure her, but knowing she wasn't the only ignorant one did little to assuage her own personal confusion.

"Most people don't even understand the basic differences between Micros and Macros," he continued. "What do you think separates people into one category or the other?"

"Their channeling?" she said uncertainly. "Macro means something large, right? So Macros have more channeling."

Lucan shook his head.

"That's the common misconception, and unfortunately, the language we use only adds to it. The terms macro and micro actually refer to how channeling interacts with the body. Macro can mean large, but it can also mean that something has a larger scale or scope. On the other hand, micro can refer to something small, or something that is more localized."

Thea nodded. She understood that much at least, though she didn't understand how it pertained to abilities.

"Now, when we talk about channeling, we're really talking about the act of channeling the kinetic energy that our body produces. For Micros, this energy is localized in the brain, and the act of channeling maintains that central pocket of energy. For Macros, the energy is in a more constant state of flux throughout the body, and their abilities often require that the energy be channeled outside the body. Thus, Macros channel energy on a larger, more external scale, while Micros keep their energy more localized."

"That explains why Macro energy is easier to detect," Thea said. Somehow, Lucan's explanations made much more sense than anything she'd ever learned before.

"It's also why channeling sickness is something only Macros experience," he explained. "And why Macros often have a much more difficult time controlling their energy."

"Is there any way to stop it?" she asked, "channeling sickness."

Lucan shook his head.

"Unfortunately, there is no known cure, and the reasons why it occurs aren't fully understood. There are treatments that can help, however. If you feel comfortable with it, I believe I can design a plan that will help you."

Thea nodded. Lucan wasn't a researcher. He was kind, and he really wanted to help her. She felt she could trust him.

"Thank you," she said.

"To begin with, I'd like you to work on increasing your physical strength," he said. "I know they aren't pleasant, but the most effective way to do that is to take channeling suppressants. This will ensure you can increase your strength without relying on your enhancement."

Thea swallowed, trying to force down the sudden nausea that came with the memory of the medicines they'd given her in the lab.

It wasn't just the thought of the medicine that made her stomach twist. Without her channeling she wouldn't be able to defend herself.

She hadn't seen him since Gram had left, but she knew Nix was still there, lurking around the base. Would Lucan be able to stop him if he decided to attack her? Lucan was a Macro, but he didn't seem like much of a fighter. What if Nix had help?

She shuddered, but Lucan didn't seem to notice as he had returned to writing on his tablet. Thea took a deep breath and tried to calm herself. It didn't matter if she had her channeling or not. She couldn't stop Nix, not the way she was. She couldn't protect herself or Kai.

She had to get stronger.

She clasped her hands in her lap, squeezing them together until her knuckles turned white and her fingers ached.

"Okay," she said. "I want to try."

Nix's stomach rumbled as he pulled the back off the old comm monitor on the table in front of him. That morning he'd eaten the last of the meal bars that he kept in the workshop—a large three-walled garage where he spent most of his time. He hadn't wanted to risk going to the kitchen for food.

It wasn't a big deal. He was used to going long periods of time without eating. It was how he'd spent most of his life.

His stomach rumbled again, and he sighed.

The girl was in Lucan's office. It sounded like their conversation would go on for a while. Nix only needed to be in the kitchen long enough to warm a meal and grab another box of meal bars from the cupboard. If he went in the front door he could easily get in and out of the kitchen without the girl ever knowing he'd been there.

It would be fine.

The house was quiet when he entered. Lucan was still talking with the girl. He'd offered to make a training program for her.

She trusted him.

That was good. Lucan could be oblivious to the way other people reacted to him sometimes, but he was a kind man, and a good doctor.

The more she trusted Lucan and Gram, the lower her anxiety would be. That would only make it easier for Nix. It didn't matter that she was still afraid of him or that she thought he might do something to hurt her. All he had to do was stay away from her.

He found a plate of leftover food wrapped in plastic in the fridge, likely saved for him by Lucan. After throwing it in the microwave, he opened the cupboard to search for another box of meal bars.

"Oh, hey."

Nix jumped at the sound of the brother's voice behind him and hit his head on the corner of the cupboard door as he turned around.

"Sorry," the brother said, as Nix rubbed his head. "You probably aren't used to us being here." He gave Nix that strange look again.

"Yeah, I guess." The truth was, it was easy for Nix to forget about the brother, since he couldn't hear his thoughts over the girl's.

"Well, we met the other day, but not really. Your name was Nix, right?" There was no hesitancy in his tone, only friendliness.

"Yeah."

Nix turned back to the cupboard and pulled out a box of meal bars as the microwave beeped, signaling that his food had finished heating. He turned toward the microwave, then stopped and reached back into the cupboard for a second box. The less he had to come to the house, the better.

"I never got the chance to actually introduce myself. If you didn't already know, my name is Kai, and my sister is Thea."

Nix nodded as he opened the microwave and pulled out his food.

"Yeah, I knew."

Nix was used to people reacting to him the way the girl did. He didn't even know why half the time. In town, people gave him a wide berth. Gram said it was because he always looked angry. Nix knew that was only part of it. Micros knew how much channeling he had, even if their sensing was weak. That made them nervous, and that nervousness was often infectious.

For some reason, Gram had never displayed any of that apprehension. Instead, he'd only seemed amused by Nix's surly attitude.

The brother was like him. He would fit in well here.

Nix yanked open the drawer with utensils, suddenly feeling irritated.

To his surprise the other man let out a quiet chuckle. Nix picked up his food and the boxes of meal bars and turned to leave.

"You were the one who followed my sister back to our village, right?"

Nix eyed him warily, wondering why he wanted to know. Maybe, like his sister, he was suspicious of Nix's motives after all. Maybe this was his way of trying to get information from him.

There was no point denying it though, so Nix nodded.

This time, the brother laughed.

"Man, I didn't know what to do when I sensed you. I've never seen channeling like yours, and Thea was exhausted from her trip to town. I was really worried, but then you just sat there, not doing anything, so I was relieved but pretty confused, too."

Nix shifted his weight awkwardly, not knowing how to respond.

"Well thanks," the brother said, surprising him again. "Gram said you followed her to make sure the soldiers didn't. And if you hadn't been there when the Syndicate showed up, I don't know what we would have done."

Nix just shrugged. He looked down at his food, then towards the doorway.

The brother chuckled again.

"Sorry to keep you from your meal. I just wanted to say that."

"Thanks," Nix mumbled. "And..."

What was he supposed to say? Sorry people are always afraid of me? Sorry I used to be in the Syndicate? Sorry I'm not like Gram or Lucan?"

"Never mind," he grumbled and moved toward the door.

"See you later," the brother said as though the conversation hadn't turned awkward.

Nix rounded the corner into the hallway and nearly bumped into Lucan. Startled he craned his neck to make sure the girl wasn't with him. Had he gotten distracted and missed her approach again?

No, she'd gone outside to the courtyard.

Lucan is okay actually. I like him. If only Nix wasn't here...

Nix scowled.

"Sorry, Nix." Lucan said then looked down at the plate of food in his hands. "I see you found the leftovers. Good."

"Sorry," Nix mumbled. "Thanks."

He started to walk away but Lucan stopped him.

"You look like you aren't feeling well. Are you alright?"

"I'm fine," he grumbled. Instead of letting him past, Lucan pointed at the meal bars tucked under one arm.

"Is that all you've been eating?"

Nix shrugged and Lucan sighed.

"You and Gram, I swear," Lucan muttered, sounding exasperated.

"I wasn't that hungry. I'm eating the food you left now, so what does it matter?"

Lucan shook his head with another sigh.

"Do you want me to bring something out to the workshop after dinner?"

Nix shook his head. He'd rather not give the brother, who he was sure was listening, an excuse to follow him.

"I'll get some later. Thanks."

He turned away before Lucan could say anything else.

There was that feeling again. The itchy, prickly feeling as tiny bumps formed on her skin even though she wasn't cold.

Thea felt like she was being watched.

She hadn't seen Nix since Gram had left, but she knew he was there, lurking around the base. Signs of his presence were everywhere. The extra bedroom that must be his, though she'd never seen him enter or leave it. The plate of food Lucan set aside at meals. The occasional sound of a bike's engine that never strayed too far from the outer walls.

She shivered. He was there, watching them.

It made her feel jumpy, like her senses were constantly on high alert, waiting for him to make his move.

Her head ached as Lucan scooped some kind of stew into large bowls. She wasn't really listening to what Lucan and Kai were saying until Kai shouted, "This is it!"

Thea looked up from her own bowl to see him looking down at his.

"This is our mom's stew," he said, looking up at Lucan.

Lucan smiled.

"I don't know that mine is as good as your mother's."

"Our dad always tried to make it, but never got it right. This tastes almost exactly like it, though."

Thea took a bite. The stew was hot and burned her mouth a little. It had a simple, mild flavor. The vegetables were cooked well in a light-colored broth. The primary flavor came from the vegetables themselves, with a few fresh herbs adding a refreshing taste. The stew was made mostly of root vegetables, which made it hearty and filling.

Tears stung her eyes.

Mom's stew. It was simple, but there was an elegance to it, just like their mother.

"I can see why dad had a hard time getting it right," she said after clearing her throat. "It's too simple of a dish for him. He was probably always trying to add additional seasonings or ingredients."

"Our father is a cook at the local tavern," Kai told Lucan. "He loves cooking, and he's really good at it, but he could never make Mom's stew the way she made it."

"Will you tell us about her?" Thea asked Lucan as he set aside an extra bowl before filling one for himself.

Lucan's sad expression wasn't what she expected, and she immediately regretted asking. Before she could apologize, Lucan spoke.

"Gram is the storyteller," he said in his usual calm voice. "You should ask him when he gets back."

Thea was disappointed. Besides wanting to know more about her mother, she'd found that she enjoyed listening to him. His voice was soothing. She would have liked to hear him tell a story.

"Gram is better at telling the fun stories," Lucan went on. "About the times he got us into trouble and Iris got us out of it. I'm afraid my stories won't be as exciting. When I was adopted, Iris went with me, to help with the adjustment. That was how she met..."

Lucan paused with a glance toward Kai and cleared his throat, like he'd changed his mind about what he was about to say.

"It was a terrifying time for me," he continued, "but Iris made it easier. She made my new home feel like home, and my new family feel like family— because that's what she was to me."

Thea thought of nights spent curled under her mother's arm, a blanket wrapped around them both. Her mother pointed out pictures in the stars, and told her stories of creatures, heroes, and adventures. Of sunny afternoons sitting on her mother's bed as she showed them pictures of flowers and different plants in her favorite book. Kai was always more interested in that than Thea was.

"You're my family now," Lucan said, surprising her again. "I only hope I can give you some of the same strength Iris gave to me."

Tears filled her eyes.

Family.

They weren't alone.

"Thank you," she whispered. "For everything. I'm sorry I—"

She couldn't finish as the tears spilled over and her throat closed.

"You have nothing to be sorry for," Lucan said with a sad shake of his head. "I'm sorry for what you've been through. I wish...I wish I'd found you sooner. I wish I'd been there for you, after Iris's passing."

"You knew?"

"The matron of our orphanage kept in touch with Iris. She never would tell us where she had gone, but Gram and I had resources. We could have found out. We could have been there for her. Next to my time in the research facility, it's one of my biggest regrets."

"I think our mom would just be happy that you're doing well," Kai said. Thea nodded her agreement.

Lucan smiled again.

"I think you're right. Thank you."

Family.

Nix should have known. Of course Lucan and Gram would feel that way about the siblings. Of course the siblings would fit right in with them. They were the same. They belonged.

He didn't.

He shrugged off the thought. It didn't matter.

But Nix isn't like them.

It was a constant reminder that he couldn't ignore.

Evening finally came along with the blissful dampening of the girl's thoughts. It was easier to find ways to distract himself when she was asleep. It wasn't much, but it was the closest thing he got to a respite, though her disturbing dreams allowed for little peace.

He rubbed his head and took a deep breath, forcing himself to lower his channeling. Normally, raising it helped him focus his telepathy. It was how he filtered out specific thoughts in a group, or pushed the noise to the back of his mind when he didn't want to listen to them. He found himself doing it subconsciously a lot of the time—an automatic reaction after so many years of using the technique to shield himself.

It didn't work on her thoughts. Raising his channeling only made them louder.

He'd always thought of his telepathy as a burden, but now that he couldn't rely on it, he appreciated the ability more. Not being able to avoid Lucan or the brother when he wanted to was a problem. He hadn't even sensed Kuda and the others when they'd approached the siblings' camp. Catching him off guard was something that usually only Kaori could do.

He didn't like it.

That night, as her dream resembled all too clearly the research facility and the experiments done on her, Nix found even the workshop to be too confining of a space. He picked up some parts from one of the two long tables that took up most of the space and tossed them into a box along with a set of tools.

He didn't usually have a particular goal in mind when he worked on old devices or tinkered with spare parts. He just enjoyed taking things apart and putting them back together for no other reason than because it kept his hands busy and provided a distraction from his ever-present telepathy.

He carried the box outside along with a chair. As he sat down, he closed his eyes, enjoying the soothing relief of the cool night air on his face. He took a deep breath, trying to slow his heart rate as the girl's fear made his own heart race and his muscles tense. The sight of the long pod in front of her made his body itch. The machine, he knew, was used for measuring channeling, and the procedure was not pleasant. He rubbed his arms, trying not to remember the burning, tearing feeling of his energy being ripped from his body.

He dropped his head into his hands and rubbed them over his face as though he could rub the images away.

He couldn't.

He'd been too hard on her before. Of course she was scared and overwhelmed. Of course she didn't trust him. What other reaction could she have, given what she'd been through? He'd been an idiot.

He went back inside and tossed the parts back onto the table before moving toward his bike. He couldn't go far, with Gram gone, but he had to get away, at least for a little bit. He couldn't stay here. Not like this.

The girl's nightmare shifted into a series of distorted images. A researcher leaned over her, his eyes cold and calculating. She tried to run but someone caught her from behind, slammed her hard to the cold floor. She cried out in pain as she looked up into the face of her attacker. It was Nix. He loomed over her, his face shadowed and full of malice. She managed to break free from his grasp and from the lab, or maybe the dream had just changed.

She was running through a dark forest, with the trees so close together she hardly had room to maneuver. She broke free of the trees, into a wide, round clearing. Sharp pain burned her side, spreading through her body like fire. She saw a shadow of a figure on the ground, but before she could move towards it everything went black.

The dream hadn't stopped. Everything around her was simply dark, the blackness hot, thick, and suffocating. He could taste it, filling his mouth and throat, tightening his chest. He gasped for air. He couldn't breathe. He couldn't think. He had to get out. He had to stop this.

He stumbled to the cabinet against the wall and rummaged clumsily until his hands grasped a small bottle—channeling suppressant. He took a long drink straight from the bottle. His stomach twisted with nausea but he reached into the cupboard for another bottle—a sedative. He took another long drink then stumbled towards the bed in the back of the room. The medicines acted quickly. He collapsed to the bed, trying to take slow breaths, trying to keep the drugs down when his stomach wanted to reject them. The workshop spun around him. He felt like he was falling though he knew the bed was solid beneath him. His channeling grew too weak to sustain his telepathy. His eyes closed in relief as the girl's thoughts and the workshop slipped away.

Something wasn't right.

Kai was distracted, tense. He barely protested when she told him she wanted to make breakfast for them and Lucan. She was sure he would fret or worry that she was too tired. He knew she hadn't been sleeping well. He knew she'd had another nightmare.

Yet he said nothing about it. He simply sat in the kitchen quietly, his fingers under his chin and his brows pulled together in contemplation.

It made her even more jumpy.

What did he know that he wasn't telling her? Did he sense something? Was it related to Nix?

She shivered as she beat eggs in a large bowl. She couldn't remember much of her dream, as usual, but she remembered his face, dark and shadowed, and the tight grip of his hand on her arm.

She was glad that Lucan had told her to wait a bit longer to start the channeling suppressants. He wanted to make sure she was fully recovered first. She wanted to wait until Gram returned, though she doubted there was much he could do to stop Nix.

Not like there was much she could do either.

"Hey, you okay? You don't look so good."

Thea jumped at the sound of Kai's voice. A quick glance showed her that he wasn't speaking to her. She looked behind her to see Nix standing in the doorway of the kitchen, a dark scowl on his face. She spun around in surprise, spilling egg all over the counter. Her elbow brushed against the hot pan on the stove, and she yelped in pain.

"Thea!" Kai jumped up and moved to her side. "Are you okay?"

She nodded without taking her eyes off Nix. He turned around to leave the kitchen but before he had rounded the corner, the sound of the front door crashing open in the other room made Thea jump again.

"You all okay? What's going on?" Gram's voice shouted from the living room.

Kai guided her toward the sink to rinse her hands and put cool water on her elbow. She followed him numbly, her channeling rising as she strained her senses. Her muscles snapped tight in anticipation.

What was going on? Were they under attack?

"You dumbass! What did you do?" Gram shouted, closer now, though still out of sight. Nix stopped, his body rigid.

"What is it?" Lucan's voice from the other side of the hallway, quiet but clearly alarmed. "You don't look well, Nix. Are you alright?"

"No, he's not alright!" Gram shouted. He came into view as he stepped closer to Nix. His face was red with anger and his muscles bulged as he clenched his fists. To her surprise, Nix shrank away a step.

Sure, Gram was large, and his appearance was intimidating, but he was a Micro. Nix was a powerful Macro. There was no way Gram could beat him in a fight. So why did he suddenly look like someone who felt powerless and terrified?

Gram took a deep breath and tore his hand through his hair.

"Damn it, Nix," Gram said, his voice quieter but clearly still angry. "I told you I needed you here to make sure nothing happened while I was gone. What the hell were you thinking?"

Thea's eyes widened.

She'd been right. Gram had been wrong to leave Nix here with them. He'd done something, something to make Gram this angry, something that put them in danger.

What did Gram know? Was someone coming for them?

"Thea," Kai whispered, giving her a little shake before putting his arm around her. She hadn't realized she was shaking. "Thea, it's okay."

She shook her head. It wasn't okay. It would never be okay. So many people were after her, it was foolish to think hiding at the base was all they had to do, that Gram and Lucan could protect them on their own.

Lucan was saying something, but she couldn't seem to hear him over the buzzing in her ears. Her vision blurred and the lights overhead seemed too bright. Her head hurt and her body felt hot as the energy inside her rose in a sharp torrent.

Memories and nightmares filled her vision, blocking out the kitchen, making her forget where she was or what was real. Men dressed in black loomed above her, surrounding her, threatening and angry. They stepped closer and her panic sent her energy whipping into a storm she couldn't control.

"Stop!" she shouted.

Something solid hit her back, followed by a crash. Her hands and clothes felt warm and slick with sticky liquid. Just like her nightmare.

"No!"

It couldn't be real. She didn't want it to be real.

"No, Kai!"

It was too late. It was her fault. It was always her fault.

"Thea!"

Kai's voice. He was there. She reached for him blindly through her tears and instead felt something cold brush against her hand before finding her lips. The liquid stung as it slid into her mouth and down her throat. She felt the buzz of energy and recognized the drink Lucan had given her on her first day at the base.

That's right, she wasn't in Senari or the forest that haunted her dreams.

"Thea are you alright?"

A sob tore from her throat as Kai's long arms wrapped around her, pulling her close.

"It's okay. You're okay."

She blinked until she could see through her tears. There was no sign of Nix, only Lucan's worried face in front of her. Gram still stood near the doorway, looking toward the back door with a frown. The cupboards above her hung open, their contents strewn around her on the floor and countertops. Raw egg puddled on the floor, soaked her clothes, and dripped from her hands.

She'd lost control again.

"Please," she choked out between sobs. She buried her face in Kai's shirt, but her words were for Lucan. "Please, help me. I don't want to hurt anyone."

She felt a hand on her shoulder, followed by Lucan's soothing voice.

"It'll be alright. We'll figure this out together."

The muffled sound of shouting from
outside the thick and heavy door
that holds me captive
reaches me.

As shadows race along the wall,
I stand in shaking dread for what
new pain or horror waits me next.

The lights go out, replaced by red
that flashes with the distant sound
of the alarm before my door
clicks open.

A hesitant, unbelieving step and then
another. I wait.

One breath, then two
and then I open the door.

The hall is clear, the shouts are far
away and down another hall.
I take a step and then I try
to run on weak and shaking legs.

My vision blurs as dizziness
and weakness slow my pace.

My heartbeat races much too fast.
I'm falling.

A flash of dark, a ghost or man,
then gentle hands encircle me
and hold me up before I fall
asleep.

When next I wake, the nightmare ends.
I'm free.

My brother finds me, lost between
dream and memory, uncertain how
my salvation came to be.

Chapter Eight

Where are you? We need to talk.

It had been almost a week and Nix still hadn't returned to base. He hadn't even responded to the message Gram had sent him. Every time he looked at it, he remembered the girl, her eyes wide with terror as she stared at him, her out-of-control energy whipping around the room like a storm, ripping the cupboards open behind her, their contents flying through the air before crashing to the floor.

Nix understood then why the Military and Syndicate were both after her, and how she could have injured trained fighters in Senari. She had a lot of power, but she was also scared, impulsive, and out of control. If something didn't change, someone else was going to get hurt because of her.

Monster.

He knew all too well what had made her the way she was.

"You've got guts coming here at a time like this, I'll give you that."

Nix nearly dropped his phone at the sound of the voice from behind him. He'd parked his bike in a secluded corner of town, near the outer wall, not wanting to draw any more attention to himself than necessary. Of course, since it was impossible to hide his energy without channeling restrictors or a channeling suppressant, he wasn't surprised someone had decided to come looking.

Nix reached out his telepathy as he climbed off his bike, but didn't sense anyone else besides the approaching soldier nearby—just the rumble of thoughts coming from the rest of the town.

"And you've got guts taking me on yourself," Nix said, reaching for his sword.

Nix thought the man looked familiar, with his bronze skin and close-cropped hair, but he'd also seen a lot of soldiers in his life. The man was shorter than Gram, but it was obvious he was at least as muscular, if not more so.

"Alright, easy," he said, stopping several feet away with his hands up. "I just want to know if Gram is coming back."

Nix relaxed after checking the man's thoughts. He was a friend of Gram's and had been expecting to meet him in Karza several days ago.

"I can't imagine he sent you here," the man continued, "not with this many bounty hunters around."

"I'm not his pet," Nix growled. "I don't need to be sent anywhere."

"Alright, kid. I didn't mean anything by it. Just making conversation."

Yeah, this guy was definitely a friend of Gram's.

Nix rolled his eyes and turned away. He wasn't there for conversation.

"So, you know every Micro in town sensed you arrive, right?"

To his annoyance, the man fell into step beside him as he began to walk toward the center of town.

"I swear every bounty hunter and peacekeeper in the Wilds must be here," he continued, "except for Gram, of course. There're a lot of soldiers and Syndicate, too."

Nix almost replied that he could handle himself, but thought better of it and clamped his teeth together. Talking would only encourage him. Why was he following him, anyway?

"I suppose you think you can handle yourself," the man chuckled. "Well, Gram's right about one thing. You're cocky as hell."

This time Nix did roll his eyes.

"I'm meeting someone," Nix grumbled as they stepped out into the square.

If Nix hadn't known better, he would have thought it was Market Day. A few local shopkeepers and food sellers had set up stalls, hoping to profit off the unusual activity. It appeared some merchants had even decided to stay in town with their wares.

Unlike Market Day, the thoughts and sounds in the square were more subdued. Instead of the noise of bartering, sharing news, and greeting acquaintances, a hum of quiet murmurs buzzed around him.

"Sometimes I wonder if it's even worth it," a nearby merchant said in a hushed voice.

"Of course it is," the man next to him laughed. "With all these bounty hunters, we can set our prices as high as we want and call it a hazard fee."

"And what's to stop a crowd like this from taking what they want and leaving us with nothing? They're no better than the Syndicate, and the peacekeepers only care about their bounties, not actually keeping the peace."

Nix walked past them, his head down and his chin tucked into the collar of his jacket as he crossed to the tavern.

"You're going in there?" the soldier asked as he climbed the steps. "Maybe it's not guts. Maybe you're just crazy."

Nix didn't answer. The man shook his head and followed him inside.

The room fell silent as they entered, even though the tables were almost as full as they had been on Market Day.

Rumors say he's a monster.

That guy with him is no pushover.

Isn't that Jaxon? Why are they together?

If we try to take him here, we'd have to fight everyone in this room over him. If we can find him alone later...

Nix resisted the urge to rub his head as he moved toward the stairs. If Kaori was still in town she'd find him. He stopped, as his eyes fell on her, already sitting at a table with an older man he didn't recognize.

"Why's he here?" the soldier said, looking at the man sitting with Kaori.

"Who is he?" Nix asked.

"Intelligence officer."

"Shit."

Kaori met his eyes and gave him her usual smile, as if she'd expected him all along. He didn't miss the toss of her hair or the way her eyes narrowed. She wasn't happy to see him, or at least she wasn't happy that he'd seen her.

"Are you crazy?"

Nix nearly jumped as Kay's voice hissed in his ear.

They pulled him by the arm, dragging him toward a small alcove by the kitchen. He'd never been comfortable with Kay's habit of standing too close, but now he didn't even have room to step away.

"What the hell is wrong with Gram?" they asked without looking at him, as though they were talking to themself. "He knows half the Wilds are here in town. How could he let you come here alone?"

"I'm not here because of Gram," Nix snarled. Why did everyone seem to think he needed Gram to tell him where he could and couldn't go?

Kay shook their head.

"I don't know if you're an idiot or what, but you need to leave. Right now. You know I like you Nix, but I'm not about to let you turn my tavern into a crime scene. You can go through the kitchen. Go."

They shoved him into the kitchen as the soldier's voice drifted from the entrance.

"Ah, just the two idiots I was looking for."

"Get out of our way Jaxon. We have business that doesn't concern you."

"I highly doubt you have business in Kay's kitchen," he said with a laugh. "And you know there'll be hell to pay if they catch you back there."

"Now, now boys," Kay said in their friendly, teasing tone, "you know better than to stand around in my way. Go sit down and I'll bring you some drinks."

There wasn't much else Nix could do unless he wanted to start a fight with the whole tavern. He'd rather not owe Kay for that, so he sighed and made his way through the kitchen to the back exit.

As much as he didn't want to, it was time for him to return to the base.

Thea had never been very good at controlling her abilities. She always used too much channeling, her instructors had told her in school. That was why she felt so drained after difficult classes, why she experienced headaches and fitful sleep.

Channeling sickness, the local physician had told her father—the same illness that had taken her mother. There was no cure, but the researchers at the Military lab might be able to help.

Her father had opposed the idea, of course, but she couldn't let herself continue to be a burden on him and Kai, not after her mother's death.

She couldn't stay the way she was. Something had to change.

Her time in the lab had only made things worse. She could feel it every time her channeling tore through her body. Instead of merely struggling for control, it felt like she had no control over her energy whatsoever. When she was afraid or upset, it would lash out on its own, latch onto whatever it could. It had happened in Senari. Kai's knee injury had happened because of her. She couldn't let that happen to anyone else.

Lucan's training plan wasn't easy. She was sure it wasn't supposed to be, but the medications made her nauseous and left her with a pounding headache, which only made the exercises that much harder. It was hard to push her body physically when everything else made her feel too exhausted to move. Her concentration only seemed to worsen with each passing day.

She felt like she wasn't making any progress, and it was frustrating.

Kai was worried about her. She could see it in the way he looked at her. He tried to get her to take more breaks, but she needed to get stronger.

She couldn't keep being such a burden to him. She couldn't keep making him worry about her.

So, even though she was tired, she pushed herself to go to the gym whenever Kai was busy with Lucan or Gram. She didn't like that Gram was training him to shoot or teaching him fighting techniques. She wasn't particularly skilled at fighting, nor did she like the thought of hurting someone, but at least she had the abilities for it. Kai was a Micro. She should be the one protecting him.

The house was quiet that day. Lucan was busy in his office, and Kai was outside with Gram. Thea strained through another set of exercises, her muscles aching with the effort. She thought she heard the sound of footsteps in the hallway and wondered if Kai and Gram had come back already.

"You're doing that wrong."

The deep voice startled her, and she lost her grip as she looked up toward the door. Rather than set up the weights on a different machine, she had found it easier to reattach the bar so she could do a pushing exercise with the same machine. Now she understood her mistake. As the heavy weights behind her crashed back into place, the bar shot toward her face. She cringed and threw up her hands on instinct. She heard the crash of the weights and felt a hot sting against her arm, but not the pain she was expecting.

She opened her eyes and lowered her hands. Nix was standing right in front of her, holding the bar at his side, the snapped end of the rope dangling to the ground.

She gasped and took a step back, her back hitting the machine behind her.

"Why were you doing that?" he snapped. "Are you stupid?"

"I—"

Her throat closed up as she looked from him to the bar in his hand. He must have pulled it so forcefully that it snapped.

Why? What did he want?

His scowl deepened when she didn't answer him. He moved forward slightly, slowly. She was trapped against the weight machine, unable to escape.

"Get away!"

Her voice cracked. Not the forceful command she was hoping for, but it worked. He dropped the bar and backed away.

"Do the exercises the way Lucan taught you, or don't do them at all," he growled as he turned away.

Before he could leave the room, Kai appeared in the doorway.

"Oh, hey," he said, not looking surprised to see Nix. Of course. He must have sensed him.

Nix pushed past him without any acknowledgment. Kai frowned as he watched him go, then turned to Thea. His frown deepened to worry when he noticed the bar lying on the floor.

"What happened?" He moved to her side. "Your arm."

She sucked in a breath as he touched her arm and looked down to see a red mark like a burn. The rope must have hit her when it snapped.

"Nix, he..."

Tears filled her eyes, and her throat closed up, cutting off the words.

"Come on, let's get this taken care of. Then you should try to rest."

He grabbed her hand and led her down the hall to the kitchen. Before they rounded the corner she heard the low rumble of Nix's voice again.

"You can't hide them here forever. They're going to come for her and there won't be anything you can do about it."

Was he making a threat?

She stopped. She didn't want to go in there, not with him.

Kai gave her arm a gentle tug without looking back.

"It's okay, Gram's with him."

Instead of a reply from Gram, Thea heard a shushing sound followed by the screech of a chair.

"Oh hey Kai, it's sparring time! Nix is going to join us!"

Gram grabbed Nix's arm as if to say he had no choice. Nix shrugged him off with a low grunt, his eyes darkening when he saw her.

"Just a minute," Kai said as he led her toward the cupboard where Lucan kept extra medical supplies. "Thea hurt her arm in the gym. I want to put something on it first."

"What happened?" Gram asked with a frown. "You okay? Want me to get Luc?"

Thea's face burned, and she stepped closer to Kai.

"No, I..."

She could blame Nix for what happened, but even though he had frightened her, it really had been her own fault. She hadn't followed Lucan's instructions, and once again, she'd caused trouble for everyone else.

"The rope snapped on the weight machine," she said quietly. "It hit my arm. I'm fine."

"Shit, I'm sorry Thea!" Gram exclaimed. "I guess I should check all the ropes to make sure none of them need replaced."

"It's not your fault," she replied quickly.

Her eyes darted to Nix and his eyes met hers. She expected him to tell Gram about her mistake, in that same harsh tone he'd used every time he'd spoken to her.

Do you know the best way to deal with a bully? her father had always told her. *Look them square in the eye and make sure they know they can't push you around. And if that doesn't work, punch them in the nose.*

Her mother hadn't liked that last bit of course but otherwise her advice was the same. *You are just as good as anyone else and the best way to show them that is to act like it.*

So even though she wanted to hide, she raised her chin and held his gaze. His eyes were blue, she realized, dark like the color of the night sky. She'd never really looked at them before. It would have been a nice color on anyone else.

To her surprise he said nothing about the gym, and to her satisfaction, he was the one to look away first. He stepped away from Gram toward the door, but Gram grabbed his arm again.

"Nuh uh," Gram said. "I owe you an ass-kicking, remember?"

Nix tore his arm away again with a snarl.

"I didn't come back for that."

He stormed toward the door and this time Gram let him go.

"Oh, welcome back, Nix. How are you feeling?" Lucan's voice came from the hallway.

She didn't hear a response from Nix, just the sound of the back door slamming shut. Lucan stepped into the kitchen a moment later with a sigh.

"Gram, you should really give him a break. You know this has been hard on him."

He looked startled when he noticed Thea and Kai, as though he hadn't realized they were in the room as well.

"Yeah, I know," Gram said, and his expression looked almost sad as he glanced at Thea then quickly looked away.

What did that mean?

"It doesn't change the fact that he needs his ass kicked."

Thea let out a snort. She couldn't believe Gram thought that was even a possibility.

Gram chuckled and his expression returned to normal.

"What, you don't believe I can?"

She looked down and wrung her fingers together.

"You're a Micro." Her voice came out small. She didn't want to be rude, but it was the truth.

"There's no reason a Micro can't hold their own against any Macro," Gram said with a mischievous twinkle in his eye. "Want to give it a try? You might learn a thing or two."

"Thea's on channeling suppressants today," Kai protested as he covered her wound with a bandage.

"Do you really have to try and fight everyone you meet?" Lucan said in exasperation before stepping closer to Thea. "What happened to your arm?"

"Just a little scrape from the gym. It's not a big deal, but I wanted to get something on it before we went outside," Kai answered.

Lucan peered at her more closely.

"You look pale," he said. "Are you feeling alright?"

"I'm just a little tired," she answered without meeting his eyes.

"Maybe you should go rest," Kai suggested as he put away the salve he'd used and closed the cupboard.

Thea shook her head. Now that Nix was back at the base. She'd much rather stay with the others even if she didn't think there was much they could do against him. Besides, lately she found the dim barracks to be suffocating. She'd rather not spend any more time there than she had to.

"I'll make you some tea, at least," Lucan said as he moved toward the cupboards.

"Thank you, but I think I just need some fresh air."

"So, are you going to tell me what really happened in the gym?" Kai asked once they were outside.

Thea didn't answer, but instead moved toward the bench under the large tree. She felt sore and tired, and it was a relief to sit down.

"Are you sure you're alright?" Kai asked, and she knew he wasn't asking about the gym this time.

She didn't know how to answer either question.

"I think you're pushing yourself too hard," Kai continued as he plopped down beside her. "I was surprised to realize you were in the gym again. You worked out earlier this morning, didn't you?"

"Yeah, I just felt like I could do more."

"I'm worried about you," Kai said. "I know you haven't been sleeping well, and I know you aren't telling the truth whenever you say you're fine. Even when I can't sense your energy, it's obvious that you're exhausted. Even Lucan can tell."

"I have to get stronger," she muttered.

Kai sighed and Thea bit her lip. She'd made him worry again. Wasn't she doing this so he wouldn't have to?

"Sorry," she said quietly as she leaned her head against his shoulder. "Maybe you're right."

She thought he was about to say something else, but the back door opened, and Lucan entered the courtyard, followed by Gram.

"I brought you some tea," Lucan said, eying her with a look of concern.

"Thank you." Thea took the cup and drank a small sip to satisfy both him and Kai.

"Well, that decides it," Gram said with a grin, as though they'd been discussing a problem, and he had found the solution. "You'll have to spar with me, Luc."

Lucan sighed, but a hint of a smile spread across his lips, contradicting the words he spoke next. "If that's the only way to get you to shut up, then I guess I have no choice."

Thea smiled. Whether he intended it or not, Gram had managed to shift the attention away from her and she was grateful. She was also curious and eager to see what each of them could do.

"It's been a long time, Luc. This is going to be fun," Gram said as he reached for the gun belt draped over the nearby wall. He pulled a cartridge from one of the pouches and loaded it into the gun.

"You're going to shoot him?" Thea asked incredulously.

"Nah, they're blanks," Gram said, flashing a mischievous grin. "They aren't dangerous, but they do hurt like hell."

Thea couldn't believe he was so eager to shoot them at his friend, even if they weren't dangerous.

"You fight?" she asked Lucan, once again noticing the toned muscles of his arms.

"I prefer not to," Lucan admitted, "but I'll make an exception to shut up this loudmouth."

"Just for that, I'm not going to take it easy on you, Luc."

"That's good. You'll definitely lose if you do."

Lucan always seemed so cool-headed and serious—a stark contrast to Gram's loud, sometimes childish, behavior. She saw a new side to Lucan now. Between the two men's banter and competitive grins, she thought maybe they were more similar than she had initially realized.

Gram grew quiet and serious as he dropped his stance. He suddenly seemed much more powerful and dangerous. Lucan, on the other hand, seemed much the same as he always did. He circled the yard slowly, considering Gram as though puzzling out the most optimal move to make. She supposed he had no reason to look concerned. From his standpoint, he had all the time in the world.

To her surprise, Gram made the first move. In one fluid movement, he fired his gun and lunged to one side, as though trying to anticipate the coming counterattack.

As she predicted, Lucan moved as soon as Gram raised his gun. He charged from the direction opposite where Gram had moved. Gram was ready for him, though, and fired again. Had his movement to one side been a ploy to direct Lucan's movements? Or was it simply dumb luck? Gram seemed more like the impulsive type than the type to think that far ahead, but maybe she had been wrong.

Lucan moved to dodge Gram's shots, but lost his balance, falling to a crouch. Gram fired another shot before Lucan could get back up. Thea was sure it would hit. She cringed in anticipation, but the bullet bounced harmlessly away as the air shimmered in front of Lucan.

Thea had never known a Waller before so even though he had told her about his ability, she was still surprised.

Gram straightened with a sigh, his usual casualness returning.

"That's why you're no fun, Luc. How am I supposed to prove my point if you go and throw up a wall?"

"I suppose you think I should just let you shoot me then. It's embarrassing enough that you knocked me down. Besides, your point was to prove that you could hold your own. I think you've done that."

"I guess," Gram said with a shrug, "but shooting you would be more fun."

"I don't understand," Thea interjected. "You said he knocked you down, but he never even got close to you. And his shots missed."

Lucan sighed as he brushed himself off.

"Gram can manipulate chance," Lucan explained. "The problem with speed enhancement is that it makes our footing much less stable. There's an increased chance we could slip or stumble. Gram can take that chance and make it a certainty."

"And you're saying I can learn to do this?" Kai asked, looking at Gram thoughtfully.

Gram shrugged.

"Depends. Chance manipulation takes a lot of concentration. There's a lot of information to keep track of. But you don't necessarily have to do what I do. My point is that there are ways to counter a Macro. Ideally, when you can use their own abilities against them. The more cocky and hot-headed a Macro is, the easier it is to find a weakness to exploit. Also, the more satisfying it is when you knock them on their ass."

Gram looked up toward the roof with a grin. Thea followed his gaze, wondering what he was looking at. She thought she saw a shadow of movement from the top of the roof and realization made her skin prickle. Had someone been watching them?

Nix?

Thea shivered.

Gram cleared his throat and shook his head, his grin quickly fading to a frown.

"Anyway, since you're good at sensing energy, that's probably the best place to start. I've seen Micros who can tell what move a Macro is about to make just by reading their channeling. Some can manipulate a person's perception, make them think they are seeing something they aren't or the other way around."

Gram frowned, like he was thinking of a specific person that he didn't particularly like.

"Micros aren't like Macros," he continued. "Our abilities aren't so constricted by a linear progression. You can learn to do just about anything, but it helps to start with what feels the most natural."

Kai nodded distractedly as he turned his attention back toward her.

"You really don't look well," he said. "I think you should go rest."

Thea shook her head.

"I heard you talking to Nix earlier," she said to Gram. She was tired of not knowing what was going on. "It sounded like he was warning you about something."

"I hope what he said didn't scare you," Gram said with a sigh. "I didn't want to make you worry, but there are a lot of people in Karza looking for you. Bounty hunters mostly."

Nix was in Karza talking to bounty hunters? About her? Why did Gram seem so calm about it?

Thea crossed her arms over her body, hugging herself tightly.

"I assure you, we are doing everything we can to keep you safe," Lucan said.

Lucan too. How could he say they were doing everything they could when they let Nix come into the place that was supposed to keep her safe? When they knew he was talking to bounty hunters and yet did nothing to stop him?

"Well, that's all for today," Gram said. He sounded suddenly annoyed. "I've got an asshole I need to talk to, but first, here."

He moved back toward the wall and picked up a small bundle.

"I got these for you, just haven't found the right time to give them to you."

He held the bundle out to Thea and she took them, feeling curious.

"What is it?"

"Throwing daggers."

She felt Kai stiffen beside her. She had to admit, she didn't love the idea of using a weapon either.

Their reaction must have been evident on their faces because Gram chuckled.

"It's just an extra precaution," he said. "Believe me, I'd much rather you didn't have to fight either, but if it comes to it, I want you to be prepared. I'll show you how to use them later, okay."

"Thank you," Thea said tentatively. She didn't want to hurt anyone, much less with a weapon, but there could certainly come a time when she might not have a choice. If she wanted to protect herself and Kai, then Gram was right. She should be prepared to do whatever it took."

"For now, I think you should get some rest," Lucan said. "When you feel up to it, I'd like to discuss your training schedule. I think it would be best if you took a break from the channeling suppressants for a while."

Thea nodded.

"You sure you don't want to go lie down?" Kai asked after Lucan and Gram had left.

She shook her head before leaning it against his shoulder.

"It's nice out here."

"I'm relieved that Lucan is going to change your training," he said. "If you won't listen to me, I think you'll listen to him."

She chuckled slightly. "You were right, as usual. I'm sorry I made you worry."

"I'm your brother," he said. "Worrying about you is my job."

"It shouldn't have to be."

Kai sighed. "How about if you promise not to push yourself so hard, I'll try not to worry so much?"

"What if I don't think that's a deal you can stick to?"

He laughed.

"I could say the same about you."

She bumped her shoulder against his.

"I guess I can try harder not to try so hard," she said.

He put his arm around her and squeezed her shoulder.

"Then I guess I won't have to worry quite so much."

I see my home from far above,
a dollhouse, small and quaint, with
an open roof so I can see inside.

The flowers in the garden pop with color,
their scent filling me with longing for a time
when life was not exactly simple,
but I was happy and content.

I see myself running through the halls,
bouncing with each eager step.
I'm still too young to know
that life is full of cruelty and pain.

Into Mother's lap I dive,
not noticing her tired eyes or
my father's hollow face.
I ask her for a story.

She pulls me close,
and brushes back my hair
with tender hands before she hugs me tight,
though not as tight as once she did.

My father calls my brother's name.
I see him peek around the corner.
His smile is timid, guilty.
He was supposed to watch me.

"Take care of your sister,"
my parents always tell him,
but now our mother beckons him
and smooths his hair with caring patience
before telling us a story spun from
starlight and faraway dreams. The story ends.

No longer am I watching from above.
I've grown, and now my house is not a game.

My mother seems to fade away before me.

As tears stream down my face,
her freezing hand finds mine
and places it in Kai's warm grasp.

"Take care of your sister,"
she tells him one last time.

Chapter Nine

"*Stop trying to force me to be around them,*" Nix snapped telepathically before Gram had even entered the workshop. "*You're only making things worse.*"

Gram just laughed. Of course. It was so like him to find the whole situation entertaining, and to provoke it on purpose.

"Maybe it would be easier if you tried actually talking to them yourself," Gram insisted. Before Nix could interject, he added, "without being an asshole."

"It wouldn't matter," Nix said, thinking back to the gym. He had tried to help her, hadn't he? It had only made her more afraid. "She doesn't trust me. I don't really care one way or the other, but you are only scaring her more by trying to force us to be around each other."

"Well, if you hadn't rushed off like a dumbass to fight the Syndicate that night, maybe she wouldn't have gotten the wrong idea in the first place," Gram grumbled.

He was usually quick to let things go, but ever since the girl and her brother had come to the base, it seemed he and Gram always ended up in the same argument.

"If I'd told you, you would have hesitated, and then the Syndicate would have taken them," Nix countered, not for the first time. "You worry too much and overthink, then make stupid decisions."

Gram's laugh was cold.

"You think I make stupid decisions? How many times have you run off on your own recently even though you know everyone who's looking for her would be just as happy to get their hands on you? I can't believe you went to Karza on your own!"

"I don't need you to worry about me," Nix snapped back. "I'm not your pet."

Gram had treated him like a kid since the first day they'd met, but Nix didn't stay at the base because he needed protection. He could take care of himself. The base was simply more convenient.

"Why did you go to Karza?" Gram asked suspiciously.

He sounds like he's been talking to Kaori again.

"I knew she was there," Nix mumbled. "I wanted answers."

"Damn it Nix!" Gram cut him off before he could continue.

"I haven't talked to her since the day she found me," Nix spat. "I saw her in town, meeting with an Intelligence officer. I came back to tell you that, but if all you want to do is argue, then I'm leaving."

I don't want to argue.

Gram ran his hand through his hair with a sigh.

"How did you know he was Intelligence?"

"Some soldier was waiting for you. He followed me to the tavern, and that's where we saw them."

"Jax," Gram said with an amused smile.

"I can't believe she'd actually work with the Military," Nix said, shaking his head. "Maybe if I go back, I can learn something. Maybe she'll tell me—"

"Hell no!" Gram shouted, cutting him off.

I swear, every damn time. This dumbass never learns.

"She knows something she isn't telling me," Nix argued.

"She always knows something she isn't telling you, and she knows just how to play you to keep you from finding out what it is. When are you going to learn that? Stay away from her, and don't let her anywhere near this base, do you hear me?"

"I'm not a kid," Nix spat.

Gram laughed without amusement.

"Then stop acting like one."

Nix scowled and turned toward his bike.

"I only came back to tell you what I learned," he snapped. "Whether it's from Kaori or someone else, we need answers."

"Wait."

Gram sounded tired and Nix could feel the regret in his thoughts. Regret that they always seemed to argue lately. Regret that he couldn't do anything about the way the girl's thoughts were impacting him. Regret that the circumstances seemed to be pushing him away.

"You look tired," Gram said. "You should stay here and rest today, try to get some real sleep. Luc says Thea's channeling shouldn't recover until the morning. If you want to leave after that, I won't stop you."

Nix opened his mouth to protest, but Gram cut him off.

"Stay," he said firmly, "or I'll shoot you with a stun bullet and tie you to a bed."

Nix smirked and shrugged.

"Fine," was all he said before turning back to his workbench.

"And come get some real food later. You can't live on meal bars alone."

Gram really did treat him like a kid.

He supposed sometimes that wasn't such a bad thing.

Nix was disappointed when he opened the fridge and didn't find a plate of food waiting for him. Of course, he'd been gone for almost a week, and had returned unexpectedly in the afternoon. There'd been no way for Lucan to know to save a plate for him. He closed the fridge and pulled two packaged meals from the cupboard.

As his food cooked, he made a mental list of the maintenance he needed to do on his bike. He'd been neglecting it lately, and he didn't want to miss the opportunity to make sure everything was in working order. He realized his mind had already started planning ahead for a time when he would leave the base without plans to return. He didn't want to think about that at the moment, so he pulled open the nearest cupboard absently.

The truth was, he missed the familiarity of his regular routine. He'd grown comfortable here, and he was loath to give it up. Unfortunately, that familiarity he'd grown accustomed to was already a thing of the past. Gram thought it would be easier for him to have her thoughts silenced? It only made it harder to avoid her, which made him feel even more on edge.

He swore and slammed the cupboard shut as he heard the brother's thoughts drawing closer. Nix jerked open the microwave, even though his meal was only half heated, and grabbed a utensil before turning to leave. It was too late. The siblings were already turning the corner into the kitchen.

"I'm not too tired, Kai. I like having the opportunity to cook again, and I want to give Lucan a break."

"If you're sure," her brother responded doubtfully. He looked up at Nix with a smile, clearly unsurprised and unfazed to find him there. The girl froze with her mouth open, her eyes wide with surprise and fear.

"Hey, Nix. You should have dinner with us now that you're back," the brother said. "Thea's cooking, so it should be really good."

Nix frowned and resisted the urge to roll his eyes. Gram wasn't the only meddlesome one. Instead, he shook his head and held up his half-cooked meal to show that he already had food.

"Too bad. In spite of how she acts, I think Thea would like the chance to impress you. You're totally her type."

Nix coughed in surprise. The brother grinned at his reaction.

"Ha! Thought so."

"Shit," Nix spoke out loud before he could stop himself.

"You have a problem?" the girl snapped. Her voice shook slightly, but she squared her shoulders and raised her chin. Her attempt at bravery would have been comical had he not just messed up in more ways than one—and if the brother's thought wasn't repeating itself in his head.

The brother tried and failed to stifle his laugh, and Nix turned away to hide his embarrassment.

"Do what you want," he grumbled.

"We need to talk later," he transmitted to the brother.

This time it was the brother's turn to speak out loud from surprise.

"Whoa, that's weird," he said, to which his sister replied, "Yeah, he is."

Thea had been relieved that Nix had refused to join them for dinner. She'd been angry enough at Kai for inviting him that she'd snapped at Nix without thinking. Normally, she'd be too afraid to get any words out. She wasn't afraid to speak her mind to Kai, though. He knew how she felt about Nix, and yet he'd wanted him to eat with them?

"I don't like it, Kai," she said to him as they exited the house after dinner. "He's dangerous. I don't trust him. I don't want to be around him. I can't stand that he's here at all."

Kai winced. Her channeling was still little more than a faint hum in her body, but he must have been able to sense her agitation, anyway.

"Sorry," she mumbled.

Kai sighed.

"I just figured it might help if we spent some time around him, got to know him a little. Maybe we'll learn something. Maybe he's not up to no good after all."

Thea shook her head in exasperation. Her brother trusted people too easily. He relied on his ability to read people—and he was usually right—but it couldn't tell him everything. He'd admitted that the others were keeping something from them. His ability couldn't tell what. In spite of that, Kai still believed that Nix might turn out to be trustworthy. She was surprised, but she also wasn't. That was just how Kai was.

"I can't, Kai," her voice shook, "I just can't."

"I know," he told her softly, his voice sad. "I know. I'm sorry, okay."

"It's not your fault."

He stepped next to her and placed a comforting hand on her shoulder.

"You really should try to get some sleep now. It's been a long day, and I know you're tired."

Thea stifled a yawn.

"What about you?"

Kai shook his head. "I'll be there soon. I've got some things to talk to Gram about. I'll see what I can find out about Nix, okay? We can talk about it tomorrow."

Thea hesitated, still not wanting to return to the barracks alone. She thought about insisting on joining him, wanting to know as much as she could, but she could see stubbornness in his face. She sighed and relented.

"Fine, but I expect you to tell me everything," she said, making sure he knew she could be just as stubborn.

He smiled and patted her shoulder.

"Do you want me to mix up something to help you sleep?"

She just shook her head. "I'll be fine."

Instead of returning to the barracks, Thea made her way back to the courtyard. She was tired, but not eager for sleep. The strange dreams seemed to be worse on nights when she was coming off the channeling suppressant, like they had been waiting patiently to sink their claws into her thoughts. She shuddered, not from the chill air of the night, but from the thought of being alone. Lately, the thick darkness of the barracks at night felt oppressive, like something tangible that could swallow her whole if she didn't get out.

She couldn't explain why she felt that way. She'd never been one to be afraid of the dark. In fact she loved the night sky, filled with glittering jewels overhead. Moonless nights like this one were her favorite. Without the additional light from the moon, the stars stood out even clearer in the blackness that wasn't just black but deep purple and navy blue folded together behind twinkling white, yellow, red, and blue gems of light. Thea had once loved leaning against her mother's shoulders as they found pictures in the stars together.

As she sat, remembering the stories her mother would tell her about those pictures in the sky, and trying to pinpoint the stars that made those shapes, the sound of an engine cut through the quiet stillness of the night, catching her attention. Was Nix leaving again? But the sound was getting closer, rather than farther away.

❖

You're totally her type.

Nix knew that wasn't true. The brother had only been trying to shock him enough to confirm that he really did have telepathy.

Still, for some reason, he couldn't get the words out of his head.

A quiet chuckle from behind him told him the brother could sense his agitation. He turned around with an annoyed frown.

"I brought you a plate," the brother said. "I could tell you actually wanted some."

Nix scoffed as he took the plate, wondering if other people found it this annoying when he knew what they were thinking. The brother just let out another chuckle.

The food was good. Even better than anything Lucan ever made.

"Thanks," Nix mumbled before shoveling a few more bites into his mouth.

"So this is where you're always hiding out. It's a pretty cool space." The brother gestured to the parts in front of Nix on the table. "What are you working on?"

Nix shrugged and set down the unfinished plate of food, somewhat regretfully. "Nothing really. Just passing time."

He frowned and crossed his arms over his chest. It had been so hard for Nix to get a read on this man, with his sister's thoughts dominating everything else.

"How long have you known? Did Gram tell you?"

"About your telepathy?" He sounded amused. "I really didn't know until today, but I knew something was going on. I saw how you reacted around Thea, and I knew you were a Macro, so I guess it was the only thing that made sense."

Nix didn't know what to say. To most people, telepathy was only a myth, a story the Syndicate had made up to aggrandize their founder, but the Military knew the ability was real, and the siblings had suffered the consequences. He shouldn't be surprised one of them had figured out he had it.

"I know my sister," the brother continued. "I know better than anyone that she can be a lot. Even for me."

Nix looked away, feeling embarrassed and frustrated. He didn't need anyone's pity.

"It was Kai, right?"

He knew the brother's name, of course, but it still felt strange to use it when they'd only spoken a few times. The brother nodded, so Nix continued with the question he couldn't resist asking. Their abilities weren't the same, but he guessed they experienced something similar because of the girl's thoughts. "How do you do it? How do you deal with it?"

Kai didn't answer him. He turned away from Nix suddenly, worry and unease filling his thoughts. "Something's wrong."

Nix stretched out his telepathy. He was surprised Kai could pick up her energy so easily. The faint hum of her thoughts had been growing all afternoon and evening. He still couldn't read them without concentrating. He couldn't pick up anything concrete, but he could sense the fear and panic that Kai must also be feeling. One thought surfaced in the hum. Someone was there.

Nix frowned as he moved outside. If someone besides the five of them were at the base, he should be able to hear their thoughts easily enough when hers were so quiet. Was she letting her fear create a threat that wasn't there? It wouldn't be the first time. Nix almost turned around and went back inside the workshop. Almost told Kai it was probably nothing, let him go soothe whatever anxiety she was feeling, as he always did. But he stopped, another possibility suddenly occurring to him. He swore and started to run.

❖

Thea's heartbeat quickened as the engine's roar drew closer and stopped outside the base. She strained to listen. Though her channeling was weak, she could hear the sound of footsteps crunching on the gravel road that separated the courtyard from the outer wall. Someone was inside the base.

Terror froze her in place as the sound of footsteps drew closer. A woman stepped through the shadows into the dimly lit courtyard. She was tall with long, dark hair. She wore a dark, cropped jacket over a tight-fitting shirt and pants. There was no friendliness in her smile as she appraised Thea, only cold condescension.

"You must be the peacekeeper's new pet I've heard so much about." Her tone was just as unfriendly as her smile. "I'm looking for Nix. You know where he is?"

Thea managed to squeak out a single word, her voice thick like sludge in her throat.

"Nix?"

He'd told this woman about her? Did that mean she was one of the bounty hunters he'd been talking to in town? Thea forced her legs to take a step back.

"Yeah, he's supposed to tune up my bike," the woman said. She paused and tilted her head to one side, her mouth pulling into a frown before continuing. "I've heard a lot about you, you know, but I'm not sure I see what all the fuss is about. You seem more like a scared little animal than some Military secret weapon."

The woman locked eyes with Thea and took a step closer. Thea stepped back as she continued.

"I know what it's like to have your whole life taken from you." In spite of her words, there was no sympathy in her tone, only patronizing nonchalance. "There's no going back to who you used to be. Once you're a pawn in someone else's game, there's only one thing you can do."

The woman paused like a teacher waiting for her students to come up with the right answer.

Thea said nothing.

"You have to change the game," the woman went on. "They say you're dangerous. Instead of sticking to this mousy little victim act, why not embrace whatever power they think you have? Turn it against them, and fight back?"

Thea just shook her head because she didn't know how to respond. She didn't know why the woman was telling her all this, or what she really wanted. The woman gave a patronizing sigh, like she was explaining a difficult concept to a child.

"The Peacekeeper can't protect you forever. He knows that, and I think you do, too. If you want security, you won't find it here, but I know people who can really help you."

Thea shook her head again and managed to squeak out a quiet, "No."

She didn't know this woman or what she wanted, but she did know that she wasn't about to go anywhere with her or trust anything she said.

"How disappointing."

The woman's voice turned cold and her body shifted slightly, her casualness turning to something more threatening. Thea looked around the courtyard frantically, as if help would materialize in front of her. A dark blur moved past her, and instead of help, she found Nix standing in front of her.

"I told you not to come here," Nix growled in his low voice.

"Don't be like that, Ghost," the woman said with another toss of her hair, her demeanor turning casual again. "I wanted to meet your new friend. Aren't you going to introduce me?"

Nix whirled toward Thea, and she scrambled away from him, her legs hitting the bench behind her. She lost her balance and plopped down, trembling as Nix towered over her.

"What are you doing?" he snarled. "Hurry up and go inside."

The woman stepped around him with a shrill laugh.

"I see you aren't any better at playing nice with others," she said. "Hasn't the peacekeeper taught you anything?"

The woman now blocked her path back to the house. She was trapped. Dirt and gravel swirled at her feet as her channeling spiked, her fear allowing it to break free from the last remains of the channeling suppressant. The branches above her groaned and a rain of leaves fluttered around them. The woman raised one eyebrow.

"Maybe you're more interesting than I thought. What a shame."

"Thea!"

Kai entered the courtyard, somewhat breathless. It seemed he hadn't come from the house. Where had he been? She heard the sound of the backdoor and Gram rounded the corner a moment later.

Thea exhaled in relief.

"What's going on?" Gram asked, stopping when he saw the woman. His face darkened and he closed the remaining distance across the courtyard in a few quick strides, positioning himself between Thea and the woman. Kai, limping slightly, moved to help Thea stand up.

"Kaori." Gram's voice was colder than she'd ever heard it before. "What are you doing here?"

The woman laughed. "No need to be so cold, Peacekeeper. What if I said I'd missed you guys?"

"Then I wouldn't believe it." Gram's hand itched at his side, as though searching for his gun. Thea's heart sank when she realized he didn't have it.

"You two really have been spending too much time together," the woman answered. "You're starting to sound alike. I just wanted to meet your new friends and offer my help."

Gram snorted.

"Your help is the last thing anyone needs."

The woman spun on her heel and tossed her hair over her shoulder.

"Well, I'll be in town if you change your mind," she threw a pointed look back toward Thea, then stepped closer to Nix. She said something as she brushed her hand over his chest, but Thea couldn't hear the words. Then she left the courtyard the same way she'd entered. Gram exhaled as she disappeared through the archway.

"Kai, take Thea inside," Gram's voice was a low snarl as he glared at Nix.

"Come on, Thea," Kai helped her stand and pulled her away from the two men. She followed him numbly, casting a last glance at Nix. His face was unreadable. She shuddered as she let Kai lead her back toward the barracks.

My frantic search begins again
Within this knot of tree and dark.
I know that only sorrow and
Regret wait for me ahead.

I turn and run away,
Unwilling to accept this fate,
To see you lying there and know
I cannot save you.
So I run.

My vision blurs.
The world around me shifts and
I leave behind one destiny
To change it for another.

As sunlight fills my sight and
My breath begins to slow,
A haze of lazy drifting dust
Glitters all around me,
Calming me.

My terror turns to curiosity as
I search the unfamiliar room.
I hear a noise,
I turn around
To see him standing there—
My nightmares manifested.

As blood drips from his hands,
And shadows hide his face,
There's nowhere to run.
I can't escape.

He slams me hard against the wall,
Malicious fury burning on his face.
A glint of metal, cold and sharp.
It presses into flesh.
One small movement
Is all it takes.

A smile spreads across his lips
As hatred burns in eyes the shade
Of night.

I tear my eyes away from his.
The dark and swirling marks
Upon his arm unmistakable—
A clear sign of what he is:

A monster.

Chapter Ten

Nix picked up the parts he'd been tinkering with before Kai had interrupted him. He frowned at the cold metal in his hand, then slammed them back down onto the table with enough force to break off several pieces. He swore and scowled at the scattered metal as though the pieces were to blame for his temper.

It was really himself that he blamed. He'd been careless and foolish, caught off guard time and time again—first by the girl, then her brother, now Kaori.

Gram had been pissed, of course. He was sure Nix had invited her to the base in spite of his warnings to keep her away. He'd hardly waited for the siblings to be out of earshot before launching into his lecture, giving Nix no chance to explain.

Another fight widening the rift that had been growing between them ever since they'd run into the girl in town.

Gram was usually pretty tolerant of Nix's surly attitudes and isolated behavior, but it seemed his patience had finally run out. He had new people to take care of—new pets, as Kaori would say—and Nix had become nothing but a problem.

He rubbed his face with both hands. Gram was right about one thing, he was tired. He needed a night of actual sleep. He doubted he'd get it. Lucan had thought the girl's channeling wouldn't recover until morning, but her thoughts had been drumming louder and louder ever since Kaori's appearance, like they'd broken through some kind of barrier keeping them in check. Even if he could fall asleep, which was difficult for him under normal circumstances, he doubted he would be able to sleep for long.

He grabbed a wrench off the worktable and slapped it against his hand as he approached his bike. He might as well start on the maintenance he'd been planning earlier.

At first, the distraction worked. His mind emptied, and he didn't think about his recent arguments with Gram. He didn't think about Kaori or the verbal jabs that always seemed to eat away at the back of his mind. He couldn't ignore the girl's thoughts, but they were dulled by the turning of each screw and the repetition of each step.

It didn't last long. As her dreams grew more urgent, so did their demand for his attention. His eyes stung and his forehead throbbed. His frustration grew as he worked on a particularly stubborn bolt.

The dream was familiar. She'd had a similar one several times, of searching through a dark forest with a fearful sense of dread. She knew there was something waiting for her, a horror she couldn't escape.

It was suffocating.

This time, the dream was different. Her subconscious forced herself away from the forest, the scenery blurring around her as she pushed herself faster and faster through the darkness, branches tearing at her skin and clothes.

The scenery shifted and light flooded her mind, sending spikes through his vision. His hand slipped, knuckles scraping against rough metal. He swore and sat down heavily on the floor, cradling his fingers in his other hand.

Her dream had shifted to the workshop.

Nix's forehead wrinkled in confusion as he heaved himself up from the floor while wrapping his bleeding knuckles in his shirt.

The details of her dream seemed too precise for her to have simply glanced inside in passing. She must have been in here sometime while he'd been away. He snorted. Gram couldn't have told her that the space was his or she would have stayed far away. He scanned the room, looking for any sign that she had been there, or that something had been moved. Since most things didn't have a set place, there was no way to tell.

She explored the room curiously, wondering at its purpose. She reached for the stack of old bounty cards next to the computer when she heard a loud clatter behind her.

She whirled around and found Nix standing at the entrance to the workshop. His hands were slick with blood and his breath came out in heavy rasps. Shadows covered his face, making his expression unreadable and menacing. She was trapped.

The dream shifted again, and Nix slammed her hard against the stone wall of a dimly lit room. His hand gripped her shoulder, his fingers painful like a vice. His other hand held his sword to her throat. The cold metal pressed against her skin. With only the slightest movement its sharp edge would bite into her flesh, drawing blood. His eyes were wide and full of hate, his jaw clenched with his teeth bared. It wasn't just that he could end her life, she could see in his face that he wanted to. He would enjoy it.

Her eyes fell to his sword arm, where his shirt sleeve had pulled up on his bicep. The dark marks of the tattoo swirled around the muscle, unmistakable. She recognized it for what it was, the mark of a member of the Syndicate.

He sank down onto the bed, numb. Over and over, the scene replayed. His hands trembled. He clenched them into fists and the pain in his bleeding knuckles pulled him back to reality. He swore, his voice barely a choked whisper, and dropped his head into his hands, forcing himself to breathe slowly as he tried to think about anything other than the scenes replaying in his head.

He could rationalize it easily enough. Her subconscious was trying to deal with her anxiety. It made sense that he would be the one to manifest as the personification of all her fear. Gram and Lucan were both too easy to like, too easy to trust. He was not.

It made sense in his head, but that was little comfort against the reminder that he could never escape his past or who he was. He'd left the Syndicate, tried to start a new life at the base, tried to be who Gram seemed to think he could be. What the girl saw was the truth. His worst self. His reality.

He didn't know how long he sat there, frozen, trying to keep the past at bay. He looked down at the dried blood on his hand and stood with a sigh. He should take care of the wound before Gram or Lucan woke up. He didn't want to have another argument with Gram. He didn't want Lucan's pity. Heavily, he left the workshop and made his way toward the main house.

As she lay in the darkness of the barracks, waiting for her heartbeat to slow, Thea couldn't rid herself of the images from her nightmare. The blood on Nix's hands. The hatred in his eyes. The bite of metal against her skin. The tattoo around his arm.

Every creak and groan of the surrounding room sent her heart racing again. She clutched her blanket close, as though it could protect her.

She didn't know how long she lay awake, gripped by fear. Dim gray light began to creep through the cracks in the closed shutters. Not wanting to continue chasing shadows and remembering nightmares, she slipped silently from her bed and crept to the door.

She made her way to her usual spot in the courtyard, but hardly noticed as the sky transitioned from gray to faint pink before breaking into the vivid colors of sunrise. Her thoughts remained fixated on the darkness of her nightmare.

It was just a dream, but she knew there was truth in it, too. She'd seen it the night he'd confronted the Syndicate. The look on his face had been almost the same—the hatred and the bloodlust. He was dangerous.

She shivered even though the morning air was warm. Goosebumps broke out on her arms, and she shook her head as she tried to rub them away. Sitting there in her thoughts wasn't helping. The others would be awake soon. Maybe she could distract herself by starting breakfast. Besides, even if they were still asleep, it would be comforting to know Gram and Lucan were nearby.

She expected the kitchen to be empty, so she was surprised to find it occupied. She let out a small yelp as Nix turned around, a look of surprise on his face. Her eyes traveled from his face to the defined muscles of his bare torso before landing on his arm. He swore and reached for the shirt lying on the counter, but it was too late. She'd seen the tattoo. She didn't know the meaning behind the swirls and symbols circling his right bicep, but she knew what the tattoo stood for.

"That tattoo." Her voice rose in pitch as fear burned in her throat like bile. "You really are one of them."

His jaw clenched, the muscles in his arms bulging as he tightened his hands into fists.

"I was," he said after a long pause, his voice low and threatening.

She took one step back, away from him. The tattoo. The blood on his hands. The sword against her throat.

He raised his hand, took a step toward her. He was going to attack her. She spun towards the hallway and sprinted, crashing into the wall as she rounded the corner. She heard a shout behind her but didn't stop until she crashed breathlessly through the door of the barracks.

"Kai!"

Kai sat up, looking around in blurry-eyed confusion.

"What is it?" he asked sleepily, his voice scratchy and dry. "What's wrong?"

"We have to leave, Kai. We have to hurry."

"What are you talking about? Why?"

"I was right! He's one of them! He's been with the Syndicate all along!"

"Wait, wait," Kai said, holding up his hands placatingly. "Come sit down, tell me exactly what's going on."

Instead of answering him, she turned to the small chest of drawers where they stored their few belongings. She reached for her pack and started frantically stuffing their clothes inside.

She jumped when she felt Kai's hand on her elbow.

"Come on, Thea, come sit down."

Thea exhaled and let herself be led by her brother.

"I was in the kitchen," she told him as she sat stiffly on the edge of the bed. "Nix was there and he wasn't wearing a shirt and I saw it. I saw his tattoo. I asked him if he was one of them and he said he was. And he moved toward me. I thought he was going to attack me, so I ran."

Kai put his arm around her.

"Hey, it's okay. Try to calm down."

Her breath caught and turned to small hiccups as she tried to hold in a sob. Gram couldn't protect her. That woman from the night before had said so. Thea buried her face in her shaking hands to catch the tears that she couldn't hold back anymore.

"I'm so scared, Kai."

"I know, it's okay."

"I thought maybe it was safe here, that we could stay here, but I don't know anymore."

"It's going to be okay."

He moved his hand to rub slow, soothing circles on her back.

"I trust Gram," he said quietly. "I don't think he'd let Nix be here if he thought he might hurt us. You saw Gram fight. And Lucan too. I think between the two of them they could stop Nix if they felt like they had to. But they let him be here. Remember that, okay."

"But maybe he's fooling them. Or maybe you're just wrong Kai."

"Let me get you something to drink."

Thea hesitated for a moment then let go of her brother and nodded. She wiped her eyes with the back of her hand and let out a ragged breath. Crying and being hysterical wouldn't do any good. Kai was right, she needed to calm down so they could make a plan. She squeezed her eyes tight, trying to force the tears to stop. The images of her nightmare seemed to be permanently etched into her eyelids, melding with memory, making it hard to remember what was real and what wasn't.

Blood on his hands. Standing in the kitchen with hatred in his eyes. The tattoo.

Kai handed her a steaming mug, filled with Lucan's sweet herbal tea blend. Her hands still shook as she held the cup to her lips. She thought the tea had a slightly different taste than usual. She felt lightheaded as she finished the cup. Tired.

"No."

That taste. It was a sedative. Kai had given her a sedative. She didn't want to sleep. She didn't want to be vulnerable and powerless. She didn't want to return to the nightmares.

"Just try to rest," Kai said as he took the cup from her hand. "I promise everything will be okay."

No.

She didn't know if she managed to get the word out. Her tongue felt heavy, her thoughts sluggish.

The room spun. She was falling, and couldn't keep her eyes open. She felt Kai's hand on her back, easing her down, then the soft bed beneath her. Her eyes closed and she couldn't open them again.

Nix banged his fist against the counter, then squeezed his fingers tighter to stop his hand from shaking.

Monster.

That's what she saw when she looked at him.

He swore and sank to the floor, burying his face in his hands. He gave up trying to make them stop shaking.

Blood on his hands. The hatred on his face. The blood pouring from the wound as he buried the knife to its hilt. The heat of adrenaline fading as he realized what he'd done.

Monster.

Shouting pulsed in his head, pounding with each beat of his own anger in his chest. Sweat dripped down his neck with the oppressive heat of bodies pressing and jostling around him.

Monster. He's caused enough harm already. He should be locked up. Fix it.

His hands felt slick and sticky. Blood? That couldn't be right. He wasn't holding a knife. His hands were covering his face, weren't they?

He lowered them and shook his head.

Monster. He should be locked up.

His chest closed tighter and his breaths came faster. A strong smell burned his nose, and his body tensed. Smoke? His sword pressed to her throat. The still form of the guard on the ground. Blood on his sword and a scared boy standing in front of him.

Monster.

A hand gripped his shoulder. They wanted to take him back to the darkness. He didn't want to go. He couldn't breathe. He couldn't escape. He swung his fist but someone caught his arm.

That smell again, stinging his nose and throat. He started to cough.

Not smoke, he realized. Herbs.

He blinked until he could focus on Lucan's worried face in front of him, holding his arm with one hand and a small bottle with the other. It was Gram's hand that gripped his shoulder, its weight familiar and comforting.

"You alright?" Gram asked as he reached down with his other hand to help him up.

Nix took a shaky breath before nodding. He sank into a chair and buried his face in his arms on the table. No one spoke, but he could hear them moving around him. He took slow breaths and concentrated on those sounds: the sound of a cupboard opening and closing, then the microwave, footsteps moving away from the kitchen. He brushed his fingers against the bare skin of his arm, slick with sweat, not blood. The sound of footsteps returned to the kitchen, and he felt fabric brush against his arm.

"Here, you probably want this." Lucan's calm voice.

Nix sat up and took the long-sleeved shirt Lucan had placed on the table next to him. He nodded gratefully before pulling the shirt over his head and arms, hiding his tattoo with a feeling of relief.

Monster.

He frowned. Hiding the mark was meaningless in the end. He couldn't change what he was any more than he could remove the ink tattooed to his skin. He'd been fooling himself.

"Let me see your hand."

Lucan set bandage tape and a salve on the table next to him. Nix looked down at his raw knuckles and let out a bitter chuckle before placing his palm flat on the table in front of Lucan. He'd forgotten about the foolish injury that had brought him to the kitchen in the first place.

Gram sat at the table opposite Nix and slid a warmed-up meal towards him. Nix's stomach lurched at the smell of the food. He shook his head and pushed the tray to one side. Gram frowned.

"What happened?" he asked, his voice uncharacteristically soft.

"The girl was here. She saw my arm. She knows."

Nix rubbed his tattooed arm with his free hand and took a shaky breath.

"I figured as much," Lucan said as he finished bandaging his hand. He stood as Kai entered the kitchen. Nix was only vaguely aware that he could hear the other man's thoughts. He'd given his sister a sedative. Nix had been so consumed by his own nightmares, unable to tell which thoughts were his and which were hers, he'd hardly noticed when hers slipped to the quiet rumble of sleep.

"How's your sister?" Lucan asked.

Kai's eyes slid toward Nix and Nix looked away. Kai shrugged.

"She's sleeping now. I gave her a sedative. I figured it was best for her, and for him." He gestured toward Nix. "She wasn't about to calm down on her own."

Gram's eyebrows shot up in alarm.

"He knows," Nix said before either Gram or Lucan could comment.

"What?" Gram asked. "For how long? How did you figure it out?"

Kai shrugged again.

"It was just a theory at first. I couldn't quite figure Nix out. I can always tell when someone is hiding something from me, or not telling me the truth. People's energy changes based on what they're feeling. It changes when they lie. So I knew you were all hiding something from us, but I couldn't figure out what."

Gram looked away guiltily and rubbed the back of his head.

"I get why you didn't tell us," Kai went on, as he sat down, "and I don't plan to tell my sister, not yet anyway. No reason to add fuel to the fire, right?"

Nix groaned and leaned back in his chair. Kai was right. Everything about him was just something else for her to hate.

"So how did you figure out he was a telepath?" Gram asked, not seeing the connection.

"I know how intense Thea's emotions are," Kai said with another chuckle. "It can be a lot sometimes. Even for me. Her emotions can be as erratic as her channeling. The experiments only made it worse. It's like water being poured through a sieve. They're always there, raw and unfiltered."

He gestured to Nix. "I knew Nix was a Macro, so when I saw his reactions around her, telepathy was the only thing that made sense."

"You never answered my question," Nix grumbled, looking away. "How do you deal with it?"

Kai rested his elbows on the table with his fingers laced under his chin.

"Well, you have to remember that I have more experience with her than you do," Kai said after a moment of contemplation. "I've gotten used to it."

He paused, frowning slightly as he thought about how best to explain his own experience.

"I'm not sure how helpful my advice can be. The truth is people call my ability empathy, but I don't really feel people's emotions. It's actually just an advanced form of energy sensing. It's like people's moods and feelings are tied to their energy wavelengths. Those wavelengths change and form different patterns depending on what they are feeling. It's a lot easier to intellectualize someone's feelings, like reading a chart."

He shrugged. "It's true that with Thea there's a lot more information, so it can be overwhelming—especially when she's panicking. I guess I've just learned to redirect her feelings, or to try to get her to focus on one thing at a time."

Nix snorted. Being overwhelmed by too much information was an understatement.

"It sounds challenging," Lucan said.

Kai cast a sympathetic glance at Nix before frowning. He shrugged again and didn't meet Lucan's eyes.

"It's better than the alternative."

He didn't elaborate, but Nix could see it in his thoughts. After escaping from the research facility, she'd been so frail and hollow, hardly saying or feeling anything at all. It was a shocking contrast to the vividness of her emotions now. Kai blamed himself, though Nix didn't understand why.

If anyone was to blame, it was Nix.

Kai furrowed his eyebrows and met his eyes, looking confused. Nix looked away and Kai cleared his throat before continuing.

"For you Macros though, everything is so much more tangible. Every one of your abilities is so physical and sensory. I'm guessing your telepathy is much the same way. I bet the thoughts and feelings you get from her are a lot more overwhelming, as if you were feeling them yourself?"

Nix hesitated with a glance toward Gram before giving a slight nod. Gram frowned and crossed his arms over his chest, realizing Nix still hadn't told him everything. His jaw clenched before he let out a disappointed sigh.

Well, that complicates things, he thought.

"*It doesn't change anything*," Nix transmitted without looking at Gram. "*I'd already made up my mind. I'm leaving.*"

"Like hell you are!" Gram shouted out loud as he jumped to his feet, startling Kai and Lucan with his sudden outburst.

"Well, I can't stay here!" Nix spat.

He was annoyed and frustrated, but more than anything he was tired. Tired of the weight of the girl's thoughts in his mind, tired of the sleepless nights, tired of the arguments with Gram.

Monster.

He was tired of trying to be someone he could never be.

The siblings belonged here, safe with Gram and Lucan. The truth was, he never really did.

Before the others could say anything, Nix stood and stormed out of the kitchen. He was leaving and there wasn't anything Gram could do to stop him. He was certain, this decision was best for everyone.

Nix looked around the workshop regretfully, then kicked the nearest table so hard it slammed into the table next to it. Tools and bits of metal skittered noisily to the floor. He swore and picked up the parts he'd removed from his bike earlier. He shouldn't have taken it apart. He should have known he would need it. He started putting the parts back into place on the bike without bothering to finish the detailed cleaning and maintenance he'd planned.

"I'm sorry."

Nix didn't turn around as Kai entered the workshop. He wasn't in the mood to talk. "I wanted to help, but all I did was start an argument between you and Gram."

"Gram just doesn't like the idea that he doesn't know what's best for everybody, that's all," Nix said. "It's not your fault."

Kai hesitated. There were questions he wanted to ask and reassurances he wanted to give, but he didn't know where to start. Nix stood and turned toward him with a frown before setting his tools down roughly on the table.

"I used to be in the Syndicate," Nix said before Kai could try to convince him to stay. "I'm not anymore. I don't know why they're after your sister, but I don't think it's just about what happened in Senari."

He crossed to the cabinet by the entrance and jerked it open.

"That's good enough for me," Kai said placatingly. "Everyone has done things they regret. I can tell that you don't want to hurt us. And I can tell that you're suffering. Not just because of my sister's thoughts. I can tell it's hard for you, the way she thinks of you."

"I don't need your pity," Nix snapped before slamming the cabinet shut.

"That's not what I meant," Kai continued, unruffled. "You feel responsible for what happened to her because of your telepathy, don't you?"

Nix stopped and looked at Kai in surprise before looking away again.

"Sorry," Kai said. "I probably shouldn't have brought it up."

"What about you?" Nix mumbled. "Why do you feel like it's your fault?"

He didn't know why he asked. Maybe he was curious. Maybe he actually wanted it to be someone's fault other than his own. Or maybe he was just angry and wanted to make someone besides himself feel hurt.

It seemed the last one worked, whether he wanted it to or not. Kai's shoulder's slumped and his face paled.

"It was my fault," Kai said quietly, his voice cracking with the agony Nix knew he felt. He paused, and Nix thought he wouldn't continue. He didn't need to. Nix could read his thoughts, and he regretted asking the question. Kai didn't deserve it.

"Sorry," Kai said before Nix could turn back to his bike. "I've never really talked about it with anyone. I..."

His expression was one of pleading, like Nix was some sort of lifeline he desperately needed. Nix supposed he owed it to him to hear him out, since he'd asked the question in the first place. He nodded and leaned against the table with his arms crossed.

"After our mom died, I wasn't in a good place," Kai said. "I was sad of course, but mostly I was angry. Angry at our town for all the years they treated my mom like an outcast. Angry at my dad for shutting down, for not being able to help us when we needed him most. Angry at my birth father for not being there at all. And then there was Thea, going through her own problems and I couldn't deal with that on top of my own, so I pushed her away. She went to the research facility because she had nowhere else to go. So believe me when I say it's not your fault. You didn't choose to be a telepath, but I chose not to be there for her when she needed me the most."

Nix shook his head, and Kai let out a bitter chuckle.

"I guess none of us are good at dealing with this stuff," Kai said.

Nix could at least agree with that.

"The thing is, I know my sister," he continued. "She has strong feelings and strong opinions, and sometimes she jumps to conclusions. She also hates to lose, by the way. I think that's a lot of why she acts the way she does around you. And she tends to let her fears get the better of her. She's been through a lot, and it's been really hard for her."

Nix let out a long exhale. "I know."

"Give her time," Kai said. "It may not seem like it, but she's actually better than I am at processing this stuff. She'll come around."

Nix let out a snort of disbelief, but the truth was, his anger had already faded.

"Look, I appreciate it," he admitted, "but it doesn't change anything. You'll all be better off with me gone."

He picked up his tools again and turned back to his bike. Kai could sense the finality in his mood and left him without saying anything else.

Gram entered the workshop just as he was climbing onto his bike. Anger simmered beneath his regret. He was still upset with Nix for being so stubborn, but mostly he regretted that they'd argued and there was nothing he could do to make things easier for him—or to convince him to stay.

"Here," Gram said, holding out a large pack, "at least take this with you."

"Thanks."

Nix didn't meet his eyes as he took the pack and slung it over the back of his bike. Gram slapped a hand on his shoulder as Nix started the engine.

"Take all the time you need," Gram said over the engine's roar, "then come back."

Nix didn't expect he'd ever come back, but he couldn't bring himself to contradict Gram, so he just nodded.

"Don't die out there," Gram said, releasing his shoulder with a half-hearted grin. "If you do, I'll come find you and kick your ass."

Nix didn't smile or respond. He pulled his bike out of the workshop and drove away without looking back.

Thea cracked open her eyes and shut them again with a groan, confused by the light streaming through the open shutters. Kai usually left them closed when he got up before her. She rolled over, away from the light, her thoughts muddled. As she tried to remember falling asleep, she recalled the events of that morning. Her eyes flew open, and she shot up in bed. Her head spun with the sudden movement and her stomach lurched with nausea.

"Here," Kai was at her side with a cup of cool water. She eyed it suspiciously but took it and drank a sip.

"You gave me a sedative," she grumbled accusingly.

"I'm sorry." He laid a hand on her arm. "I thought the rest would be good for you."

She looked at him through narrowed eyes. He just smiled in return. She thought the smile looked sad. Did it mean he'd learned something that he knew would upset her?

"Did you learn anything?" she asked. "I assume you talked to Gram."

Again, a pained expression crossed his face.

"Only that we have nothing to worry about. Nix is gone and I don't think he'll be coming back."

His words only made her feel more anxious. Did he leave because he knew he couldn't fool them anymore? Was he returning to the Syndicate? Would they be coming for her again, with fresh information and a powerful ally?

In spite of her worry, she couldn't deny that she felt relief, too. At least for the moment, the immediate threat was gone. He couldn't hurt her.

"What are we going to do?" she asked him.

"We're staying here."

There was a sense of finality in Kai's tone that left little room for protest. She knew he always had a good reason for taking a firm stance, so she waited for him to elaborate.

"If we leave here, all we'll do is go back to running and hiding. I don't think either of us wants that, and I do think we're safe here. Gram's doing everything he can to keep it that way."

"But how? He's just one man. How can he keep us safe from both the Military and the Syndicate?"

Kai shrugged. "I guess he has some connections. For now at least, he's keeping the Military from believing we're here. How long that will last, I don't know."

Thea knew that wasn't a long-term solution. She thought again of that strange woman's words. *The peacekeeper can't protect you forever.*

Was it wise to wait around for their situation to spiral out of control?

"I wish I could say what's going to happen in the future," Kai said, his voice soft and reassuring. "I wish I could say this really is the right thing. But I do know this, I like it here. I like Gram and Lucan, and it's nice to not have to do this alone."

Thea smiled. He was right.

"I like it here too," she confessed. "And if Nix is really gone then I feel a lot better about staying."

Kai frowned again at her mention of Nix.

"Is there something you aren't telling me about him, Kai?"

He shrugged. "I think maybe you're being too hard on him. It's not like you. But I guess it doesn't matter anymore."

It was so like Kai to want to be lenient, even to someone undeserving, but she didn't think he was being fair to her. She shook her head, not wanting to think about whether he was right. As he said, it didn't matter anymore. She could push Nix from her thoughts, hopefully for good.

I run and never look behind
To where my past is ever following
I know it's drawing near
I can't escape
I can't break free
I try to be enough
But always falling short
I turn my back
I try to hide
But never seem to rid myself
Of this regret

Chapter Eleven

Nix wanted to drive far away from everything and not look back. He wanted to forget. He wanted not to care.

Instead, he turned toward Karza.

The streets were even more crowded than they had been the day before. Everywhere he looked, he saw soldiers, peacekeepers, and bounty hunters. The tension in the air felt thick enough to slice with his sword. He didn't have to look around to know the majority of the eyes were trained on him. He glared at those he passed, every muscle in his body tense, his head pounding with thoughts and adrenaline. Any person here would be all too eager to attempt to claim his bounty for themselves if they weren't worried about being stabbed in the back by the competition.

He smirked. No one was likely to make a move against him openly, but he hoped there were at least a few idiots foolish enough to try. A good fight was exactly what he needed.

He reached the tavern without incident. He ignored the line and moved straight to the ordering machine. Protests died on the lips of those who recognized him. Kay started weaving their way toward him with a surprised expression, but Nix ignored them and moved upstairs. He tossed his pack onto an empty chair in the farthest corner of the room and flopped down to wait. He didn't need to search for Kaori. She would come to him.

He slid his phone from his pocket and frowned, hesitating a moment before opening the map. He zoomed in and out of different areas absently before shoving the phone back in his pocket with a frustrated snort. After another moment, he pulled it back out and tapped a quick message.

More soldiers and bounty hunters in town. Be careful.

The reply came seconds later.

That's my line, dumbass.

He sighed and put his phone away, ignoring the guilt that wouldn't let him stop thinking about the base. If these thugs really did locate the girl, Gram wouldn't be able to hold them off on his own.

He tried to push away the thought. They didn't need him. Gram had Lucan. Kai seemed pretty smart, too. They would figure something out.

That's what he kept telling himself.

His food arrived, and he had nearly finished eating before Kaori finally slid into the empty chair beside him. She'd attracted almost as much attention entering the tavern as he had, only for different reasons. When Kaori walked into a room, everyone noticed—the way she swayed when she walked, the way she tossed her hair, the way she looked at you like she knew she'd won the moment your eyes locked onto her. He knew because he'd spent half his life noticing her and losing the game he didn't know he was playing.

"No need to be jealous," she half-laughed as he glared at the leering men at the nearest table. She smiled and wiggled her fingers at them. "They're just looking."

Her smile broadened when she turned back to him. His eyes trailed over her mouth, down her neck, over her tight shirt, and back up. He usually tried to hide it. This time he didn't.

"You're here earlier than expected," she said, raising one eyebrow. "What happened? Did the peacekeeper get tired of you after all?"

He scowled and looked away before shoving another bite into his mouth. She laughed and leaned close, reaching out to stroke a finger down the crease in his forehead.

"Guess I hit a nerve," she said, her voice soft and breathy. "You don't belong there anyway."

He let out a snort of annoyance, but didn't shake her off or contradict her. She leaned back again with a sigh.

"You always were the sentimental one."

"What's that supposed to mean?"

"You don't have to pretend with me, Ghost. I know you. I know you spent the last few years playing good boy with the peacekeeper because you thought he might actually want you around."

"You're the one who said I don't play nice with others," he grumbled, recalling the words she'd said at the base.

"And thus is the contradiction that is Nix."

It was unusual for her to use his real name. The way her voice caressed the word made him forget about his sandwich. Her face softened momentarily before she looked away, with a toss of her hair.

"The thing is Ghost," she continued, her voice rougher, "people like us don't belong. Not with do-gooders like him. We aren't good enough for that. You were a tool to him just like you were to my father. Instead of wasting your time trying to prove your worth to someone who will ultimately reject you anyway, you should just focus on looking out for yourself."

Nix shrugged. "Maybe you're right."

He shoved the last of his food away and stood. He didn't want to talk about Gram, not with Kaori.

"Where are you staying?" he asked.

"The safe house, where else?"

He raised his eyebrow.

"Do they know about your meeting with that Intelligence officer yesterday?"

Kaori frowned then tossed her hair with a shrug.

"It's not like I tried to hide it."

That was apparently all the answer she was going to give him. Not that he cared. The Military wasn't his concern, and neither was the Syndicate. As Kaori had said, the only thing he needed to worry about was looking out for himself.

"Let's go," he growled, throwing his pack over his shoulder.

She grinned maliciously and stood to follow him.

"Oh, this is going to be fun."

Karza, like most of the Wilds, served as a sort of neutral territory between the Military and the Syndicate. With only limited access to resources or the bulk of their fighting forces, neither side had an easy way to route the other from the Wilds entirely. Any victory would be temporary, as the other side would soon send reinforcements or set up a new foothold in a new location. Yet neither side was willing to abandon the territory completely. It was the primary reason the war had come to a standstill in the first place, and the primary reason the two sides managed to coexist in Karza with little more than the occasional scuffle between aggrieved individuals.

Similarly, the Syndicate's safe house was no secret. The Military knew about it, where it was, and probably even how many Syndicate were there at any given time. But doing something about it and the many similar safe houses throughout the Wilds wasn't worth their time. At best, the Syndicate would simply send more members. At worst, they would launch a large-scale retaliation. Either way, it was in the Military's best interest to leave them alone, so long as they stayed out of Military territory.

The safe house was more of a complex than a single house. It sat prominently at the end of a street of mostly abandoned, larger residences. An outer wall encircled the house itself, along with a small courtyard, unattached garage, and storage unit.

The complex had likely belonged to an important figure in town long ago, but like most buildings in Karza, it was now rundown and derelict. Its outer wall had caved in several places, and the garage was missing its doors. Cracks spread across the stone surface of the main house, and several of its windows were missing shutters. Still, it was relatively intact compared to other houses, and large enough to house several Syndicate teams at once.

The main room in the house had been outfitted with a bar style kitchenette and several tables, like a tavern. The chatter in the crowded room fell silent as Nix entered, though the noise he heard in his head only grew. A mixture of outrage and alarm crashed into his mind even before the room's silence broke, transforming into a tumult of angry voices and angry thoughts. He tried not to wince at the screech of chairs scraping noisily against the hard floor as several people jumped to their feet.

"What's he doing here?" Kuda's nasal voice stood out from the noise as he stomped closer to them. His eyes darted between Nix and Kaori with a look of confusion before they narrowed in resentment.

"Shut up, Kuda," Kaori responded before Nix had a chance to probe his thoughts further. "He's here for the same reason as the rest of us. To avoid all those idiots filling up this stupid town."

"He's a traitor," another man protested angrily. "He isn't one of us. If your brother—"

"That's not for you to decide." Kaori whirled around, her bored facade stripped away in a rare show of rage. The man backed away, wide-eyed, and Kaori sighed before turning back toward Nix and Kuda with a toss of her hair. "My brother isn't here. The one you need to worry about is me. Now back off."

Hesitantly, the ring of people that had slowly been closing in around them dispersed. With another scrape of chairs, most of them returned to their seats, though their thoughts remained a disgruntled rumble. Kuda didn't budge.

"Seems like all you can do is hide behind Kaori, Ghost Boy," Kuda sneered, "just like you've always done."

If Kuda wanted a fight, Nix was more than happy to give him one. He wasn't worried about what the others would do. Let them come at him. He'd remind them why no one had succeeded in taking him in before now.

It had been a long time since Nix had let his channeling go unchecked. Those who didn't know him well were too surprised to move as his body began to blur before their eyes. The Micros in the room could sense the enormity of his energy and they were afraid.

Ghost. Monster.

He dropped his pack and pulled his sword from its sheath before slamming Kuda against the wall. His free hand gripped Kuda's shoulder while his other held his sword to the man's throat, the blade tilted at just the right angle that it wouldn't draw blood. For now. With the slightest movement, the sharp edge would bite into the other man's flesh. With only minimal effort, he could end his life. Nix wanted to do it. He'd wanted it for years. Kuda had always looked for new ways to provoke him or belittle him. Nix had always held back. He didn't have to anymore. A malicious smile spread across his lips as Kuda's eyes widened in fear.

The desire fled him in an instant, and he stumbled back from Kuda in shock. His grip on his sword felt weak, and he clenched his fist to keep himself from dropping it.

The girl's dream—it had been the same.

The room tilted and he barely noticed Kuda's fear turn to a sneer.

"Guess it's true then. You've never been anything but an out-of-control monster, a nuisance to the entire clan, but now you're a pet with a muzzle."

He heard the shuffle of footsteps as the others regained some of their courage. If he didn't do something, they would attack him. Swiftly but precisely Nix swung his sword in a short arc, the tip grazing Kuda's face. Kuda doubled over with a scream of pain as blood stained his hands.

Nix didn't look around to see if the others were coming. He didn't have to. Kuda's scream was the only sound in the room.

Kaori broke the silence with her cold laugh.

"I tried to tell you to back off, Kuda, but you never listen. Someone better clean him up."

She turned away with an amused smile and Nix followed her out of the room.

It was no surprise that Kaori had the best room in the safe house all to herself, even though the rest of the building was crowded. It wasn't just her ties to the head of the clan that earned such respect. It was Kaori herself. She knew when to intimidate and when to manipulate in order to get what she wanted.

Nix threw his pack into a corner and flopped down on his back on the bed, his head throbbing. He covered his face with one arm, not wanting Kaori to see how shaken he was. He hated the version of himself that the girl's nightmare had shown him. He hated even more that he'd lived up to the nightmare.

Monster.

They were right.

"You really haven't changed, have you?"

He felt the dip in the mattress, then Kaori's weight pressing against him. He let out a snort as he moved his arm away from his face to look up at her. It was easy to forget she was there, since he couldn't hear her thoughts. He couldn't have that with anyone else.

Her dark hair spilled around him, its familiar scent filling his head, overpowering any thought that wasn't her. Her smile was uncharacteristically soft as her fingertips brushed his cheek.

"The peacekeeper must really be getting to you," she mused.

He frowned and wrapped his arms around her waist, pulling her on top of him. He didn't want to think about Gram or the girl. Kaori made for a welcome distraction.

She lowered her mouth to his, and he kissed her hungrily as his hands traced over the curves of her body, the perfect balance of softness and muscle. Her hands slid under his shirt to pull it over his head, her breath hot against his mouth. His passion and desire took over, burning away any other thoughts.

He traced his hand down the bare skin of her back as he waited for his breathing to slow and his heartrate to return to normal. Her head was on his chest, her dark hair spilling around her. He moved to kiss her, but she sat up and let out a laugh, all trace of warmth or affection gone.

"Well, that was fun, as always," she said as she climbed off the bed. "We should do that more often."

He sat up slowly as she disappeared into the small bathroom that was attached to the room.

"Are you just going to sit there?" her voice called from the bathroom. "Come get cleaned up."

He clenched his jaw in frustration. It was always this way with Kaori. It didn't matter how much he tried to distance himself from her. In the end, he couldn't stay away. In a moment of weakness and self-loathing, he'd sought solace in Kaori, and once again, he was left with only hollow disappointment.

"Come on, don't look so serious, Ghost." She stuck her head around the corner. He could hear the water running in the shower.

He sighed and ran a hand over his face. Kaori was right, he needed to stop being so sentimental. He'd given up on having a genuine relationship with Kaori, or anyone else, a long time ago. It was better to only think about whether he wanted something and if he could take it.

She kissed him again when he stepped into the shower, tangling her fingers in his hair. He ran his hands over her body once more, enjoying the slippery feel of her wet skin. He wanted Kaori, and for the moment he could have her. Nothing else mattered.

Nix didn't belong at the base. Watching Gram and Lucan with the siblings had made that realization painfully clear to him. He and Gram had both lived at the base, but they were almost always separate, each with his own space and priorities. They didn't go out of their way to spend time together. They only ate together when making plans or when they both happened to be eating at the same time.

Nix had left, but that didn't really change anything for either of them.

After only a few days in Karza with Kaori, Nix was just as sure that he didn't belong there either. The Syndicate didn't want him, and only tolerated him because they were too afraid to stop him from being there. He left the safe house when Kaori left and returned when she did, but the distance between them remained the same as it had for years. It didn't matter that they shared a bed or their bodies, she was as elusive and out of reach as ever.

He couldn't go on like this. The money he'd had with him would soon be gone. Then what, return to a life of taking what he wanted? Become a bounty hunter on his own?

"So what are you going to do now?" Kaori asked as he sat in a chair, asking himself that very same question.

He realized, then, that he already knew the answer. He'd decided even before he'd left the base.

"I'm going west," he said with a shrug, like it was a natural thing for him to do and not a death sentence.

Kaori nearly choked on her drink.

"To Senari?"

Nix shook his head.

"To Chusan."

"You know they want to kill you, right?"

He smirked at her reaction and shrugged.

"I can't tell if losing your master has given you a death wish, or if your time with the peacekeeper has made you as foolish as my brother," she said as she cocked her head to one side.

"And whose fault is it that they think I'm solely to blame for what happened?" he snapped. "I take it Ryu doesn't know whose side you're really on?"

She sighed, as though his words only proved her point.

"My brother should know I'm only on my own side. And so should you."

No reaction. No apology. He should have known he couldn't bait her into giving up any useful information.

"My brother knows exactly what I need him to think he knows," she continued. "It's the only way to keep him from running the Syndicate into the ground with his idiotic ideas."

"I thought running the Syndicate into the ground was exactly the reason we did what we did?"

She smiled patronizingly, and he turned away. It wasn't the first time they'd had this same argument. He knew he would never get a real answer from her, would never understand why she'd gone back to the Syndicate after everything.

"Well, I'll come with you, I guess," she said with a resigned sigh, as though that had been the topic of their conversation all along. "It should be entertaining, at least."

"I don't need you to come."

"I guess it's the death wish after all, then," she mused. "Either that or you're missing that room of yours in the prison?"

Goosebumps prickled his skin, even though his body felt suddenly hot.

She was right. If he tried to enter Chusan on his own, those were the only possible outcomes.

She laughed at the look on his face.

"Do whatever you want," he grumbled. "You always do anyway."

"Yup."

She grinned, an eager mischievousness in her expression that he hadn't seen in a long time. It reminded him of the way she'd looked long ago, before she'd become someone he hardly recognized. His own expression softened, and she turned away, her usual mask returning with a toss of her hair.

"I've got to take care of some things before we go. Why don't you see what you can do about my bike in the meantime?"

Chapter Twelve

The western Wilds, where the brown desert began to give way to rugged foothills, was considered the unofficial boundary of Syndicate territory. Residents in these western villages considered themselves to be members of the Syndicate, even if they weren't combatants themselves.

Chusan, located deep in the mountains beyond, was the heart of Syndicate operations. This was where the Syndicate leaders lived and where their combatants were trained. It was where Nix and Kaori had grown up, and where they were now headed.

They stopped for the night at an outpost near the border, an old stone building they'd used many times while on various assignments.

"What's your plan?" he asked Kaori, knowing she had one. It was easy enough for him to slip into following her lead. It was what he had always done.

"Well, that depends." Kaori pulled something from the pack on the back of her bike. A mischievous grin spread across her face as she held up a pair of wide metal cuffs. "How much do you trust me?"

"Not a bit," Nix said without hesitation, but he grinned at the sight of the channeling restrictors in her hand.

It was a tactic they had used plenty of times before to sneak into Military facilities. He'd wear the cuffs in order to remain undetected until he was right outside the facility walls. Having channeling like his suddenly appear was enough to make even veteran soldiers believe in the supernatural. Kaori had laughed when he told her they thought he was some kind of ghost.

His grin turned to a scowl.

"The question is whether you have more to gain by just turning me in. I know you would in a heartbeat if it would benefit you."

He would have liked to pass off his remark as a joke, but he couldn't make light of the very real possibility of her betraying him. Again. Maybe she was right. Maybe he did have a death wish.

As usual, her response was anything but reassuring.

"It's either this or you give up on making it to headquarters," she said with a shrug. "I don't care either way. I think you're being foolish, but if you want in, this is the only way."

His scowl deepened. She was right. He was being foolish. He hesitated, wondering not for the first time why he was stubbornly sticking to this course of action. Hadn't he decided to move on and forget about the others?

He sighed and took the cuffs from her.

"What's he doing here?"

Two guards stepped onto the path—one of many that led through the mountains into Chusan. The nearest drew his sword with a look of panic in his eyes. The other held back and pulled out her radio to call for backup.

"Oh, calm down," Kaori sounded bored. She gestured to the cuffs on his hands. "What do you think he's going to do with those on?"

She grabbed Nix's arm and stepped forward. The guard who had spoken moved to block her path. Kaori sighed and rolled her eyes.

"I would think it was obvious," she said in reply to his question. "I've brought my brother a present."

The guard scoffed.

"You think I believe for a second that he can't take those cuffs off any-time? I know all about that strategy, Kaori."

Kaori rolled her eyes again and turned to Nix.

"Go on then, take them off," she told him with a taunting smirk.

Nix pressed the release button on the left cuff and was rewarded with a red flashing light. The cuffs remained securely latched onto his wrist. Kaori had insisted on coding them so he couldn't remove them himself, a precaution for just this scenario, a fact that made the hairs on his neck stand on end.

The guard didn't seem impressed.

Kaori grabbed Nix's arm with an exaggerated groan and began to tug him away.

"I guess you're just going to have to be the one to explain to my brother that you let the Syndicate's most wanted man go. I'm sure he'll be so pleased."

"Wait," the guard said. "Fine. Hand him over. We'll take this traitor to the prison."

"Absolutely not," Kaori spun back around, and Nix could hear the amusement in her voice. She was enjoying this. "Do you have any idea how hard it is to track this one down? And making him behave? Even harder! I'm not about to let you take credit for my hard work."

Nix let out a snort and Kaori shot him a warning look before continuing.

"I'll settle for nothing less than taking him directly to my brother."

The guard glanced between them suspiciously. He wasn't buying it, but it didn't matter. He had no choice but to take them to Ryu.

The other guard stepped up and whispered something in the man's ear.

"Fine," he relented, "an escort's on its way."

Nix's first thought when he saw Ryu was how much he looked like his father. It was more than just his features. It was the rigid way he stood, with his hands behind his back, an expression of cold placidity on his face. Nix shivered. He hadn't believed Kaori, but the truth was staring him in the face. Ryu had changed.

He'd made a mistake coming here.

"I want to be alone with him." Ryu's voice was low and even, a cold slap in the face that didn't need to be loud to pierce every corner of the large room.

"Don't be like that, Ryu." Kaori tossed her hair over her shoulder before crossing her arms to hide her agitation. "It's been a while since we've all been together like this."

"Don't make me repeat myself, Kaori." Ryu's voice remained even, though his face had turned red, and Nix could see his jaw muscles clenching.

"I'm not one of your pawns," Kaori snapped, her voice rising in pitch as her composure slipped with each word. "You can't order me around."

Ryu took a deep breath and smoothed his shirt with his hands, his cold mask returning with the motion.

"But I can have you removed." His words were a command, and he expected to be obeyed. "Leave us, Kaori."

She ground her teeth so hard the sound was audible.

"Fine." She spun on her heel with another toss of her hair. "I have better things to do, anyway. Just remember, I'm the one who brought him to you."

Without a second glance at Nix, Kaori stormed out of the house. Nix wondered if she was leaving him to whatever fate Ryu had planned for him. There was never any telling with Kaori. She could just as easily wash her hands of him and the Syndicate in her anger as she could free him.

Nix turned his attention back to Ryu. His face remained calm, though his brow wrinkled, and his mouth turned down in a deep frown.

Time seemed to stop as they stood in silence, frowning at each other.

"Why did you come here?" Ryu asked at last. Though his voice was quiet, it seemed to echo after the silence that had frozen them in place.

Nix opened his mouth to answer, but closed it again.

Why had he come here?

It made no sense, even to him. Yet here he was, prisoner to the Syndicate, facing his worst fears and the fate he'd been avoiding since he left five years ago. All so he could understand why Ryu had sent men after that infuriating girl.

Silence stretched between them again until Ryu let out a heavy sigh, passing one hand over his face. With that one gesture, the facade of leadership seemed to drop away. Beneath it, Ryu was still there. When he spoke again, his voice had lost its cold indifference, replaced by frustration and a hint of the uncertainty Nix remembered.

"I know both of you well enough to know this prisoner act is a sham. My sister isn't so loyal to me that she would ever give me you. Though I suppose she'd just as easily sacrifice you if there were some kind of benefit to her."

Nix let out a snort and Ryu smiled slightly, not looking at him, but rather out the cloudy pane of the window in front of him. The mottled glass wasn't clear enough to see anything but hazy shapes, and so Nix knew Ryu wasn't really looking at anything at all. The old habit put Nix at ease.

"I came for answers," he told Ryu.

Ryu's eyes narrowed as he turned back to Nix.

"There's a girl," Nix said, looking away, "a Macro girl the Military has been after for a while. I ran into her in Karza and a few days later I ran into Kuda and about nine others. They were after her. Kaori says you sent them. It didn't make sense, so here I am."

The explanation sounded even more ridiculous when he put it into words. Why was he here?

"Are you helping the Military capture her?"

"I don't help the Military," Nix answered coldly.

"You work with a peacekeeper," Ryu argued.

"That's different. Besides, it's your sister who's been meeting with Military Intelligence officers."

Ryu's eyes widened with surprise, making him look even more like the young boy Nix remembered.

"You say my sister is working with the Military. She says the same of you. I don't know who to believe."

Nix let out another snort. Ryu was still Ryu, naive and uncertain. He hadn't changed at all, in spite of the convincing facade he wore.

"Kaori tried to kill you," he stated trying not to sound impatient, "or have you forgotten that detail?"

"And you killed my father!" Ryu snapped, the color rising to his face again.

Nix looked away.

The truth was, he deserved whatever punishment Ryu wanted to give him.

A long time ago, Ryu had come to Nix when everyone else thought his ideals were nothing more than a nuisance. It was a time when Nix found himself distanced from Kaori, isolated and alone. Ryu's admiration had been a comfort to him, as Nix's nonjudgmental practicality had been for Ryu.

All that had changed when Nix helped Kaori betray the Syndicate. Though it had been her plan, it had been Nix's sword in the end that had ended her father's life, making Ryu the next leader of the Syndicate at only fifteen.

Ryu exhaled slowly. As he buried his face in his hands, he looked more young and uncertain than Nix had ever seen him. Nix could only imagine how hard the last five years must have been.

"At least that's what my sister told me. I don't know what to believe anymore." Ryu's voice shook, little more than a strangled whisper.

"I didn't come here to hurt you," Nix said, before holding up his wrists. "Take these off and find out for yourself."

Ryu let out a dark laugh as he looked toward the cuffs blocking not only Nix's channeling, but Ryu's ability to read his thoughts.

"You must think I'm a fool. My telepathy, if you can even call it that, is nothing like yours. I imagine you could make me believe anything you wanted. If this is my sister's plan, then I'm disappointed in her. I expected better."

Nix shook his head stubbornly. He didn't know what Kaori had told him, but his telepathy didn't work that way.

It wasn't a point worth arguing, so instead he said, "it takes time for my channeling to return completely. Several minutes at least. And my telepathy returns last. It takes time for me to focus. It should be enough time for you to know I'm telling the truth. I didn't come to hurt you or the Syndicate."

Ryu studied him for several moments, frowning. At last, he let out a sigh, the coldness melting once again.

"I can't," he said, sounding as though he wanted to. "I'm sorry."

Nix stiffened, expecting Ryu to finally pronounce his sentence. Instead, Ryu surprised him by gesturing toward the chair opposite him.

"For now, sit down. We'll talk about this girl."

Nix sat, dumbfounded.

"You heard about what happened in Senari?"

Nix nodded.

"I couldn't just ignore three men getting injured by an unknown Macro from the east. I sent a few teams out to look for her, but it was Kaori who informed me she was a research subject the Military were planning to use against us. She also told me the girl had been seen in Karza."

"And you sent Kuda?" Nix asked in disbelief.

Ryu shook his head.

"I sent Maro," Ryu corrected. "I don't think you knew him. He was a good man, reliable but compassionate. I made him a squad leader about a year ago. I didn't send them to hurt her. I wanted her brought back here."

Nix frowned.

"When I ran into them, Kuda was the one giving orders."

"I thought it was odd when Kuda and his squad volunteered to go with Maro," Ryu said. "Kuda never leaves Chusan, unless Kaori wants him to. Were you able to pick up anything from their thoughts?" Ryu asked.

Nix grimaced. He wasn't about to tell Ryu how unreliable his telepathy had been ever since meeting the girl.

"Nothing," was all he said.

Ryu's eyebrows raised slightly, but he didn't ask for Nix to elaborate.

"Tell me about this girl," he said instead, the last of his walls coming down at once. Whatever Nix told him now, he would believe. "Is she really a threat? Like my sister says?"

"Hardly."

The snarl in his voice didn't match his answer, though he spoke the truth. She was clumsy. She used too much channeling too quickly, leaving herself vulnerable. Her fighting was predictable.

And yet she had surprised him more than once.

His frustration quickly faded as he remembered her nightmares, her memories, and the terror she felt every time she saw him.

Monster.

"She's not a threat to anyone. She just wants to be left alone."

The sad empathy Nix saw in the other man's expression was so characteristically Ryu.

After a brief silence, Ryu asked, "Do you know how the Syndicate was first formed?"

Nix nodded and the corners of his mouth turned up in a small smile. How many times had Ryu told him this story?

"During the war, right?"

"My great-great-grandfather never wanted to start a war. He started the Syndicate to protect people from the Military."

Nix wasn't sure he believed Ryu's story, but he was sure that he'd rather see a Syndicate like the one Ryu envisioned than the one that existed currently.

"I have no intention of doing things the way my father did," Ryu continued. "Ability research is wrong. I wanted the girl brought here so I could learn if she was truly a threat, and to protect her if she wasn't. The other clan leaders don't always agree with me, though. I wouldn't put it past Kuda to be following someone else's orders.

Nix scoffed. "Kuda never does anything that Kaori doesn't tell him to do."

Ryu didn't smile or even seem to acknowledge Nix's remark.

"I believe you," Ryu said. The coldness that had returned to his voice made his words anything but comforting. "I believe that you didn't come here to harm the Syndicate. Rest assured, I have no intention of harming the girl, but I can't allow the Military to capture her either. I'll do everything I can to help her have a good life here."

A door opened off to one side and Nix jumped to his feet, his chair banging noisily to the floor. The man who entered the room—Nobu—had been Reizen's right-hand man. The sight of his powerful biceps, even bigger around than Gram's, reminded Nix of all too many painful strikes—to his face, his ribs, his stomach. Anger and loathing welled up in Nix at the sight of him, but so did a feeling of powerlessness. He was a lone little boy again, with no way to fight back. A dark room waited to imprison him and there was nothing he could do. He looked down at the channeling restrictors on his wrists and balled his hands into fists so they wouldn't shake.

"I'm sorry, Nix." Ryu's voice remained emotionless. "You know I can't let you leave here."

Nix backed away from Ryu and the approaching Nobu. There was nothing he could do. Fighting back without his abilities would be pointless, but he wasn't about to do nothing and let them take him. His hands itched for his sword as he scanned the room, looking for anything that might help him. He knew there was nothing that would make the difference. Best case scenario, he'd be executed sooner rather than later. Unfortunately, Ryu was more likely to think it merciful to keep him alive.

"Let's not get ahead of ourselves," Kaori's voice came from the entrance. How long had she been standing there? None of them had noticed her until she spoke.

"What are you doing, Kaori?"

Ryu's eyes darted between Nix and his sister, as though he suspected they had some plot after all. Nobu stepped towards her, but Ryu held out his hand.

"Wait, Nobu," Ryu warned.

"I'm not sure you appreciate the gift I brought you," Kaori said with a toss of her hair, "so I've decided to take it back. Sorry, but Nix is coming with me."

Nobu let out a snort that was uncharacteristic of his quiet, stoic nature. Ryu's expression remained calm, though his eyes narrowed. He clenched his jaw and took a deep breath before speaking.

"Father underestimated you," he told her. "I don't intend to do the same, but you're outnumbered, Kaori. Against two Macros. There's nothing you can do. Turn around and leave, and I'll forget this incident happened."

Kaori's lips curled into a sneer. She let out a cold laugh as she sauntered closer.

"You really are foolish, aren't you? You think I'm outnumbered? You have no idea."

Ryu took a step back as Kaori drew near. Nobu moved to position himself between the two of them. Kaori just laughed at her brother's reaction. Nix reached out and grabbed Kaori by the arm.

"What are you doing?" he seethed in a low voice.

"What does it look like?" she answered without looking at him, a smirk on her lips. "I'm saving you. Or would you rather I leave you here to rot in prison? We both know my dear brother doesn't have the stomach to execute you."

Ryu cleared his throat, regaining his composure. "I already told you, Kaori, you can't win. Back off—"

His voice trailed off as shouts rose from outside. Kaori flashed a triumphant smile as the door slammed open. A man ran in, panic on his face.

"There's been a prison break," he exclaimed, stopping behind Nix. His eyes darted between Kaori and Ryu and his hand hovered over the handle of his sword.

"From the prison? How?"

The sound of clanging swords echoed from outside and Nobu took a step toward the door, looking torn between running outside and staying to protect his leader. There was no question though. Everyone present knew Ryu was his top priority.

"You think you know who your enemies are?" Kaori told her brother. "You think you have control here? You have no idea."

Before Ryu could respond Kaori disengaged Nix's channeling restrictors.

Nobu stepped forward but Kaori moved between him and Nix, stopping the larger man in his tracks. He was stronger and faster than her in every way, but he knew enough to be cautious around her. Kaori laughed and turned her back on him.

The man who'd come in from behind raised his sword, ready to stop them from leaving.

"Let them go."

Ryu's voice was calm, but his face was red with a fury that was itself a mask. Nix didn't need his returning energy to recognize the hurt in Ryu's eyes. He'd seen it before.

"I'm sorry," Nix said quietly, "I really didn't know."

Nix turned his back on Ryu as Kaori reached the exit. Her bike was waiting by the door. Nix didn't climb on. He was sure they weren't going to be able to leave Chusan without a fight.

"Let's go," he growled.

"Don't be mad, Ghost," she laughed over the roar of the bike's engine. "If a prison cell is what you want, be my guest. I'm sure Ryu would gladly welcome you back, in cuffs."

She wasn't wrong. He supposed he should be grateful Kaori hadn't left him behind this time. It didn't change the fact that she had used him. Again. Was he ever going to stop falling for her plots? Was he ever going to stop losing to her?

A few Macros attempted to pursue them. With his channeling returned, it was easy enough for Nix to dispatch anyone who tried to block their path. Once they were free of the village, he jumped on the back of the moving bike. Kaori revved the engine, pushing it to its limit as they climbed into the mountains, leaving Chusan behind.

Nix was relieved when the outpost, and his bike, came into view. Kaori pulled her bike to a stop next to his, the engine ticking with heat, and climbed off after him.

"Well, that was fun," she said, as though nothing out of the ordinary had happened. As though she hadn't just instigated rebellion in the Syndicate. Again.

"Don't give me that," Nix growled. "You were using me. I was just a distraction, wasn't I?"

Kaori let out one of her patronizing sighs.

"You're the one who wanted to walk into Syndicate territory with no plan and hope they wouldn't execute you on sight. I'm the one who got you

151

in, and the one who got you out. The truth is, I had no intention of showing my hand to my brother today. Instead of being childish, you should be thanking me."

He knew Kaori hated having to make adjustments to her plans, but she had because it was the only way to get him out. He didn't like feeling like he was part of her plot to betray Ryu—again—but he was grateful.

He let out a sigh of defeat. "So why did you bother? I thought you only looked out for yourself?"

She laughed and stepped close to him, so close her breath tickled his cheek.

"You'd be no fun locked away in a prison cell."

His anger dissipated almost instantly. He reached for her waist, but she spun away.

"So, what now?" she asked as she rummaged through the packs on her bike.

He frowned as he leaned back against the cool stone of the building. Ryu was going to go after the girl. Nix was sure his promise to keep her safe was genuine, but he didn't like the thought of the Syndicate showing up at the base to take her by force. No matter what assurances they made, Gram and Lucan would never let them take her, not without a fight. And she would never trust them. Someone was bound to get hurt.

"There you go again," Kaori said with a laugh as she held out two meal bars. He nodded apologetically, taking the food from her. He'd gotten lost in his own thoughts again, forgetting to answer her question.

He shrugged. "Go back to Karza I guess."

Kaori sighed, "I thought you were done with the peacekeeper? He's bored of you, Nix. It's time to move on."

"I didn't say I was going back to Gram," he growled, his words sounding childish in his own ears. "What do you expect me to do? I can't stay in Syndicate territory."

"I don't see why not," Kaori dropped her mocking tone. "Any of the other clans would welcome you with open arms. Forget about my brother and the peacekeeper. You don't owe them anything."

Nix let out a snort. As if she was any better at letting go.

"Any other clan would welcome me right up until they turned me in for the bounty." He shook his head with a scowl. "And if they didn't, it would only be because they're looking for any advantage to overthrow Ryu. Unlike you, I'm not interested in a clan war."

He shoved the meal bars in his pocket and moved toward his bike. The sooner he got word to Gram, the better.

"Oh Ghost, a clan war? You always did think too small." She was closer than he thought, her voice right in his ear.

Before he could turn around, hot pain bit into his side. He pulled away from her too late. She smiled at him, a long knife in one hand, red with his blood.

"There are much bigger things happening than just some silly clan war," she said pityingly. "If only you'd just stayed away, it wouldn't have had to turn out like this. The Military is ready to make their move, and I can't have you getting in the way."

She stepped between him and his bike, cutting off his escape. Fire spread through his torso. Poison. As usual. He knew he didn't have long before he'd barely be able to move. He channeled as much energy as he could and sped away from Kaori, deeper into the cover of the surrounding trees. She wouldn't follow him. She knew she didn't have to. Using his channeling to enhance his speed would only make the poison spread faster. He'd be dead long before he had any hope of reaching Karza.

When he could no longer see Kaori or the outpost behind him, he stopped to lean against a tree. Already he felt weak, like he could barely stand. He slid to the ground and leaned his head back, closing his eyes. He wanted to rest, to sleep.

The Military was going after the girl. They would attack the base without warning, and Gram wouldn't be able to stop them. Nix had created yet another problem for him. He wasn't going to die without at least trying to fix it.

He forced his eyes open, each lid heavy. Lifting his arms felt like lifting heavy weights as he struggled to remove his jacket. His fingers fumbled in his pocket and pulled out a channeling booster. It would only make the pain worse, and the poison spread faster, but he didn't care. It was the only chance he had of making it back to the base. He only had to accomplish that one thing. Warn the others. His life didn't matter after that.

The fresh hum of energy from the medicine gave him the strength to peel off his shirt and rip it into strips. His hands shook as he pulled a small medical kit from another pocket. He used part of his shirt to wipe at the blood, gritting his teeth through the pain. Next, he squeezed a numbing salve over the wound and pressed a thick white bandage over it. He wrapped the remainder of his shirt around his waist, securing the bandage in place.

He knew it wouldn't be long before blood soaked through the bandage and the thin fabric. The poison was Kaori's specialty. She'd explained the ingredients to him once, though he didn't really understand it. All he knew was that the wound would bleed like hell and burn like fire. Using his channeling would only make it worse.

His vision blurred from the effort it took to stand. His body shook as though it were cold, though his veins burned like they were on fire. He ground his teeth and tried to take even breaths. Slow and stumbling, he began to make his way back toward the outpost. He could only hope Kaori wasn't there waiting to finish him off.

Every step felt heavier than the last. Spots danced in his eyes, but at last, his bike came into view. Kaori was nowhere in sight. He pulled himself onto the seat and draped and closed his eyes in a moment of tired relief. He opened them again with effort and gripped the handlebars weakly. Now he just had to stay conscious long enough to make it back to base.

I was wrong to let you go
And now it's too late to undo
The damage that was done
You've moved on
And I've tried to
But really I never could
Instead I buried my heart
And let it grow cold
Ignored what you were to me
And what we became
So why are you writing me now
After all this time?
We can't go back to who we were
I can't become the man I was
Because if I let myself remember you
I won't be able to face
The mistakes I've made
And the hole inside me that you
Left behind.
So I put your words away
Unopened
And pretend like I can go back
To who I was before I knew you.

Chapter Thirteen

After learning the truth about Nix, Thea had begun practicing with the daggers Gram had given her. It hadn't been easy to control them enough to hit the target Gram had set up for her with any reliability. She'd only ever used her manipulation to haphazardly fling rocks or sticks, and never with precision. If she didn't maintain the right balance on the daggers, they would simply fly sideways harmlessly. Gram had told her to practice with one dagger at a time until she could make it fly straight. Once she could hit the target accurately, she could try adding more daggers.

Thea lifted a dagger into the air and let it hover for a moment, making sure it was balanced, adjusting her aim. It was getting easier, and she was getting faster. She gave the dagger a push of energy, and it flew towards the target on the other side of the courtyard with a whistle of air. It sunk into the target with a satisfying *thunk*.

"Impressive," Gram said from behind her. She turned to see him and Kai enter the courtyard.

"You're improving fast," Gram said.

"I can hardly get her to stop practicing," Kai grumbled with a frown.

"Practice is good," Gram said with a shrug. "Just don't wear yourself out too much or Luc'll have my ass."

Thea chuckled.

"Have you tried two yet?" Gram asked her.

Thea shook her head.

"I think you're ready, go ahead and try it."

Thea felt her face burn. Having an audience made her nervous, but she bent and picked up two daggers from their storage case before letting each hover above her hands. She didn't know if it was because Gram and Kai were watching, or because she was trying to focus on two objects at once, but she found it much more difficult to keep them steady. She took a deep breath and shot the first one forward, followed by the second. The first dagger flew in a straight line toward the target, but the second started to turn to the side. Convinced the first dagger would hit its mark, she turned all her focus to the second and gave it a nudge to get it back on course. She wasn't fast enough. The dagger's point barely grazed the edge of the target before clattering against the wall behind.

Gram let out a low whistle.

"Did you change the second dagger's course after firing it?" he asked.

Thea nodded. "It started to turn, so I tried to fix it. I wasn't fast enough, though."

Gram shook his head.

"That's a high-level skill most Manipulator's don't learn until they can easily control multiple daggers. The fact that you picked it up on your own is impressive."

Thea's face burned hotter at his praise.

"I wonder if it's because of that trick mom taught you," Kai said.

Thea shrugged.

"What trick is that?" Gram asked.

"My mom taught me to use my manipulation by balancing leaves," she said.

"Leaves? Isn't it hard to control something that lightweight?"

"It's more like balancing them than controlling them," Thea explained, as she reached up to pull a leaf from one of the lowest branches of the nearby tree. She let it go, then gave it a nudge to make it float higher. The slight breeze caught the leaf, and she nudged it back toward her. The leaf swayed back and forth gracefully as she gave it little nudges, trying to hold it in one place.

Gram let out another whistle.

"I've known a lot of Manipulators," he said, "but I've never seen anyone do that."

He let out a laugh and added. "Now that I think about it, that's just the sort of thing I'd expect Iris to come up with."

Thea smiled.

"Lucan said you have a lot of great stories about her," she said, letting the leaf fall. "Will you tell us some."

Gram beamed, but before he could answer, Kai asked, "You...You know my father too, don't you?"

He sounded like he'd been thinking about it for a while and had finally found the courage to ask. She supposed it made sense. Their mother had gotten pregnant before she left the city, so there was a good chance Gram knew his father too. Still, the question surprised her. She'd never once heard Kai express an interest in wanting to know about him. Sometimes she even forgot they were half-siblings.

"I guess you know, then," Gram said, rubbing the back of his head the way he did when he didn't want to tell them something. "I wasn't sure she'd told you, so I didn't want to bring it up. His name is Nolan—Nolan Astley. He's a...uh...commander in the Military, oversees the peacekeepers and Military Police."

"Does that mean he's one of the people trying to find me?" Thea blurted out as soon as the thought popped into her head. She regretting saying it before she'd even finished her sentence.

Gram looked away with a regretful frown. It was all the confirmation she needed.

"Does he know?" Kai snapped. "Does he know who we are?"

Kai left the real question unspoken. It didn't need to be asked. It hung so heavy in the air Thea could taste it on the tip of her own tongue, could see it in the way Kai's jaw clenched and the way Gram's shoulders sagged. They were all thinking it.

Why isn't he helping us?

"Yeah, he knows," Gram said with a sigh and tore his hand through his hair. "Nolan and your mom, well, things got messy. Nolan's family—"

Kai turned away, cutting him off with a shake of his head.

"I'm going to go help Lucan."

"Kai—" Thea started to follow him, but he waved her off with a sad smile.

"I'm okay."

Thea hesitated, unsure whether to follow him anyway or give him space.

"Give him a bit," Gram said.

She hesitated another moment before sitting down on the bench under the tree. Gram swore quietly and let out a sigh before plopping down next to her.

"Sorry," he said. "Maybe I shouldn't have said anything. Nolan isn't actually a bad guy. Believe me, I've wanted to hate him. I probably should, but I guess I know him too well."

Thea wanted to ask more, but it felt wrong without Kai present.

"How about I tell you about some of the times your mom got me out of insane amounts of trouble?"

Gram grinned, but his voice sounded forced, like he was simply trying to lighten the mood. Thea appreciated his effort and nodded. It didn't take long for Gram to have her laughing until her sides ached as he told her stories from his childhood. Besides Lucan, many of his stories also featured a girl named Aly. His voice caressed the name softly, as though it were a fragile thing that could break if he spoke too loud. Thea wondered where she was now, and if they would ever meet her.

"So, there we were, hiding in the closet, absolutely dripping wet. Ms. Margaret came in and we were sure we were dead. She was going to open the closet, and we were gonna be done for. Then Iris shouts, 'Be careful! I saw the biggest spider in there earlier!' Well, Ms. Margaret was terrified of spiders, so she got out of there real quick. We had to give Iris our desserts for a week to make up for it, but believe me, it was worth it."

"I'm not sure any of your schemes were ever worth it," Lucan said with a sigh as he entered the courtyard, shaking his head. Gram grinned.

"You heading out?" he asked.

Lucan nodded. "I have to attend to some things in the city. I'll come back as soon as I can, but it will likely be close to a week."

"Where's Kai?" Thea asked, her amusement from Gram's story quickly fading.

"I thought he was with you," Lucan said, looking around the courtyard in confusion. "Did something happen?"

"I told them about Nolan," Gram said. Lucan's eyes widened, and he nodded in understanding.

"I'm gonna go check on him," Thea said, brushing off her pants as she stood.

Gram nodded, then turned back to Lucan.

"Be careful," she heard him say as she crossed the courtyard. "If you find out anything, let me know."

"I will. If any trouble comes up, contact me."

Their exchange reminded her of all the things she had to worry about. Right now, she couldn't think about them. This time, she was going to be the one to comfort Kai. She couldn't do that if she let herself get distracted by worry.

Thea hesitated as she entered the barracks. Kai was sitting on his bed, fiddling with something small in his hands. She wasn't sure what she was supposed to say to him. Nothing she could say or do could fix what he must be feeling. If anything, her presence might only make things worse.

She took a deep breath and crossed the room. She plopped down beside him on the bed and bumped her shoulder against his.

"What's that?" she asked, gesturing toward his hands.

He held open his palm to show her a silver band dotted with tiny blue stones. It was simple, but beautiful.

"It was Mom's. She gave it to me when she told me about my father. Said he'd given it to her."

"What did she tell you about him?" she asked.

"Nothing really. She seemed sad, so I didn't want to make her talk about it."

Thea leaned her head against her brother's shoulder.

"Gram seems to know him pretty well. Maybe you should ask about him."

Kai shook his head. "I don't want to know about him."

He clenched his fist around the ring, his fingers turning white. He exhaled and relaxed his grip before holding the ring out to her.

"Here, you should have this. It would look good on you."

She hesitated before taking it.

"Thank you. And I agree with you. It's just..." She stopped, realizing what she was about to say was selfish and insensitive. She was supposed to be trying to make him feel better.

"Just what?"

"Nothing. Never mind."

"Just tell me. I won't feel bad, I promise," he said, reaching over to poke her cheek.

Thea took a deep breath. "I guess I couldn't help but be curious. He was part of mom's life after all."

Kai didn't say anything, and Thea hunched her shoulders guiltily.

"Sorry," she said.

"Don't be," he sighed. "You're right. We should ask Gram about it some-time. I just...not today."

Thea nodded.

"Thanks for worrying about me," Kai said with something close to his usual smile. "I'm okay though."

"You sure?"

He nodded. "Yeah, I just. I don't know." His voice shook, and he stopped to clear his throat. "It makes me feel responsible, I guess. For what's hap-pened to you. I know that doesn't make sense but—"

"Hey," she stopped him, resting her hand on his arm. "I don't know an-ything about this guy, or how involved he is in what happened to me. It doesn't matter, because there's one thing I do know. Our parents are Iris and Jonah Copelan. You're my brother and you're always there for me. I wouldn't be able to do any of this without you."

Kai wrapped one arm around her shoulder and rested his chin on top of her head.

"Thanks," he whispered as he squeezed her shoulder tight.

Thea could hardly remember what it was like to be passionate about anything. Their time at the base had given her the opportunity to rediscover her love for cooking. Memories of days spent in the kitchen with her dad were a comfort to her that she hadn't realized she'd missed. Hearty stews paired with crusty bread. Savory meats with crunchy vegetables. Flaky pas-tries and spongy cakes.

She'd spent so long simply surviving, she'd forgotten how to live. For the first time in a long time, she finally felt like herself.

Gram sat back with a sigh after scraping his plate clean after dinner that evening. To her surprise, he sounded more sad than content.

"You alright?" she asked him.

Gram shook his head.

"Your cooking is way better than Luc's, you know. It's a shame."

"Thank you?" Thea wasn't sure whether Gram was complimenting her or not.

Gram laughed. "Sorry, never mind. It's nothing. Thanks for the meal. It was really great."

Thea looked at him quizzically as he left the room.

"He's worried," Kai said.

"About Lucan?"

Kai didn't elaborate. Thea crossed her arms and puffed her cheeks, irritated. It felt like they were keeping something from her, and she didn't like it.

"Don't worry about it," Kai said, patting the top of her head as he stood. "Come on, I'll help you clean up."

The next afternoon, Thea found herself with nothing to do while Kai was with Gram, learning to drive his motorcycle. She'd already finished her exercises for the day, and had attempted to practice with her daggers, but found concentration difficult. Her head was hurting, and she was tired from another poor night's sleep. She decided instead to explore the base, something she had started doing when she had nothing else to do.

The base was larger than she'd first realized, stretching out in a long rectangle away from the main house. Most of the buildings and extra rooms were stacked haphazardly with spare equipment or furniture. She thought maybe she could find some additional furnishings to make the barracks more comfortable. At the moment, their quarters were simply one long, dreary room with extra beds pushed against the walls. Two beds and a few chairs had been dragged to the center for her and Kai to use.

There didn't seem to be any particular system used to store the items in the various buildings and rooms she searched. Furniture was stored right alongside radio equipment and old cleaning supplies. Some of the rooms looked like they'd been rummaged through already, adding to the disorganization. She found some additional cookware, which she moved to the kitchen.

She wandered into a large, three-walled structure near the rear gate—a sort of vehicle bay. Several partially disassembled vehicles remained parked on one side of the structure. Two long tables took up most of the remaining space. Tools and spare parts littered the tables. Along the back wall, a row of communication monitors and computers sat on a long table. Cabinets lined the remaining wall, with a bed pushed into the corner. A layer of dust covered everything except the computers, as though they were the only things that had been used in some time.

Thea was sure she hadn't explored this building before, and yet she felt an odd sense of familiarity as she circled the tables. Warm sunlight filtered through the open side of the building, lighting up the specks of dust that floated lazily through the air. She reached for a stack of small black squares next to one of the monitors, wondering what they were. Some had notes attached to them, written in tight, slanted handwriting.

She was startled by the loud clatter of metal behind her, and she spun around.

"Why are you here?"

The voice was strained and breathless, but she recognized it even before she saw him.

He was back.

Nix stood across from her, leaning against the cabinet by the entrance. The vivid memory of her nightmare sprang to her mind immediately. She took a step back, though there was nowhere for her to retreat. Her eyes were drawn once again to the dark mark on his bare arm. Was that blood crusting his hands and arms? She noticed the torn fabric tied around his waist in place of his shirt—or maybe it had been his shirt. His face was shadowed by the sun streaming in behind him, but it didn't mask the sweaty shine on his skin or the lack of color in his olive complexion.

"Gram." His voice came out rough and raspy. He fumbled with the latch on the cabinet, his hands shaking. "Go get Gram."

"You're hurt," she said quietly, taking a hesitant step forward.

"I'm—" He glared in her direction, but his eyes seemed to glaze over, not seeing her. He closed them as he leaned against the cabinet. "I just. Go. Hurry. Please."

The last word came out as a strangled plea.

She had been so afraid of him before, but now she only felt pity. She forced herself to move toward him.

"Let me help you."

"No—"

His legs gave out and he began to fall helplessly toward the floor. She rushed forward and caught him, easing him down to lean against the cabinet.

"What happened?"

Thea's head whipped up at the sound of Gram's voice coming from the entrance. Kai entered a few steps behind him.

"Kaori," Nix responded weakly, his words slurring as he began to slip into unconsciousness. "Military. And Syndicate. . . They're coming."

Part Two

To Blackest Night

Two pasts haunted by darkness and nightmares.
Alone. Betrayed. Afraid.
Two futures careening toward bitter fates.
Darkness. Disaster. Regret.
We are the same.
I cannot save you from this pain
So instead I create a chance, a choice
A single step toward tomorrow.
By embracing my fate can I rewrite yours?
By facing my fears can I give you courage?
By resigning my safety, can I bring you home?

Chapter Fourteen

Gram cursed and crossed to the cabinet Nix had been trying to open. He wrenched open the door above Thea's head and began searching through its contents.

"Damn it, what did I tell him? This happens every damn time," he grumbled, his voice higher and tighter than usual. "And now of all times. Without Luc here. I'm going to need your help, Kai."

Kai was already kneeling beside Thea. He carefully pulled away the strips of torn fabric from Nix's wound. Beneath the blood and dirt, the skin looked swollen and red. Fresh blood seeped out around the edges of the wound.

"He's burning," Thea told her brother.

"The wound looks infected," he said, "and it looks like he lost a lot of blood. That's probably why he collapsed."

"Here, give him this." Gram handed Kai a small bottle. "It's not just an infection. If Kaori did this, then he's almost surely been poisoned. That'd be her trademark."

Kai nodded and instructed Thea to tilt Nix's head so he could pour the antidote into his mouth. He poured slowly, closing Nix's mouth between drops to give him a chance to swallow.

"We should get him in the house so I can take care of his wound," Kai instructed once the liquid was gone.

She channeled her energy as she lifted Nix from the ground. More blood oozed from his wound, making her stomach clench with nausea. She stumbled slightly, and Kai put a steadying hand on her back. She took a deep breath, trying not to let her nightmares creep into her thoughts.

"Take him to the room next to mine, Thea. Kai, we can contact Luc from here." Gram gestured toward the monitors on the long table in the back of the room. "You can ask him how to treat the wound."

The room Gram had indicated was empty aside from the bed along one wall, a tall wardrobe, and a chair in the corner. Thea laid Nix as carefully as she could on the bed before sitting down in the chair.

The Military was coming. She was in danger. They all were. She tried to keep the familiar sense of panic at bay by concentrating on something else. Her eyes were drawn to the dark tattoo on Nix's arm. Instead of distraction, her mind had merely found a different reason to feel anxious.

She tore her gaze away from the tattoo and moved her chair closer to the bed. Tentatively, she reached out to brush Nix's dark hair off his forehead. His skin burned beneath her fingers. Even in sleep, he had a scowl on his face. Maybe he was in pain, or maybe that was just how his face always looked.

She looked away.

He was Syndicate. He was dangerous, and she didn't trust him.

He had come back to warn them, though. Kai had told her that she'd been too hard on him. For the first time, she wondered if he was right. He was rude and abrasive and always seemed to call her out on her insecurities, but had he ever really done anything to hurt her? Or had she simply chosen to blame him rather than accept her own shortcomings? Maybe she had never seen him at all.

The girl is mine, he'd said.

She shivered.

"You okay?"

She jumped at the sound of Kai's voice. He was looking down at her with the familiar worry on his face. He held a small box in his hands, the glass bottles and jars rattling together.

She nodded. "What do you need me to do?"

"Can you bring a table or something? And another chair?"

Thea carried one of the small side tables from the living room and a chair from the kitchen and placed them near the bed.

"Here," Kai handed her one of the bottles he'd pulled from the box. "We need to bring his fever down. Get him to swallow some of that, just a little at a time."

Thea sat on the edge of the bed, and with her free hand tipped Nix's head back slightly. She dropped small amounts of the liquid into his mouth, as she'd seen Kai do with the antidote.

Meanwhile, Kai soaked a cloth in a different liquid and began to wipe the wound carefully. Fresh blood welled up as he wiped the dried crust away. Thea turned away, her stomach twisting at the sight.

"That should be enough," Kai said. "Here hold this."

Thea set down the bottle she was holding and moved closer to Kai so she could take another jar from him. He scooped a thick-looking paste from the jar and spread it over the wound and surrounding skin. After taking the jar from her, he handed her another bottle of liquid and a folded bandage.

"Soak that bandage in the liquid."

She did as he instructed. He took the soaked bandage from her and placed it over the wound, then took the bottle and instructed her to prop Nix up so he could wrap his torso in a long white bandage. When they finished, she realized the sun had begun to set, making the room dim.

"How is he?"

They both turned as Gram entered the room. Kai shook his head, his expression grim.

"I've done what I can for the wound," Kai told him, "but his channeling is so weak I can barely detect it."

Gram shook his head, his face pinched with a frown of worry.

"We need to get him to Luc. This poison isn't easy to treat."

"Isn't Lucan in the city?" Thea's voice rose in pitch, the fear closing her throat, squeezing her chest. Her body tensed with the itch to run. "We can't go there."

"We can't stay here either," Gram said with a shake of his head. "The three of us can't defend against a Military attack. Or a Syndicate one, for that matter."

"But the Military," she said, unable to finish her sentence. She didn't need to tell him that the capital, Andewarden, was one of the most dangerous places she could choose to go.

"Sometimes the best hiding spot is where they would least expect you," Gram answered with a half-hearted smirk. "It's your choice, of course. I don't want to put you in danger, or leave you on your own, but Nix won't make it without Luc's help."

Gram's voice hitched. He cared about Nix, she realized. He wasn't just a mercenary or a bounty hunter Gram chose to work with. To Gram, he was as much family as they were.

Thea felt Kai's hand on her arm. She hadn't realized she'd started to tremble. The thought of going to the city filled her with a panic that she couldn't control, but there was no question. Gram was worried about Nix, and she couldn't leave him to face this alone.

"We're going with you," Kai said softly but firmly. Hearing him say the words out loud made Thea relax. She couldn't think about the danger. This was the right thing to do. She just had to focus on that.

She met Gram's eyes and nodded.

Gram seemed to relax as he gave them a grateful smile.

"Thea, come help me hook the trailer up to my bike. Kai, you go pack up whatever supplies you think we'll need."

Thea followed Gram back to the workshop. Once again, she was struck with an odd sense of familiarity as she moved about the space.

"Won't they be watching the base?" Thea asked as she held the trailer in place while Gram attached the connectors to his bike.

"I contacted a...uh...friend in the Military," Gram told her with a quick glance out of the corner of his eye, as though he were wondering how she would react.

Thea froze.

"I trust her with my life," he assured her, his voice gentle. "She says the patrol is small, only a few soldiers meant to keep an eye on us. If we slip out the back gate in the night, we might be able to get out unnoticed. Even if they spot us, I don't think they'll try to stop us. They're a just a recon squad after all."

"Won't they alert the others that we're headed for the city?" Thea asked, liking Gram's plan less and less.

"We'll go south first before doubling back toward the east," he said. "I doubt they'll expect us to head for the city. They don't know Nix made it back or that he's injured. They'll probably think we're going west, or trying to hide out down south."

Thea didn't say anything. She didn't like it, but since they'd already decided to stay with Gram, going to the city was their only option.

When they finished attaching the trailer, Gram rummaged in the cabinet again. He groaned as he pulled out a near empty bottle.

"I knew that little shit had used channeling suppressants, but I didn't realize he'd taken this much. Dumbass."

Gram shook his head before pulling out two small vials sloshing with reddish liquid. He handed them to Thea.

"These are channeling boosters for Macros. You'll be dead tired once they wear off, but if we run into any trouble getting out of here, you'll be glad to have them."

Thea mumbled a numb thank you and took the vials with trembling hands, trying not to think about the bitter, sludgy taste. This time she would be taking them not because she was powerless but because the others were counting on her.

Thea eased Nix onto a pile of blankets in the trailer as Kai arranged himself and their belongings into the remaining space. She felt Gram's hand rest on her back. There was something comforting about its weight.

"You can ride behind me on the bike," he said. "I'm going to need you to help me keep a lookout for trouble."

Gram kept the headlight off as he drove at a speed faster than she thought a bike could go. The device he wore over his eyes must allow him to see in the dark. He dodged obstacles as if it were full daylight. Watching the ground blur beneath them made her dizzy, and she gripped the back of Gram's jacket so tight her fingers ached.

A headlight lit up the darkness—another bike trying to cut off their path. Gram swerved to the side. The movement put them nearly parallel with the trailer behind them, as it couldn't turn at such a sharp angle. Just when Thea thought they would crash into it, Gram gave the bike a jerk in the opposite direction, and the trailer straightened behind them. Thea turned to see Kai clutching the rails with wide eyes, then swung her head around toward the other bike. Gram had managed to get around it and was pulling away in a cloud of dust.

A flash to their left caught her attention, but before she could find the source, a loud boom made her ears ring. Silver flashes rained down in front of them, littering the ground with metal spikes. Gram drove over them without slowing.

The headlight fell away behind them, and they saw no other signs of pursuit. After some time, Gram slowed the bike and called over his shoulder, "Any sign we're still being followed?"

"No!" Thea called out.

Gram pulled the bike to a stop and shook out his hands before shifting in his seat to look behind him.

"Sorry about that, Kai! You okay back there?"

Kai nodded, but Thea could see that his eyes were still wide, and his chest was rising and falling like he was trying to catch his breath.

"I think all the jostling reopened Nix's wound though," he called.

"We'll be in the city by morning," Gram said, flicking on his headlight and gripping the handlebars again. "We just have to hope he can hold on until then."

"Why didn't the spikes damage our tires?" Thea asked in Gram's ear as he drove. The engine was quieter now that he wasn't pushing it so hard.

"Anti-puncture tires," he called back. She felt his back rumble as he chuckled. "I've never been so glad Nix insisted on them."

The tall skyscrapers of Andewarden came into view as the sky was beginning to lighten from black to gray. Gram pulled the bike to a stop, well away from the distant buildings, his eyes scanning their surroundings.

"What is it?" Thea asked, her chest tight with worry.

Before Gram could answer, the sound of an approaching vehicle cut through the quiet of the early morning. The vehicle turned in front of them and stopped. A woman stepped out. She was pretty, with dark skin, wavy brown hair to her chin, and a smattering of freckles across her nose.

"Lucan's already at the clinic," she said to Gram.

Thea stepped nearer to Kai as she studied the woman. Kai reached up from the trailer to give her arm a reassuring squeeze.

"I can take those three in my car. You can follow us on the bike. Here." The woman opened the back door of her vehicle and pulled out a dark, hooded jacket. "You should put this on, so no one recognizes you."

"Thanks Mel." Gram grinned as he took the jacket.

The woman stepped toward the trailer. Thea took a fearful step back, but the woman just looked down at Nix, her mouth pulled into a frown of worry.

"What'd he do this time?"

"That damn woman of his," Gram grumbled.

She shook her head.

"I didn't know she was working with Intelligence. Things have gotten complicated. Intelligence and Research have the backing of the Grand Marshal and the council. They're forcing Marshal Barton's hand and bypassing Nolan completely. I'm sorry I couldn't warn you sooner, we only just learned what was happening."

"I know Mel," Gram said softly. "I wouldn't fault you even if you knew. You know I never want you to have to compromise your position for me, or put yourself in danger of reprisals."

The woman smiled, looking a little sad. She shook her head and turned her attention to Thea and Kai. Thea wished she could hide behind Kai, but he was still sitting in the trailer.

"Sorry," she said, "I should have introduced myself sooner. I'm Mel. Gram and I have known each other for a long time. I wish we were meeting under better circumstances. I wish..."

Her voice trailed off, and she turned away.

"We'd better go. I have to get back before anyone starts looking for me."

"It's okay," Kai whispered in Thea's ear. "I don't sense any reason not to trust her. Gram trusts her, and she's worried about us."

The woman and Gram had moved close to each other and were talking quietly with their heads close together. Gram reached down and took the woman's hand. She laced her fingers in his and stretched up to kiss his cheek, before pulling away.

It seemed they were more than just friends.

Thea let out a shaky breath before moving to lift Nix from the trailer. The woman opened the back door of her vehicle so Thea could ease him onto the back seat. Kai met Thea's eyes and smiled reassuringly before climbing into the front passenger seat. She took a deep, shaky breath before sliding in beside Nix.

"There's more jackets on the floor back there," the woman said, as she took her seat in front of Thea. "When we get to the clinic, you should each put one on. Especially him. If anyone recognizes him, it would not be good."

Thea could see the worry in her eyes through the mirror. It calmed her. Whoever she was, she cared a lot about Gram, and Nix too.

They drove through narrow streets with buildings packed close together, casting their surroundings in shadow. Thea shuddered and tried not to focus on the dark alleyways or mirrored windows. She turned to look for

Gram, but he wasn't behind them. He must have taken a different route. Their vehicle stopped in front of a two-story building that was separated from the others by a wide paved parking lot in front and a small grassy park to one side. Gram's bike was already parked in front, and she could see him standing by an outer stairwell.

Thea arranged one of the jackets over Nix's shoulders, pulling the hood up over his head before putting one on herself. Once she'd pulled the hood up over her hair, she opened the door and stepped out, blinking in the morning light. She hadn't realized how dark the car's windows were. They'd kept out not only the light, but any prying eyes. She felt a wave of relief and gratitude. As she ducked back into the car to lift Nix out, she turned to the woman, who remained seated behind the wheel.

"Thank you," Thea told her.

The woman flashed a smile and winked.

"Good luck," she responded as Thea pulled Nix from the vehicle. Thea thought she meant it.

They followed Gram up the external set of stairs to a door at the top. They entered and found Lucan already waiting in a small living area, furnished with a couch, a few chairs, and a small dining table.

"I've already got things set up in the bedroom," he said, jumping to his feet. "Kai, I could use your help."

Thea followed Lucan into a bedroom off the main room and laid Nix carefully on the bed. Medical instruments, bandages, and jars of medicine were already set out on a small table. She closed the door behind her as she left and took a moment to look around the small apartment. The living room opened into a small kitchen and there were two other doors down a short hallway, one of which was probably a bathroom.

Gram was standing in the kitchen, assessing the food stock in the cupboards.

"I'll have to go out for some supplies later," he said grimly.

"Is this your apartment?" Thea asked him quizzically.

"It's Luc's," Gram said with a shrug as he pulled two packaged meals from the cupboard. "His family owns the building and runs the clinic downstairs. Luc's the only one who uses the apartment, though."

He held up the meals.

"You look tired. Do you want to sleep? Or do you want to eat first?

After staying awake through the night, her eyes burned. She could feel a dull ache building in her forehead. The thought of food only made her queasy.

"I think I'd rather just sleep," she confessed.

Gram chuckled.

"It was a rough night, wasn't it? You can use the other room there." He pointed toward one of the doors. "That other one's the bathroom."

"What about you?"

Gram waved her off. "I'm gonna eat first. And wait out here for Luc."

Thea felt guilty leaving him to wait alone, but figured it was better if she slept now, while the others were busy, so she could take her turn staying awake later. She nodded gratefully before pulling a change of spare clothes from the pack Kai had carried in.

She filled the bathroom sink with water and let her shirt soak while she showered. The hot water helped ease the tension she'd been carrying through the long, anxious night. She was reluctant to leave, but she was feeling dizzy from the heat and her own exhaustion. After her shower, she scrubbed her bloodied shirt and hung it on a hook to dry. She changed into clean clothes and emerged from the bathroom, rubbing her hair with a towel.

The bedroom where she'd taken Nix had been small and bare—only the bed, a small table, and a chair in the corner—as though it were so rarely used that it only needed the bare necessities for furnishings. The second room was different. A desk was pushed against one wall, books and files lined up on a shelf overhead. Office supplies were arranged neatly on the desk's surface. A wardrobe stood in one corner of the room and a plush chair in another.

Thea melted into the softness of the bed and closed her eyes. She was worried about what their next steps would be. Thinking about the fact that they were sitting right on the Military's doorstep made her chest tighten. She tried to push the worries from her mind. She was too exhausted to focus on any one thought anyway.

Yet she found sleep to be difficult. She tossed and turned. She knew she had fallen asleep, but when she woke, she didn't feel rested. She sat up, rubbing her tired eyes and pushing her hair from her face. She could see light around the edges of the curtains, but had no idea how late in the day it was or how long she'd slept.

Kai was slumped in the chair in the corner, asleep. She thought about waking him and offering him the bed, but he was snoring softly, so she let him be rather than disrupt his sleep.

The curtains in the living room were open. There was no sign of Gram or Lucan, but she did hear water running in the bathroom. The door to Nix's room was open a crack so she peeked in, wondering if either of the two men was inside.

The room was empty aside from Nix, still sleeping on the bed. A chair was pulled up close to the bed. Thea sat down quietly.

His face was relaxed now. It was the first time she'd seen him without a scowl, and she realized there was a handsome boyishness in his features that didn't match the visible scar on his chin or the many other old wounds marring his body. She wondered which face represented the real Nix. This one or the hardened glower that haunted her nightmares? Was he someone to be feared? Or was it all a mask to hide the young, vulnerable man lying in front of her—the one Gram worried about, who had risked himself to warn them? Thea didn't know.

The only thing she did know was that there was more to him than she'd allowed herself to acknowledge. Gram trusted him. Kai did too.

Her eyes strayed to the tattoo on his arm again, and she was reminded of all the reasons why she couldn't.

The Syndicate had attacked her and Kai in Senari without provocation. She'd lost control and injured several of their members, and Kai as well. They'd been looking for her ever since. Nix was one of them, or at least he had been once. How could she possibly trust that he wouldn't turn her in?

She jumped when she felt a hand on her arm.

"There you are."

It was Gram.

She stood abruptly, embarrassed that he'd found her sitting by Nix.

"Sorry," he said softly, "I didn't mean to surprise you."

She shook her head and moved toward the door. Gram followed her out of the room, closing the door behind him.

"I was looking for you or Lucan," she told him, feeling like she had to explain herself.

"Lucan's downstairs in the clinic," Gram said before gesturing toward Nix. "How is he?"

Thea shrugged.

"Just sleeping." She hesitated a moment before asking, "will you tell me about him?"

Gram's eyebrows shot up and Thea looked away, her cheeks warming. Gram let out a sigh and moved into the kitchen. He pulled two meals out and began to heat them up before answering.

"You've pretty much summed him up right. He's a total dumbass. A complete jerk. Pretty much the worst a guy can be when it comes to dealing with other people. He's a clueless asshole and an idiot."

Thea choked back a laugh. She'd expected Gram to defend him, not ridicule him.

"But if you can get past all that, he's not a bad guy." His voice grew softer and his unmistakable tone of affection surprised Thea. "His life has just been...complicated."

"You mean because he was in the Syndicate?" She wanted to sound objective, but couldn't keep her throat from tightening in automatic fear. The words came out in a high squeak.

Gram let out another sigh and rubbed his forehead with one hand.

"Like I said, complicated. I can say this with absolute certainty, he has no loyalty to the Syndicate. In fact, he has as many reasons to want to avoid them as you do, probably more.

Thea picked at her food speculatively. Gram cleared his throat before continuing.

"Look, I'm not expecting you to like the guy or anything. He's pretty much been an asshole to you. Just don't take it too personally. He's an asshole to everybody. But if there's one good thing about Nix, it's that backstabbing isn't his style. If there was ever anyone I would want watching my back, it would be him."

Gram looked away and rubbed the back of his head, looking embarrassed. She guessed it wasn't often that he gave such a genuine compliment.

"Thank you," she said. "Thank you for telling me that. The fact that you trust him and consider him a friend is probably the best endorsement anyone could have. I thought maybe he was fooling you before, but I can see now that I was wrong. I'm sorry."

"Nah don't be. Like I said, he's an asshole." Gram stretched his arms overhead as he stood, "Anyway, you look like you're still tired. Why don't you try to get some more sleep?"

"What about you?" Thea asked, noticing the dark shadows under his eyes. "Have you slept at all?"

"I slept a little. Now I've got some things to take care of."

Thea yawned. She'd been too anxious to sleep well before, so she didn't feel rested. She still didn't know what to think about Nix, but after her conversation with Gram, she felt like some of her worries had been alleviated. It helped that Gram didn't simply gloss over his faults. It told her his praise was genuine. If Gram could look past those flaws and see the good that lay beneath, maybe it was time she started trying to do the same.

Never anything else.
Visions fill my thoughts with
Violence, anger, darkness.
Is this all that I've become?

A quiet gasp and I look up
To see myself standing there,
Shock and horror on my face.
Words are needless and I know
She sees me as I am:
A monster.

Wait,
I want to say.
I'm sorry.

But answering with fear is all the other me can do.
She runs, and I know I can't escape the past.
A monster is all I'll ever be.

Chapter Fifteen

When Thea woke, her face was wet with tears. She curled into a ball on her side and wrapped her arms tight around herself, shaking as she tried to hold in her sobs. Kai was already sitting next to her, rubbing her back with soothing circles.

"Hey, what is it?" he asked, his voice gentle but full of worry.

Thea couldn't find her voice as the tears closed up her throat. She pressed her fists into her eyes in a futile attempt to stem her crying.

"You were right," she managed to choke out between sobs. "I was wrong. So wrong."

Kai didn't respond, just continued to rub her back. Once the tears finally began to slow, he stood.

"Let me get you some water."

He left the room and came back with a glass. He put one hand under her shoulders to help her sit up. She swung her legs over the side of the bed and took the glass from him with shaky hands. Kai sat beside her as she sipped the water, wrapping one arm around her and pulling her against his shoulder.

"Now why don't you tell me what's wrong?"

Thea shook her head.

"I don't know," the tears started to stream again.

She didn't know how to articulate what she felt, and she didn't want Kai to see her that way.

Like a monster.

"Hey, it was just a dream," he said. "Can you try to tell me about it? Maybe we can make sense of it together."

She set down the glass on the nearby side table and wrung her fingers together in her lap.

"Do you remember the day Nix left?" she asked through tearful gasps.

Kai stiffened. "Yeah."

"I had a nightmare that morning. In my dream, I was in the kitchen at the base, thinking about that nightmare, like I was reliving it over and over

185

again. And then there were these other thoughts, they felt like memories, but they weren't. They were terrible." She shuddered. "I don't know."

She choked on a sob.

Why? Why did it feel like she had done those things? The killing and the violence and the pain? It wasn't just this dream, she was sure. She felt like her dreams lately were nothing but darkness and anger and hurt.

Was that what she had become inside? Was she so polluted by the deceit and cruelty of others that she'd become that way herself?

A monster.

"Was there anything else?"

Thea hunched in shame.

"I just want to help," Kai said soothingly, making her feel even worse. "You can tell me about it."

Thea took a deep breath as she set the water down on a nearby table before wringing her hands together in her lap.

"I said I was standing in the kitchen," she said shakily. "But I saw myself walk into the room, like another version of me. She looked so afraid, and shocked to see me. I could feel what she was thinking, like...like...maybe that's what telepathy is like, I don't know."

Kai stiffened, his hand going still on her back. Thea buried her face in her hands as tears shook her body again.

"What was she thinking?" Kai asked quietly, "This other version of yourself."

Monster.

Her tears came harder, and she couldn't have spoken the word even if she wanted to. She shook her head, with a choked sob as she buried her face in her hands.

"The last few days have been stressful," Kai said as he pulled her into a hug. "You must be exhausted, and I know you're scared. You aren't being fair to yourself. You've been through a lot, and it takes time to deal with that. I'm proud of you for agreeing to help Nix. I know that was hard, but it just shows you're a good person, one of the kindest people I know."

Thea choked out a bitter laugh.

"I'm not," she insisted. "I was wrong about him. I treated him like a monster, but I'm the monster."

There it was. She'd said it. She couldn't meet Kai's face, but she could feel him shake his head.

"Is that what you meant when you said you were wrong?"

She nodded. She didn't know why her dream had made her think about Nix. Maybe because it resembled that day in the kitchen. Had she looked at him the way she had looked at herself? She didn't know, but somehow, she was sure that she had hurt him.

"He left because of me, didn't he? That means he got hurt because of me."

She choked on the last words, the tears closing her throat once more.

"It's not your fault," Kai said as he squeezed her shoulder. "Someone did that to him. They're the ones to blame, not you. We don't know what happened, but it sounds like it probably would have happened either way, okay?"

She shook her head as she reached up to wipe futilely at her wet face.

"You came around on your own and realized you were misjudging him. That means you're a good person."

"I don't understand why I keep having these dreams," she said, burying her face in his shirt. "It's like, like that's all I am. Just broken. And tainted. I feel like the way I looked at myself in my dream is the truth, like I can never go back."

Kai sighed. "Dreams are strange things. Sometimes there's no point trying to figure them out. It's been a stressful few days. A stressful few months actually. You have to give yourself time. I know things will get better."

When she didn't respond he said quietly, "I wish there was something more I could do to help you. Your nightmares have been pretty bad lately. Maybe we should talk to Lucan about it. He might know something that can help you sleep better or reduce your stress."

Thea suppressed another shudder. She knew Kai was probably right, that getting help was the best solution, but she didn't want to have to talk about her nightmares with anyone else. She didn't want to have to remember them.

A sudden thought struck her, and she grabbed Kai's arm in alarm.

"What? What is it?" he asked.

"My dream last night. It made me think of Nix because it was so similar to what happened the day he left. It was like it wasn't me in the kitchen, but him, his point of view."

Kai looked speculative. "Dreams are often the way our brain processes our feelings, so maybe it was your brain's way of realizing that you'd misjudged him."

"That's not what I mean," she insisted. "I dreamt about his tattoo before I even saw it."

"You were already suspicious of his connection to the Syndicate."

She shook her head.

"No, that's not it. That garage at the base. I dreamt about being there and then Nix came in. It was just like when he came back to warn us. I dreamt about it before it happened."

She felt dizzy. What did it all mean? Were her dreams really just dreams? Kai shook his head.

"I don't know, Thea. Like I said, dreams can be weird. And you have a hard time even remembering them most of the time. Maybe your mind is inserting details into those dreams now, when they weren't there in the first place."

"But Kai—"

She was interrupted by a loud sound from the living room.

Thea followed Kai out of the room, her heart thundering against her ribs. Lucan came running out of the other bedroom with a similar look of panic on his face.

The sound had come from Gram throwing open the front door. He was just closing it behind him as they came out. His eyes were wide and his breathing heavy.

"What is it?" Lucan asked.

"They're watching the clinic. Probably listening too. They know we're here."

He pulled open the door next to the entrance—a closet—and took out a black metal box. He set it on the table in front of the couch and flipped a switch, causing a low whir to emanate from the box.

"This will keep them from listening. Just keep your voices low," he told them.

Skeptically, Thea enhanced her hearing and was rewarded with a high-pitched screech in her ears. She shook her head to stop the ringing and returned her hearing to normal. Though it couldn't do anything to her unless she used her ability, Thea still moved away from the box with a wary look. She sat on the furthest end of the couch, and Kai sat down beside her.

Gram didn't sit, but instead paced anxiously in front of them.

"If I were better at sensing energy, I might have noticed them sooner. They saw me when I came back. I don't know if Nolan sent them or someone else." He looked to Lucan. "Intelligence and Research are taking the lead on this one."

"I'm sure Nolan could have guessed you'd come here," Lucan said speculatively. "He knows us both too well. Mel didn't say anything?"

Thea didn't see whether Gram nodded or shook his head. She'd turned to look at Kai instead. She was worried about how he would feel after hearing the two men mention his father.

He'd balled his hands into fists, and she could see the muscles in his jaw clenching. She leaned her head against his shoulder, hoping to reassure him.

"How long do we have?" Lucan asked, drawing her attention back to the conversation.

"I don't know," Gram admitted. "They won't come unprepared, but they know I saw them. They won't want to risk us getting away again. I'm sure it'll be tonight."

"I don't think we'll be able to get Nix out of here unnoticed," Lucan said speculatively. "If they realize he's incapacitated..."

His voice trailed off and Gram's face paled.

"We're lucky they can't sense him," Kai said after clearing his throat. "His energy is still too weak."

"He's in no condition to travel either way," Lucan said with a frown.

Gram shook his head, looking conflicted.

"I don't think they'll attack the clinic on a hunch," Lucan added. "Maybe if—"

"Don't say it Luc," Gram interrupted. "I'm not using them as bait."

He ran both his hands through his hair, looking more frustrated than Thea had ever seen him.

"If we're gone, do you think the soldiers would still come to the clinic?" Thea asked, guessing what Lucan had in mind.

"Thea!" Kai said at the same time as Gram said, "It's too dangerous."

"We don't have another option, do we?" she asked. "If we stay here, we're in even more danger. If we leave, and make sure the soldiers see us go, then Nix and Lucan will be safe, right?"

"I never wanted to ask you to put yourself at risk," Gram said with a sigh.

"We owe Nix that much," she said.

Kai took her hand and squeezed it. In spite of his objections, he knew she was right.

It wasn't just Nix's warning, she knew. Ever since he'd come back, she hadn't been able to stop thinking about their interactions. Maybe he'd confronted that group of Syndicate fighters in order to keep them away from her. Maybe he'd only fought her that night because she'd been out of control. Maybe he had no choice. He'd frightened her in the gym, but he'd kept her from getting seriously hurt by her own stupidity. Maybe he didn't have the best personality, but maybe he'd been protecting them all along.

She had been wrong about him before. She had acted like a monster, but she could choose now to act differently.

Gram nodded to them thankfully and some of the tension seemed to release from his shoulders.

"We need a plan," he said. "Any ideas?"

Kai sighed in resignation and rested his chin on his interlaced fingers before asking, "The goal is to get them to follow us, right? Then we need to make sure they see us leave."

Lucan nodded his agreement. "It would help if we knew how many are already watching the clinic. Then we can formulate the best plan."

"Kai?" Gram asked, "What are you able to sense?"

Kai shook his head.

"It's hard, with so many people around. I can't tell what doesn't belong because it's all unfamiliar to me."

"There shouldn't be too many in this area with high energy," Lucan told him. "If they were skilled enough, they'd join the Military and be able to obtain housing in the city."

"What if I went outside with Kai?" Thea suggested. "If he points out the highest energies, I might be able to see them or hear them."

Kai shook his head. "It's too dangerous."

"They already know I'm here," Thea argued stubbornly. She wasn't going to sit there being useless. "The safest thing for me to do is make sure we can escape successfully."

"That might be the best option," Lucan agreed calmly.

Kai let out another sigh, but didn't protest further.

"I don't think we should try anything before dark," Gram said, rubbing his chin. "If we need to lose them, it'll be easier that way. There's not much point in you trying to spot them until right before we leave, in case more of them come. In the meantime, try to rest and make any preparations you need to."

"Where will we go?" Thea asked. "Back to the base?"

Gram frowned, as though the question hadn't occurred to him. He was only thinking about getting them away from the city.

"We can't," he said slowly. He let out a groan and tore his hand through his hair again. "I don't know. I—"

"Ryu."

They turned at the sound of the raspy voice behind them. Nix was leaning against the doorway of his bedroom, his hand clutching his side. His breathing was heavy, as though crossing the room had required all his strength.

"You shouldn't be up," Lucan said at the same time as Gram exclaimed, "Like hell!"

Lucan crossed the room quickly to help Nix over to the couch. Thea and Kai stood to make room for him. He closed his eyes in a grimace as Lucan lowered him down.

"Ryu said he'd keep her safe," he continued, his words slow and slightly slurred. "I was coming back to tell you. When Kaori..."

He stopped and frowned.

"Even if that's true, it's too risky," Gram argued. "Kaori would be all too happy to bring the entire Military down on her brother and the Syndicate, you know that. These two would only be the bait. Hell, maybe that's been her plan all along. It wouldn't surprise me if she'd thought that far ahead. Maybe Ryu can be trusted, I don't know, but I sure as hell don't trust the rest of the Syndicate."

Thea's stomach twisted. Nix was talking about the Syndicate? He wanted them to go to the Syndicate for protection? All her fear and mistrust came rushing back at the sound of that one word.

Nix just shook his head slowly, heavily. "There's nowhere else."

"There's other old bases out there, aren't there? Or remote villages?" Thea countered. There was no way she was going to hand herself over to the Syndicate willingly.

"That's worked out for you so far," Nix snapped, turning to look at her with a scowl. His voice was too weak for his words to sting, though. He leaned his head against the back of the couch again, like he didn't have the strength to argue with her.

"Do what you want," he conceded. "Just don't get Gram killed doing it."

Gram cleared his throat.

"First things first," he said, like he wanted to steer the conversation away from a potential argument. "We have to get away from the city."

He pulled a folded paper from his pocket—a worn map.

"There are some old outposts," Gram said, as he spread the map on the table in front of them. "We can head for this one near the Syndicate border. That should at least keep the Military from making too aggressive of a move. We can decide what to do from there."

Gram explained the course they would take through the canyon to the north. They would be close to the Garrison, but should be safe as long as they stayed on the northern rim. The forest cover would help them more easily avoid their pursuers. Thea wrung her fingers and tried to pay attention, but she couldn't stop the nagging voice in her head telling her they were making a mistake.

We weave at a reckless pace
Between the looming trees
And grasping, scratching branches,
Unable to see what lies ahead.
I worry she'll fall behind,
Tired and alone.

The roar of engines fills the night,
And light cuts through the darkness
As they close in around us.
We can't go forward,
And we can't go back.
We're trapped,
And she's alone.

"Take the bike and go,"
You say,
But you can't do this on your own.
I have no choice.
I have to find her.
She's all alone.

Another danger blocks my path
And I lose control.
I can't fight back.
My body burns with fire.
"Take care of your sister,"
My mother said,
But I didn't,
And now she's all alone.

Chapter Sixteen

"Are you sure about this?" Kai asked as she pulled her hood up over her head. "I know you feel bad about Nix, but you don't have to try to make up for it by putting yourself in danger."

Thea had started moving toward the door, but she stopped and turned toward him.

"I'm in danger either way," she said quietly, not meeting his eyes. "At least this way I can be useful."

That woman, regardless of what she'd done, was right about one thing. She was tired of hiding. She was tired of being a victim. She was tired of people getting hurt because of her. Maybe it was time to change the game, to embrace her power, and turn it against the people who wanted to hurt her and use her.

Maybe it was time to fight back.

Of course, she couldn't say all that to Kai.

Before Kai could respond, she turned back toward the door. He let out a sigh and placed a hand on her arm.

"Just be careful," he said.

Thea took a shaky breath and nodded.

"We're only checking to see how many soldiers there are." Her voice sounded a lot less confident than she'd hoped. "I'm sure it'll be fine."

She pulled open the door and stepped outside. Kai followed. They hesitated a moment before descending the steps, as though they each expected an attack to come the moment they walked through the doorway.

Thea enhanced her senses, her muscles coiling tight as they reached the parking lot. The muffled sound of radio static, followed by a voice, filled her ears. It was close.

"The girl is moving."

Before she could say anything to Kai, he grabbed her by the arm and jerked her back toward the stairs.

"Get back inside," he hissed.

Thea saw a flash of silver before the crack of a single gunshot rang out through the quiet night, making her ears ring. There wasn't time to think. She stepped forward and pushed her channeling from her body in one large explosive blast. Kai stumbled and nearly lost his balance, but Thea reached out to steady him. The bullet clattered harmlessly to the ground.

"I'm sorry," she said.

Kai shook his head. "I'm okay. Come on, we have to get back inside."

It was too late. Two men were rushing toward them from the small park.

"Go get Gram," she said as she pushed her channeling into her legs. "I'll distract them."

She barely heard Kai's cry of protest as she sprang forward. All her attention focused on the attackers rushing toward them and the rising spike of channeling in her body. She'd always been so afraid of losing control, but maybe now was the time to let herself go. As long as Kai went inside, she didn't have to worry about hurting him.

She cast one last glance over her shoulder and was relieved to see him charging up the steps to the apartment. Rocks skittered at her feet and her hood flew back from her face as she let her channeling continue to rise. She took a deep breath and tried to gather all that wild energy before pushing it out toward two nearby garbage bins, grinding her teeth with the effort. They were heavier than they looked. The bins lifted slowly from the ground, and she pushed them toward the soldiers.

The first soldier managed to dodge, but the other was too slow. He fell to the ground as the first bin struck him. Thea let the second bin crash into the first, hoping it was enough to keep the soldier incapacitated long enough for Gram and Kai to be ready to leave.

The other soldier closed in. She spun away as he reached to grab her but collided into something solid behind her. A third soldier had snuck up behind her. He reached around her torso, pinning her arms with enhanced strength. She struggled to break free, but the pressure of his grip made it hard for her to even breathe.

Another gunshot rang out from the park. She wouldn't be able to break free from the enhancer's hold. Her energy spiked in panic and the enhancer squeezed tighter, trying to keep his hold on her as her energy pushed him back. The stun bullet whizzed past her, and then she heard another shot, this time from behind. The enhancer stiffened and then crumbled to the ground as an engine roared to life behind her.

It was Gram. She spun around and ran for the bike as he fired another round of shots. She'd almost reached it when hot pain seared her leg. A metal prong clattered to the ground at her feet. A stun dart. It had just missed her.

"There's a manipulator!" she called as she jumped into the empty trailer.

"Stay down!" Gram hollered as the bike raced away from the clinic, tires screeching and hot.

Her leg burned, and her head pulsed with the beginning of a headache. She'd used too much energy, but they weren't safe yet. She pulled a channeling booster from her pocket as Gram turned sharply into the nearest alley.

"They're above us!" Kai shouted as more shots rained down on them. Somehow Gram managed to swerve enough in the narrow space to dodge all the shots. Even if his ability was aiding their luck, Thea was sure one of the bullets would hit them. Gram couldn't fire back while driving, and Kai wasn't a good enough shot to make the difference. That left her. She had to do something.

Kai cried out as she stood up in the moving trailer before springing to the rooftop above. She heard the crackle of another stun bullet and released another blast of her channeling to knock it back. The move used a lot of her energy, but it was effective. She still had another channeling booster in her pocket if she needed it.

There were two attackers. She concentrated on the soldier still aiming her gun and pushed. The woman's eyes went wide as her foot slipped over the edge. Thea heard the sick crack of her shoulder hitting the edge as she fell, but she didn't have time for nausea. The metallic flash of another dart flew toward her. Pressure built in her head as she strained her concentration to redirect the dart's trajectory. It wobbled as it flew back toward her attacker. His eyes widened, and he moved too late to dodge the dart completely. The dagger embedded into his arm, and he fell to one knee with a groan.

Thea jumped back down to the alley and ran to catch up to the bike.

"That was stupid!" Gram shouted over his shoulder. "I said to stay down!"

"I took care of them!" she shouted back before climbing into the trailer.

The pain in her head spiked with every bump in the road and worsened as they left the city behind.

The fight had definitely cost her, but she'd helped them escape. She hoped it was enough.

"I sense a lot of people ahead!" Kai shouted as the terrain began to rise in elevation.

Gram swore and slowed to a stop.

"I was hoping it wouldn't come to this," he said. "We're going to have to go off-road, and the trees are too dense here. We'll have to leave the trailer."

"What about our supplies?" she asked him. She'd noticed they hadn't packed very much. Only one large pack in addition to the satchel Kai wore slung over his back.

"We can tie it to the back of my bike," Gram said.

"You can't really expect Thea to run the whole way," Kai protested. "Is there no other route we can take?"

Gram shook his head.

"If we try to backtrack, we'll run into soldiers that followed us from the city. Cutting over the canyon rim is our best option right now. I'm sorry Thea. Hopefully, we won't have to go far before we can stop for a break, but call out if you can't keep up, okay?"

"I'll be okay," Thea insisted. "Lucan gave me a couple of channeling boosters."

She didn't tell him that she'd already used one of them.

Gram sighed and rubbed his head.

"Stay close and tell me if you need me to slow down."

Thea nodded.

The dense forest and steep incline forced Gram to drive much more slowly than he had on the flat roads leading out of the city, but Thea still struggled to keep up as he wove dangerously between trees. Her legs burned from running and her body ached from her previous fight. She pulled out the second channeling booster and gulped it as she ran.

Kai cried out in alarm at the same time Thea noticed shadowed movement from the corner of her eye. Another headlight cut through the darkness as another bike roared to life, cutting off Gram's path. They'd been waiting for them. The sudden light seared her eyes, momentarily blinding her. She stumbled and fell with a cry, rolling a few feet before slamming hard into a tree.

"Thea!" she heard Kai cry out. She blinked to clear her vision as she pulled herself up to a seated position. Bloody knees peaked through her now ripped pants. Light bounced off the trees, making the dizzying labyrinth even more disorienting. Several more bikes circled around them, ridden by soldiers with guns trained on Gram and Kai.

Before Thea could try to stand, a shadow moved in front of her, cutting off her view. She was pulled to her feet roughly and slammed against the tree.

"Careful Walt," snapped a voice to her right. "There's no need to be rough. Just get her in cuffs."

Thea blinked to clear away the rattling in her head. The man holding her didn't seem to be much older than Kai. He was short and stocky, with a thick neck and even thicker arms. The man who'd spoken was tall like Gram, but not as broad or muscular. He was older, with streaks of gray showing at the side of his hair. He pulled his gun out as he turned away from them and started walking closer to Gram and Kai.

"Well if it isn't Gram Wyman, helping another fugitive escape."

"I shouldn't be surprised you're part of this Zane," Gram shot back. "You get tired of beating up cuffed prisoners and decide to go after helpless girls instead?"

The older man barked a humorless laugh.

"Helpless?" he replied. "I see you're as delusional as ever, Wyman. You're as bad as the animals you insist on protecting and I'm going to enjoy finally taking you in."

Thea couldn't pay attention to the rest of their conversation. The man holding her reached for her arm and twisted, trying to pin it behind her so he could turn her face against the tree, probably to allow him to more safely put cuffs on her. This was it. They were taking her back. Once he got the channeling restrictors onto her wrists, it would be over. She'd be helpless.

She felt him tense and take a step back as her channeling tore through her body, pulling up a swirl of leaves and sticks as her instinct fought to push him away. His grip loosened slightly, and she ducked under his arm, pivoting behind him. She remembered what Lucan had said about Macros having less stable footing. She moved uphill from him and shoved with all her strength, barely keeping her own balance as he lost his and tumbled to the ground.

"Run Thea!" Kai cried out, but she was already sprinting, tears streaming down her cheeks.

The other soldiers turned toward her with their guns. The soldier she'd pushed was already back on his feet and lunging for her. She didn't have time to think. She jumped to the branches above her. One of the soldiers fired, but the bullet bounced off the trunk of the tree with a sizzling pop. She jumped away to the next tree, then the next, trying to put more distance between herself and the soldiers. She didn't want to leave Gram and Kai, but the soldiers were there for her. Maybe if they didn't have to worry about her, they'd be able to find a way to escape as well.

"Go after her," she heard the older soldier shout. "Get these two restrained."

Thea continued jumping from tree to tree, but she couldn't pull away from the soldiers following her. She had to move slowly in order not to fall. She might be able to outrun them on the ground, but it would burn through her energy faster.

She probably wouldn't be able to get away from them without a fight, but they were trained soldiers. Maybe she could take out one of them if she could surprise them.

She stopped to catch her breath, keeping herself pressed against the trunk of the tree so they couldn't shoot at her. The sudden roar of an engine startled her. Had Gram and Kai managed to get away, or was it more soldiers joining in her pursuit?

She peered down at the soldiers as they caught up to her position. The stocky one held his hand against his earpiece then nodded to the other.

"You go after the girl," he said to his partner. "I'll take care of this."

"The girl is our priority. We should focus on apprehending her. Let the others worry about Wyman and the brother."

"What, you don't think you can handle one little girl?" the stocky soldier asked.

"You couldn't."

The stocky man shoved the other soldier then snapped, "If she's able to rendezvous with them, she'll be more likely to escape. I'm going to make sure that doesn't happen."

"If she gets away, I'll make sure Zane knows who to blame."

The stocky man shook his head again as he walked away.

"Don't worry. Like I said, I'm going to make sure that doesn't happen."

Thea jumped to another tree, then climbed higher, listening. She could hear the sound of engines but couldn't tell which direction they were going or how many there were. Had Gram and Kai managed to escape somehow? Should she try to find them?

She had no way of knowing where they were, or which bike was there's. If she turned around, she might just be walking into more danger.

Besides, she still had one soldier following her. If Kai had gotten away, he would find her. She needed to make sure there wasn't a soldier waiting for him when he did.

Even from her higher vantage point, Thea still couldn't see much through the dense canopy of branches, but she thought she could see a break in the trees ahead of her. The ground had continued to rise steeply, and she could tell the soldier was struggling to keep up with her. Maybe if she could lure him to that clearing, she could find a way to use her speed to surprise him.

The moon had risen and was shining overhead as she entered the small clearing, like a spotlight shining on her. It made her shudder, but she held her ground, her enhanced sight piercing the darkness of the forest. She could just make out the soldier's shadowed figure quickening his pace. He must have caught sight of her standing in the open clearing. She turned and began to run, feigning a limp in order to draw him in. Her heart rate rose as the sound of his footsteps drew closer. She felt the familiar burning as her channeling began to spike. She couldn't afford to lose control and waste it.

She took a deep breath. Once she was sure he was far enough into the clearing, she pushed a burst of energy into her legs. She sped toward the opposite side of the open space, then jumped to push herself off the trunk of a tree. She tucked herself into a ball as she flew back towards the soldier, then stretched out her legs as she crashed into his chest. She couldn't control her fall and landed hard on the ground. Her side throbbed with dizzying pain, but she raised her head to see the soldier crash back into a tree with a crack, his head slamming backward with the impact. He slumped to the ground and didn't move.

Thea didn't wait to find out if he was still conscious. She dashed back into the cover of the trees, not stopping until she was out of breath. Finally, she leaned against a tree, her muscles aching and her head pounding. She tried to listen for the sound of the bike, but it was hard to hear anything over her own breathing and the ringing in her ears that told her she'd used too much channeling.

She knew she didn't have enough energy to get caught up in another fight while she was alone. She needed to find Gram and Kai.

The closely growing trees were disorienting. Thea could only hope she was running in the right direction. She could still hear the sounds of engines, but didn't know if Gram's bike was among them.

How was she going to find Gram or Kai without getting caught by the soldiers?

What if they hadn't been able to escape?

Would she be able to help them without putting them all in more danger?

There was no way to know the answers to her worries. All she could do was run and hope they found her before the soldiers did.

A silver glow filled the darkness and Thea turned toward the light, straining her senses. As she neared, beams of light cut through the trees, too bright for her enhanced vision. She pulled back her channeling and blinked to clear her eyes. A bike was lying on its side, its headlight still lighting up the dark. She thought it looked like Gram's, but she wasn't sure.

Where were they?

Thea approached the bike cautiously, searching the shadows beyond the light. Her tired muscles snapped tight with anticipation and her heartbeat thudded in her ears, drowning out the sound of her own footsteps. She wasn't watching her step and tripped over something soft.

Kai's satchel lay on the ground at her feet, its strap cut. The light fabric was discolored by a dark stain.

Kai had been here. Was he hurt? Where was he?

"Kai!" she called out, turning around in a frantic attempt to find him.

A strangled cough made her jump. She whirled toward the sound, her stomach dropping as a weak, breathy voice filled her ears.

"Thea. Go."

"Kai!" she shouted again, this time spotting him crumpled on his side on the ground.

"No," she whispered, stumbling forward, her vision already blurring with tears.

He raised his head slightly. She couldn't see his face well in the dim light, but it was clear that any movement was a struggle.

"No. Kai. I'm here," she choked out as she fell to her knees at his side. She rolled him onto his back with shaking hands and let out a gasp as she felt the sticky blood soaking his clothes.

"You have to get away," Kai said weakly, his eyes fluttering in an attempt to look at her.

"No, Kai," she sobbed as she pulled her jacket over her head and began wiping the blood, trying to find its source. There was so much. Too much.

"Where's your wound? I don't know how to stop the bleeding. Tell me what to do. Tell me how to help you."

He reached up with one hand, and she took it with hers, trying to ignore the squish of blood beneath her palm.

"Run."

The word slurred as Kai's head rolled to one side and his arm went limp.

She had to help him. Maybe if she could get him on the bike, but she didn't know how to drive it. She had to try anyway.

The crunching sound of leaves behind her made her turn, hoping Gram had found them. He could make this right. He could help Kai.

"What a shame." It wasn't Gram.

"I would have left your brother alone, if he hadn't gotten in my way. It's laughable that he thought he could stop me on his own."

It was the woman who had come to the base. Kaori. Her long hair was tied into a high ponytail and she carried a short, flat sword in each hand—one stained dark with blood. She sauntered forward with the same look of cold condescension that Thea remembered from the night they'd met.

"You did this." Thea choked, the words a numb statement rather than a question. "You hurt Kai."

"Don't worry, you'll be joining him soon."

She stepped closer.

"And Nix," Thea said, as though Kaori hadn't replied. "You hurt him too."

The woman stopped.

"I guess he didn't die then. The truth is I never wanted to kill him, but it would be a real problem if he was here. It would make it so much harder to kill you."

"Why?"

Thea's body shook as anger and denial burned hot inside her. Her channeling rose, scraping her insides raw, as though her body were trying to gather every last bit of energy it could. She pulled a dagger from the pouch at her hip with trembling fingers.

The woman laughed, the sound harsh and shrill in Thea's ears.

"I see you took my advice," she said with a smirk, "but it's too late. You could have been useful to me, but I don't have time to play around with you anymore. I can't take the risk of letting the Military get what they want."

Thea hardly registered her words. She'd hurt Kai, and Nix, and she didn't even seem to care. Someone had to stop her. Thea sprang forward, a cry of fury escaping her throat as she lunged with her dagger. To her surprise, the woman made no move to dodge or get out of the way. Thea swung.

And missed.

The woman hadn't dodged. She hadn't moved. Thea's swing had simply been off by several inches.

The woman stepped lazily into a thrust with her sword. Thea tried to spin away, but the second blade sliced into her abdomen. The cut wasn't deep, but it burned like fire. Thea gasped and dropped into a crouch, clenching her teeth through the pain. She launched her dagger from her hand, but it flew wide, missing the woman again.

Thea sprang away with a groan, trying to put distance between them. She couldn't just run. She had to find a way to get both Kai and herself to safety.

But how?

She didn't even know where Gram was. Her thoughts felt sluggish and her body slow. The heat of her wound seemed to be spreading through her body, burning her from the inside.

"You poor Macros," Kaori said as she strode toward her with a toss of her ponytail. "You always think speed and strength are the most important things you need to win. It's always so disappointing when you realize how little those things matter, that you aren't actually as superior as you thought you were."

Thea's vision blurred, and she stepped backward, her legs wobbling.

"You're probably feeling the poison by now. Burns, doesn't it? Even if you could beat me in this fight—which you can't—you'd still die. Both you and your brother."

Thea's channeling spiked with a fresh surge of anger. Leaves and dust swirled around her as she pulled at everything she could. This time she wouldn't miss. The nearest trees groaned. Rocks rumbled along the ground. Nausea welled up in her stomach as pain tore through her body, but still she pulled. The swirling debris cut her skin and ripped her clothes. She thrust her hands forward to help her focus, launching the storm toward Kaori, forcing her to stumble back as debris collided into her.

Thea's legs trembled and then gave out as the last of her energy was spent. The storm died away in one sudden crash as the remaining debris fell to the ground. Thea couldn't hold her body up anymore. Every part of her burned as she tried to claw her way closer to Kai. Her blurred vision began to dim. She couldn't reach him.

Before she sank into unconsciousness, her last sight was of Kaori standing over her, her face twisted with rage.

Chapter Seventeen

After the others had finalized their plans, Lucan had insisted Nix return to bed. He couldn't really argue. It had taken all his strength to drag himself to the living room. In spite of his frustrations with himself for not being able to help the others, sleep found him quickly.

When he woke, gray light seeped around the edges of the curtains. It was morning.

His side ached and his body felt weak and heavy as he sat up. He swung his legs over the side of the bed and tried to stand, but a wave of dizziness forced him to stay seated. Despite that, he could feel the energy humming in his body. His channeling was returning and soon it would be strong enough to detect. By the time his telepathy returned, it would be too late. The Military would know he was there.

He swallowed down the nausea that accompanied another wave of dizziness as he forced himself to his feet. He pulled fresh clothes from the nearby wardrobe with painful effort.

Lucan frowned as Nix hobbled out of the bedroom.

"You shouldn't be up," he said, sounding exasperated.

Nix waved him off as he switched on the emitter, still on the table in the living room.

"I can't stay here," he said matter-of-factly. "The sooner we leave, the better, before my channeling is detectable."

"You know, it's a wonder you're even alive right now. You need time to heal. You need to rest."

Nix shook his head.

"I can already feel my channeling returning. You know it won't be long before they can sense me. It's better to leave now."

Lucan frowned. He didn't answer immediately. Nix knew him well enough to know he was mentally weighing all the options against each other, carefully trying to find the best one.

"If I weren't like this, you would have gone with them, wouldn't you?" Nix pressed. "They might need you. I don't need my telepathy to know you're worried. You grind herbs when you're worried."

Nix pointed to the bowl in front of Lucan.

"I am worried," Lucan admitted with a sigh, "but I'm grinding these herbs so I can change your bandage. I have to take care of this foolish patient before I can worry about anything else."

Lucan remained quiet, still thinking, as he poured water over the herbs, making a paste. He carried the paste, along with a pile of fresh bandages, over to the couch. Nix ground his teeth impatiently as Lucan unwound the bandage around his waist. Nix knew there was no point trying to further his argument. Lucan would make his decision when he was ready, and nothing Nix said would hurry him along.

"I'll need to take care of some things before we can leave," Lucan said at last, as he applied the paste to the angry red skin around Nix's wound. "Gram was sure they would have to leave the trailer behind once they reached the canyon, so they weren't able to take much with them. We should take food and extra medicine with us."

Nix let out a sigh of relief, then winced as Lucan wound a fresh bandage tight around his waist. Once he'd finished, Nix replaced his shirt, his movements stiff.

"You should try to rest while I'm gone," Lucan said pointedly.

Nix was about to encourage Lucan to hurry, when the door slammed open, startling them both. Lucan stepped protectively in front of him. His quick reaction told Nix the other man was even more on edge than he'd realized.

They both let out a sigh of relief and relaxed as Gram entered the apartment carrying the girl in his arms. Lucan tensed again, though, as they both noticed her bloody clothes and the numerous cuts and scrapes on her arms and face.

"What happened?" Lucan asked at the same time Gram said, "Glad to see you're still alive, Nix. Take her."

Nix wobbled slightly as he stepped forward, but Lucan moved ahead of him and scooped the girl into his arms.

"Nix is only barely alive," he said after clearing his throat. "I still have my supplies in the bedroom. I'll take her in there. Where's Kai?"

Gram shook his head with a grim expression as he leaned tiredly against the wall. Nix felt his stomach drop. His vision swam with another wave of dizziness, and he sank back into the couch numbly.

"He...didn't make it."

Gram's voice cracked and he swallowed before nodding toward Lucan. "It's probably poison."

Kaori.

Lucan nodded before hurrying into the bedroom with the girl.

Nix stood staring at the floor, not knowing what to say. From the corner of his eye, he saw Gram turn back toward the door.

"Where are you going?" Nix asked, looking up. His voice sounded wrong in his own ears.

"To take care of Kai."

"I'll help you." Nix struggled to stand, feeling even heavier than he had before Gram's return.

Gram just shook his head.

"You can't."

He pulled the door open and was gone before Nix could reply.

Nix sank back into the couch, alone again.

He slammed his fist angrily against the couch beside him, the soft cushion absorbing the impact in an unsatisfying way.

If he hadn't gone with Kaori this never would have happened.

Suddenly the apartment felt too small, too quiet. He stood with a groan and hobbled to the window, feeling restless.

He brushed his fingers against the curtain and stopped. It would be stupid to open the window. He swallowed and rubbed his face before turning away.

Instead, he moved into the kitchen, hoping food could distract him from feeling like the room was shrinking around him. He warmed up a meal but pushed it away after only a few bites.

He couldn't eat. He couldn't sit still. He was too tired to pace but did anyway.

He hated it.

He hated that he'd been stupid enough to trust Kaori. Now he was without his abilities little more than an enhanced throw away from the Military and sure imprisonment.

And Kai was dead.

Just don't get Gram killed, he'd told the girl the night before. He really was an idiot.

If he could take back those words, he would.

"I thought I told you to rest."

Nix jumped, startled by Lucan's voice.

"You look tired," Lucan added. "Maybe you should try to sleep."

"I'm pretty sure I slept for like two days."

Lucan sighed.

"Being unconscious and sleeping aren't the same thing. I'll keep watch until Gram comes back. You should try to rest in the other bedroom."

"What about you?" Nix asked.

"I didn't nearly die yesterday. I can make you a sedative if you'd like, but either way I'm taking over the watch, and you are going to lie down."

"Fine," Nix conceded, "I'll rest, but I'm not taking a sedative. If anything happens, I'd rather not be killed in my sleep."

Lucan chuckled. "I see you have very little faith in my abilities. Fine. No sedative, but at least drink some tea. It'll help you relax and will help with the healing process."

When Nix didn't protest, Lucan moved into the kitchen.

"So how is she?" Nix asked when Lucan returned with two steaming mugs.

"I think she's through the worst of it. Her recovery might be even longer than yours, though. In addition to the poison, she had some pretty serious cuts and bruises. She used a lot of energy too, even more than when she fought you. That will make it harder for her body to fight the effects of the poison. I suspect she'll be facing some serious mental trauma too..."

His voice trailed off to almost a whisper.

"Gram said he'd take care of Kai," Nix said to break the weight of the silence. It was too heavy.

"I hope he's careful." The worry in Lucan's voice only made the air in the room feel heavier.

Nix rubbed his forehead, wishing for fresh air, wishing he was outside, wishing he wasn't useless and helpless.

He frowned and gulped down the rest of his tea.

"Wake me up if you get too tired," he said as he stood.

"I think it's fine if you open the window," Lucan said. "Just leave the curtains closed."

Nix nodded gratefully before closing the door behind him. Relief washed over him, and his shoulders sagged as he slid open the window. The curtains swayed slightly, and he took a deep breath of the fresh, cool air. He sank into the bed and closed his tired eyes. With the cool air from outside and the knowledge that Lucan was keeping watch, he sank quickly into sleep.

Running
Darkness chasing close behind
I fight alone
No home or sun to
Bring me help or comfort
Panic pushes me on
Where is he?

Blinding light cuts through the night
Searing sight like a burning wound
There I see him
Lying there

No

Held by unseen barriers
I cannot reach him
I cannot save him

From the shadows steps another
Gleaming cruelty burning in her eyes
She laughs
Stabbing swords and deep wounds
Running red with blood and
Still I cannot move

Crimson rain stains my hands and
Splashes on my face
Stumbling and dizzy I fall
Mocking whispers fill my ears
Stealing any trace of hope
"Don't worry, you will join him soon"

Chapter Eighteen

Nix couldn't remember where he was when he woke up. The base? The forest? His stomach lurched and his head spun. The dream had been so vivid, he could still see Kai's bleeding body, even after opening his eyes.

No. It wasn't a dream. Not his anyway.

It was hers.

He jumped to his feet, sucking in a breath and steadying himself through the sharp pain in his side. His legs still wobbled as he threw open the bedroom door and rushed toward the room where the girl was sleeping, still dreaming her horrific nightmare.

Kaori was standing over her now. The blade pierced her flesh slowly, burning with hot, agonizing pain. Nix sucked in a breath as he crashed against her door.

"What are you doing?" Lucan cried out in alarm as he followed Nix into the room.

"We need to wake her up."

She was screaming while Kaori laughed. Blood filled her vision, poured from her side, dripped from the branches above. Lucan said something.

Nix couldn't focus on his words, so he simply said again, "She needs to wake up."

He could almost feel the poison spreading through his own body again. His legs shook, and he placed a steadying hand on the wall for support. He was vaguely aware of Lucan's hand on his shoulder.

"She's having a nightmare," Nix managed to gasp, "and she's in pain."

Lucan moved to her side to feel the pulse on her wrist. He nodded grimly.

"Her heartbeat is too fast." Lucan's voice sounded far away and muddled. Nix tried to focus as Lucan bent to give the girl a gentle shake.

"Thea, wake up," he said. "You're dreaming."

She didn't stir. The gruesome images began to flash in a nauseating montage. Her brother's still form lying in a heap on the ground, blood covering her arms and dripping from her hands. Kaori's taunting laugh as she plunged her sword into her body again and again.

"Lucan, you have to do something."

"She isn't waking up. She's still too weak from the poison. I can give her something for the pain. Maybe that will settle her nightmare as well."

Lucan rushed out of the room. Nix staggered to the bed and collapsed on its edge. He put his hands on her shoulders and gave her another shake, harder than Lucan had done. He tried to sit her up, but she remained limp in his arms. He had to do something.

Maybe...

He slid next to her on the bed. Mindful of the IV in her arm, he wrapped one arm around her shoulders, leaning her against him in a sitting position. Maybe he could fill her thoughts with something else, something other than her brother's gruesome death. He thought of his own memories of her brother.

Kai had been understanding. Non-judgmental. He saw Nix not as a monster, but as someone of value.

Nix swallowed the lump in his throat and concentrated instead on his observations of the siblings. Kai had always known what to say to calm her down. That's what she needed now.

He focused on projecting those memories into her mind. His gentle words. His light-hearted teasing, mellower than Gram's. The comforting arm around her shoulder. It felt like trying to whisper over a yell, but gradually her breathing slowed. Her mind grew quiet. He didn't stop, though. He wasn't going to give the nightmare a chance to return.

Lucan reentered the room, carrying a tray with a large bowl of steaming liquid and a heap of white bandages. A mug also sat on the tray. Lucan raised his eyebrows when he saw Nix sitting next to her, cradling her against him.

"Here, you look like you need this," was all he said as he passed Nix one of the mugs.

Nix took it with his free hand. He could feel the tension in his forehead that had become such a familiar sensation whenever she was around. As uncomfortable as it was, he was surprised to feel a sense of relief. Somehow his head had felt emptier the last few weeks, even with all the noise of the crowded places he'd been.

Lucan checked her pulse again and nodded.

"Her heartrate has slowed. What happened?

"I'm projecting memories into her mind. Keeping her from having nightmares."

"You can't keep doing that indefinitely, Nix," Lucan said with a worried frown.

"This is better than her nightmares. If you want me to get any rest, this is as close as it's going to get."

Lucan sighed. "Well for now I need to change her bandages. I've mixed painkillers into an ointment."

Lucan took Nix's empty mug from him and set it back on his tray. Nix stood and laid the girl gently back on her pillow. Though the nightmare had stopped, her mind felt heavy, tinged with a grief that would only grow once she was awake. She seemed small lying there, broken. She'd endured so much already, but still managed to keep a firm determination hidden underneath her fears and anxieties.

She'd had her brother to help her heal after the nightmare of the research facility. Would she ever be able to heal from his loss?

Nix continued to project into her thoughts as he left the room. He was tired, and his channeling still wasn't fully recovered. It made concentrating difficult.

He rubbed his forehead as he tried to recall anything he could about Kai. He'd slipped so naturally into life at the base, it almost felt as though he'd always been there. She probably didn't realize how much she'd adapted too, better than Nix ever had. He'd spent years keeping Gram and Lucan at a distance. A lot of the time he still did.

He and Gram had been through a lot since he'd first come to the base, but Nix still didn't feel like he belonged there with the others—not the way Kai and the girl did. Unlike them, Nix had never been able to distance himself from the past.

Kaori's words popped into his head, cutting like a knife. *People like us can't belong, not with do-gooders like them. We aren't good enough for that.*

The girl's panic stirred as he thought of Kaori. He cursed himself for letting his memories stray to her while he was projecting. How stupid was he? He moved across the room to the window and opened it to let in the cool air.

As a slight breeze ruffled the curtains, he inhaled and forced thoughts of the past from his mind. He thought instead of his favorite places—the places he went when he needed to recharge. He tried to make the memories as vivid as he could. The rustling sound of leaves as thin rays of sunlight found openings in the canopy of branches overhead, warming the cool shade enough to be lazily comfortable. The scent of grass and bark and wind that stretched out into the valley below. The sun-warmed rocks worn smooth by wind and rain, grounding him with their solidity.

He yawned and rubbed his neck before stretching out on the couch. Her thoughts felt hazy, lulled by the soothing scenery he projected. His eyelids grew heavy as the memories pulled him with her into sleep.

Nix sat up in a panic. Had he only nodded off or had he been asleep for hours? He relaxed again after checking the girl's thoughts. Her dreams were quiet, no nightmares.

"I've been keeping an eye on her," Lucan said, startling him. "I would have woken you if it looked like she was having nightmares."

Nix sat up as Lucan handed him a mug of tea. He held a second mug up to his own lips. Nix noticed the dark shadows beneath his eyes and frowned.

"You should have woken me, anyway. You still haven't slept."

"I actually slept for a little while after Gram came back. I did insist that he woke me after he'd eaten and showered. He was more in need of sleep than I was."

Nix turned and saw the door to the other room now closed. He had slept right through Gram's return. He gulped down the rest of his tea and stood up with a groan.

"Well, now the couch is all yours. Get some sleep."

Lucan shook his head and quickly finished his own drink. "I want to check your bandage again first. I've been caring for Thea and haven't had the chance."

"You can check it later. It's pretty much better, anyway." Nix gave his side a pat with his hand to prove he wasn't in need of attention, but ended up wincing.

Lucan sighed. "What would you and Gram do without me? On your own, you'd both end up dying of stubbornness. It'll only take a few minutes. I promise I'll sleep as soon as I'm done."

Nix sat back down with a sigh and took off his shirt. Lucan stood up wearily to retrieve his supplies from the kitchen. After removing the old bandage, he gave a satisfied nod.

"These poisoned wounds take a long time to fully close, but this one is healing faster than the last one. The inflammation is nearly all gone."

"I told you it's fine," Nix insisted, then winced again as Lucan applied ointment to the wound."

Lucan chuckled. "Like I said, stubborn to the death."

Instead of wrapping long bandages around Nix's torso, Lucan retrieved a smaller, adhesive bandage from the kitchen, just large enough to cover the wound.

"This will keep water from getting into the wound," he explained as he placed a clear film over the bandage. "You should be able to shower with this on, but we'll have to keep an eye on the wound to make sure the inflammation doesn't return."

"Is that a hint?" Nix asked with a smirk as he stood up from the couch.

"Well, I doubt the Syndicate offered to let you take a shower," Lucan mused with a hint of a smile. "You probably haven't showered since you were in Karza."

Nix frowned and Lucan let out a small chuckle. "I put fresh clothes in the bathroom for you already."

"Fine. I'll shower if you sleep," Nix said as he bent down to pick up the old bandages and Lucan's other supplies.

The hot water of the shower was invigorating. Muscles he hadn't realized were tense relaxed. He felt lighter, like he was washing away his anxiety and regret along with the grime. Even the girl's thoughts, buzzing in his mind, felt less draining than they had in the past. He wasn't sure if it was because they were both still recovering, or if he was simply growing more accustomed to them.

Hadn't Kai said something similar? That he could deal with her emotions because he was used to them?

He ran his hand through his wet hair and let the vividness of the girl's dream pull his attention away from his own memory. He didn't want to think about Kai or what his loss meant for all of them. He took a deep breath, as if the dappled sunlight and gentle breeze of her dream were real. He smiled at the realization that her dreams continued to replay the scenes he'd projected to her, her mind's gloom thinning with the comfort the warm imagery provided.

"You're in a good mood," Gram whispered as Nix entered the kitchen.

Nix's smile turned into a scowl.

"Oh sorry, I didn't mean to spoil it. Believe me I'd rather you grin like an idiot than make such scary faces all the time."

Nix just rolled his eyes as he pulled a meal from the cupboard.

After he'd finished heating his food, Gram motioned toward the bedroom. Lucan was asleep on the couch, breathing deeply, so Nix followed him, shoveling food into his mouth as he walked. After closing the door, Gram flopped down on the bed, his shoulders sagging as he rested his elbows on his knees.

"What happened out there?" Nix asked as he moved toward the window.

Gram let out a heavy sigh and rubbed his face before answering.

"Zane was waiting for us in the canyon," he said. "They had us surrounded, but Thea managed to break away. I made an opening so Kai could go after her on the bike."

Gram shook his head, his face pale and his eyes tired and hollow looking.

"I don't know what happened after that. When I found them, they were both hurt, and Kaori looked like she was about to finish Thea off. She ran when she saw me. I didn't have time to look for her. I knew I needed to get Thea and Kai back to Lucan. If only I'd been faster, maybe Kai would have made it."

Gram's voice tightened, and he rubbed his hand over his face with a shaky breath.

"So what now?" Nix asked to keep Gram from spiraling any further in his own regret.

"I don't know," Gram said, his voice just above a whisper.

"Did anyone see you come back?" Nix asked.

Gram shook his head. "I don't know. I'm sure they're still watching the clinic. I guess I should have paid more attention."

"They have to know I'm here. My telepathy is back. I might as well be sending out a signal to every Micro in the city," Nix said.

Gram frowned as his eyes scanned Nix's face, as though really looking at him for the first time.

He still looks pale, he thought. *He's in no shape for the Military to come storming in. We have to get out of here. But Thea.*

Instead of voicing his concerns, he said, "Tell me what happened with you. You went to Chusan?"

There was a hint of accusation in Gram's voice and Nix looked away. He didn't need to be reminded that what he'd done was stupid.

"Kaori had made it sound like Ryu was after the girl. It didn't sound right to me. I had to find out for myself. I thought at the very least I might be able to convince him to back off."

Dumbass.

Nix just shrugged before continuing.

"He said he would protect her."

"And you trust him?" Gram asked. "Didn't you say the Syndicate was coming too?"

"He didn't exactly want to let me leave," Nix admitted, again not meeting Gram's eyes. "He said he'd send a team to get her. I knew you'd put up a fight if they showed up out of the blue."

Gram sighed.

"I still don't like it. Nothing good ever comes from getting caught up in Kaori's schemes, and her schemes always lead back to her brother."

Gram didn't like it, but they were out of options. He dropped his head into his hands and sighed.

"I don't know what the right thing is," he said, his voice pained.

Maybe if I'd done things differently in the canyon...

"It wasn't your fault," Nix growled quietly, clenching his hands into fists. "You told me not to trust Kaori, not to go off on my own. If I'd listened, this wouldn't have happened. I wouldn't have been lying here in bed while they were out there, fighting her."

Gram straightened, running both hands back through his hair.

"As much as I want to call you a dumbass and tell you that you're right, I can't," he said. "Sure, you made a bad call. You've already paid the price for it. I made the wrong call out there and I have to live with that. Beating ourselves up isn't going to change anything. All we can do is make damned sure we protect that girl. I'll do whatever it takes to make sure the same thing that happened to Kai doesn't happen to her, even if it means going against my better judgment and trusting the Syndicate."

Nix clenched his jaw. Gram was right. He usually was. And now Nix knew what their only real option was. He opened his mouth, but before he could speak, the girl's despair slammed into him like a weight.

She was awake.

Her nightmares were real.

Her brother was dead.

She was alone.

He was drowning.

He couldn't breathe.

The images overrode his other senses. The darkness of the forest surrounded him. Kai's blood-soaked body filled his vision—real memories this time, undistorted by dreams. He couldn't push past them to recall any of the memories he'd used to stop her nightmares before.

"She's awake," he managed to gasp through the sudden nausea and vertigo. He grasped the edge of the window frame to stabilize himself before swinging one leg through the curtains.

"What the hell do you think you're doing? You can't go out there!"

"I have to," he didn't even care that his voice shook. "I can't be in here. I can't help her if I am."

"Dammit Nix," he heard Gram say as he jumped out.

Hot pain flared in his side as he landed. He sucked in a sharp breath and bent over slightly to brace against the pain before hobbling into the shadows of the buildings across the from the clinic. He sucked in several more breaths before jumping to the roofs above.

He wasn't far enough away for the distance to really dull her thoughts, but at least outside he didn't feel like they were smothering him. He took several slow breaths as he slumped against the low wall surrounding the rooftop. He rubbed his forehead and turned his focus back to what was happening inside the apartment.

Gram and Lucan had both gone into her room. Gram placed a torn bag gently on her lap, Kai's bag. Her fingers brushed the edge of the blood-stained strap numbly but made no move to open it. She didn't look up at Gram or Lucan. She hardly even registered that they were there.

She was just empty, like her mind had dropped a heavy curtain to block out every painful memory or feeling. He pressed his hands against the rooftop below him, forced himself to feel the rough texture beneath his fingertips grounding him in reality as he let himself sink deeper into her numbness.

There, beneath the surface, he could sense the storm of grief waiting to break through, the horrifying images crashing against the barrier over and over again.

Kai's body. The blood she couldn't stop. Kaori.

The darkness pulled him under. He was drowning and there was only one way out—force the curtain open and release the storm raging underneath. He had to find the right memory. Something she couldn't ignore. Something to make her feel.

Thea!

Kai called out to her, shaking her awake after one of her nightmares. She clung to him as though she'd never hear his voice again.

This time it wasn't a nightmare. It was true. She never would hear his voice again.

Cracks began to form in the haze, and the images began to pour through. She couldn't stop them.

The only thing I care about is that you're safe, Kai had said. *End of story. Whatever it takes.*

The numbness dissipated into a storm of emotion, stealing his breath. Grief sharp as a knife and regret that ached like a wound that wouldn't heal.

An anguished cry tore from her throat. Gram pulled her into his chest as her body shook with sobs. Lucan stood at her side, patting her back reassuringly.

Family.

All three of them were hurting, but together they would be alright.

Nix leaned his head back against the stone behind him and clenched his hands into tight fists before releasing them with a long exhale.

All of this had happened because of him. There was nothing he could do to make it right, but he could bring it to an end. He could give the Military what they really wanted.

It was time for him to stop running.

He was tempted to leave right then, but he owed Gram more than that. He owed him a goodbye at least.

Nix jumped down from the roof with another stab of pain. He scanned the parking lot and surrounding buildings as he climbed the stairs back to the apartment. His skin itched with the sensation that he was being watched. If they were there, he couldn't sense them, not with the girl's thoughts returned to their usual intensity.

Before Nix could even close the apartment door behind him, Lucan snapped, "You're in no condition to be jumping out of windows, Nix."

Lucan stopped and moved closer with a grim frown.

"You don't look well. Are you alright?"

Nix shrugged, wondering what he must look like to make Lucan's attitude change from exasperated to worried so quickly.

Gram didn't seem worried, at least. Or maybe he was just trying to distract himself from his own pain. He slapped Nix hard on the shoulder before handing him a steaming mug.

"Told you, dumbass."

"I'll want to check under your bandage later to make sure the wound hasn't reopened," Lucan said. "But first, Thea would like to speak with you."

Nix grimaced. Gram laughed and shoved him lightly toward the door.

"You look like you'd rather get stabbed again, you dumbass."

Nix gulped down his drink, then shoved the mug into Gram's hands with a scowl. His obvious annoyance only made Gram's grin widen. As annoying as his teasing was, Nix was glad to see him acting like his usual self, even if it was forced.

With a sigh, he gripped the doorknob and entered the bedroom.

The small room felt even smaller as her thoughts, her grief, her regret all pressed down on him. He took a shaky breath and hesitated before letting the door click shut. His throat closed with the sound, making it hard to breathe.

He stayed by the door as though the distance were enough to protect his mind from hers. It wasn't. Of course it wasn't. He looked longingly toward the closed window by her bed, but didn't move. Instead, he crossed his arms over his chest and leaned against the door, waiting.

She sat propped against several pillows, looking small and frail, with her face turned toward the window rather than him. Her fingers fidgeted with the edge of the blanket as her thoughts fumbled for the right thing to say.

She didn't have to say anything, of course. He knew. And yet he waited.

"My brother knew you were a telepath, didn't he?" she said at last, avoiding the more difficult conversation. Her voice came out hoarse, barely above a whisper.

Nix didn't answer immediately. Finally, she turned to look at him, a spark of curiosity brightening the hollowness in her eyes.

He looked away and nodded.

"He trusted you," she continued, "though he never would tell me why. He tried to convince me to trust you, too. I'm sorry..."

Her words slurred as tears began to spill down her cheeks.

He was reminded of the last conversation he'd had with Kai, and he projected it to her on instinct.

That's good enough for me. Everyone has done things they regret. I can tell that you don't want to hurt us.

He hadn't realized it while she was asleep, but his ability to project to her, to share only the information he wanted her to receive, was as difficult as trying to quiet her thoughts. She caught a glimpse of the rest of the memory, before he could cut it off.

I can tell it's hard for you, the way she thinks of you.

She seemed to shrink even more as regret flooded her thoughts.

Nix ground his teeth as he pulled his thoughts back by force. He'd have to be more careful.

"Thank you," she said, though her thoughts said *I'm sorry.* "I felt like I was trapped in that nightmare. I saw Kai, over and over. And that woman."

Her voice cracked and her hands began to tremble. Again, his response was almost automatic. Blue sky, cool shade, the feeling of a gentle breeze on a hot day.

Her eyes widened before she closed them with a shake of her head.

"Sorry," he mumbled.

The barest trace of a smile spread across her lips.

"It felt like...like I was drowning in freezing water."

He'd felt the same way, trying to swim through the dark depths of her grief.

"I couldn't pull myself out or stay above the surface," she continued. "But then you reached in and pulled me out."

Her eyes stayed closed as she tried to remember. He was annoyed to realize that she remembered more than just the memories of Kai he'd shared. He really was an idiot. He'd shared his own feelings too, about his history with Gram, and his observations of her.

She shivered as she remembered what Kaori had told him, that he didn't belong with the others.

"She hurt you too, didn't she?" Her voice was so soft it could have been a thought. She opened her eyes and met his for a moment before he looked away again.

"I'm sorry," she choked with a sob. "I'm so sorry."

It's my fault. Because I drove him away. He got hurt. And Kai...

"It's not your fault," Nix snapped, pulling her from her thoughts with the sudden harshness of his voice.

"*It's mine*," he transmitted as he turned away to leave. "*I intend to make it right. And if I ever get the chance, I intend to pay Kaori back for all of it.*"

"Wait," she said softly. "Will you stay with me? For a little while at least?"

Under different circumstances he would have laughed. It hadn't been that long since she'd run from him in terror. He supposed it was the same for him. It hadn't been that long since he'd done everything he could to avoid being in the same room as her. Now he found himself moving closer.

He knew he should leave. He should send Gram or Lucan in to sit with her.

Instead, he moved the chair that was by her bed closer to the window before reaching behind the curtain to raise the glass. He leaned his head against the wall and tried to focus on the cool, fresh air, instead of the way his head throbbed.

She let out a half-hearted chuckle and he looked at her in mild surprise.

"Sorry," she said, leaning back with a half-smile. "The look on your face, you look like you'd rather be stabbed again."

He let out an annoyed snort and closed his eyes with a small smile of his own.

Nix swore silently. He had not meant to fall asleep again.

Memories had plagued his dreams, memories brought on by the dread of knowing what he had to do.

His own dream had woken him, but it was hers that filled his head now.

Darkness—so thick he could feel it on his skin, closing around him. He stood and staggered to the window, throwing back the curtains, letting the chill air ground him. He sucked in several deep breaths as he focused his senses on what was real in front of him. The rough windowpane beneath his fingers. The faint pink light that tinged the sky telling him it was morning. The rustling of branches from the trees outside.

He took a deep breath, focusing on the lightening sky outside. He sent the image into her thoughts until the darkness dissipated. Once he could breathe again, he straightened and closed the window.

The girl was curled up on her side, whether from cold or fear, he wasn't sure. Most of her blanket was hanging off the bed. He reached out one hand, hesitantly, hovering for a moment before brushing her hair back from her face. He let his fingers trail down her bare arm. Her skin felt cold. Carefully, he pulled the blanket up to her chin, then straightened and stretched his stiff body, wincing as the movement pulled at his wound.

He closed the door softly behind him as he left the room. Gram was up, pacing in the living room.

"Good. You're up," he said as he tore one hand through his hair. He opened the closet by the door and pulled out extra ammunition before checking that his gun was loaded properly. "We're out of time. We need to get the two of you out of here, now. Luc went out to get some extra supplies. Once he's back, we'll leave. We'll go to Ryu. I don't like it, but I don't think we have much choice at this point."

Nix clenched his fist. They were out of time. He wasn't fully recovered, but that didn't matter. He didn't need his full strength for what he was planning to do. The only issue now was telling Gram.

"I'm not going." His throat tightened on the words.

"What the hell are you talking about?" Gram's eyes narrowed and his voice turned cold.

Nix cleared his throat. His tongue felt heavy in his mouth.

"They want me. They always have. That's what all of this is about. Once they have me, they won't have any more reason to come after her. I'm turning myself in."

"Like hell you are!" Gram shouted. "This is no time for your nonsense, Nix. If I have to knock you out and tie you up in Luc's car, I will, but you are coming with us."

"I've already decided," Nix said, shaking his head stubbornly. "You can't change my mind, and you can't stop me."

Gram tightened his grip on his gun. He was serious. Nix could tell by the look on his face, by the way his stance widened, and his knees bent slightly. He was prepared to unload every stun bullet he had on Nix if he had to.

Nix had still been young when he'd met Gram, too confident in his abilities. He'd lost to the peacekeeper more times than he could count, but that was one of the reasons he'd come to respect him, to trust him. They'd sparred and fought side-by-side for so long, Nix didn't need his telepathy to know exactly what Gram would do.

Nix dove behind the couch at the same time that Gram fired. In spite of everything, a grin spread across his lips. He was lucky to get this one last chance to fight Gram for real. If they weren't going to see each other again, then there was no better way for them to say goodbye.

Gram was already circling slowly toward him, trying to get a clear shot or flush him out from hiding. Nix enhanced his strength and lifted the bottom edge of the couch, knowing there was only one thing he could do to avoid getting hit with a bullet. He flipped the couch toward Gram. Gram tried to dive to the side while firing a round of haphazard shots, but there wasn't enough space in the small living room to avoid the couch. It knocked him back against the wall. Nix didn't wait. He kicked the door from its hinges and ran from the wreckage of the room.

"I'll be sure to buy you plenty of time," Nix strained through the girl's sleeping thoughts to transmit the message to Gram. He was sure he only managed to succeed because he was so familiar with Gram's mind. *"Get the girl to Ryu. Keep her safe."*

"We'll come for you." The replying thought was faint. Or maybe it wasn't a thought at all, but only what Nix thought he would say. It didn't matter. Either way, Nix's final message would be the same.

"*Forget about me.*"

This wasn't a diversion. This was a chance for the girl to be free, without having to look over her shoulder. That could only happen so long as the Military had him, and she had the protection of the Syndicate.

"*Goodbye, Gram. I'm sorry. Thanks. For everything.*"

He didn't try to listen for a reply.

He slowed as he approached the city's main gate, his hands clenched to keep them from shaking.

He'd avoided being captured for so long, he couldn't deny the panic boiling inside of him, making his breathing shallow and his legs weak. He'd rather do anything other than what he was about to do. The only thing that stopped him from turning and running was his resolve to protect the others. It was stronger than his fear or his sense of self-preservation. It was the only thing that kept him moving forward.

He could feel the shock and disbelief of the city guards on top of the wall. He could use their surprise to his advantage. There was no way he could hold out for long, especially once more soldiers showed up, but the longer he fought the longer Gram would have to get out. Nix smiled grimly to himself. If he was going to go down, the least he could do was give them hell first.

A dark expanse,
Limitless as the sky,
Stretching around me
Farther than I can see.

I do not feel confined or trapped
Within this void,
But instead I feel a freedom
Unknown to me before,
With all of time and space at my feet,
Ready to be explored.

Tiny points of light glimmer to life
Growing closer and brighter—
Windows softly glowing in the darkness,
Casting paths of light to guide my steps
Toward scenes of other lives, in other times and places.

The nearest scene reveals a boy,
Dark hair and darker eyes
Clouded by a loneliness
That does not belong on a face
So young.

Why did I never notice
When he was here,
That same hunger for belonging
That I see in every window?

I recognize the girl
That stands before him,
With dark hair and mischievous eyes.
The eagerness in her expression
Does not match the cold indifference
Of the woman that I fear.

She accepts him,
I realize—
In a way I never did.
My shame is hard to reconcile
With what I know about her,
With the grief and anger that I feel
Because of what she's done.
There's more to their story
Than just the wounds she's given him
And me.

I want to look away
But instead I look ahead
To the next window.
To know him means to face his darkness
And his past, to accept that
I might not like what I see.

He's older now and
Dark ink swirls around his arm.
The haunted longing in his eyes
Has turned to anger
And resentment.

Monster.

In every window it's the same.
The others look at him
With hate
With fear
With envy.

They use him like a tool,
Discard him when they're done,
Blame him when his strength alone
Is not enough.

Always, he's alone,
Except when he's with her.

And then the darkness comes.
The blackness that has haunted
My nightmares.
Not a dream, but his reality.
Thick.
Hot.
Choking,
It presses all around,
Closing tighter.

I feel a tug, pulling me away
From the darkness and the windows.
Faint pink light turns to orange and gold,
Chasing away the cold and the fear,
Helping me to breathe again.

I see myself lying there.
I see myself through his eyes.
Broken.
Helpless.
Small.
I know I must protect her.

Whatever happens to me,
It's time to face my fears
And my past,
So she won't have to suffer
For my mistakes
Anymore.

I say goodbye,
Approach the wall
With pounding heart and
Aching wounds.
No time is left for my regret.

Chapter Nineteen

A loud crash from the living room woke her. She sat up in confusion. The last place she'd been was a cold prison cell, her hands shaking and her breath ragged. Before that, she'd been in a fight, hadn't she?

No, it was a dream. A dream that wasn't just a dream.

She swung her legs over the side of the bed and tried to stand up, but crumpled back down, her body still too weak. She let out a frustrated groan, then braced herself as she tried to stand again, slowly this time, using the nearby table for support. Her legs wobbled, and she stumbled toward the wall, crashing against it heavily. She inched toward the door, every step an exhausting effort. Her vision blurred and she closed her eyes, taking slow breaths as she waited for the dizziness to pass. She clenched her teeth and pulled open the door. Her legs nearly gave out again when she saw the scene in the living room.

The couch was flipped over across the room from its normal position. The door was splintered, hanging off its lower hinge. Gram stood facing the door and didn't seem to notice her enter.

"What happened?" she croaked weakly, a sick sense of dread settling in her stomach. Gram spun around, then rushed to her side to help her wobble to a chair. She noticed a trace of blood on his lip.

Before he could answer her question, his phone rang. He pulled it from his pocket swiftly, as though he'd been anticipating the call.

"Mel," he began, but it seemed he was interrupted. Thea wanted desperately to listen, but her channeling was still too weak to enhance her hearing.

Gram swore. "We have to stop him."

Silence as he listened.

"You're saying we should let him go? You know as well as I do—"

Gram swore again as he hung up the phone and tore his hand through his hair.

"Where's Nix?" Thea asked tentatively.

Gram's expression grew pained, confirming what she already suspected.

"Buying us time." His voice shook, his words thick with emotion. "We have to get you out of here."

"He's turning himself over to the Military, isn't he?" She almost couldn't hear her own voice over the pounding in her ears. The sick feeling in her stomach turned sour with anger. Her voice rose and hot tears pricked her eyes. "He's sacrificing himself? For me?"

What right did he think he had to decide that on his own? Did he really think so little of her? Did he think she was so useless and fragile that she needed him to throw his life and freedom away to protect her? She knew what it would do to him. She was sure now that it had been his past she'd seen in her dream.

Was there really no way to stop him?

She knew there wasn't. She was weak. That's why he'd done this.

"Thea, I—" Gram paused, his voice full of pain, his eyes full of loss and indecision.

He'd lost Kai too, she realized with an ache in her chest. And now Nix.

He probably blamed himself, but it was her fault. All of it was her fault.

She blinked away her tears. This wasn't the time. Gram was worried. He was suffering. She didn't want to add to that. She couldn't be the broken, useless girl who needed protection anymore. It was time to stand up.

"Where will we go?" she asked.

"I don't know," Gram admitted hesitantly. "Nix, he—"

"He wanted us to go to the Syndicate," Thea interrupted, rolling the possibility around in her mind.

"I don't know what the right thing is," Gram said with a sigh, sounding a little like his usual self. "Maybe we can hide out somewhere for a while until you recover, but that's only a short-term solution. Going to the Syndicate, though, that's a big risk. I know it's not something we should take lightly."

"We're going," Thea told him firmly. Nix was right. Running and hiding hadn't worked. She'd been reckless and selfish. She hadn't trusted Nix. She hadn't been there for Kai. It was time she learned her lesson. "We're going to the Syndicate, but I have no intention of running away. We're going to save him."

Gram grinned and the usual mischievous sparkle returned to his eyes, erasing the worry that had been clouding them. Her own shoulders relaxed. It was reassuring to see his usual confidence returned.

"You're as crazy and stubborn as he is, you know that? Well, if you can't stop someone from being an idiot, I guess the next best thing is to do something stupid yourself."

"Do I want to know what reckless thing you are encouraging my patient to do?"

They turned toward the door at the sound of Lucan's voice. He picked his way carefully over the splintered door, his face pinched with anxious surprise as he surveyed the room.

"What happened?"

"Our favorite dumbass did the most dumbass thing to date, so Thea and I are going to join the Syndicate so we can rescue him."

Lucan sighed and pinched the bridge of his nose.

"I can't even begin to digest everything that is wrong with that sentence. What exactly did Nix do this time?"

"He turned himself over to the Military so they would stop coming after me."

Thea felt her anger spike again as she spoke the words. She was starting to understand why Gram spoke about him the way he did.

Lucan's expression was speculative as he scanned the room again.

"I was worried something like this might happen."

His eyes narrowed as they stopped on Gram, and he pursed his lips before continuing.

"It doesn't surprise me to hear about Nix being reckless. It doesn't even surprise me that you want to upstage him in the most asinine way you can think of. But joining the Syndicate? That's too reckless, even for you. I know Nix thought getting protection from them was the right move, but we've already established that his ideas are terrible. I'd like to think I can count on at least a little more sense from you, Gram, but you've proved me wrong."

Lucan's voice grew more heated with every word. Thea had seen him exasperated, but never truly angry. It seemed Gram's words had pushed the normally calm man too far.

"Now hold on Luc!" Gram held up his hands in defensive protest. "This one wasn't my idea. I was all set to be the responsible one this time, but she insisted."

Lucan whirled around to face her. He looked tired, she realized. Dark circles rimmed his eyes, and his face seemed a little paler in spite of his anger. Of course, caring for her and Nix must have kept him busy and worried, not to mention Kai.

Thea blinked and set her jaw defiantly. She couldn't think about Kai right now. If she didn't want to be treated like a helpless little girl, she couldn't act like one either.

Lucan's words died on his lips, and his shoulders dropped in defeat.

"What did I do to deserve being stuck with so many stubborn, foolish, reckless people?" he muttered, rubbing his forehead with both hands. He looked up at Gram and added, "I guess the fact that he's gone means he really has been holding back after all."

Gram scowled and shrugged.

"Well, I figured that was the case. Let's just say I taught him everything he knows and leave it at that."

Thea didn't understand how they could take this so lightly. She was about to voice her disapproval, but Gram spoke first.

"Luc's right, though," he said. "You're in no shape to barge into the Syndicate and start making demands. If Nix is right about Ryu, then I'm sure he'd take you in. But to march up to the head of the clan and demand that he take on the Military to help Nix of all people. Well, it won't be as simple as saying please. There's plenty of reasons for there to be bad blood between those two."

"I think Nix is probably right that they would protect you," Lucan agreed as he moved to flip the couch to its normal position. "But if you are serious about convincing the Syndicate to help, then you'll need to give them a good reason. I'm not sure simply offering to join the fight will be enough."

Thea frowned. Once again, her plan wasn't enough. She hadn't thought it through.

"Hey, don't worry so much," Gram said, placing a reassuring hand on her shoulder. "We don't have to figure out everything right now. First, we have to get you better, then we start training."

"Training?" she asked in confusion, only half registering Gram's words.

"You're strong. There's no denying that." Gram said. "You've improved a lot with only a little bit of training, but Syndicate fighters start training when they're kids. We can't make you the kind of fighter they are, but if you want them to take you seriously, you need to work on your basic skills."

Thea closed her eyes, a sinking sorrow twisting in her stomach as she thought of her dream. She had seen Nix as a child, being attacked by several older boys at once. One of them had a knife. Was that what they considered training? Were those the kind of people she really wanted to get involved with?

Wait. She had an idea. Her eyes flew open.

"I know what we need to do," she told them. "I know how to convince the Syndicate to help us."

Her confidence waned as both men sat across from her, waiting expectantly. She looked down at her hands as she wrung them together, trying to find words to explain what she had suspected for some time. Her face felt hot as her disorganized thoughts churned in her head.

"Ever since..." Her voice squeaked, and she paused to clear her throat.

"Would you like me to make you some tea first?" Lucan asked.

Thea smiled appreciatively but shook her head. She was tempted to put off her explanation, but she knew the waiting would only increase her anxiety.

"Maybe later," she said, and took a deep breath before continuing. "When I was in the research facility, I started having really vivid dreams."

She wrapped her arms around her body, wishing for the reassuring weight of Kai's arm on her shoulder. Tears stung her eyes, but she blinked them away.

"Every night after they'd performed tests, I would have these dreams. I could never remember much after I woke up, but I always knew that they'd felt so real, like they were actually happening."

She shuddered and rubbed her arms, trying not to remember her recent nightmares.

"Lately, I feel like they've been different. Less abstract, and I remember them more."

"The first day you came here," Lucan said softly, "You had a nightmare."

Thea nodded. "That was one of them."

Tears filled her eyes, and her throat closed with emotion.

"I dreamt I was in a really dense forest at night." Her voice came out high and tight as she struggled to hold back her tears. "I was hurt, but I was running anyway, trying to find something. I was afraid, worried I was too late. I saw a bright light, and then a dark shape on the ground. Then there was blood everywhere."

She wiped her eyes and looked pointedly at Gram. His face had turned pale at her description, and she knew that even though the dream was more gruesome and abstract, he saw the similarities too.

"I think that dream was about Kai," she choked out and her body began to shake. She couldn't hold back the tears as she said, "About the night he died."

She couldn't see their reactions through her tears. She covered her face with her hands, trying not to lose control. She couldn't break down. Not now. There wasn't time.

She felt a weight next to her on the couch and wiped her face with her hands before looking up. Gram handed her something to wipe her eyes and placed a hand on her back. Its weight and warmth were comforting, but it wasn't the hand she wanted to feel.

Neither man spoke as she wiped her eyes and nose.

Finally, Lucan said, "Dreams are strange things. Especially nightmares. When our mind is trying to process something like trauma, the way it does that isn't always linear. Our brain uses symbolism and imagery to help our subconscious process our anxieties, fears, and experiences. It's easy for our conscious mind to try to assign the wrong meanings to those symbols instead of letting our subconscious process them. It's usually better to simply accept dreams and let them go."

Kai had said something similar, but she shook her head because she knew she was right.

"The day Nix left," she croaked, shame warming her face and tightening her chest, "the day that I saw his tattoo, I had a dream that I was in that garage at the base. He came in with blood on his hands and arms. I'd never been in that building before. In my dream, I was afraid. I thought he had hurt someone and that he was going to hurt me."

She took a deep breath trying to stop the tears from spilling over again—this time tears of regret.

"That day he came back it was the same. I was in the garage. Everything happened the same way. Everything looked the same. At first, I was afraid when I saw him, but then I realized he was hurt and I tried to help him."

"It's possible your memory of the dream is altered by your experience," Lucan said, still sounding speculative.

"That's what Kai said," Thea told him, "but I know I'm right. Last night, I dreamt that Nix was fighting soldiers at the city walls. Before that, I saw him—his past. I saw him fighting for the Syndicate."

Her voice caught again. She didn't know how to make them understand, but she knew these weren't just dreams. They were real.

Gram leaned back, removing his hand from her back to brush it through his hair.

"You're saying you have an ability to see the future? Or the past?" he asked. His tone sounded more contemplative than skeptical, and Thea let out a sigh of relief. He believed her.

But what she was about to say still scared her.

"I think...I think when they tried to give me telepathy something went wrong. I think they gave me this instead."

"But you can't control it?"

Gram was rubbing his chin now, and she could see in his eyes that he was thinking.

She shook her head.

"No."

"Luc, you've never heard of anything like this?"

Lucan frowned and shook his head.

"I have never heard of anyone having clairvoyant abilities, but that doesn't mean it doesn't exist." He studied her in that way that made her shiver, even though she knew how kind he was. "Remember, telepathy was little more than a folktale until a few years ago. Some claim that the Syndicate's founder was a telepath. Others say he was simply very intuitive. I always believed the latter was true until Nix came along."

He shook his head, as though trying not to get distracted from the main subject.

"Sometimes abilities might not be recognizable as abilities. They might present like a trait. As those traits get passed on, they may become stronger and more noticeable. My guess is that maybe you had one of these traits, and somehow the research experiments had the side effect of bringing them out or enhancing them. Did you ever have feelings of déjà vu or feel like you had a strong intuition for things that were going to happen?"

Thea frowned. She'd never considered the possibility that this was something she was born with. She didn't think Kai had either, but she also knew he hadn't always told her everything.

"I don't know." She squeezed her eyes shut and shook her head. It was too much to think about.

She took a deep breath and changed the subject.

"You said Nix bought us time?" she asked Gram. "How much time?"

Gram sighed, the pained look returning to his face. "Not enough time to figure this out. There's one thing I'm certain of, Nix won't just hand himself over without a fight. It's not in his nature. They'll be trying to deal with him for a while, at least. Enough time for us to get you out of here, but that's about it. We'll have to lie low somewhere for a while, get you back on your feet."

Lucan nodded. "I understand Nix's reasoning, but it's too optimistic to think they'd simply leave you alone."

"That idiot never thinks things through," Gram grumbled.

Lucan nodded and continued. "It's best to assume they will still come looking for you here. Gram's right that the first step is to get you better. Then you can worry about training and trying to control this ability."

Gram reached into his pocket and pulled out the folded-up map he'd shown them earlier.

"I don't want to risk going through the canyon again," he said, trailing his finger over the map as though looking for something. "And we don't want to risk going too near Karza or the base, either.

"My dad lives near Cross Point," Thea said hesitantly. "I don't really want to get him involved, though."

Gram shook his head. "It's best if we get out of Military territory. I'd like to meet him someday, though."

Thea smiled and turned back to the map, allowing Gram to study it without interruption.

"Here," he said, pointing to a location southeast of Senari, on the western border of the Wilds. Thea shuddered, remembering the incident with the

Syndicate that had led to Kai's injury. She couldn't keep being afraid of them if she was going to do this.

Lucan stood.

"You'll need supplies. I'll prepare what I can for you and prepare some herbal mixtures that might help with your ability."

"Aren't you coming with us?" Thea had never considered that he might not. She'd come to rely on him, and she was sure they were going to need his help many times before this was all over.

Lucan shook his head. "I'm afraid going to the Syndicate is a line I'm unable to cross. I have responsibilities here, and people who need me."

"Don't worry," Gram said after Lucan had gone. "It's always been like that with Luc. He's willing to help us out when we need it, but ultimately his place is here. He's never liked fighting, but he's saved our asses more times than I can count. When we need him, he'll be here, waiting for us. He always is.

"Besides," he continued, crossing his arms with a grin. "Luc's family has a lot of influence here in the city. I'm sure he's going to try to find some way to help Nix. It'll be good to have him here."

Thea nodded. She felt guilty for assuming he would go with them. It was too much to expect anyone to follow her with what she was about to do. She bit her lip and glanced sideways at Gram. Was she expecting too much from him too? She was asking him to throw everything away and put himself in danger.

"You know," Gram went on. "I joined the Military the first chance I got, as soon as I was old enough. I thought I would spend my whole life as a soldier."

Thea swallowed. Of course. He couldn't easily give up the life he had here, either.

"Turns out, that was just about the dumbest decision I ever made, joining the Military," Gram said, surprising her. "It didn't take me long to learn all the problems with the organization. Thing is, once they have you, they aren't too eager to let you walk away. No matter how much of a headache you cause them. Doesn't mean they won't demote you and send you out to some hellhole in the Wilds, though."

"What did you do anyway?" she asked curiously.

Gram grinned. "That's a long story, best saved for when we have nothing else to do. Let's just say, what we're about to do, you and I, isn't even the craziest thing I've ever done."

Thea smiled and felt her shoulders drop in relief. Not only was he going with her, he seemed to be trying to reassure her that he was okay with it.

"Anyway, you ought to drink some of that tea, like Luc suggested, and get as much rest as you can before we leave." Gram moved toward the kitchen. "How about something to eat too?"

Her stomach rumbled. Since waking up, the only thing she'd eaten was some broth Lucan had brought her. She needed to do whatever she could to begin recovering her strength.

"That sounds great."

Lucan returned before evening. He was insistent that Thea wasn't well enough to ride behind Gram on his bike, and they had too many supplies, anyway. Gram had managed to replace his trailer, though the new one didn't seem quite as sturdy. While Gram loaded the trailer on his bike, Lucan began explaining the treatments he'd prepared for her.

"Is there anything that stands out as a possible trigger for your ability?" he asked, his forehead wrinkling as he scribbled notes on his tablet.

Thea tilted her head, thinking back.

"They seem to happen more when I've used my abilities a lot. And they seem to be clearer when my channeling is lower."

Lucan frowned.

"Interesting. I would expect the opposite."

He scribbled some more notes.

"And maybe..." she hesitated, feeling her cheeks warm, "maybe when I'm thinking about a particular person a lot, my dreams end up being about them. I hadn't noticed before, because I wasn't sure the dreams meant any-thing."

Lucan nodded. He remained silent as he wrote, his lips pursed together. At last, he clicked the stylus into its holder and handed the tablet to her.

"I'll explain all your treatments to you, but I've also made notes in case you forget something. I believe it would also be helpful for you to record your dreams in as much detail as you can. It's surprising how much more we can remember when we take the time to record things. It might also help you see patterns or sort out what has already happened from what is going to happen."

Thea nodded and took the tablet gratefully.

"I'm not certain this will help," he continued, "but this is what I want you to do. Before you go to sleep, I want you to do the channeling exercises I taught you. Try to really stretch your channeling. Then, I want you to take these."

He held up two small jars. One held crushed herbs, similar to those used in the herbal tea she'd grown accustomed to drinking every day. The other held tiny round capsules that shimmered blue in the light.

"We've been treating the damage caused by the experiments with herbal remedies until now. These capsules are a stronger medication that should speed up that process. I want you to continue drinking the herbal teas, though. I've modified this blend with herbs that will not only help you relax, but also help your memory and the clarity of your thoughts."

He set the two jars down and picked up another.

"This blend is for you to drink in the morning. It will give you energy and help speed up your healing.

Thea nodded. She was glad he'd written this all down. It was a lot to remember, and he hadn't even started on the ointments, salves, and bandages that were meant for her wound.

"Any questions?"

Thea bit her lip. She was sure she would have questions later when he wasn't around to answer them. Right now, she was too overwhelmed by the deluge of information.

He smiled.

"I've tried to be as thorough as possible in my notes. Read over them and you'll be fine."

She nodded and he leaned back again with a sigh.

"I wish you had a few more days to recover, but it's just not possible."

"I appreciate you doing all of this," she said with a sad smile, "and for everything you've done for me so far. Not just treating me. I don't know what I would have done without all of you after..."

Her voice caught and the words died on her lips. Lucan reached out to squeeze her hand.

"We'll see each other again," he said, his voice soothing. "I'm sure of that. All of us will be together again."

With those words, she couldn't stop the tears anymore. For her, *all of us* would never happen again. She would never stop feeling the emptiness of missing Kai. How could she ever feel whole or complete again? How could anywhere ever feel right without him there with her?

She wiped her eyes and took a deep breath. All she could do was move forward and make sure they didn't lose anyone else. She was going to get Nix back, and for that to happen she had to be stronger.

"Sorry." She gestured toward the box of herbs and medicine. "Go ahead. You were going to teach me how to take care of my wound."

The dark again,
heavy and hot.
The air's taste
thick and acrid
on my tongue,
in my lungs.
Anything is better
than this place.
Still, I question
if I should
do this.

Before I can
find an answer
the door scrapes
open and light
burns my eyes,
sharp and piercing
as needles driving
deep inside
my head with
a drumming ache.

She stands there
like she doesn't
care, but the
wild way her
eyes dart around
tells me otherwise.
I follow her
no longer questioning
but still with
a sinking feeling
of regret for
what I know
I must do.

Thoughts of fear
and shock
fill my head,
and blood stains
my sword,
but the body
I see is
his.

The hallway blurs.

The lights are
gone and instead
trees surround me,
closing in, pinning
me down.

I see him
lying there again,
so still and
there's nothing I
can do to
stop the blood,
to stop time,
or to stop
him from fading
away in front
of me again.

Chapter Twenty

Thea woke with a cry. Her stomach lurched. She pulled herself up and wretched over the side of the trailer. Gram noticed and slowed the bike to a stop.

"You alright?" he asked.

She squeezed her eyes shut so tight they hurt, forcing the red to give way to blurs of color. When she opened them again, she saw spots instead of blood. Her head swam and her stomach churned with lingering nausea, but she took a deep breath and nodded. Gram fished water from their supplies and handed it to her. She took several slow sips, the cool water easing her dry throat and queasy stomach.

"Can you hang on for a bit more? There's a place we can camp just ahead."

"I'm fine," Thea assured him, though her voice cracked. "We don't have to stop. We can keep going."

Gram shook his head.

"Nah. I never planned to push through the night. Just wanted to put some distance between us and the city. There's a spot up ahead where I'd planned to camp."

He let out a yawn and Thea bit her lip guiltily. He must be tired. She nodded.

"Let's stop there then."

He let out a chuckle and patted her arm.

"Good. If Luc thought I was driving all night without letting you rest or take your medicine, he'd probably follow us out here just so he could kick my ass."

Thea smiled, glad for his humor to help chase away the darkness of her nightmare.

Gram climbed back on the bike and accelerated slowly. Her body ached with every bump. Gram and Lucan had tried to make it as comfortable as possible for her, but there wasn't anything they could do about the roughness of the terrain or the soreness of her healing wounds. She tried to shift the blankets around her, but nothing seemed to help. She doubted she would be able to fall back asleep.

Instead, she tipped her head back so she could look directly above her at the sky. The night was clear, with a half-moon and the bike providing the only light. The tiny points of starlight far above danced and glittered, cradled in velvet folds of the dark sky around them. This darkness was nothing like the endless choking blackness of her dream, of the prison cell where Nix had spent so much time. She shivered at the memory and focused again on the sky, an endless, soft blanket, wrapping her up and carrying her far away, freeing her from her worries.

She wondered if Nix ever felt the same way when he looked at the sky, or if he only saw darkness.

He'd suffered so much. Not just the prison cell, but loneliness and rejection. She understood now why he acted the way he did. How could he let anyone in when everyone he'd ever known had only ever hurt him?

She understood the gratitude he felt for Gram. Gram had reached out a hand to him and accepted him when no one else ever had. Gram had saved him from the darkness.

And she'd pushed him right back into it.

She wiped her eyes to keep her tears from falling.

It wasn't too late. They were going to save him. Once they did, she was determined to never let him feel alone in the dark ever again.

Maybe together, with Gram and Lucan, they could both find a way to let go of their pasts and move forward.

Eventually Thea had fallen back asleep. With thoughts of Nix and her regrets fresh in her mind, she found herself back in the same dream, only time had moved forward. Fortunately, she found she was no longer in the hallway but outside in a town's open square. Wooden buildings with peaked roofs surrounded her, and smooth cobblestones lined the ground at her feet. The evening sky burned orange, though the sun had long set, and a haze of smoke stung her throat and lungs, making her cough.

Across the square stood a boy in his mid teens. Even if Thea hadn't seen him in other dreams, she could have guessed who he was. The resemblance to his sister was unmistakable. They had the same dark hair, the same red-brown eyes, the same small nose and chin.

He held a sword, his stance firm, but his hands trembling. His eyes grew wide with hurt and betrayal, and she could sense the fear and sorrow in his thoughts.

Thea lowered her own sword. When she spoke, her voice wasn't her own. She wasn't surprised. She already knew this wasn't a dream, but a memory—Nix's memory.

"Put down your sword, Ryu. I don't want to hurt you."

The boy hesitated before gripping his sword tighter and taking a small step forward. Before he could move, motion caught Thea's attention from behind Ryu. Kaori emerged from the shadows with a look of triumph as she raised her own sword to attack. Ryu didn't see her. His attention was on Nix. He didn't realize Kaori was there or the danger he was in. Without time to think Nix rushed forward to intercept Kaori's attack.

Ryu let out a cry, thinking Nix was attacking him. Thea could sense his surprise when, instead, Nix caught Kaori's sword with his own and grabbed the second sword with the palm of his free hand. He pushed all the channeling he could into his palm, trying to prevent the sword from slicing deeper, but it was too late. The blade had already pierced his skin, and Thea could feel the poison burning in his arm.

"What do you think you're doing?" Kaori growled angrily, not easing the force of her attack.

"That's my line!" Nix seethed. "This wasn't part of the plan."

Ryu simply looked between them with wide eyes, unsure what to do. He'd thought Nix had betrayed them, along with his sister. Why would Nix protect him now?

"Go, Ryu!" Nix said to him. "Run!"

His voice seemed to snap Ryu from his stunned immobility. He lowered his sword and ran.

Kaori tried to pull back her own sword, but Nix grabbed it, keeping her from chasing after Ryu even as the poison burned up his arm and into his shoulder and chest.

"You're a fool, Ghost." Kaori spat angrily, her eyes growing wild as they darted between him and the direction Ryu had gone. "Why would you choose to die for the sake of my useless brother? You're worth a thousand of him!"

Before Nix could answer, shouts and gunfire sounded from a nearby street. Kaori let go of the sword Nix was holding and stepped away with a sad shake of her head.

"The soldiers will be here any minute. I can't afford to take you with me now. I guess this is goodbye, Ghost. I never meant for things to end this way. It's a shame."

Kaori turned away and melted into the shadows before Nix could try to stop her. Thea's vision blurred, and she felt the heaviness of his body as he stumbled away from the square, toward a nearby alley. The sounds of footsteps grew closer. She didn't know who was coming. Soldiers? Or Syndicate? Either way, she knew Nix was in trouble. He slid to the ground as the surroundings began to fade away, leaving only the burning feeling of fire in her veins and the aching of her wound in her side.

Thea hissed as she sat up and the dull pain in her side grew to a sharp bite. She blinked as she looked around, trying to remember where she was. The dream had felt so real, like she had been the one swinging her sword, hearing thoughts inside her head, burning with poison in her veins.

The last one, at least, she had her own memory of, but the others had felt just as real.

That was because they had been real.

She didn't know why she was able to see them so clearly now. Maybe Lucan's treatments were already making a difference. Regardless, she knew she'd seen another glimpse into Nix's painful past.

It was a lot to process.

He and Kaori had betrayed the Syndicate in order to gain their own freedom, but it seemed Kaori had other motives that included killing her brother. Nix had saved him, and Kaori had left Nix to die.

Hot anger flooded Thea's body, making her weak channeling surge a little stronger. Gram stirred and Thea took a deep breath to calm herself, not wanting to wake him.

She would rather save thoughts of Kaori for another time, anyway. It would be all too easy for her thoughts to stray from Nix's nightmare to her own.

She scooted closer to the fire and added wood to the dying embers so she could heat water for her morning tea. Even that small task took a lot of effort. By the time the water was hot, Gram rolled over with a sleepy groan. He ran a hand through his hair absently as he sat up.

"You're awake," he stated, sounding a little surprised. "How're you feeling?"

"Sore," Thea admitted as she poured hot water into her cup and measured the appropriate amount of herbs into a small pouch. "But it feels good to be out of that trailer."

"I bet," he said with a chuckle. "You look like hell, though. Nightmares?"

She shook her head.

"No, not like...not like that. I did have a dream, though. One of the dreams I told you about." She paused, not sure how to explain it. "It was about Nix. Not Nix now, but in the past."

Gram shook his head, looking confused.

"I'm still not sure I get it," he admitted. "Do you see the future or the past in these dreams?"

She smiled a little. She didn't really get it either.

"I've only recently been able to remember them at all. And a lot of the time they don't make sense. But I think maybe the past, the present, and the future get all jumbled up. It's hard to tell until something happens, then the dreams make more sense. This one was different, though. It was clear, like I was really there."

She described the dream to him, omitting the fact that she had seen the dream from her own point of view. She was certain this had been a moment from Nix's past. She had been in his place. The feelings she'd felt were his.

When she finished, Gram didn't say anything. He just sat, staring at the fire with his arms crossed over his chest, his expression pained and distant.

"Do you know? Did all of that actually happen?"

Gram smiled sadly and shrugged.

"The truth is, I don't know the whole story myself," he confessed. "You may have noticed, Nix isn't really the talkative type."

She shrugged and he let out an exasperated chuckle.

"But from what you described, that's about the time I first met him. The Military raided the Syndicate's headquarters, and I found him in that alley."

He didn't continue but instead stood and moved to the trailer. He pulled two meal bars from their packs and handed one to her.

"I was still with the Military then," he continued as he sat back down on the ground next to her. "I was just a regular soldier. At the time, the Syndicate was causing a lot of trouble. More than usual. Their leader was obsessed with ability research. They'd hit research facilities to steal documents, equipment, formulas—anything they could. There was even a rumor that they'd developed a new ability. The higher-ups in the Military weren't happy, but the Syndicate was stronger than they are now. We couldn't take them lightly."

Thea nibbled on the meal bar as she listened.

"The truth is I don't know very much about the Syndicate," she said. "Everyone in the Eastern Territory just says they're dangerous and that the Military keeps us safe from them."

Her own experiences had done nothing to dispel what she'd always been taught.

"That's the Military for you," Gram said with a sigh. "Do you know why the war started in the first place?"

"Because the Syndicate tried to overthrow the government?"

Gram shook his head.

"The Syndicate claim the Military were the aggressors and they were just trying to protect themselves."

Thea wrinkled her nose.

"So which side is right?"

"I expect neither of them," Gram said, running his hand through his hair. "What I do know is this. The Military has a lot of problems, but so does the Syndicate. I heard you were attacked in Senari?"

Thea nodded with a small shudder.

"Kai and I went there after I left the research facility. He thought it would be the safest place, since the Military doesn't have much presence there. He tried to find work at the local inn—and a place for us to stay—but a group of Syndicate members got aggressive with us. They accused us of being spies for the Military."

The truth was, those first months after she left the research lab were little more than blurry memories to her, including that encounter with the Syndicate. She remembered the group of big, strong looking people dressed in black. She remembered shouting and the fear that made her channeling spike out of control. She remembered the loud buzz in her ears. She remembered Kai crouched on the ground in pain, unable to stand.

They never talked about it, but she was the one responsible for his injured knee. It wasn't the Syndicate who had hurt him, it was her. Because she'd lost control of her channeling.

"I don't think everyone in the Syndicate is like that," Gram said, his voice startling her out of her memory. "Most people who we call 'Syndicate' aren't even combatants or involved in the war in any way. They're just ordinary people. But there's no doubt that life for the combatants is a harsh one. They start combat training as children, and give special treatment to the strongest. Life in the slums was tough, but it was nothing compared to that. I'm sure Nix is the way he is because of it."

Gram's voice turned to a low growl. It was clear he disapproved of the way his friend had been treated—of the way all Syndicate children were forced to live, and think, and fight.

Thea nodded. She'd seen it.

"I don't think it was just the training, that was harsh, or the lifestyle," she said contemplatively. "I think raising children that way leads to a lot of jealousy and bullying. I think that was probably harder on him than anything else."

She looked away and let her hair curtain around her face in an attempt to hide her burning cheeks.

"You're probably right," Gram said with a sad sigh. He paused and rubbed at his chin, as though trying to remember where he'd left off.

"Anyway, around that time, the Syndicate always seemed to know what our plans were," he continued. "We couldn't stay one step ahead of them. There was one squad in particular that always seemed to be able to get past our security, no matter how tight it was."

"Because of Nix," Thea cut in. "Because he's a telepath."

Gram nodded.

"The Syndicate Ghost, they called him," Gram said with a smirk. "The stories were mostly exaggerations of course, an excuse made up by idiots who didn't want to admit their own incompetence.

"The higher ups wanted him stopped but they didn't know who he was or why he was able to do the things he could do. They found an informant in the Syndicate and that's how the Military learned about his telepathy. It was a prize they couldn't pass up."

Gram paused, his expression distant.

"We had two objectives the day we were ordered to raid Chusan. The first was to take out their leader. The second was to find the telepath, and take him alive if possible."

He shook his head in disgust.

"When we arrived, the whole town was in chaos, and not because of us. It seemed like some kind of internal conflict was going on. Half the higher-ranking leaders were already dead, including the Syndicate's head. We found Nix too, half dead, even though he only had one cut on his hand. Didn't make sense until the medic figured out it was poison. They barely managed to keep him alive long enough to get him out of there. He's lucky he's got so much channeling. That's probably the only thing that saved him."

"Kaori was the informant, wasn't she? The internal conflict was something she planned, I think."

Thea scrunched her forehead as she tried to remember more details from her dreams. It was a lot to digest—half a lifetime that wasn't her own.

"For a long time, it was only a guess," Gram said with a frown. "Like I said, Nix doesn't talk about it. Whether she always intended for him to get captured by us, or whether she simply left him behind because he was injured, I don't know. But I do know she lied to him about her plans."

Gram had picked up a stick while he'd been talking and had begun to break off small pieces to throw into the fire, staring at the orange flames like he wasn't really seeing them. His meal bar still sat unopened in his lap.

"So, what happened after that?" Thea asked.

Gram startled as though he'd forgotten she was there.

"Now that the Military had him in custody," he continued, "they had to decide what to do with him. The researchers wanted him, of course. There was a small group in Operations who said it would be a waste not to try to use his abilities to the Military's advantage. But most of the upper ranking officers just wanted him dead. They said he was too dangerous to be left alive."

A hard edge of disgust crept into his voice.

"All I saw was a kid. A kid who'd probably never been a kid before. A kid who'd been left behind by his own people. The whole thing didn't sit right with me. I tried to stand up for him, but I was only a soldier. I didn't have any sway or authority. So, I did the only thing I could. It was probably the dumbest thing I've ever done, but it's also one of the few things I don't regret. I helped him escape."

Thea let out a gasp of surprise. Gram's mouth turned up in a small grin at her reaction.

"And they didn't arrest you?" she asked in disbelief.

Gram laughed and threw the last of his stick into the fire. He opened his meal bar at last and took a bite before continuing, as though intentionally drawing out the suspense.

"Oh, they did. But even though I had no power, I had friends who did. Nolan...ah, he's Kai's..."

He paused awkwardly and Thea nodded in understanding.

"Nolan managed to get me out. Mel helped too. Nearly ruined their own careers in the process, but they were able to get me reassigned to that middle-of-nowhere hellhole as a peacekeeper. They told me the only way back was to capture Nix and turn him over to the Military."

Gram chuckled, as though the events were somehow funny. Thea didn't see how. She was surprised to learn that Kai's father had done so much for Gram. Sick anger twisted her stomach at the thought. Why hadn't he been willing to help them?

She took a deep breath and blinked away the tears threatening to form. It wasn't time to think about that now.

"And you did find him," she said, "though obviously you didn't turn him in.

Gram nodded.

"Yeah, it wasn't easy, but I did track down that little asshole," Gram went on with another chuckle. "Even though he ran off without even a thank you for saving his ass, I knew he was going to need help. The Military wasn't going to stop going after him. Not that he was appreciative. I had to kick his ass a few times before I could finally get him to come to the base. In the beginning, he never stayed for long, but eventually he'd start coming back without me having to track him down again."

Gram stopped and his face grew pained.

"You're worried about him," Thea said.

"I guess he's not coming back on his own this time," he said quietly. He shrugged and his grin returned, though Thea thought it looked a little forced. "We'll just have to go get him so I can kick his ass again."

Thea nodded. "We'll get him back."

They finished their food in silence after that. Gram took a walk away from the campsite to give her some privacy while she changed her bandages. When he returned, instead of packing up their supplies, he cleared his throat and tore his hand through his hair, looking nervous.

"There's something else you should know," he said, "something Nix wouldn't want me to tell you."

Thea tilted her head quizzically, but Gram wasn't looking at her.

"What is it?" she asked, his nervousness making her nervous.

"The thing is, I told you that the Military researchers wanted him. Before I could get him out of there, they did run tests on him."

Thea shuddered, remembering her own time in the research facility. Gram frowned.

"I'm okay," she assured him. "Go ahead. I'm okay."

Gram nodded.

"That was when they started experimenting in earnest to recreate telepathy themselves."

"And that's why Nix blames himself for what happened to me," Thea said suddenly, interrupting Gram. He looked surprised, then nodded.

Thea bit her lip, once again feeling regret. It couldn't have been easy, the way she treated him, the things he knew she thought. Gram didn't say anything. His expression looked uneasy as he watched her, waiting to see how she would react.

"No one is to blame," she told him, "except the world we live in and the people who run it. The ones who care more about power than people. If Nix were like them, he wouldn't feel guilty about what happened to me, and he wouldn't have done so much to try to help us. If he were like them, he never would have sacrificed himself to protect me."

Her voice hitched and she blinked back her tears. She'd been wrong about him, and she would probably never stop regretting it, but this wasn't the time for regret.

Gram smiled and his shoulders sagged with relief.

"That's why I like you," he said, his voice warm.

She shook her head. "I wish I had realized it sooner."

"Nah. He doesn't make it easy. Because he really is an asshole."

She choked out a laugh in spite of the tears still stinging her eyes. She was grateful for Gram. He made it so much easier not to dwell on her mistakes.

She had thought losing Kai meant losing everything, but as Gram grinned, she realized she wasn't alone. She still had a family with him and Lucan and Nix. She belonged to them, and they belonged to her.

She would do anything to protect her new family, but she realized now that she didn't have to do it alone. Saving Nix was something they would do together.

If she had realized that sooner, could she have protected Kai? Would Nix still be here?

She shook her head. It wasn't too late to save Nix. They would save him, and they would make sure he never had to feel alone or like an outsider ever again.

"Try not to worry so much," Gram said as he helped her stand. "You don't want to end up with a permanent scowl like Nix."

Hammering heartbeats,
And stuttering breath,
I sit in the dark,
Waiting.
The rumors say
They've found us.

Marching footsteps,
And murmuring voices,
I sense them
Before I hear them.

Splintering wood
And shattering glass.
Light floods the room,
Distorted by shadows.
Guns and shouts,
Before I hit the floor.

Behind the soldiers
Eyes like night
And hair like shadow,
A crooked frown
Pulling down
The edge of his mouth,
And the scar on his chin—

His face,
Not from the past,
But just as when
I saw him last,
Only then he had smiled.

Chapter Twenty-one

The outpost was really just an old storage facility. Gram had told her that it had once been used to store supplies for traveling troops, and usually housed only a few guards at a time. The tiny living quarters still surprised her—a single room with a row of cots, a bathroom, and a small kitchen in the corner.

"There should be a water circulation system installed," Gram said as she surveyed the room with a frown. "May need some work to make it usable, though. You feel up to checking the supply room to see if there's anything useful?"

Thea was surprised by the question. She had already begun to mentally prepare herself for weeks of dull recovery on the uncomfortable-looking cots.

"I doubt I can lift anything yet," she said, absentmindedly running her hand along her side.

"Oh, I don't expect you to. Just see if any of the boxes look like they might have food. I'll take a look at the circulator and come join you in a bit."

Thea nodded, grateful for the opportunity to keep herself occupied.

Unfortunately, even the walk back outside to the storage room left her feeling breathless and dizzy. She leaned against the wall inside the dusty room as she waited for her eyes to adjust to the dim light. She wasn't even going to bother trying to enhance her vision. It would only give her a headache.

Rows of boxes filled one side of the room. Thea swayed as she stepped closer and had to brace herself with one hand on the wall to keep from falling over. A hand on her other elbow made her jump.

"You alright?"

Thea nodded.

"Just a little dizzy."

"I guess you won't be going through any boxes today," Gram said. "Come outside. I want to show you something."

Gram offered her his arm to hold onto and Thea took it as she followed him back outside.

"See the red tape on that tree?" Gram asked, pointing ahead of them.

Thea squinted, then nodded once she saw the tape. It was further than the walk to the storage room had been, and that distance had taken all her strength.

"Today you're going to rest," Gram said matter-of-factly. "Tomorrow you can start training. Your first goal will be to make it to that tree and back without getting tired. I don't expect you to walk that far tomorrow, and you had better not try, but if you add a little distance every day, you can start regaining some of your stamina. You'll need it before you can start training for real."

Gram wasn't going to baby her like Lucan or Kai, but he wasn't going to let her push herself before she was ready either. Somehow, his straightforward instruction gave her confidence. He wasn't going to let her do too much too soon, so she could feel comfortable pushing what small limit she had.

She needed to get stronger, and this time, she was going to do it right.

By the end of the first week at the outpost, Thea had made it to the tree but was too exhausted to make it back. She slid to the ground, leaning against the trunk, wondering if Gram would come help her back to the building. Instead, he walked outside, looked in her direction and called out, "You alright?"

"I made it to the tree," she answered.

"Good job! Can you make it back?"

Thea shook her head. She realized he probably couldn't see the motion, so she called, "not without resting first."

"Take your time," he answered, "and think about what you can do differently next time."

It was an obvious lesson Thea had missed. She'd made reaching the tree her only objective and hadn't thought about what would come next. She had burned herself out just getting there, and now she was stuck. Gram wasn't going to save her.

As she sat there, she realized she was always this way, always charging ahead, fixating on a single goal without thinking about her next steps.

Gram had been teaching her an important lesson without her even realizing it.

He was good.

It wasn't until the third week that Thea could easily walk to the tree and back without feeling exhausted afterward. Gram flashed a big grin when he saw her.

"Alright, now we can get serious," he said.

Thea knew the weeks of waiting had been hard on him. More than once, as she made her slow attempts to reach the tree, she'd noticed him pacing around the building in bored agitation. Now he leaned against a tree with the same look in his eyes that he'd had when sparring with Lucan, like he was trying to decide if shooting her or knocking her off her feet would be more fun.

"Unfortunately, we don't have the time to get you where you need to be," Gram continued. "I'm not as nice as Lucan, so I'm just going to be blunt and say it. Your fighting is clumsy and predictable. You use your enhancement all wrong and waste your channeling. You push yourself too hard and don't conserve your energy. Then you can't use your manipulation when you need it, because you're already exhausted."

Thea felt her face burn hot with embarrassment and defensiveness. She wanted to hunch her shoulders in shame and throw them back in defiance at the same time. Tears filled her vision, and she blinked to clear them away with a shake of her head.

She knew that Gram was blunt and jokingly critical of Nix, but she had thought that was just the nature of their relationship. He'd only ever been kind and patient with her, so this new side of him threw her off. She didn't know how to respond.

To her added surprise, Gram let out a loud laugh.

"That right there," he said, pointing at her with a grin. "You let your emotions get the best of you. That's the real reason you lose."

"I..."

Thea wanted to protest, but she knew he was right and there was nothing she could say to deny it.

"Sorry," he said, his voice changing to a softer tone. "I don't mean to be harsh or upset you, but in a fight it's hard enough to take stock of your own situation and condition. It's best to learn your limitations and weaknesses when it doesn't count, so that when the time comes, you know how to handle them better."

Thea nodded and took a deep breath.

"I'm ready for whatever you want to throw at me," she told him, willing herself to believe her own words.

Gram chuckled again, like he recognized her attempt at confidence for the bluff it was.

"Well, I'll say one thing, you're already one step ahead of Nix," he said. "He'd still be sulking if I told him something like that, and it would make it ten times easier to knock him on his ass."

After that, Gram's remarks were only encouraging and instructive. He didn't need to be critical. Every time she found herself flat on her back, the air knocked from her lungs, she heard his words clear in her head: clumsy, predictable, wasted channeling. She could see what mistakes she had made and what she needed to do differently.

"That was better," Gram said, calm and matter-of-fact, as he helped her up. "Remember, a slight increase in your overall speed is better than large bursts. You'll give yourself an advantage without burning yourself out."

Thea had thought her injuries had made her body ache. That had been localized pain. Now every muscle seemed to be bruised from all the falls and hits she'd taken during their sparring matches. She'd expected Gram to hold back, focus on form or theory more than anything, but she'd hit the ground more times than she could count and had hardly landed a blow in return.

She hadn't believed him when he'd said a Micro could beat a Macro. Now she knew firsthand that he hadn't been exaggerating. It wasn't simply his ability to manipulate chance that gave him the upper hand. It was his skill. Gram's movements were so effortless and fluid. Nothing was ever wasted, even when he feinted. He had very few tells, making it hard to predict his next attack. Maybe that lack of waste was why he seemed to have limitless stamina. Or maybe it was simply the amount of time he'd invested into staying in peak physical condition.

Either way the difference in their capability was a daunting hurdle. She doubted there was any amount of training that would ever allow her to gain the upper hand over him.

It made her all the more grateful to have him as her teacher.

Training was better than waiting, but it wasn't long before Thea began to feel restless again. Gram insisted she wasn't ready, but she felt like they were wasting time.

Her dreams didn't help.

"You seem distracted today," Gram said as he helped her up from the ground again.

"Sorry," she grumbled as she rubbed her bruised elbow.

"Let's take a break."

He poured them each a cup of water from a filtering pitcher and handed one to her.

"So, what's on your mind?" he asked when she didn't take a sip but simply fidgeted with the cup in her hands, running one finger absently along the rim.

"Something's changed." Her throat felt tight with worry, so she took a sip of water before continuing. "Or maybe it's going to, I don't know."

"The dreams?" Gram asked, his eyes narrowing.

Thea nodded.

"I..." She paused. She hadn't told him much about her recent dreams. She didn't want to worry him. "They've been pretty bad lately. I don't know. I..."

"You don't have to tell me if it's too hard," he said, his voice slightly higher pitched than usual.

Thea shook her head.

"I'm just worried about Nix. I don't know for sure what's happening to him, and it makes me feel anxious. I just wish I wasn't so useless."

She set her water down with a clang and buried her face in her hands. She always told herself she wasn't going to cry, but her frustrations, her anger, her sorrow always brought the tears back.

Gram sighed.

"It is frustrating," he said. "Believe me, I get it. I'd love nothing more than to charge into the city, guns blazing, and bust him out of there. Knock some sense into Nolan while I'm at it. But all that would do is get me a prison cell and you a one-way ticket to the research lab. We're doing this the right way. We just have to be patient."

He frowned and tore a hand through his hair. He sounded like he was trying to give himself a pep talk as much as her. She felt a little better knowing she wasn't the only one feeling helpless.

"But like I said, something's different now. I don't really understand it," she said.

"You mean your dream?"

Thea nodded.

"Until now, I've either dreamt about his past or else how they've been treating him—I think. But last night—I don't know what to make of it."

"Tell me about it."

Thea closed her eyes, trying to remember details.

"I was hiding in a room with no windows. I knew someone was searching the building. I was trying to be quiet so they wouldn't find me. I heard footsteps and then soldiers burst through the door into the room. Then I saw Nix. He was helping them. After that he went back with the soldiers, not to the prison, but to a room, like a small apartment or dormitory."

Gram straightened.

"Can you remember any other details? Like about the building they raided, or its surroundings? Even the room where you saw Nix after."

Thea did her best to remember. She could see Gram's jaw working as she spoke.

She found herself holding her breath after she finished, waiting for him to respond.

"I'm not completely sure yet," he said with a slight smile, "but this might be good news. I assume your dreams have been pretty grim until now, since you haven't been telling me much. You don't have to worry about me by the way. I can handle knowing whatever is going on."

"Sorry," she began sheepishly, "I—"

He held up his hand to interrupt her.

"When that idiot turned himself in, I gave Nolan a call. I begged him to do whatever he could for Nix..." His voice cracked and he looked away. "I begged him to do whatever he could to keep Nix alive."

His voice was quiet now.

"Nolan's not the biggest fan of Nix so asking him was a stretch, but I knew one thing for certain—the Military has been trying to rid the Eastern Territory of Syndicate hideouts for months and not having much luck. I knew Nix could be the key to making that happen. Looks like Nolan took my advice."

Thea nodded, feeling the same spike of anger she felt whenever Gram talked about Kai's father. She had been curious about him once, about his time with their mother. Now she couldn't get past the fact that he'd turned a blind eye to his own son. She was grateful he had agreed to help Nix. Maybe Kai's death had taught him a lesson, but she didn't think she would ever be able to forgive him for not doing the right thing sooner.

"There's no way to tell if these dreams are in the past or the future, is there?" Gram asked as he stared at the map he'd laid out on the table. It had been another week with several more dreams about Nix raiding Syndicate hideouts.

Thea shook her head.

"Not until we know for sure an event has happened."

"Well whether it's the past or the future or right now, one thing is clear," Gram said, tracing his finger across several locations he'd circled. "They're moving west."

Thea nodded, trusting his assessment. None of the locations were familiar to her.

Gram picked up the map and folded it before placing it back in his pocket. He slapped his knees and stood, as though he'd made a decision. She held her breath, anticipating his next words.

"It's time. You're ready."

"Really?"

"You're fighting could be better, but you've come a long way. The important thing is that now we have a reason to make the Syndicate listen."

Thea swallowed. She didn't feel ready. She wasn't strong. She probably never would be. But she wasn't useless either. She had a way to save Nix. She had a way to make the Syndicate help.

She felt the familiar tightening of fear in her chest, and the quiet voice in the back of her mind telling her again that it was too dangerous, too risky.

She took a deep breath and told herself that there was no other way.

She was afraid, and she wasn't ready, but that didn't matter. This was the only way to save him. This was the only way to make things right.

It was time for her to stop hiding.

The way his hair hangs
over his forehead
and his eyebrows pull
together in concentration,
the dark tattoo on his arm
stretching and rippling
with every movement
of hardened muscle.

The way his voice
vibrates and rumbles,
somehow both
smooth and rough.

The way one corner
of his mouth pulls up
in a crooked smile
and he pauses before
every answer.

His tanned skin
and deep blue eyes,
the scar on his chin,
a symbol of his
loneliness and pain,
so different from mine
and yet a connection
that makes us the same.

Now all that is gone
as we point our swords
at each other.

All I can see is the blood
on his hands,
and the smoke
choking my heart.
He lowers his sword
but I cannot—
love brings only hurt,
but its loss is something
I will never forget.

Chapter Twenty-two

"So you're saying we're going to march right up to the Syndicate front door and demand to talk to their leader?" Thea asked skeptically.

"Of course not," Gram said with a grin, "That would be crazy. We'd get thrown in prison for sure."

Thea let out a breath of relief. He'd been teasing her. He had a real plan.

"We're going to use one of the back entrances in the mountains. There'll be guards there of course, but they'll probably be more willing to hear us out than an entire village full of Syndicate."

"Isn't their job to throw us in prison? Or just kill us?"

Gram laughed.

"Oh they can try, and they probably will. Once they lose, they'll be that much more likely to take us to see Ryu."

Thea had been skeptical of Gram's plan from the start, but as they hiked higher and higher up the narrow mountain path, she was convinced things wouldn't work out the way he'd planned. Her chest heaved, and she felt light-headed. No matter how much air she tried to suck into her lungs, she still felt like it wasn't enough.

They'd left the bike in the foothills, hoping to avoid attracting unnecessary attention. Thea wondered now if that was the right decision. She was exhausted. She was sure she would be useless in a fight. Their effort to go unnoticed seemed wasted, anyway. She was certain they were being followed.

Gram seemed unaffected by it all. He forged ahead, his long legs hardly slowing even on the steepest parts of the climb. Occasionally, he would stop and give her a sheepish apology before letting her catch her breath. If he noticed they were being followed, he didn't seem bothered by it.

It was early evening before he grabbed her arm and held a finger up to his lips. His body tensed, like he'd finally become aware of their circumstances. He handed her a channeling booster, and she felt the hairs on her skin rise with tension as she drank it.

Gram pulled his gun from its holster at his side and waved her forward, his expression serious. She followed him, enhancing her senses to scan their surroundings for any signs of an attack. She caught sight of movement in the trees, little more than flitting shadows, and heard the rustling of footsteps in the underbrush—but no attack came.

The path wound toward a narrow gap in the mountainside. As they neared, two figures stepped out to block their path. One was a large man, older than Gram, but still strong and intimidating. The other person had a smaller build, and a gun strapped to their hip. They held one hand up as though listening to the earpiece clipped over one ear.

"Stop!" the man called out, one hand reaching for the sword on his back. "Who are you, and what are you doing here?"

To Thea's horror, Gram holstered his gun and sauntered toward the two Syndicate guards with a friendly grin on his face.

"We're here to see Ryu, uh, the clan leader," he drawled.

"I don't recognize you," the man pulled his sword out of his sheath a few inches and narrowed his eyes.

Gram stopped. His expression didn't change but Thea noticed the way his hand twitched toward his side.

"You can't tell me you recognize everyone in the Syndicate," he countered with a chuckle. "There's no way. There're too many people."

"You trying to tell me you're Syndicate?" the man scoffed. "You look like you're from the east."

"Well, that's 'cause we are."

Thea flinched as the man drew his sword in one swift movement, the sound ringing out in clear echoes off the mountainside.

"Now hold on," Gram chuckled again as he held up his hands to wave off the man's suspicion. Thea didn't miss the way he stepped back into a lower stance, ready for the attack that was sure to come. "We were sent here by someone in the Syndicate. Well sort of. Anyway, the clan leader wants to see her. You really going to tell me that you don't know who she is?"

"Who sent you?" The man didn't lower his sword or relax in any way. His eyes darted between Gram and Thea, as though expecting one of them to make the first move.

"Well, that's beside the point. Just trust me and ask your boss."

The guard didn't respond at first, but his eyes stopped on Thea, studying her. She felt her cheeks burn. She wanted to hunch her shoulders, pull up her hood, hide. Instead, she held his gaze, trying to appear confident though her legs tensed with the urge to run. Finally, the man tilted his chin toward the other guard, who reached for their earpiece again as they retreated further away. Thea forced herself to exhale. The forest itself seemed to be breathing, moving, closing in, as the shadowy figures who'd been following them drew closer, cutting off their escape.

Before the guard on the radio could return another figure stepped into view.

"I know this one. He's a peacekeeper," he spat, gesturing toward Gram. "I've seen him with the Ghost."

The first guard clenched his jaw, his nostrils flaring as he set his stance, preparing to attack. Thea tensed.

"Take them," he said.

Attackers rushed out from the shadows. At least five, she thought, though there wasn't time to count them. They went for Gram first. She didn't know if it was because they'd identified him as a peacekeeper, or simply because he appeared to be the bigger threat. It didn't matter. She needed to have his back.

Gram drew his gun in one swift movement, firing a rapid volley of shots. One attacker went down with the sizzle of a stun bullet. Another hung back at the edge of the path.

Thea gathered her channeling, trying to keep it steady without overdoing it. She didn't need such a big burst of speed, Gram had told her, only a slight increase to give her an advantage. She pushed a bit more channeling into her initial burst and closed the distance to her target easily before letting her speed drop to just above normal.

The woman sidestepped gracefully, without a hint of surprise. Thea heard the sound of a blade cutting through the air and dropped to a crouch. Air ruffled her hair as a dagger sliced the empty space above her shoulder, barely missing the fabric of her jacket. She spun one leg out, trying to sweep the woman's legs out from under her. Instead of falling, the woman caught herself dexterously and landed in a crouch before shooting another dagger toward Thea.

The dagger flew wide, easily missing without Thea having to dodge. *Thanks to Gram*, she thought with a smile.

She heard the sizzle of a stun bullet before the woman collapsed. Thea used another burst of speed to close the distance to the two guards who were blocking their path. From the corner of her eye, she saw Gram avoid an attack before spinning his opponent hard onto his back. She cringed, remembering all the times she'd fallen to the same move.

The fighters on the path had their swords drawn and ready. Thea didn't have a lot of experience fighting against someone with a sword, but she was sure they would have the advantage in a close-range fight. She pulled two daggers from the pouch at her hip, letting her energy flow into them before launching one toward the man who'd identified Gram. He dodged, his foot slipping on the loose dirt beneath him, unable to find any traction. The blade sliced through the fabric of his dark jacket before clattering against the stony mountain behind him.

Maybe she shouldn't have felt relieved that her dagger had missed, but the thought of the blade slicing through soft flesh made her stomach lurch.

Thea shook her head and shot forward before the guard could regain his balance. She gave her arm an additional push of strength as she embedded her fist into his stomach. He doubled over, his large form folding over her body. His exhale was loud in her ear, the oily smell of sweat strong in her nose.

Incapacitate your opponent as quickly as possible, Gram had told her countless times. *Aim for joints, look for unstable footing, use your opponent's size against them.*

Thea could see the opening. One solid kick to the side of his knee would take the guard down and keep him down, but she couldn't bring herself to do it. Instead, she stepped her leg behind his and pushed hard against his chest, knocking him flat onto his back with the last of his air escaping his lungs in a rush. Confident he wouldn't be getting up easily, Thea turned toward her other opponent.

The pop of another stun bullet filled the air. Thea straightened to catch her breath, waiting for the shot to hit the other guard.

"Thea watch out!" Gram shouted before colliding into her, hard. She grunted, her own breath knocked from her by the impact of his weight. She fell hard to her hands and knees as she heard the sizzle of the stun bullet above her. Gram froze momentarily before collapsing to the ground beside her. He'd been hit.

Her eyes darted around wildly. Shadowed figures stepped out from the trees as more footsteps crunched on the path behind her. She threw herself over Gram as the Syndicate fighters began to surround them.

What would they do to him? What would happen to her?

Her hands began to shake as images of the research lab flashed in her thoughts. She heard another pop, felt the electrifying heat sear her shoulder. Her vision began to dim as she slipped into unconsciousness.

The room was dim, rather than black, but she recognized it. Rough stone walls. Warm air, stale and acrid in her mouth. The hard stone bench with a thin mattress that took up most of the space.

At first Thea thought she was dreaming again, but when she moved and her head spiked with pain, she knew she was awake.

As she reached one hand up to rub her forehead, she noticed the thick bands clamped around each wrist. Channeling restrictors. She wrapped her arms around herself to keep them from trembling and closed her eyes. The worst that could have happened had happened. They had failed, and now she was at the mercy of the Syndicate. Would they use her for experiments like the Military had? Or would they simply keep her locked away in a dank prison cell—forgotten—as they had with Nix?

She reached out a shaky hand to touch the rough stone wall. He had been here. Maybe not in this exact cell, but one like it. A sickly light buzzed above her, keeping her from being drowned in darkness as he had. She was grateful. Her own fears and nightmares were enough to leave her shaking. She wasn't sure what she would do confronted with his worst fear as well.

She shook her head and leaned her forehead against the wall. It was surprisingly cool in contrast to the warm air. She curled her knees to her chest and rolled her forehead toward the stone, its coolness a relief for her headache.

Where was Gram? Was he in the prison too? Was he alive? There was nothing she could do for him. Tears stung her eyes, loneliness and pessimism threatening to overwhelm her.

If only Kai was here.

The thought came unbidden, and a sob broke free from her throat.

The urgency of leaving the city, her recovery, her training. All these things had been enough of a distraction to let her bury her grief, but as she sat alone in the tiny prison, with no one to allay her fears or tell her what she should do next, she couldn't stop the pain from ripping through her chest.

He was gone.

Things weren't okay. Maybe they never had been, but at least his words, his worry, his gentle touches, had helped her believe they could be.

The sound of metal grating against stone startled her. She sat up straight and wiped her face with a shaky breath as the door to her cell slid open.

The man who stood in the doorway was broad chested and muscular, even more so than Gram. Deep lines stretched across the dark tan of his face as he looked down on her with distaste, as though he'd rather kill her and be done with it than follow whatever orders he'd been given. He wore a dark, short-sleeved shirt, stretched tight over his powerful arms. The sight of the tattoo circling his bicep made her stomach twist. She swallowed and tried to keep her fear from showing on her face.

"Get up."

His deep voice was hardly above a whisper, but it made her jump.

Her legs trembled as she stood. Her headache spiked and dizziness made her vision swim. She stumbled as the man grabbed her roughly by the arm, like he was impatient with her slow, clumsy movements.

"Hurry up," he snapped in his rough, quiet voice as he pulled her down the long, garishly lit hallway. The familiar sight was disorienting, like she wasn't really there, but back in her dream. Her stomach clenched as she remembered the dead guard lying slumped against the wall, his blood pooling around him. She swallowed to keep the bile from rising in her throat as the man pulled her along.

Brightness blinded her as they exited the hallway. She swayed on her feet, but the man pulled her roughly, causing her to tumble after him. She tried to raise her free arm to shield her eyes and crane her neck to look at the rows of wooden houses. Her head pulsed and her body ached with every jerking step, so it was almost a relief when the man finally pulled her up the steps and through the large double door of the main house.

She blinked to clear her vision again. The spacious room seemed dim as her eyes adjusted, though large windows covered one wall all the way to the ceiling. The glass was mottled and cloudy, softening the light from outside.

Thea looked around and recognized the large hall. Wood-paneled walls stretched to meet crisscrossing beams high overhead. Benches and tables filled most of the space and a long-faded rug softened the footsteps of the people shuffling around the edges of the room. Their whispers echoed, soft but indistinguishable, off the high walls.

They all seemed to be avoiding the far side of the room where several people stood. Two large men held another by the arms. His bruised and bleeding face was scrunched in a grimace of pain. His hair, that was usually so carefully styled, hung over his forehead, sweaty and disheveled.

"Gram!"

Thea tried to break free from her guard's firm grasp, but his grip was too tight. His fingers pressed so hard into her skin she could almost feel the bruises forming.

Another man stood to the side of Gram and his guards, facing away with hands clasped behind his back. Everything about him, from his clothes to his posture, seemed crisp and stiff—not a hair, a wrinkle, or a breath out of place. He turned slowly when she called out. His red-brown eyes looking down on her from across the room made her gasp and take an involuntary step back.

She had seen Ryu before, in her dreams, but she'd never noticed until then how much he resembled his sister. Their eyes were the same—cold, disdainful, merciless. Thea began to tremble. If her guard hadn't been holding her so firmly, she may have collapsed.

"Bring her." Ryu's eyes narrowed as he spoke, his voice flat and emotionless, as though he were bored.

She stumbled numbly behind her guard as he hauled her across the room. He shoved her as they reached the others, and she fell to the ground in front of Gram. She tried to crawl closer to him, but her guard positioned himself between them.

"Thea, are you hurt?" Gram asked worriedly, his voice hoarse with pain.

"Quiet!" her guard ordered before she could find her voice. He turned around and punched Gram hard in the stomach. Gram let out a wheezing groan and Thea squeezed her eyes shut to hide the desperate tears that had begun to blur her vision.

This was all her fault.

"Stop it!" she croaked, her voice shaky with tears and fear.

She couldn't stop them. She couldn't do anything.

The big man whirled back toward her, and she fought the urge to shrink away. She couldn't do anything, but Gram had told her the Syndicate didn't tolerate weakness. They only acknowledged strength. She blinked the tears from her eyes and took a deep breath.

"We didn't come here to fight you."

The man reached down and yanked her to her feet. She flinched, sure he was going to hit her too.

"Enough, Nobu."

The voice wasn't loud or particularly deep, but it cut through the room like a blade. It was the voice of someone who knew he would be obeyed regardless of how he spoke. That surety commanded attention in a way shouting never could.

Silence hung in the room like someone holding their breath. Ryu kept his back to them, staring at the hazy glass of the window like he was unaware of their presence entirely—his hands clenched tightly behind him, his fingers white and his forearms taught,

Gram let out a ragged cough, and the room seemed to breathe again. Thea took a subconscious step to the side, wishing she could go to Gram. The man in front of her tensed and Thea froze before Ryu's quiet, even voice called her attention again.

"My advisors thought I was crazy when I didn't have Nix executed on sight. It appears they were right. I believed him when he said the only thing he wanted was for you to be safe. I let him go. Since you came here with this Peacekeeper, I can only assume this was one of Kaori's games all along."

"No, you're wrong," Thea started to protest before she could stop herself.

Ryu whirled toward her, all his calm vanishing in an instant. His face flushed red but before he could speak, the man in front of her gripped her arm in one of his powerful hands and slapped her hard across the face with the other. Her vision turned white hot as her head exploded in pain. Static and ringing were the only sounds she heard. If he hadn't been holding her arm in his vice-like grip, she would have collapsed.

She blinked and wiped her eyes with her free hand. When her vision cleared, she saw Ryu had stepped closer to them. Her eyes met his. Was that concern she saw? Regret? Before she could decide, the look was gone. The cold calm returned, and he faced away from her again.

"I want everyone out," he said—another simple command. "You too, Nobu."

"But sir—" the man protested, tightening his grip on Thea's arm. She ground her teeth to keep from crying out, which only made her cheek hurt more.

Ryu whirled around again and grabbed Nobu by the forearm. The man's eyes widened as Ryu's narrowed.

"I won't repeat myself, Nobu."

Slowly, she felt the man's grip slacken. He seemed to hesitate again before finally releasing her. Her fingertips tingled as blood returned to her arm. Footsteps echoed behind her as the room's occupants obeyed Ryu's command. Nobu and the two other guards left last, out a door on one side of the room.

Gram wobbled on his feet without the support of his guards holding him up. Thea stumbled to his side and attempted to ease him to the floor.

"You're hurt," she whispered, her throat tight with worry.

He tried to brush her off with a wave and a chuckle but sucked in a pain-filled breath instead.

"Help him up and follow me."

Thea jumped at the sound of Ryu's even voice behind her. She turned her head to see him step towards the side of the room, toward a different door than the one the guards had exited through. He didn't look at her, but simply motioned for her to follow.

Thea hesitated and looked down at the cuffs on her wrists. She couldn't lift Gram on her own, not without her channeling.

"It's alright," Gram assured her. "I'm fine, I can manage."

Gram let out a groan of pain as he tried to stand.

"No, don't." Thea tried to stop him, worried he might make his injuries worse.

"I forgot about the cuffs," Ryu said as he returned to her side. He reached down and slid his arm under Gram's. His tone hadn't changed, but his voice seemed less menacing somehow, like he'd let out a breath he'd been struggling to hold in. His shoulders hunched slightly, and his chin lowered, like he was embarrassed by his mistake.

Gram groaned through gritted teeth as Ryu hauled him, less gently than Thea would have liked, to his feet.

"Can you stand?" Ryu asked her in his even tone. Thea nodded and heaved herself to her feet, not sure what to think of him. Her legs still wobbled, and her head throbbed even more than it had before, but she took a deep breath and waited for Ryu to lead the way.

Ryu led her down a narrow, wood-paneled corridor. He opened one of the doors near the end of the hallway and motioned for her to enter ahead of him. She stepped into the small living quarters and looked around. She could see a sleeping area through a doorless archway on one side. A couch sat by the door with a small kitchenette in the opposite corner.

Thea jumped and whirled around at the sound of a lock clicking behind her. Ryu's baffling behavior, combined with the disorienting familiarity of the hallways, had caused her to let down her guard.

"I'm sorry," he told her, holding up his free hand placatingly. "I didn't mean to startle you. I simply don't want anyone disturbing us. I promise, I mean you no harm. You should sit."

He gestured toward the sofa and surprised her with a small smile, though his voice remained oddly monotone. Instead of accepting his invitation, she backed away warily. He frowned as though he wasn't used to his suggestions being disregarded and walked Gram toward the couch. He slid his arm out from supporting the other man. Gram let out a groan as he flopped onto the couch. Thea's nostrils flared and she let out a disapproving breath at Ryu's lack of gentleness.

Ryu turned back toward her. His eyes seemed to widen slightly as he met hers. He looked away and let out a sigh as he turned to the small fridge. He pulled out several pieces and wrapped them in a towel.

"I'm sorry Nobu struck you." He didn't meet her eyes as he held the ice out to her. "It was never my intention for you to be hurt."

Thea shook her head. She didn't understand how he could make such an obvious effort to be considerate of her, and yet show so little sympathy for Gram, whose condition was far worse than hers.

"What about him?" she asked accusingly as she motioned toward Gram.

"He's a Peacekeeper," Ryu replied, like he didn't understand why she would ask a question with such an obvious answer.

Thea bristled. Instead of taking the ice he held out to her she crossed her arms stubbornly over her chest.

"He's with me."

Ryu lowered his hand with a frown. Thea flinched as he suddenly stepped closer and raised the cloth-wrapped ice to her cheek. The subtle shift in his expression was hard to read. Confusion maybe? She couldn't be sure.

Her skin stung as the coldness of the ice sunk into her cheek, but the cold also brought relief. She tried not to think about the bruise that must already be forming on her face. With some resignation, she took the ice and held it to her cheek herself. Ryu's shoulders relaxed slightly, and he took a step back from her.

"Nix said I should come here," she went on. "He thought I would be safe here. But if it's not safe for Gram, then it's not safe for me either."

"You don't know what you're saying," Ryu said, his voice harsher than it had been. He smoothed his shirt with both hands as though wiping away his emotions. When he continued, his voice was even and toneless once more. "He's the enemy, simple as that. The moment he crossed our border, his life ended. Even with my position, there's nothing I can do to change that. Once the others are sure we can't learn any valuable information from him, he will be executed."

Thea stepped back in horror but to her surprise, Gram let out a hoarse laugh.

"Don't flatter yourself," he said. "Me? Your enemy? I've got much bigger things to worry about than a kid like you."

He met Thea's eyes and smirked.

"Don't worry about me. Just do what you came here to do."

Ryu's frown deepened, and the flash of anger in his eyes reminded Thea of his sister. She shuddered. Ryu seemed to notice, and the hot anger cooled to something softer.

"Don't get me wrong," he said. "I can offer you my full protection. You are safe here. Nix may have lied to me. I don't know. But what I told him is true."

Thea shook her head and squared her shoulders as she thought about Gram's words. She hadn't come here so Ryu could keep her safe. She'd come here to save Nix.

If she was going to do that, she was going to have to borrow a little bit of his attitude. She crossed her arms over her chest and narrowed her eyes, doing her best to impersonate his surly arrogance.

"Protection?" She tried to snort as he would have, with all the disdain she could muster, as though protection was the last thing she needed from anyone. Her confidence grew as Ryu's expression, so carefully placid until then, fell away in surprise. "I didn't come here for protection. I came here to join you—and to help you—but in return, there's something you have to do for me. Well, two somethings actually."

"What is it?" Ryu asked hesitantly, his voice no longer able to hide behind cold indifference.

"First, this guy is off limits," she said, gesturing to Gram. "From now on, he's under my protection, and I want him under yours as well. I don't care if you think that's impossible. You need to make it possible. No more beating him up. No executions."

Ryu opened his mouth to protest, but Thea didn't give him a chance. She had to keep control of the conversation.

"Second," she said, holding up two fingers. "Both of these things are non-negotiable, by the way. If I don't get either one, I take my friend, and I walk."

She narrowed her eyes and paused, waiting for him to acknowledge his understanding. He clenched his jaw, staring back at her stubbornly before finally giving a slight nod. "Go on."

"Nix has been taken by the Military." Her voice cracked on the words and her bravado slipped. "We want to get him back. You're going to help us."

Whatever Ryu had expected her to say, it wasn't this. Shock spread across his face. He opened his mouth, then closed it again. Finally, he looked away and let out a dark laugh.

"You've got to be joking."

His voice turned quiet and cold. This wasn't indifference or surprise. This was years of pent up hurt and anger. She clenched her fists tight and lifted her chin stubbornly, but her voice still shook when she answered.

"I'm not."

"You don't know what you're asking," he spat. His eyes narrowed, and he squared his own shoulders like someone issuing a command.

"Even if it were possible," he continued, "why would I agree to help a traitor? Even if I were willing to help, most of my clan would be all too happy to let Nix rot in a Military research facility. The only thing that would make them happier would be if they could kill him themselves."

His words didn't surprise her. She knew what Nix had done. She knew how the Syndicate must view him. She knew how Ryu had felt about him, and how much his betrayal must have hurt. In spite of all that, she didn't miss the desperation in Ryu's voice or the frantic panic in his movements as he began to pace.

"You don't understand!" he pleaded when she didn't react to his words. "I have a responsibility to my people. Even if I wanted to, helping Nix would be as much a betrayal as what he's done."

He wanted to give in to her demand, she realized. He just needed her to convince him that it was okay. Any remaining fear she felt melted away with the realization. He no longer seemed intimidating or commanding. Underneath his cold exterior he was still the same hurt, scared boy she'd seen in her dream.

"I know what they did." Thea's voice softened. "Nix and your sister. I also know Nix saved you. Did you know he nearly died because of it?"

Ryu stopped pacing and stared at her in surprise. His eyes darted to Gram as though questioning if he was the source of her information.

"Don't look at me," Gram said with a grin. "Nix didn't suddenly become the talkative type in the last five years."

Ryu looked back at her, searching her face in confusion, as though he could find the answer there. He looked down at her wrists, then his jaw clenched, and he met her eyes, his expression hardening again.

"If you know all that, then you know there's nothing I can do. I didn't have Nix killed when he was here. As far as I'm concerned, my debt to him is paid. Besides, his past actions aren't even the issue anymore. I don't know where you got your information, but it's clearly incomplete. Nix isn't being held prisoner by the Military. He's joined them. He and my sister both. They've been raiding Syndicate hideouts for weeks. Nix doesn't need to be rescued. He needs to be stopped."

"Oh, I know all that," she said patiently, trying to sound confident without coming across as patronizing. "Nix turned himself over to the Military because he thought it was the only way to protect me. Looks like things didn't quite go the way he planned, which is why I'm so mad at him. Now we not only have to rescue him, we have to stop him, your sister, and the Military all at the same time. Like I've been saying all along, you are going to help me. That's not negotiable."

"That's not—" Ryu tried to correct her, but she continued.

"Now I don't know exactly where all these places are, so I'll just have to describe them to you. You tell me if they've already been attacked."

Now she was the one who began to pace back and forth as she listed off locations. Ryu's eyes grew wider with each one. Even knowing the locations themselves would have been a surprise, but she could tell him details no one should know unless they had been there.

"Wait," Ryu stopped her. "There's been no report of the Military moving that far west."

"Then that's probably where they will move next," Thea told him with a nod. "Unfortunately, I can't tell you when."

"How did you—?"

"I told you I came to join you. Did you think I would make such a difficult, non-negotiable request if I didn't have something to offer in return?"

The last of Ryu's coldness seemed to crumble away all at once and for the first time, he seemed to be just himself. He stared at her with wide eyes and his mouth slightly open. His face reddened—not with anger, but with something like admiration. Her own face flushed, and she looked away.

He cleared his throat before stammering, "How...How did you know all that?"

"I saw it," her face burned hotter, and her voice squeaked. Now that she had his full attention, her confidence plummeted. She felt exposed as she explained, "I can't really control it, but I can see things that are going to happen. And things that have happened."

"How long have you been able to do this?"

He looked at her with a kind of sad empathy, like he recognized something in her he could relate to. It made her feel vulnerable, like he could see past her bravado to the broken cracks she was trying to keep hidden.

"I think you already know that I was in a Military research facility." Her voice came out quiet and shaky. "I don't know if this was something I could do before or not. I..."

She'd been trying so desperately to hold herself together ever since Nix had left, but as she saw the pity in Ryu's eyes, she was reminded just how broken she was. Now all the cracks she'd so carefully covered up felt like they were growing and expanding. Her mother's death. Her father's grief. Her struggles with her own health. The experiments. Kai's injury.

Kai.

His loss was the final blow that had left her shattered, a heap of the pieces of her former self. She had tried to pick up those pieces, hold them all together, but she couldn't. She was just as broken as she'd ever been. More broken.

Ryu said something. She couldn't hear his words over the ringing in her ears, but she thought maybe he was apologizing.

A hand touched her elbow gently, making her jump. It was Gram. She could see the worry in his expression even through his grimace of pain. She didn't resist as he led her toward the couch.

"You alright?" he asked her.

She nodded numbly, though of course she wasn't.

"Here." Ryu pressed something into her hands. Something to drink. She raised the cup to her lips, half expecting Lucan's citrusy herbal tea. Instead, she was met with a pungent smell and a bitter taste. It reminded her of something Kai would have made. She choked on a bitter laugh, and then the tears came.

Her body started to shake with sobs as tears poured down her cheeks. She felt someone take the cup from her hands, felt the comforting weight of Gram's large hand on her back. He wrapped one arm around her shoulders as she curled her knees up between them, forming herself into a ball against him.

She cried until she was dry and spent. As her sobs finally stilled, she kept her swollen eyes shut though she doubted she would find any comfort in sleep.

Part Three

Out of Darkness

Here I sit alone
With the metallic taste
Of chemicals on my tongue
And my body aching
To my bones

I don't regret the choice
I made for you
To give up everything
And face my darkness
And my past
To save you

Here I sit alone
In this unfamiliar
Place so far from
Anywhere I ever
Called home
Surrounded by
wary glances
And whispering voices
Discontent for who I am
And what I want
From them

I don't regret the choice
I made for you
To face my fears
And run toward everything
I ever ran away from
Just to save you

Now that silence fills my thoughts
I miss the comfort of your voice
And though you're far away
I hear you
Like a memory
Or maybe a wish
For what can never be
Maybe the one thing I regret
Is that I wasted the time
We could have had
By running from what I
Wanted to be
From what I saw in you
That reminded me of me

Chapter Twenty-three

Nix wretched, though there was nothing left in his stomach to throw up. His evening meal sat uneaten on the small table of the room where he was being held. He'd returned to his room from the research lab, too weak and sick to do anything other than collapse on his bed. His stomach had other ideas, though. He'd barely had the strength to make it to the toilet, and after emptying his stomach, he didn't have the energy to return to the hard bed or attempt to eat his food when it arrived.

Not that he'd had much of an appetite since turning himself in.

He let out a shaky breath and leaned his head back against the wall, closing his eyes.

His body hurt, inside and out. His skin felt raw, like he'd been pricked by a thousand needles, and his muscles ached from the physical and mental stress of the experiments.

He'd felt it all before, of course. His telepathy had made him a prime research subject for both the Syndicate and the Military.

It wasn't his own experiences that came to mind, though, when every shift of his weight made him want to throw up again.

It was hers. Her nightmares and her fears.

Somehow, he'd let himself forget just how awful the experiments were, or maybe he'd simply become numb to the fear and the memories after so many years of being a target. For her, the memories had been fresh, the fear imminent.

He really hadn't made it any easier for her.

It was the first time in his life that he wished he could go back. Maybe if he'd done things differently, it all wouldn't have turned out the way it had.

He didn't regret turning himself in. He'd make the same decision again in the same circumstances, but if he hadn't tried to run from her, maybe they both could have found another way to live.

At the very least, Kai would still be alive.

The room's heavy door opened with a screech.

How long had he been sitting there by the toilet, too weak to even stand? Had he fallen asleep? Had they come to take him back to the lab already? His body tensed and his heart began to race, making his headache even worse.

He didn't want to go back.

"It's okay boys, you can leave us alone. This one's lost all his fight, it seems."

Kaori.

His eyes snapped open, and his heart raced faster, this time with anger. He could see her silhouette through the cloudy partition that divided the bathroom from the rest of the room. She stood in the doorway with her hand on one hip and he could easily imagine the smirk he heard in her voice.

The haze of numbness that had clouded his head since he'd woken up in his cell cleared, but the weakness and pain remained. He wanted to jump to his feet, slam her against the wall, wrap his hands around her neck and choke the laughter from her throat, but it was all he could do to even stand.

He stumbled toward her anyway. All she did was laugh.

"Well, I'm glad to see you haven't broken completely, Ghost. I'd be disappointed if you had."

"Why are you here?" he asked through gritted teeth as he steadied himself with one hand on the wall.

"For the same reason as you," she said, tossing her hair. "For a noble and worthy cause."

He let out a snarl and made his best attempt to lunge for her. He didn't even get close before pain shot through his body and he found himself back on the floor, crumbled in a heap as electricity poured from his kill node. Once the pain subsided, he struggled to his knees, biting back the groan of pain that threatened to escape his lips. He glared at Kaori defiantly.

"That's more like it," she said, though her smirk seemed shallow, like she was forcing herself to act nonchalant. "The only question is, what are you going to do next?"

She tossed her hair again as she spun away and stepped out the door.

Nix snorted as he struggled to his feet again. If Kaori was worrying about him, then he really was pathetic.

She was right though. He'd almost given up, wished the Military would just execute him instead of putting him through this hell.

He staggered toward his cold meal, still sitting on the table.

Hell was nothing new to him. Confinement, experimentation, cruelty from his guards. He'd survived it all before. At least the Military actually fed him.

He had no intention of ever getting out of here, but that didn't mean he had to give in to the numbness and the pain. His life belonged to the Military, but that didn't mean he had to simply accept defeat. He wasn't that weak.

He'd spent half his life playing losing games with Kaori. If there was one thing he knew how to do, it was how to get back up, and keep stubbornly, persistently trying to keep up with her.

If she was here, it meant she was still playing games. This time he wasn't going to let her win.

His newfound determination didn't make the experiments any less painful. In some ways, it was harder without the numb fog he'd let himself slip into. With his resolve came more clarity and more anxiety. He was more aware of the passage of time, of the long hours cooped up and confined in his cell. His stomach twisted every time his door opened, anticipating the grueling tests to come.

He was surprised when the door opened and instead of another name-less guard, Mel appeared in the doorway.

"Come on," she said. "Time to get you out of here."

"Why?" Nix blurted with a shake of his head.

She knew he had no desire to be set free. That would defeat the purpose of why he'd come here in the first place.

Mel jerked her chin slightly toward the guard hovering behind her and shook her head. Whatever was going on, she wasn't going to tell him until they were alone. Nix stood, his legs still wobbling slightly, and followed her out of the cell.

The guard moved to block his path, flexing his muscles with a frown.

"Step aside," Mel barked, "unless you want to be the one in a cell."

The guard flared his nostrils, his face red, but he moved out of the way. Nix threw him a sideways glance as he followed Mel down the hall.

"What was that about?" he muttered.

"They're idiots," Mel spat as she slowed to walk beside him. She leaned in close to whisper, "the truth is things have been pretty grim around here lately. There's been more and more discontent since the new Grand Marshal was appointed. Different factions are forming, and loyalties are divided, even within the individual divisions. Having you here only complicates things. It's the same old story. No one agrees on what to do with you, and the ones who didn't get their way are likely to make a fuss."

Nix wasn't sure why Mel was telling him this, but he didn't say anything as they stepped out of the Research building, where he'd been held until then. The sudden light made him dizzy, and he thought he might throw up again, but he did his best to keep up with Mel as she strode briskly across the open space toward the prison complex. Soldiers stopped to whisper and glare at them as they passed. Mel appeared to be ignoring them, though Nix noticed her eyes darting around warily. Once they'd finally reached the tall building on the opposite side of the compound, she let out a relieved breath.

"Last time I checked," Nix whispered as they entered the elevator, "the Commander was one of the people who wanted me dead."

He still didn't know what decisions had been made about his imprisonment, only that he'd been taken to the research labs for regular testing since turning himself in.

Mel shook her head again with a sad looking smile as she scanned her ID and pressed the button for the second highest floor.

"I'm sorry it's taken us so long to get you transferred," she said. "I'll explain it all later but for now try not to provoke the Commander too much, okay? He's definitely more on edge than usual."

Nix had been to the upper floors of the prison complex only once, on the night he'd escaped from the Military years ago. He'd never made it to the top floor though. He and Gram had been cornered on one of the lower floors and Nix had been forced to make a dangerous jump out the window. He'd barely made it, leaving Gram to his fate alone.

Now Nix had once again left Gram behind to pick up the pieces of his own decisions.

The elevator dinged and Nix followed Mel out into a carpeted hallway.

"The top floor is the Commander's floor," Mel explained as they rounded the corner and stopped in front of a cluster of doors. "We'll go there later, but first you need to get cleaned up."

She opened the door and motioned him inside.

"This room is yours," Mel said as she entered behind him. "Mine is across the hall."

"Why?" Nix asked again. "I'm a prisoner. Why not leave me in the prison."

"You're supposed to say thank you," Mel chided, like a mother correcting an impolite child. "There's a bathroom there and clothes in the wardrobe. Once you're ready, come to my room across the hall. I'll explain everything."

She left him alone and Nix took a moment to look around the room.

A bed stood on the far wall next to a tall wardrobe. A microwave sat on top of a small shelving unit near the door. The shelves were stacked with packaged meals along with disposable cups and utensils. The only other furniture in the room was a small round table and a single hard chair. A doorway near the bed opened into the bathroom.

Nix pulled open one of the meals and tossed it in the microwave before crossing to the window above the bed. He was disappointed to find that it had been sealed shut. He supposed they had good reason to believe he could escape out the window, even from this height, but he hadn't been wearing ability restrictors the last time.

Even so, the room was an improvement over the small dim room from the Research building, even if he couldn't open the window. It didn't feel so much like the walls were closing in. He only wished the air was less stuffy. He looked around again and found a small air unit hanging on the wall near the wardrobe. He switched it on and lowered the temperature several degrees before closing his eyes, enjoying the feel of the cool air blowing in his face.

After eating his meal and showering, Nix opened the wardrobe to find several sets of dark blue, Military-issue clothing. Though there were no markings or insignia on the uniforms, he felt strange wearing them, like it only made him stand out more. He was grateful for the jacket, even if wearing Military clothing and covering his tattoo would do nothing to hide his identity.

He looked wistfully toward the stack of meals, even though he'd already eaten one. He had kept Mel waiting long enough. He grabbed a meal bar and tucked it into his pocket before opening the door and stepping out into the hallway.

Mel snorted when she opened her door and saw him.

"A Military uniform doesn't suit you at all," she exclaimed before her snort turned into a laugh.

She opened her door wider and waved him into her room.

Her quarters were identical to his, only less sparsely furnished. The bed was piled with pillows and a curtain hung over the window, casting the room in soft color. Two stuffed chairs crowded around the small table next to a tall cupboard filled with ceramic dishes and knickknacks. A deep bookcase stood on the adjacent wall and paintings hung on the remaining wall space.

Mel slid an already warmed meal across the table toward him and poured hot water into a mug for herself. She popped a tea pouch into her mug and sat down in the chair across from him.

"I'm glad the clothes fit okay," she said, tilting her head with an amused smile.

Nix nodded absently as he pulled the meal closer.

"Have you heard from Lucan?" he asked, hoping she could give him news about the others.

Mel shook her head.

"He didn't tell me much. I think he doesn't want me to feel like I have to cover for them. Gram called me before they left the city, though. Said they were going west."

They had gone to the Syndicate then. Knowing didn't give him any sense of relief. Even if it was their only option, it was still a risk—especially for Gram.

"I'm worried about them too," Mel said, "but try to cheer up. I'm sure you'll see them again."

"Not if I can help it," Nix said.

Mel frowned but didn't press him.

"For now, you should eat," she said. "We can talk more when you're finished. We can't have you looking so thin and hungry. What do you think Gram would say?"

"He'd call me a dumbass," Nix mumbled, picking up his utensil.

"Ha! He totally would! Well, we can't have that, so eat up."

Mel picked up her tablet and started to read. Nix ate his food in silence. When he had scraped the last of the food from the tray, he pushed it away from him and waited for Mel to look up from her tablet.

Her eyes met his, and all trace of her usual humor disappeared. She slid the tablet across to him with a frown, and she no longer seemed like the jovial friend of Gram's he'd always known. She was every bit an upper ranking Military officer about to give him a briefing.

"You wanted to know why I brought you out of the prison," she said. "These are our orders."

Nix picked up the tablet, but before he could do more than scan the documents displayed on the screen, Mel began to summarize.

"Commander Nolan Astley of the Military Police, under the jurisdiction of Marshal William Barton of the Operations Division, has been granted full access to the prisoner known as Nix, for the use of field operations," Mel quoted, then smiled. "Basically, Operations is creating a special unit and you're going to be on it."

Nix looked at Mel in surprise then down at the tablet again, quickly scanning the words.

He knew that during his previous imprisonment some of the Military leaders had wanted to use him, and his ability, against the Syndicate. Too many had been opposed to the idea, including the Commander himself. It seemed that faction had won out this time.

He was indeed being assigned to a special unit for the purpose of providing tactical information on the locations of Syndicate hideouts and troop movements. The Commander was to oversee operations and Captain Melinda Gale—Mel—was to act as his handler.

After he'd finished reading, he leaned back in his chair, his brow furrowed and his thoughts racing with the implication of what this assignment meant.

"I'm sorry," Mel said, startling him out of his thoughts. "This might not be an easy assignment for you."

Nix shrugged. He had left the Syndicate, but there was still a part of him that had never stopped thinking of himself as one of them. The Syndicate called him a traitor, even though most of them were just as eager to betray each other for more trivial reasons than he had. If he did this, though—if he used his knowledge to help the Military attack the Syndicate—he really would be a traitor.

"I knew something like this was a possibility when I chose to come here," he said. "It doesn't change anything."

Mel frowned, but didn't question his response. Instead, she cleared her throat and continued her explanation.

"Our team will be centered around the use of your telepathy. Our primary objective will be intel, but if we can take decisive action, we've been ordered to do so."

Nix glanced down at the tablet again and let out a snort.

"Do they realize they're going to have to remove these in order for this plan to work?"

He held up one arm, nodding toward the cuff on his wrist as though it was something ordinary.

Mel nodded solemnly.

"I've been given the assignment to supervise you," she said, her voice slightly less steady than it had been. "The rest of our team has been carefully chosen, both for their abilities as well as their loyalty to the Commander. He's certain we can deal with any disobedience on your part."

"How many?" Nix asked.

"Four including myself. Two manipulators and two skilled enhancers."

Nix shook his head as he crossed his arms over his chest.

"It won't be enough."

He wasn't trying to be arrogant, but he wondered if Mel's superiors had really thought things through.

To his surprise Mel laughed.

"I happen to know a Micro who can take you down, so don't get cocky."

"He's not here," Nix grumbled, looking away. "I just don't want to see you get blamed if something goes wrong."

Mel's grin faded as she reached into her pocket, pulling out a small device with two buttons and a dial. She placed it on the table in front of her without meeting his eyes. Nix didn't have to be told what it was. This wasn't the first time he'd been implanted with a kill node, and he easily recognized the controller. He rubbed his shoulder absently, trying not to think of the countless times he'd felt that pain.

"Don't make me have to use this, okay?"

Nix nodded and swallowed, trying to clear the lump from his throat before speaking. Even so, his voice came out quiet and hoarse.

"I never had any intention of running."

Mel checked her watch and stood up with a tight smile.

"Come on. We should be heading to the Commander's office."

Nix hesitated, wondering how the other soldiers would react to being forced onto a team with him—the Syndicate criminal responsible for killing so many of their comrades and stealing so much of their information.

He thought of the Commander's reaction to seeing him on Market Day—red faced, angry. The way people looked at him when he walked through the streets of town—as a danger, as a threat, as a weapon.

"Why are you doing this Mel?" he asked, his voice barely above a whisper. "Why is the Commander doing this?"

Why wasn't he in a cell, where he belonged?

Mel moved her chair around the table to sit next to him. She placed one hand on his forearm, a gentle, comforting gesture. Like Gram, she had never treated him like a monster or a weapon.

"What is it that makes you so certain you deserve to be locked up?" she asked, her question catching him off guard. It wasn't what he had expected her to say. "Is it so hard to believe that there are people capable of seeing you for who you are, and valuing you for it? There are a lot of monsters here. You aren't one of them, and I know there are people who will see that. I trust the Commander, and I trust my team. I hope you will too."

Nix was so surprised he didn't know what to say, so he just nodded.

"When you left," Mel continued with a nod, "Gram called the Commander. Obviously, he wanted the Commander to help you, but he also told the Commander about his son."

Mel's voice caught. She didn't even know Kai, but it was just like her to feel sorrow for someone else's loss.

"I don't know exactly what Gram said to him, but I doubt words alone were what convinced him. I think losing his son had a big impact on him. Either way, you should know, the Commander has done everything he could to get you released. I hope you can forgive him for how he's treated you in the past."

Nix nodded again, then added, "Thanks, Mel. I'm sorry I didn't mean..."

Mel shook her head and held up her hand, cutting him off.

"I'm sorry for the things the Military has done to you. I'm not excusing any of that. I just wanted you to know that we aren't all the same. There are good people here too."

She stood up again.

"You okay? You ready."

Nix nodded and stood up as well.

"Yeah, I'm ready."

I see him sitting alone in a room without windows and only a single door. I think it might be a prison cell. I know it's not the Syndicate prison. It looks similar to the room where I was held at the research facility.

He looks younger, so I think this is the past. His hand is wrapped in a bandage, and he looks pale, the way he did after Kaori poisoned him.

Someone enters the room and deactivates the channeling restrictors on his writs. I can't see who it is because I'm seeing the dream through that person's eyes. They are taller than Nix, and every step is painful, like they've recently been hurt. That doesn't stop them from leading Nix at a run down twisting hallways and up a dim stairwell.

An alarm screeches in our ears, echoing off the walls. It makes it hard to tell whether the sound of stomping boots is coming from above or below us. Maybe it's both. His telepathy must be working again because he clutches his head in pain, overwhelmed by all the thoughts of the surrounding city.

He tells me that they are trying to cut us off from the elevator above and I know we'll never make it to the upper floor. Instead, I lead him out of the stairwell and down another hallway to an empty conference room. Tall windows line one of the walls. I can see that we're high up, but that the surrounding buildings are much higher. I wonder if he can make the jump, but he just smirks at me before breaking the nearest window with a chair.

I hand him my jacket, though it's several sizes too big, and a folded paper map. The look he gives me is hard to read. I wonder if he's worried about me, and it makes me want to laugh. Neither one of us says anything. Then he turns away, jumps, and is gone. Soldiers burst into the room, guns pointed in my direction. I raise my hands with a laugh and the next thing I know I'm on the floor, hands jerked behind my back and cuffs locked around my wrists. They don't even bother to be careful about my injuries. I don't really care. He got away and that's what matters.

Chapter Twenty-four

The Commander's office was on the top floor behind a set of thick, imposing wooden doors.

Mel knocked softly before entering, an action that seemed more like a formality than a request for permission, as she didn't hesitate before reaching for the handle and opening the doors.

Nix did hesitate, but Mel smiled encouragingly over her shoulder and gave his sleeve a little tug, so he followed her inside the spacious, wood-paneled room.

The Commander sat at a large wooden desk in front of a wall of windows. He didn't look up from his tablet or even acknowledge that they had entered.

Another man sat on one of two leather sofas closer to the door. He had a hawkish face, neatly combed dark hair, and sharply pressed creases in his uniform. Nix thought he recognized him from Market Day. His look of disdain as they entered did little to ease Nix's nerves.

"Let me introduce you," Mel said, motioning Nix toward the sofas. "This is Alec Barton, he—"

"Major Barton," the man interrupted her. "And that's all he needs to know."

Mel let out a tired sounding sigh and forced a smile.

"Let's just sit down for now."

She sat on the sofa across from the other man and Nix sat beside her stiffly. A tray sat on the table in front of them, with four ceramic cups on small plates, along with an assortment of pastries and fruit. Mel handed him a cup and motioned for him to help himself to the food before selecting a small biscuit for herself.

Nix felt more out of place than he ever had in his life. His eyes darted between the contemptuous face of the man across from him, and the still silent commander, stoically continuing to read at his desk as if they weren't even there. Only after Mel began to pile his small plate with food did he hesitantly pick up a pastry and take a bite. He could feel it in his mouth, but aside from recognizing a light sweetness, he could have been chewing on sand, his mouth felt so dry. He took a sip from his cup to help him swallow.

The Commander, at last, stood up from his desk and moved toward them.

"I trust the relocation went smoothly?" he asked Mel as he took a seat across from them and reached for one of the cups.

"One of the guards tried to give me a hard time, but nothing too serious," she said casually, as though Nix wasn't there, and they weren't talking about moving him from what was essentially a prison cell.

"And the room? Was everything arranged satisfactorily?"

Mel looked at Nix questioningly and he gave her an uncertain nod, not sure the question was meant for him.

"It looks so plain," Mel said with a shrug, "but I guess it'll do."

The Commander took a sip from his cup before setting it back on the table. He cleared his throat and interlaced his fingers under his chin. The gesture reminded Nix so much of Kai that he nearly dropped his cup. He winced as hot liquid sloshed over his fingers and dripped onto the floor. The Commander shot him a perturbed look but didn't comment. Nix set his cup on the table and wiped his stinging fingers on his pants.

"You've all had a chance to read the briefing, so I won't mince words." He locked eyes with Nix. "This team wasn't formed out of a sense of sympathy or as an attempt to subvert the Research Division's authority. This team was formed to get results. If we don't fulfill our assignment, you all will be returned to your regular duties, and the prisoner will be returned to Research. Is that understood?"

The message was clear. *I didn't do this for you.*

Nix nodded, and the others answered, "Yes, sir," though Mel's voice came out quieter than the man's. The Commander met her eyes, and something changed in his expression, something that reminded Nix of Ryu and the way he tried to hide his hurt beneath the cold mask he'd adopted from his father.

Nix realized that he didn't know much about the Commander.

The Commander turned to the man sitting across from Nix.

"You have the operation report?"

The man nodded and picked up his own tablet from the table.

"Reports from the operation teams state that though evidence has been found of Syndicate locations in the Eastern Territory, most of the identified locations have either been abandoned or housed only minor operations, such as information gathering. The conclusion is that the information provided by Intelligence has been unreliable and ineffective."

"Where have you been getting your information?" Nix interrupted. The man shot him a glare and seemed ready to reprimand him, but the Commander spoke first.

"Barton, I want you and Gale to go over the report with Nix later to compare what he knows about these locations."

Nix turned to the Commander in surprise. To his knowledge, the Commander had only ever referred to him as *the prisoner* or *the criminal*, never by name.

The Commander laced his fingers under his chin again and Nix looked away.

"Reizen Suoh's daughter has been cooperating with Intelligence to provide information for some time," he said.

Kaori.

"You can't trust her," Nix said.

"Who said I did?" the Commander snapped. "I don't want her here anymore than I want you here, but in her case, it's out of my hands."

The Commander took a deep breath before continuing.

"She's an Intelligence operative, and therefore outside my jurisdiction. Our contact with her has always been minimal, but my superiors want to ensure that this remains especially true in your case."

"Then they aren't doing a very good job," Nix grumbled. "She came to my cell before Mel did."

"You're out of line," Barton barked.

The Commander held up his hand to indicate that it was okay.

"As I said, she's out of my hands. Going forward you will be with an escort from my team at all times. If Kaori Suoh attempts to make contact with you, I want to know about it. Is that understood?"

"Yes, sir," Mel and Barton spoke in unison.

"As far as I see it, she is of little value to our operation. I don't trust her information. Whatever her motives for being here, I believe she only shares what information she wants us to know. Relying on her is dangerous.

Nix scoffed. That pretty much summed up Kaori.

"I'm counting on you to do better," the Commander added, "but let's be clear, I don't trust you either. I'm not going to pretend like you are here for any reason than your own agenda either. It just so happens that in your case, I know what that agenda is. However, if at anytime your information no longer becomes useful, or if you put my people at unnecessary risk, I will return you to the Research Division."

Nix nodded but the Commander hardly seemed to care whether he responded or not. He stood dismissively.

"Barton, Gale, I'll trust you to update me on further details."

"Yes, sir."

Barton and Mel both stood and Nix followed, feeling out of place again as the two soldiers saluted. Once they'd exited the office Mel bumped his shoulder.

"That wasn't so bad, was it?"

Nix shrugged. He wasn't being returned to his cell so he supposed it could be a lot worse.

"So how about we go meet the rest of the team?" Mel asked with a grin.

"This is the big scary Syndicate criminal everyone's been going on about? He doesn't look that impressive."

Barton didn't join them as Mel took him downstairs to one of the training rooms. The room was empty except for a man and a woman, who stopped sparring when the two of them entered.

The woman who'd spoken was taller than Mel, and younger. Her white-blonde hair was shaved short aside from a messy tuft of waves on top of her head. Her sleeveless training shirt showed off the well-defined muscles of her arms, but that didn't mean she was skilled. Nix just crossed his arms with a scowl and let out a snort to show he was the one who was unimpressed.

The man next to her let out a loud guffaw. Nix recognized him as the man he'd met in Karza, the one who had followed him to the tavern.

"Damn, please let these two fight, Mel," the man said, reinforcing the impression Nix had of him as someone who enjoyed a little bit of trouble. "I really need to see Keller get her ass kicked."

"Shut up, Jax," the woman spat before Mel could respond.

"Quiet, both of you," Mel sighed with a slight roll of her eyes before turning back to Nix. "These two are Brinn Keller and Jack Jaxon, but everyone calls him Jax."

She gestured to each in turn and added, "Keller is an enhancer and Jax is our other manipulator."

She turned to the two soldiers with a mischievous smile.

"You've probably heard a lot about this guy, but don't let his reputation fool you. He's really just a problem child, not much different than the two of you."

"What, are you our mom now?" Keller asked in a tone that did not make her sound less childish.

"That's right," Mel answered with a wave of her index finger. "Now play nice and make friends, so I don't have to knock your heads together."

"I guess that means no sparring," Jax said, sounding disappointed.

"Actually, Jax, that's not a bad idea," Mel said with a shrug. "There's no better way to orient a new squad than a good sparring match. It'd be a good way for us to get used to each other's techniques."

"Hell yeah!" Jax, said with a grin. "I've always wanted to get some payback for your escape. I can't believe Gram shot me that night!"

Nix stiffened. It wouldn't be the first time his captors had taken advantage of the fact that he couldn't fight back. He was sure Mel would try to stop him if he attacked, but what about the woman? Would Mel be able to stop both of them on her own? With the channeling restrictors on Nix couldn't do much to back her up. And what was he supposed to do when she wasn't around?

He braced himself but to his surprise Mel just laughed.

"I'm not sure how well that's going to work out for you Jax, but it'll have to wait until later." She made a face of disgust. "Barton and I have to write an operation report, and we need Nix to help us go over the report from Intel."

The large man named Jax laughed.

"Not sure what sucks more, having to write an op report or having to do it with Barton."

Mel just smirked.

"That guy is way too uptight," the woman said with a laugh. "But then his hero is Commander Astley so—"

"Shut up, Keller," Jax said, giving her a shove. The look on his face told Nix that what she'd said had crossed a line.

"What, you know it's true," she shot back. "No one is more uptight than the Commander."

"That's enough, Keller," Mel said, her tone harsh enough to make the woman hunch in chagrin before crossing her arms over her chest and looking away with a click of her tongue.

Jax rolled his eyes and turned back to Nix with a grin.

"Don't worry about her. She just doesn't know when to shut her mouth."

He dodged a punch from Keller with a laugh before continuing.

"Anyway, welcome to the team, I guess. You two want to get some food before you get stuck in report writing hell? Or we could do that sparring, no abilities of course, unless Mel wants to take those cuffs off."

He raised his eyebrows at Mel hopefully, but she just shook her head with a laugh.

"You're hopeless, Jax," she said. "But we'd better get going. I promise I'll set something up soon. You've given me an idea and I think you're gonna like it."

She winked at Nix and nudged for him to follow her from the training room. Before they'd even reached the door, Nix could hear Keller and Jax already bickering behind him.

"Can you imagine what it was like to have Gram and Jax on the same team?" Mel asked with a laugh as they rode the elevator back up to the floor with their sleeping quarters. "Those two certainly gave the Commander a lot of headaches."

Nix snorted. From what he could tell, Jax's personality was like Gram's on boosters, and the Commander only barely seemed capable of tolerating Gram. He could only imagine what the pair of them would have done to the stoic man's nerves.

"What about the other guy?" Nix asked, thinking of Barton. The others had called him uptight. Nix would have said high-strung, seemingly always ready to snap at the least bit of impertinence.

Mel laughed much harder than he thought his question warranted.

"You mean Barton?"

"Yeah," Nix said. "What's his deal?"

Mel shrugged.

"Some people say it's because his dad is a marshal, but I've known Alec since we were kids and he's always been that way. Serious. He's smart though, and in spite of what you might think, he's fair. Follow orders and do your job and you'll be alright with him."

Nix scowled and Mel laughed again.

"Yeah, I forgot who I was talking to," she said. "I guess following orders isn't your strong suit, is it? Well, to answer your question, he and Gram never really got along."

Nix smiled with another snort. That was something that did not surprise Nix in the least.

Instead of returning to their rooms, Mel led Nix in the opposite direction away from the elevators. They entered a large conference room. Barton was already there, sitting at the long table, looking at his tablet.

"What took you so long. We have work to do," he said without looking up.

"I wanted to introduce Nix to the others," Mel said with a shrug. She didn't seem put off by Barton's temperament, like she was used to it.

"Well, let's get started."

He tapped on his tablet a few times, and a projection appeared on the wall behind him. Nix scanned the words as he followed Mel to a seat, his brows already pulling together.

"These are the locations Kaori gave you?" he asked.

Barton nodded and Nix scoffed.

"She's been playing you then. Do you have a map?"

Barton swiped his screen to bring up a map, then tapped a few times so they could still see the report. Nix stood and stepped closer.

"It's not easy to get people inside the city itself," he said, pointing to the large outer wall. "The Syndicate has always managed to find someone willing to share information for a price, but that's about the best they can do."

Nix tapped the area on the map that represented the crowded, derelict outer city, sprawling away from the wall.

"The slums are a different story. The Military really takes for granted how easy it is to hide in a place filled with people that no one cares about."

Barton frowned but didn't comment on Nix's remark.

"You're saying there's a Syndicate hideout in the slums?" Mel asked, sounding shocked.

Nix nodded. All the locations Kaori had given them were further from the city, and most were little more than rest stops—similar to the old outpost he and Kaori had stopped at on the way to Chusan.

He took a deep breath and tried to ignore the uncomfortable reticence itching the back of his mind, calling him a traitor.

He'd decided to do this. There was no point feeling guilty about it now.

He pinched the map, zooming and swiping the projection until he found what he was looking for.

"Here," he said. "This shop is a front. It's close enough to the main road to allow easy access to suppliers and to transport goods away from the city. It's one way the Syndicate gets supplies from the east. It's a lot cheaper to acquire the goods locally and transport them than to buy them from merchants in Karza. Though selling some of the goods at the Market for an increased price is the main way they get money for the supplies in the first place."

"I had no idea, but it makes sense," Mel said.

Barton just nodded for Nix to continue.

"Informants from the city can visit the shop without raising much suspicion, even if it is a little out of the way compared to other shops. They can simply claim the prices are better or that it's the only store that carries exactly what they're looking for. The shop probably keeps some unique items on display to support this claim, though you'll find there's no actual stock for them."

"And how can we be sure this location is still in operation?" Barton asked, no doubt referring to the fact that several of the locations Kaori had given the Military were no longer in use.

"This isn't some ordinary hideout," Nix said, shaking his head. "Setting up an operation like this, especially without drawing unwanted attention from officials or citizens, isn't easy to do. The only reason to change the location would be if it had been compromised. Since it's not already in your report, that must not be the case."

"Then I guess we have our first target," Barton said, picking up his tablet and zooming the map out slightly to examine the surrounding area.

I don't know what's past or future. It's hard to even tell if these are Nix's memories, or my own.

The cold of the lab is a familiar contrast to the burning heat I know waits in the pod in front of me. The greenish lights aren't bright, but they sear my eyes and make my head pound. The sludgy medicine sticks in my throat, making me gag.

I think this dream is about him, though. The room where they are keeping him is different than the one in my memories. A part of me wishes I didn't have to see it, to know how he's suffering, especially when it triggers my own worst fears. Part of me is glad, though, that he's not suffering alone. I only wish there was a way to let him know I'm here.

The room changes. This one is large and brightly lit. People—soldiers—surround the edges of the room. I can hear their thoughts, a mix of anger and curiosity. I recognize a few of them. Gram's friend, Mel, as well as the older man who stopped us in the canyon.

I've never met the Commander before, but I recognize him. He looks so much like Kai. I always thought Kai and I looked alike, but really, it's just our hair that makes us look similar. No one who ever saw his father could deny that Kai was his son.

The dream changes again and now Nix is on the ground. Someone is kicking him, laughing cruelly at his helplessness. Maybe it's a memory, because next Nix is the one kicking someone else, anger filling his head like a fog, adrenaline taking control of his body until hands pull him away.

I see the Commander again, frowning. His head drops into his hands, and he looks tired. The room has changed again. It looks like an office, full of expensive wooden furniture. He lifts his head and opens a drawer with shaking hands before taking out an envelope. The paper looks yellowed around the edges, like someone sent it to him several years ago. The seal on the back remains intact. The envelope has never been opened, its contents never read.

The handwriting is small, elegant, looping.

I recognize it.

It looks like my mother's handwriting.

He slides his finger under the seal, hesitates, then breaks the glue and reads the letter.

Chapter Twenty-five

Nix had stayed with Mel and Barton until late in the night, discussing different methods for an operation against the shop. Even after returning to his room, Nix couldn't sleep. Mel had left a tablet with him, with access to the reports, but no access to communication. He'd spent hours reading through the intel Kaori had provided, and making notes, trying to figure out what she could be planning. It was early morning when he'd finally gone to sleep.

He struggled to open his eyes when Mel knocked on his door only a few hours later. She laughed when he finally opened the door and handed him a steaming mug.

"I knew I shouldn't have let you have that tablet. You stayed up all night, didn't you?"

Nix just shrugged and let out a yawn.

"Well, drink that and get dressed," she said, her grin widening. "I have a treat for you."

She turned back to her room before Nix could ask what she meant.

It turned out that Mel's idea of a treat was not anything Nix could have guessed. In fact, as he followed her into the training room, he wasn't sure he could call it a treat at all. The edges of the room were lined with soldiers. A mixture of curious looks and angry glares followed him as they walked past, along with a chorus of whispers and grumbles.

"Is it true what they say?"

"I don't know why he's here."

"Belongs in the prison."

"Better to just execute him."

"He's killed too many of our men."

Barton and the rest of their team stood in front of the Commander, and a group of senior officers, on the far side of the room.

"What's going on?" he muttered quietly as he followed Mel.

"The Commander will explain," she said with a wink. "Trust me, I think you're going to like this."

Nix ground his teeth impatiently.

The Commander frowned with his usual expression of disapproval. His coldness was something he was already used to, but the expression of the woman standing next to him made Nix's skin prickle. It was more than disgust or even animosity. He'd seen that look of calculating malice before and knew without a doubt that this woman actually did want him dead.

She wore the commander's rank on her jacket as well, along with the insignia of the Operations Division. Another man stood behind them, his jacket decorated with numerous emblems and insignia. He was older than either of the two commanders, but still physically fit. There was something familiar about his face as he looked at Nix with amused interest.

Two other officers stood to one side, away from the rest. One wore an insignia Nix recognized all too well—Research. The other wore that of the Intelligence Division. Both looked at him with a greedy interest that made his stomach turn.

"You've all been briefed on your upcoming assignment," the Commander said. Mel's team stood at attention and the Commander continued. "Today's exercise is meant to prepare you for that assignment by allowing you to familiarize yourself with the Telepath's capabilities."

"I would like to renew my objection, sir," the woman beside the Commander said, turning to the older officer behind them.

The Commander frowned.

"Your objections have already been noted and overruled Commander Stewart," the older man said. "I'll ask that you not bring them up again."

The woman simply faced forward without further argument, though she glared at Nix with renewed intensity.

The Commander—Commander Astley—cleared his throat to continue.

"Today you will be participating in a team sparring match. As you work together to subdue your opponents, learn how best you can use each other's strengths and cover each other's weaknesses. This will be vital for your upcoming mission."

Nix looked down at the cuffs still clamped around his wrists and opened his mouth to point out that he couldn't do anything with them on. He closed his mouth again as his eyes darted around the room. He didn't care about

Military etiquette, but he doubted it would be smart to speak out of turn in this situation.

"Captain Gale, remove the ability restrictors," the Commander said before turning to the other Commander beside him. "If you don't mind me making a suggestion, I believe Major Zane's team would be a good fit for this match."

Mel let out a snort, which she immediately tried to cover with a cough.

"The Commander can be so petty sometimes," she whispered, giving Jax a nudge with her elbow. He nodded with a grin of his own. Mel turned back to Nix and flashed him a wicked grin. "Ready to get some payback?"

Nix frowned in confusion until he saw the man who stepped forward. It was a face he wouldn't easily forget. The last time Nix had been a prisoner to the Military, he and his partner had decided to take advantage of Nix's inability to fight back.

Nix scowled as Mel removed the cuffs. Even as weak as his energy was, he could feel it spike with the hot flash of anger and the desire to never let himself be that helpless again.

"He's the one who stopped Gram and the others in the canyon," Mel whispered.

Nix hardly registered the gasps of surprise from around the room or Mel's hand on his shoulder as he took a step forward, anger pounding in his ears and the memory of the girl's nightmares clouding his vision.

It was Jax's loud laugh and Barton's rough jerk of his arm that brought him back to the present.

"I like this guy, Mel," Jax said as Barton barked, "That's enough."

The quiet murmuring of the onlookers had risen to an angry rumble. Before Barton could reprimand him further, a clear voice cut through the noise, drawing everyone's attention.

"I can't help noticing, Astley, that your team doesn't have a Micro. If I'm understanding your report correctly, won't your team be doing quite a lot of reconnaissance?"

The Commander turned to the Intelligence officer.

"You are correct Commander Brighton. The primary objective of this team will be to gather information. My aides and I determined that the Telepath's abilities will be sufficient for this purpose, and that a Micro would only limit their ability to strike and retreat quickly."

The other officer smirked, as though the Commander had said exactly what he'd hoped he would say.

"Then I'm afraid I must raise my own objection."

The Commander stiffened, as though realizing he'd walked into a trap.

"As I'm sure you're aware," the Intelligence Commander continued, "the gathering of information must be done under the direction of the Intelligence Division, in order to ensure the integrity of our own operations. I'm afraid as things stand, I really can't approve of the composition of this team."

"This is an Operations mission, Commander Brighton," the older officer growled. "I'm afraid even you don't have the authority to interfere. If Intelligence objects to our choice of personnel, they must do so through the proper channels."

"I'm sorry Marshal Barton, I meant no disrespect. I simply wished to clear up any misunderstandings," the Intelligence Commander said with a smile that told everyone he knew exactly how much authority he had, and it was more than the others were willing to admit. He reached into his pocket and added, "But I'm afraid you are incorrect about one thing."

"It's not your place to correct a Marshal, Brighton," Commander Stewart said, stepping forward with her shoulders squared and her face flushed with anger.

"I suppose I should have given this to you from the start," the Intelligence Commander said, ignoring her angry outburst. "Orders from the Grand Marshal."

The woman stepped back, her eyes wide. The whole room seemed to be holding its breath as the Marshal took the letter and read its contents stoically. His face paled, then turned red. The edges of the paper wrinkled under his tight grip before he handed the paper to Commander Astley.

"I'm sorry, Astley," he said. "I will bring this before the council, but for now you'll have to accept it.

The Commander looked down at the letter in confusion, but before he could read it, the Intelligence Commander nodded toward a soldier on the other side of the room.

"I've chosen this woman to represent the Intelligence Division on your team. She's a skilled Micro and her cooperation with Intelligence has been a great asset thus far."

The Commander's face turned an angry shade of red as Kaori entered the room. Nix could see the veins on his neck from where he stood.

"I won't have her on my team!" he shouted.

Nix had seen the Commander get angry. He'd heard him shout plenty of times, but there was always a controlled stiffness in his posture. He somehow always seemed calm, even when he wasn't.

Not now.

His body went rigid, but not with stiffness. He balled his hands into fists so tight they turned white as his arms and shoulders shook with self-restraint. Every muscle in his body appeared to be coiled tight, ready to spring, to tear Kaori apart with his bare hands, and it took every bit of willpower he had to hold himself back.

The Intelligence Commander moved closer, a look of triumph on his face.

"I'm sorry, Nolan," he said so quietly that Nix could only just barely hear it from where he stood. "I'm afraid you don't have a choice."

The Commander's face remained red and angry, but he turned away from the other man and clasped his hands behind his back without further protest.

Nix turned his attention to Kaori as she sauntered towards him.

"Hey Ghost," she said as she stepped too close. "This'll be fun, won't it? Just like old times?"

Nix stepped away with a glare.

"No. It won't."

Mel tugged him gently by his sleeve, pulling him away from the others so she could whisper quietly.

"I'm sorry Nix. I don't like it either, but we have to win today. Even if it means working with her, we have to win."

Nix scowled but nodded as the other team let out a laugh, jeering at Mel's words.

"*They're already listening,*" Nix transmitted to her, realizing the commanders' argument had allowed his channeling enough time to recover.

She nodded and motioned toward the rest of their team. Barton frowned. Jax smacked Keller on the shoulder to turn her attention away from glaring at their opponents.

"So, what's the plan?" Jax asked as he stepped up beside Mel.

Mel just shook her head and glanced at Nix.

Nix concentrated, trying to isolate the thoughts of the others. He'd been around Mel enough that it was easy to isolate her thoughts and slip in to transmit.

Jax was easy to pick up too, either because he was another Manipulator or simply because his thoughts were as noisy on the inside as he was on the outside. Nix focused on them, gathered them up and let them solidify until they felt tangible enough to hold.

He found Keller's next—unsure, but determined to prove herself.

Barton's were the most difficult. He could sense them but had a hard time honing in, like there was a barrier he couldn't quite break through. He closed his eyes and concentrated harder, letting the other thoughts drift to the background.

Barton was cautious, dutiful. A calm anger brewed inside him, controlled but calculating, as he observed the Commander and the Marshal—his father—and tried to emulate their behavior in the face of embarrassment and political defeat.

Nix could feel Mel's anger simmering too, but it was different. More hot and roiling. Resentful, with a strong desire to prove their team's value by winning.

Nix opened his eyes as he let all their thoughts mingle in his head until he could reach them all at once. He looked to Barton, who was watching him with wary mistrust, and nodded.

"*I'm ready,*" he transmitted to the group.

Their eyes widened with surprise—all but Mel's, who had experienced his telepathy before.

"What the actual hell?" Jax shouted out loud, earning looks of curiosity from the spectators.

"No kidding," Keller said. "That is some weird shit."

"Shhh," Mel quieted them.

"*If you want to say something, just think it as though you were speaking,*" Nix projected again. "*I'll relay it to the others.*"

Barton nodded, his face contemplative.

"*Can you communicate with us and fight at the same time?*" he thought.

Nix nodded.

"*I can't keep up constant communication, and I can't fight all out, but I can do both.*"

"*And her?*" Barton nodded toward Kaori. "*Where does she fit in?*"

Nix relayed Barton's question to the others, then answered with, "*she doesn't.*"

There was no easy way to explain Kaori to them, so he didn't try. He simply added, "*She'll fill in any holes we have without needing orders.*"

Jax shuffled his feet impatiently, itching to get the fight started.

"We doing this or not?" he asked out loud. Keller smacked him on the arm.

"He's right, we haven't got all day," one of the other soldiers called. "If you're scared to fight us just forfeit already. Quit standing around."

Mel opened her mouth to argue but Barton held out one hand to stop her.

"*I'll take Zane,*" he thought. "*Jaxon should take Reed. Gale can back us up and try to take out their Manipulator and Micro. You should focus on relaying communication from a safe distance, with Keller as your defense. They are probably going to target you, but we'll do our best to keep them off you.*"

Mel shook her head before Nix even finished relaying Barton's proposed plan.

"*Problem?*" Barton thought. Nix was surprised by how naturally he'd adapted to using telepathy for communication.

"*He's wasting your abilities,*" Mel thought.

Before Nix could relay her protest Barton shook his head, already guessing what she was thinking.

"*The purpose of this exercise isn't to avenge a five-year grudge. It isn't even to win and make Commander Astley look good. It's to help our team acclimate to the telepath's abilities. If we ignore that and only focus on attacking, then what's the point?*"

Mel ground her teeth so loud the sound was audible.

"*You don't know Barton,*" Mel thought. Nix knew the message was for him alone. "*He's smart, but predictable. They're going to see his plan coming.*"

"*It's not a bad idea to start out defensive,*" Nix transmitted to her, knowing she was right about the other team's strategy.

He strained his telepathy, listening. It was more difficult to hear their thoughts among all the others in the room, but he could feel their confidence and their eagerness. He probed those feelings until they grew clearer, trying to pick up something more concrete.

"*They plan to take out Keller first,*" he transmitted.

Keller stiffened and turned her head toward the other team, annoyed that they would target her as the weakest link. Nix continued, "*They're going to try to keep Jax and Barton occupied so Zane can rush Keller and me.*"

"*See?*" Mel thought before he'd finished. "*It's almost like they're the ones with telepathy.*"

"*That's what I expected,*" Barton thought at the same time. "*As long as we split up Zane and Reed, we'll succeed.*"

Nix transmitted Barton's thoughts to the others, not Mel's.

Jax and Keller both nodded their agreement. Mel opened her mouth, caught herself, and stopped.

"*I'll look for an opportunity and take it if I have to,*" Nix transmitted to her. She nodded.

Nix didn't think Mel was wrong. Barton's plan was fairly standard, without much flexibility, but the head-on assault Mel was envisioning wasn't any better. Barton, at least, was approaching his strategy logically, while Mel was thinking with her emotions and instinct.

Either way, Nix was confident he could adapt the strategy as the need arose.

"*Everyone ready?*" Barton thought.

Nix transmitted, and the others nodded.

"We're ready," he said aloud.

The Commander waved to some nearby soldiers, who carried two large bins to the center of the room.

"Choose your equipment," the Commander said.

"Practice weapons," Mel told Nix as she picked up a ball made of some kind of foam. She threw it down and a cloud of colored powder puffed out from the ball, leaving its mark on the ground. "If you get hit, these will leave a mark. Get hit in too many vital spots and you'll be out of the match."

Nix nodded and took a long foam stick. It was lighter than a sword, but the grip felt good in his hands.

Kaori caught his eye after taking two of the sticks for herself.

He frowned but jerked his chin toward the two enhancers on the other team, Zane and Reed. With his free hand, he gave her the signal for "Enhancer. Two. Priority."

Kaori grinned and nodded.

Regardless of the animosity he felt for Kaori, he couldn't deny there was relief in the familiarity of having her on his team. Whatever else happened in this fight, he could trust Kaori to do what needed to be done.

He scowled and turned away from her.

As he took his position next to Keller, she showed him how to strap foam pads to his knuckles and boots, allowing him to leave marks even without using a weapon.

Mel and the others took their positions in front of them. Nix frowned. It would be obvious to anyone what their strategy was. It didn't matter, though. In some ways, that made things easier for him. If their strategy was predictable, then their opponents would respond with equal predictability.

He smirked as Kaori moved to the front of the formation, near Barton. The other team threw her a confused glance before discounting her entirely. She was a Micro without a gun. What could she do?

Their ignorance alone could be the deciding factor in this fight.

"*Their ranged attackers are going to target you,*" Nix transmitted to Barton. "*Stay near Kaori. She'll create an opening for you.*"

"*We're sticking to the original plan,*" Barton thought back, his thoughts laced with mistrust, "*and she isn't part of it.*"

Nix swore aloud, earning a raised eyebrow from Keller.

He hadn't anticipated how stubbornly rigid Barton would be. It wasn't just that he mistrusted Kaori. He was simply unwilling to deviate from an already established strategy. Mel had been right.

"*I can take care of myself,*" Nix transmitted to Keller. "*Their Micro and Manipulator are going to target Barton. You'll need to intercept their Enhancer in his place.*"

Keller raised an eyebrow. She knew Barton well enough to know he hadn't changed the plan. She took only a moment to decide that getting a reprimand was worth it if she had the opportunity to shine in front of the Commanders and other soldiers.

With a quiet whir, several low, narrow partitions rose from slots in the ground, providing the barest of cover to use against ranged attacks. A buzzer sounded overhead, signaling the start of the fight.

Keller sprang forward almost instantly. She was fast for someone who didn't have enough channeling to be a Manipulator. She reached Jax even before Reed and sped past him toward Zane. Zane had held back along with their other Enhancer, providing enough cover fire for him to close the distance to Mel.

With both ranged attackers focused on Barton, he couldn't do anything but hide behind the nearest partition.

"*Mel needs to deal with those ranged attacks*", Barton thought, sounding frustrated. "*What is Keller doing? Why is she fighting Zane?*"

"*Mel's got the other Enhancer to deal with,*" Nix transmitted back, "*and you're pinned down.*"

"*Why do you think I wanted Keller to stay in the back?*" Barton's thoughts snapped.

Nix swore again. He was right and Nix had missed it. If Keller had stayed with him, she would easily be able to deal with Mel's attacker, freeing her to back up Barton.

He'd thought Barton's formation had been simplistic and predictable when in actuality it had been designed to lure their opponents into doing exactly what Barton wanted.

Nix was certain Mel could handle her opponent easily enough, and the fact that Barton had assigned Jax to intercept Reed meant he knew Jax could handle it. That left Keller.

A quick glance was enough to tell Nix that she was no match for Zane. He dodged all her attacks easily with a smirk. He could take her out if he wanted to, but he was toying with her. Her movements were sloppy by comparison and only became sloppier as she grew more frustrated.

Before Nix could move to aid her, a buzzer rang out overhead.

"Walt, you're out," the Commander said in a loud, clear voice. Nix turned to see Mel's attacker covered in red powder. She grinned toward Nix then turned forward to focus on the ranged attackers. Kaori had moved in on their Micro, every shot missing without her making any move to dodge.

"Keller you're out."

Keller swore and Nix tore his eyes back toward Zane.

"Give him hell for me," Mel said.

"*What are you doing?*" Barton thought as Nix rushed in.

Nix didn't respond. He heard the sound of the buzzer again, but the Commander's words faded out as the adrenaline took over his concentration.

Nix swung his stick in a fast arc as he reached Zane. Zane managed to dodge, the tip of the stick just grazing the front of his shirt without enough force to release the powder. Zane pulled his gun out and jumped back. Nix grinned as he prepared to dodge. He doubted the other man was as good a shot as Gram, and Nix was already used to sparring with him.

A shot rang out from behind Nix and Zane grunted as red powder exploded against his shoulder. Either Barton or Mel must have shot him. Nix rushed in before he could recover. He knocked the gun from his free hand before jabbing the end of his stick into his stomach, causing him to double over. Before Zane could collapse, he pulled his arm back, then rammed his elbow down hard on the back of his neck. Zane fell to his knees and Nix kicked him in the side, just as Zane had done to him all those years ago. The buzzer sounded overhead but Nix simply aimed another kick. Hands on each of his shoulders pulled him back.

"That's enough," Barton barked, one hand squeezing his shoulder like a vice.

As Nix let the others pull him away, the battle fog cleared from his head. Resentment simmered in the thoughts around him. Resentment that their team had won. Resentment for the blows Nix had dealt to Zane.

Barton's fury rose above everything else. It didn't matter that they'd won, Nix's actions had only done more harm to the Commander's reputation. Barton wouldn't further disrespect the senior officers by voicing his anger, but he was resolved to do whatever was necessary to keep Nix in check in the future. He wouldn't let what happened today happen again.

Mel took Nix back to his room, but he stopped with his hand on the knob.

"The report," he said. "Has Barton submitted it already?"

Mel shook her head.

"He wanted to review it again before submitting it to the Commander, make sure we didn't overlook anything."

"We did overlook something," Nix said. "We just had no way of knowing."

Mel cocked her head quizzically.

"What do you mean?"

"Kaori."

Mel's eyes widened, and she spun away from him, toward the room next to hers. Nix hesitated, then stepped behind her.

Barton opened the door a crack and frowned.

"What is it?" he asked. "What is he—"

Mel cut him off.

"Have you submitted the report?"

"I was about to send it to the Commander."

"You can't," Nix said.

Before Barton could reprimand him for his bluntness, Mel cut him off again. "Seriously Alec, will you just listen for once?"

Barton looked surprised, but unoffended by her outburst. He stepped out into the hall, closing his door behind him, like he didn't want Nix to even see inside, let alone enter. Mel rolled her eyes.

"Intelligence claimed jurisdiction over our mission, which means all reports have to be submitted to them as well," Mel said. Barton's eyes widened before she had even finished.

"And if Intelligence gets our report, that woman will too," Barton concluded.

Nix nodded.

"Until now, I think Kaori has only been feeding you bad intel," Nix said, "but there's no guarantee she won't warn the shop if she knows you plan to attack it."

"What makes you so certain she would actually sabotage our operation?" Barton asked.

"I know Kaori," Nix said with a shake of his head. "She'll never leave the Syndicate completely, which means she would never do anything to weaken them completely."

"And how can we trust that you're any different?" Barton asked, his eyes boring into Nix like he was searching for any sign of untruth.

"I don't know," Nix said honestly. How could he answer a question he'd been asking himself—and failing to answer—for years? "That's something you'll have to decide for yourself, I guess."

"Barton," Mel began impatiently, but Barton held up his hand to stop her.

"We have work to do," he said. "I think we'd better notify the Commander."

The day's events had made it clear to Nix that the Military really was no better than the Syndicate. It didn't matter how much they tried to hide beneath orderliness and decorum, their hierarchy was equally plagued by petty infighting and power-hungry individuals looking for any advantage over their own comrades.

Gram had made plenty of snide comments about Military leadership throughout the years and now Nix understood why.

Nix had always viewed the Commander as inflexible and blind to the realities right in front of him. It was hypocritical, he thought, for the man to be so upset with Gram for his refusal to follow Military protocols while actively turning a blind eye to the very people those protocols existed to protect. He was just another cog in a broken system that only benefited the few like himself.

This one meeting showed Nix a different side to the Commander.

"There's only one way to keep Intelligence out of this mission," he told them after reading through Barton's report. "And that's to ensure that your team has nothing to do with it."

"What do you mean?" Mel asked.

"We're the Military Police," the Commander said with a small smile, something Nix had never seen him do before. "If we receive a report about suspicious activity, it's our duty to investigate."

"And once we do, we'll realize the shop is a Syndicate operation and shut them down," Mel said with a grin.

Nix snorted, and the Commander frowned. He cleared his throat before continuing in his usual formal tone.

"In order for this to work, I'll have to assign the investigation to another team. Barton, you'll need to work with them quietly to write a new operation report."

"We'll need to modify the strategy as well," Barton said, as their initial plan had relied on Nix's knowledge of the location as well as his telepathy.

The Commander nodded. "I'll leave the details to you, so long as you take adequate precautions to ensure the safety of nearby citizens. I don't want anyone else getting caught in the crossfire."

That was the difference between the Commander and the rest of the Military.

He did care about the people the system was meant to protect.

It made it all the more frustrating to know that the Commander had refused to protect the one person who should have been the most important to him, his own son.

"This will only work once," the Commander said, pulling Nix out of his thoughts. "Intelligence is sure to suspect the source of our information, but without definitive proof, there won't be anything they can do. I'm sure they will take steps to stop us from doing it again in the future."

The Commander set down his tablet and locked eyes with Nix.

"Is there any other information that will help this operation be a success?" He asked. "What is the Syndicate's protocol if they suspect they have been compromised? If any of their operatives manage to escape, where will they go?"

Barton was smart, but he hadn't thought to ask Nix these questions, Nix realized. Their plan had focused solely on the shop itself, its layout, and how many operatives were likely to be inside.

Nix hesitated. A part of him was relieved that he wasn't participating in the raid, though he also knew that doing so was inevitable. A part of him still thought of the Commander as his enemy, and sharing information only made him feel more and more like a true traitor.

Nix nodded and swallowed down the anxious lump in his throat.

He'd chosen to come here, to give the Military whatever they wanted from him—his life, his ability, his knowledge. Maybe that made him a traitor, but it didn't matter. It was too late to turn back, and he didn't want to. So he told the Commander everything he knew.

This time, I see the dream from a distance, rather than through someone else's eyes. I'm not sure what causes the dreams to be from one point of view or another. It's a lot less disorienting this way, though.

I think this dream is something I've seen before, but I'm not sure. I've seen so much of his life in such a short amount of time, it's hard to keep track.

Nix is young, not much older than ten or eleven. He's with another boy who looks like he's around sixteen. They're fighting. Even though it's meant to be sparring, the older boy doesn't seem to be holding back. I think the older boy is trying to train him, but his instructions are critical and unconstructive. As they both become more agitated, Nix's control seems to worsen, causing his body to blur like a ghost with every movement.

The dream shifts and I see the same boys again. They're older now. Nix looks like a young teenager instead of a kid. The two boys fight again while Kaori and a few other men watch. Maybe it's because he's so young and inexperienced, but Nix's movements seem off, almost sluggish and clumsy. His forehead is scrunched with more than his usual scowl, like maybe he's in some kind of pain.

The older boy moves in close for an attack, but before he can land any blows, Nix doubles over, clutching his head with a cry of pain. He curls up on the ground while Kaori and the men rush to his side. The older boy shows no sympathy for his opponent's predicament and makes goading comments, dismissing Nix's agony.

The dream changes again. It's dark and Nix is with the older boy and several others outside. They seem to be having some kind of argument. Nix shakes his head and walks away before slumping to the ground, his back against a tree. The older boy looks like he wants to follow him, to continue the argument, but someone stops him. After a few quiet words, the group turns and leaves Nix behind. Nix sits in the dark alone until alarms sound in the distance. He stands up with a worried look on his face. The rest of the group returns, looking like they've been in a fight. The older boy isn't with them.

The dream speeds forward, making it hard for me to tell what happened next. I think the older boy was captured, but Nix went back to rescue him. Now they're older again. Nix is arguing with the same boy in a crowded room. It looks like a tavern or bar. I think the older boy is drunk. He says something and Nix jumps toward him, punching him hard in the face. The room explodes in chaos. Everyone else comes to the defense of the older boy. I can't see what's happening until suddenly the room falls silent and the crowd parts. Nix is standing in the center, and the older boy is on the ground. Nix is holding a knife in his hands, red with blood, and the older boy isn't moving.

I don't know what happens after that. Everything is just dark until finally I wake up.

Chapter Twenty-six

"Something isn't right," Nix transmitted. He checked again, straining his telepathy as well as his senses, but there was no question. "There's only one person in there."

"Maybe we got lucky and caught them in the middle of some kind of personnel change?" Jax questioned.

"No. There would be more people here if that were the case, not less. I don't understand it, but we should be careful."

Nix's mind raced.

While it was true that this particular safe house had gone unused for some time after Reizen's death, it had become operational again in the last few years. There was no reason for it to be empty now, unless the Military's recent attacks had led the Syndicate to pull their operatives out of the East. Maybe they didn't want to risk losing anymore members. He shook his head absently. That didn't sound like the Syndicate.

Though he could imagine Ryu wanting to avoid the conflict, he doubted the other Syndicate leaders would agree to it.

He turned his attention back to the farmhouse in the distance and tried to focus his thoughts on the lone person inside.

He swore and leapt to his feet.

"What are you doing?" Barton hissed out loud.

Nix barely heard him, his attention consumed by the thoughts in the building, thoughts he recognized.

How could he be here?

Nix had to see for himself, had to know. He took a single, hesitant step forward, then broke into a run, his own admonitions and the warning cries of his team completely forgotten.

His legs felt like gel as he threw open the door and stepped into the dim room. The man lurked in the shadows on the far side of the room, his thoughts roiling with hate-filled anticipation. He'd known Nix was coming.

Nix's breath came faster, and he couldn't force his legs to move. It wasn't just the darkness or the enclosed space. It was the knowledge that his past waited for him in the shadows.

The man's harsh, deep laugh filled the room, reverberated in Nix's head, dragging up memories he'd tried so hard to forget.

"So, it's true then," the man said as he stepped closer, into a patch of dim light, confirming what Nix already knew.

Jiren.

He was Kuda's father, but he was so much more than that.

He'd been a member of Reizen's inner circle, though he hated Reizen. Few people knew that, but of course Nix could read it in his thoughts.

"I laughed when I heard the rumors. I always knew you were a monster and a murderer, but a traitor?" He laughed again, the sound grating in Nix's ears. "You know half of us would have gladly killed Reizen ourselves given the chance, but this? Working with the Military? I was right. Reizen should have left you in that hellhole prison to rot."

"You..." was all Nix could manage to stammer. "You're..."

"Alive?" the man snapped.

The way he spoke, the way he moved, his features. Nix had forgotten how much his son resembled him—not Kuda with his weasel-like features and sniveling voice.

Ren.

Handsome, charismatic, talented.

He had been Jiren's older son and Nix's trainer.

He'd also made Nix's life a living hell.

Sweat dripped down his neck, and his hands turned slick and sticky.

Not blood, he forced himself to think as the memories flashed through his mind.

The still body on the floor. The knife in his hands.

Ren had made his life a living hell, but he'd never meant to kill him.

"I thought..." he stammered as he wiped his hands on his pants.

"That I was dead? And who told you that?"

Nix could hardly organize his thoughts as his own memories tangled with Jiren's, forming a dizzying web. Their hatred for each other pounded in the background like a heartbeat, thrumming faster and louder with each haunting image.

"Kaori. She..." Nix finally managed to say, though he doubted Jiren actually expected an answer.

It had never made sense that Jiren had died in Kaori's coup against her father. Jiren, of all people, would have sided with her.

"Does Ryu know?" Nix asked, forcing the past to the shadows of his mind where he always struggled to keep it hidden.

Jiren laughed.

"You want to know whose orders I'm following," he said with a sneer. "Well, sorry to disappoint, Ghost Boy, but I don't intend to make it that easy for you."

He reached for the pouch on his hip. Nix's reaction was slow, and the dagger sliced his shoulder, just below his neck where Jiren had been aiming.

He wasn't here to play games. He was here for Nix's life.

"Nix!" Mel shouted behind him. He'd completely forgotten about the rest of the team.

"Watch out!" Nix shouted as another dagger shot toward her.

He didn't know if she would be able to dodge it in time, but he couldn't wait to find out. He threw himself in front of her and sucked in a sharp breath as the dagger embedded into his shoulder.

"No!" Mel shouted, steadying him as he hunched over in pain.

Nix's vision blurred, but he couldn't let Jiren get away. He wasn't here by accident, and they needed to know why.

Mel said something, but he couldn't hear her over the sound of breaking glass and splintering wood. Jax came barreling through the nearby window, breaking both the pane and the shutters with his entry. Jiren's face twisted in surprise and now he was the one who couldn't react in time. He doubled over after taking a hard punch to the stomach. Nix heard a pop and watched numbly as Jiren collapsed to the floor.

Even as his body convulsed he managed to push himself up on one hand, veins standing out on his forehead and saliva dribbling from his mouth as he wheezed out a laugh.

"This isn't over, you monster," he managed to hiss through gritted teeth. Jax grabbed both his arms and pulled them behind his back. Jiren's eyes rolled back in his head, and he lost consciousness.

Nix sank to his knees with a groan, and Mel dropped to the ground beside him.

"Well, that was a stupid thing you did."

Kaori crouched behind him and rested one hand lightly on his back just below the dagger. Her other hand gripped his opposite arm.

"Leave him alone," Mel hissed.

"It's not enough that he took a dagger for you? You want to leave it in his back too?" Kaori snapped.

"It's okay," Nix said through gritted teeth. "Let Kaori take care of it."

Mel hesitated.

"You should contact the Commander," he said.

Mel released her hold on him and stood up. She cast one last wary look at Kaori before turning toward Barton and Jax, who were ensuring Jiren was properly restrained.

"You always have to play the hero, don't you?" Kaori asked quietly in his ear. He didn't have to see her face to know what expression she wore. Disapproval with a hint of amusement. He frowned, trying to ignore the way her body pressed against his, steadying him as her hand slid higher up his back, toward the dagger.

"You told me Jiren was dead," he seethed as Kaori tightened her grip on his other arm.

"I guess I was wrong," she said in his ear. "You ready?"

He tensed and nodded, a groan of pain escaping his lips as her hand found the dagger. The groan turned to a cry as she pulled. She braced him for only a moment before letting go to pull his jacket from his shoulders.

"Does Ryu know?" Nix hissed, trying to ignore the way every small movement pulled at torn flesh and muscle.

"I think we're going to have to cut your shirt," Kaori said. "There's no way we're getting it over your head.

Nix nodded.

"It's fine. Do it."

She pulled a knife from her pocket and began ripping away the fabric.

"He's going to need a medic as soon as possible," Kaori called.

"I'll tell the Commander to send someone," he heard Mel say.

"No, we need to move the prisoner. Tell the Commander we're coming back."

"But—"

"It's fine," Kaori said. "I can patch him up temporarily, but he'll need better treatment once we get back."

Nix tightened his hands into trembling fists as Kaori rubbed at the wound, cleaning it with a salve that burned almost as much as her poison. When she finished, she sprayed his shoulder with something blissfully cool. Finally, she fixed a large adhesive bandage over the wound.

"That'll have to do for now," she said.

"You didn't answer me," Nix said before she could stand up.

"You seem to think I know everything that goes on with the Syndicate," Kaori said, "but as you know, I've been here, with the Military."

Nix let out a quiet laugh, that turned into a wheeze as pain shot through his shoulder.

"You know I don't buy that, Kaori. I was there, remember? You started a prison break in Chusan."

"To keep you out of prison."

Nix shook his head and Kaori sighed.

"They were Military prisoners, if you must know," she said.

Nix's eyebrows pulled together in confusion and Kaori stood before he could respond. Mel moved to his side and reached her hand down to help him up.

"How is it?" Mel asked. "Think you can walk?"

Nix nodded and let her help him up.

He felt lightheaded and his shoulder ached with a deep pain the numbing spray couldn't counter, but Barton was right, they needed to move before Jiren woke up.

"We should go," he rasped.

"Try not to run blindly into an enemy attack next time," Kaori said to Mel with a toss of her hair. "You don't want to get someone killed."

Mel's face flushed red, and she spun toward Kaori her fists already balled.

"How dare you—"

Barton grabbed her arm to stop her.

"Let it go," he said, his voice quiet enough that only Mel and Nix could hear.

Mel's hands relaxed and she stepped closer to Nix instead, placing one arm around the back of his waist.

"I'm sorry, Nix," she whispered. "She's right, I should have been more careful."

Nix shook his head.

"Don't let Kaori get inside your head," he said, as if he hadn't let her do just that.

Mel nodded and tightened her grip on his waist.

Though every step sent throbbing pain into his shoulder, Nix could walk fine on his own. Still, he didn't protest as she led him from the building. He suspected she needed it more than he did.

Pain and exhaustion made the return trip a blur. Nix was only vaguely aware of Mel telling him they were returning to the city instead of the small base at Westwarden. He closed his eyes, but there was nothing restful about the trip. His thoughts spun with memories and his shoulder throbbed with every bump in the road.

"What are we doing here?" he asked, his words slurring together.

Instead of entering through the city gate, they had stopped outside Lucan's clinic in the slums. He recognized Lucan's vehicle outside, but not the sleek black car parked next to it.

"We need to get your wound treated," Mel said.

"Jiren..." he protested.

"The others will take care of it."

Nix shook his head with a grimace.

"The Commander...we need to..."

"He's here," she said, "but you're in no shape to report on anything right now."

Mel helped him inside the clinic on the lower floor. He was relieved that he didn't have to climb the stairs to the apartment. Lucan appeared in the doorway as they approached, a worried look on his face.

"What happened?" the Commander asked, appearing behind him.

"A Manipulator," Mel said. "I couldn't move out of the way in time, and Nix jumped in front of me."

"The details can wait until later," Lucan said as he ushered them down the hall to a treatment room.

Mel helped Nix lie down onto the padded table. He closed his eyes with a grimace, listening as their voices drifted back out into the hall.

"Do you need any help?" the Commander asked, surprising him.

"No." Lucan's voice. "You and Mel can wait upstairs if you'd like."

"We'll wait here," the Commander said. "Thank you, Lucan."

"I'm glad you called me," Lucan said.

"Why?" Nix murmured as Lucan stepped back into the room, closing the door behind him.

"Let's get this wound taken care of first," Lucan answered. "I'll need to sedate you."

He dragged an IV cart closer to Nix and wiped an antiseptic on his arm. Nix winced as the needle pierced his skin. He tensed as the cold liquid began to spread through his veins.

"Try to relax," Lucan said as he fit a mask over Nix's face.

Nix thought Lucan said something else, but he couldn't make out the words as he slipped into unconsciousness.

Nix woke with a gasp, his body shaking not with cold but with adrenaline.

Monster.

Murderer.

Traitor.

"Here."

Lucan placed a hand on his shoulder and helped him sit up before placing a steaming mug in his hands.

"How do you feel?" Lucan asked. "Does it hurt? Do you feel nauseous at all?"

Nix shook his head.

"No, it's not that."

Nix took a sip of the tea Lucan had given him.

"Nightmares?" Lucan asked.

Nix nodded.

"Your injury, it was caused by someone you knew?"

Nix nodded again.

"Yeah. Someone I thought was dead."

"It must have been a shock then, to see him there."

Nix shook his head.

"It wasn't a coincidence. He knew I would be there. Where's the Commander?"

Lucan took the mug from him.

"Waiting in the lobby. Alec...Major Barton arrived a short time ago."

Nix shifted his legs over the side of the bed so he could stand, but Lucan stopped him with an exasperated sigh.

"It won't do much good for you to collapse because you tried to walk right after waking up from sedation," he said. "The others aren't going anywhere."

"Sorry," Nix mumbled.

Lucan shook his head as he picked up his tablet.

"Your vitals spiked when you woke up, but they've settled now," he said. "It was probably just the nightmare, but you should take it easy and rest for the next few days."

He smiled like he knew that was the last thing Nix would do.

"Here." He carried a dark shirt over and helped Nix put it on. It buttoned in the front, allowing him to slide his arm in with less movement, but it was still difficult. Next, Lucan picked up a cloth sling from the counter. "You'll need to wear this for at least two weeks, until your shoulder is fully healed."

Nix just nodded again as Lucan helped him fit the sling over his shoulder.

Lucan adjusted the straps until he was satisfied.

"Does anything feel too tight or uncomfortable?" he asked.

Nix smirked. "Besides the stab wound in my back or...?"

Lucan pinched his lips.

"If you're feeling any pain, I want you to let me know."

"I'm okay, thanks."

Lucan nodded.

"I'll inform the others."

Lucan stepped out of the room, leaving Nix alone momentarily. Nix gripped the blanket that lay bunched beside him on the table and tried to push the memories away.

"Nix!" Mel rushed into the room like she wanted to hug him, but she stopped herself. "Are you alright? How's your shoulder?"

"It's fine," he said, forcing a small smile to his lips.

"You look really pale," she said, then turned to Lucan. "Is that normal?"

Lucan nodded.

"He'll need to rest for a few days."

"Barton and Gale have already reported on the operation," the Commander said, stepping into the room with Barton a few steps behind. "This wouldn't have happened if you hadn't broken protocol."

Mel shot the Commander a look but didn't say anything.

"You're right," Nix said, "I shouldn't have gone in alone."

"What do you know about the prisoner?" the Commander asked. "I find it suspicious that he was alone."

"His name is Jiren Kuro," Nix said, his fingers digging into his knee. "He isn't just some Syndicate operative. He was part of Reizen's inner circle. He shouldn't have been there."

"Because he's someone important?" Mel asked.

"No, because he's supposed to be dead. Five years ago, when the Military raided Chusan. We..." Nix hesitated. He'd never told anyone about that night, not even Gram. "Kaori told me he'd died, along with Reizen and several other high ranking Syndicate leaders."

"Do you think she knew he would be there?"

Nix shook his head.

"I don't know, but I'm sure he knew that I would be. He was waiting for me. He..." *wanted me dead.*

He cleared his throat and continued.

"I don't know if he was there because of Kaori or not. If she was behind this, I can't begin to guess why. I will say that he didn't put up much of a fight. It was almost like he wanted us to capture him."

"It was six to one," Mel said. "And Jax took him by surprise."

"Jiren was the head of Syndicate combat training," he said. "Even if all six of us were fighting him at once, which we weren't, it shouldn't have been that easy."

The Commander didn't say anything, just stared ahead in quiet contemplation.

"I don't like it, but there isn't much we can do about it other than continue to keep an eye on Kaori," he said at last.

He reached for the tablet tucked under his arm, which Nix hadn't noticed he was carrying.

"We have new orders," he continued. "I was going to push the Marshal to give us more time, but with your injury, we won't have any choice other than to proceed with this new operation."

"What are the orders?" Mel asked like she already knew she wasn't going to like the answer.

"We're being reassigned to the Garrison," the Commander said. "I'll send you the details to read over later."

"Why?" Mel asked.

"Intelligence reports an influx of Syndicate movement east of Karza. They believe that because of our operations, the Syndicate has been pulling their operatives back to Senari. There isn't much point in continuing to raid safe houses we know will be empty.

"But we don't know that," Barton said calmly.

"That's exactly why I wanted to ask for more time here," the Commander said. "But with Nix out of commission, it would be pointless."

"And what will be our goal once we're at the Garrison?" Nix asked.

The Commander narrowed his eyes and didn't answer.

"We're to assist Commander Stewart in her operations while awaiting further instructions."

Nix didn't like it, and he suspected the Commander didn't either. There was only one reason the Syndicate would pull their troops back to Senari. The retaliation he had been expecting was coming. The Military, he guessed, wasn't going to wait for their enemy to strike first.

"It will be at least two weeks before he's out of the sling," Lucan said. "And months before he regains full range of motion. Over-using his arm will only slow down his recovery."

"The Military only cares that he is useful," the Commander snapped, "not about his long-term prognosis."

Lucan pursed his lips and Mel ground her teeth.

"I'll prepare what treatments I can to help with the healing process and prevent future injury, but I can't make any guarantees."

It was unlike Lucan, to give in so easily—to allow a patient to push themselves to the point of harm.

It made the grim reality that they all knew even more clear.

Nix was a tool to be used however the Military chose. His life and well-being didn't matter, and there was nothing any of them—not even Lucan or the Commander—could do about it.

"Thank you, Lucan. We need to return to headquarters now. I'm sure Intelligence already knows about his condition, and I don't want you to face any repercussions because we brought him here.

Lucan waved him off.

"Treating the injured is my duty. Even the Grand Marshal can't fault me for that. I'm not worried for myself, but you should be careful."

"I can handle my cousin," the Commander growled. "But thank you."

Nix didn't understand the conversation, but it showed him a side to both Lucan and the Commander he had never seen.

To him, Lucan had always just been Gram's friend, the caring doctor who visited the base and chided them for not taking better care of them-selves. It was easy to forget that he was part of an important family in the capital and that the complex power struggles within Military society were as familiar to him as the medicine he practiced.

What was even more surprising to him was the obvious friendship be-tween him and the Commander.

"You must not have known," Mel said as she helped him stand. "They've been close for a long time. The Commander even trained him. Come on, let's get you to the car."

Nix let Mel support him as he walked out of the treatment room, Barton following silently behind.

Nix had been hoping for a chance to talk with Lucan, ask him if he knew anything about Gram—but of course he wouldn't. Gram wouldn't have any way to contact him, and even if he did, it would be too dangerous.

As Mel eased him into the back of the waiting car, Nix closed his eyes. They were being transferred to the Garrison—closer to Gram, closer to the girl, closer to the Syndicate. It seemed no matter how hard he tried to leave it all behind, he kept finding himself back in the same place, only this time, when they called him a traitor, it really would be true.

"Here's the painkillers Lucan sent, along with instructions on when to take them," Mel said, handing him a small package. "Do you want me to have dinner sent up from the cafeteria?"

"I'll just warm up one of these," he said, gesturing to the stack of prepared meals by the microwave.

"Are you sure?"

He nodded.

"Okay, well, if you need anything, don't hesitate to come let me know, okay?"

"Sure. Thanks Mel."

Nix sighed and closed the door before leaning his forehead against the smooth wood.

He looked down at his wrists. She'd had to activate his cuffs before they'd entered the city, which meant Nix wasn't just alone, he was alone with nothing to distract him from his own thoughts.

He'd taken it for granted over the years how comforting it was to have Gram's familiar presence buzzing in the background—how much his thoughts helped Nix to suppress his own.

If there was any time when Nix regretted not having his telepathy, it was now. Maybe he should have asked Mel to stay, because being alone with his thoughts was the last thing he wanted to do right then.

He picked up his tablet and opened the Intelligence reports that he must have read a hundred times in the last few weeks. Jiren had been waiting for them at the safe house and he was sure Kaori was behind it, but there were too many missing pieces for him to figure out what her end goal was.

He wasn't going to find the answer tonight. Instead of distracting him from the memories he was trying so desperately to push down, every word he read only seemed to unlock another regret, another memory.

Traitor.

It's his fault.

Monster.

He's done enough harm already.

Danger.

I don't trust him. I don't want to be around him.

Nix buried his face in his shaking free hand and tried to breathe.

Will you stay with me? For a little while, at least?

He let out a slow exhale and leaned back, careful not to press his wounded shoulder against the back of the chair as he let the words repeat in his head.

She'd asked him to stay.

It was the memory he clung to in these moments. It didn't make up for all that he'd done or who he was, but she'd asked him to stay.

As he repeated the words over and over in his head, he could almost believe that maybe he could be more than the monster everyone believed him to be, the monster he believed himself to be.

Because she had seen him as his worst self, as someone dangerous, someone who couldn't be trusted, a monster.

And she had asked him to stay.

It was such a small thing, but at the moment, it was all he had.

They were being reassigned to the Garrison.

One step closer to Chusan. One step closer to where she was.

He'd never intended to see her again. He'd done all this to keep her safe, but he couldn't help feeling regret for the time they had wasted stubbornly pushing each other away.

Now, as the Military moved onto the Syndicate's doorstep, he could only hope that what he feared wouldn't be true. Because now seeing her again could only mean one thing, that once again she was in danger, and once again he would be the one who had put her there.

Ryu told me that he heard from the people in Senari. They were able to evacuate in time. They're safe.

I'm relieved. It's a strange thing to feel after being afraid of the Syndicate for so long. Some of them still frighten me, but I'm starting to see that most of them are just ordinary people caught up in a war few seem to really understand. Even those who fight seem to be doing it because that's what they've always done, what their parents and grandparents did. It's sad. I understand why Ryu wants it all to end. I also understand that wanting it doesn't make it easy.

For now, I just don't want to see anyone else get hurt. I don't want anyone else to have to lose their family the way I did. I'm glad I was able to help, even if only a little.

I don't know when the attack will come, but I know they won't stop in Senari. They're coming west, and Nix is with them.

Chapter Twenty-seven

"Are you sure you should be doing that?" Mel asked as he lifted the box from the supply transport.

"Lucan said I could stop wearing the sling after two weeks," Nix said with a huff.

Mel shook her head and let out a groan of exasperation.

"That doesn't mean you should be lifting boxes! He also said that overdoing it before you're fully recovered could make the injury worse."

Nix shrugged. His shoulder was stiff, with a lingering dull ache, but it felt good to be able to move it.

"Just…" Mel let out another groan, this time in defeat. "Just try not to overdo it, okay?"

Nix flashed her a grin and nodded to his wrists.

"It's not like I can do much with these on. "I'll be careful, but I'm tired of just sitting around."

"I feel that," Jax said from the other side of the transport, as he lifted multiple boxes at once, no doubt using his enhanced strength. "Why are we even here, Mel? This assignment is about as boring as paperwork."

Their transfer to the Garrison had been sudden, but after two weeks, unloading the supply transport was the most exciting assignment they'd been given.

Mel pursed her lips together and didn't respond. Even without his telepathy, Nix recognized the annoyance that flashed across her face. She tried not to show it, but he knew she was just as frustrated as the rest of their team.

"That explains why you're willing to help with the unloading," Keller said, walking up to them. "Usually, you're the one trying to avoid work like this."

Jax aimed a kick at her leg, but Keller, unburdened by boxes, easily sidestepped.

"That's why I'm here," Mel said with a grin. "The Commander wants to see us. Once you're finished, report to the west command room."

Mel turned around to leave them to their task but stopped face to face with Zane.

"What's he doing out here?" he asked, jabbing an angry finger in Nix's direction.

"My team is unloading the supply transport," Mel said flatly, "as Commander Stewart requested."

"My understanding was that the criminal is to be used for Military Police operations and is otherwise to be kept in confinement."

"Then your understanding is wrong," Mel snapped.

"Watch it, Gale," Zane snapped back. "Whether you like it or not, I am your superior officer. Your social standing doesn't mean anything out here."

Mel stiffened, opened her mouth, and shut it again before taking a deep breath.

"I simply meant, Major Zane, sir, that there is no stipulation that Nix must be kept in confinement when off duty. He is supposed to be supervised by Major Barton or myself. As you can see, I am standing right here, supervising him."

Nix winced. Mel's tone dripped with such heavy sarcasm, there was no way someone like Zane was going to let it slide.

Zane's face turned red, and Nix could see the muscles working in his jaw.

"See that you do," he growled before spinning away.

Keller started snickering before Zane was even completely out of earshot. Mel shushed her but Jax started laughing as well.

"Looks like you're joining us after all Mel," he said.

Mel sighed but turned toward them with a grin.

"Alright, let's get this done then."

"I don't get it," Nix said as she stepped next to him and picked up a box. "I thought you were in trouble for sure."

Mel winked at him and Keller and Jax both laughed again.

"Zane was wrong about one thing," Jax explained, "even out here, status still matters. Mel is from a city family and Zane isn't. Once you're a marshal, like Barton's dad, that's enough to give you status regardless of who your family is. But Zane is just a major from the sticks trying to tell a captain from city high society what to do? Not a smart move."

"Captain's like our very own princess," Keller added with another laugh.

"That's an exaggeration," Mel said.

"Well compared to the rest of us."

Mel gave them a little curtsey and said, "You can all be my knights, then."

Nix shook his head as the others moved ahead of them.

"In the Syndicate power is the only status," he mumbled to himself.

Jax laughed again, surprising him. He hadn't thought the others would hear him.

"Well, there's quite a bit of that here too, but yeah, the rules of Military society can get pretty complicated. I find it best to mind my own business and stay as far away from all that nonsense as I can."

Since when do you ever mind your own business?" Keller shot.

The two started bickering and Mel fell into step beside him.

"I'm not actually a fan of the whole system," Mel said, "though it can be handy in situations like that. In reality, having status comes with its own problems. It can be as much of a burden as a benefit."

She winked at him and Nix let out an amused huff.

"You and Gram?" he asked.

She nodded. "Yeah, my father isn't a fan, but in the end, he'll let me decide for myself. It's not that easy for everyone though. The Commander, for example. He's an only child and his family is much more important than mine. Everything he does is scrutinized by everybody. It's hard to choose the life you want for yourself under that kind of pressure."

Nix just nodded.

It seemed like an overly complicated game with a lot of unnecessary rules, but then he had never been very good at choosing the life he wanted either.

The room the Commander used as a makeshift office while at the Garrison was a stark contrast to his plush, well-decorated office in the city. A long, rectangular table took up most of the space, its surrounding chairs hard and straight. There were no windows, only cold lights with a sickly hue. Nix felt his chest tighten every time he entered the room, and that day was no exception. His head felt stuffy, his senses dulled by the panic he could barely contain as he hesitated before taking the last step through the doorway. He tried to take a deep breath, but the lump in his throat made him want to gag instead. He clenched his teeth and flared his nostrils, forcing the nausea down.

The Commander and Barton were already seated at the table. Nix held back, letting the others take their seats before choosing one for himself, a few chairs away from the others, needing the space so he could feel less like the walls were closing in around him.

After they were all seated, the Commander nodded to Barton, who projected a map onto the table in front of them. He zoomed in until a town was visible to the southwest.

Now Nix was sure he was going to throw up.

Senari.

The border into Syndicate Territory.

"Commander Stewart has been issued orders to take control of the town of Senari and set up a base of operations there. We are to assist her in gathering intelligence prior to the mission."

"What?"

Nix jumped to his feet, his chair banging noisily to the ground behind him. His ears buzzed and his body felt hot and prickly. He couldn't tear his eyes away from the map.

"You're out of line," Barton snapped. "Sit down."

"Our occupation of Senari will serve as a launchpad for further operations in the Western Territory," the Commander continued calmly, as though Nix hadn't interrupted.

Nix sucked in a sharp breath.

The idiots in charge really did want to start another war.

The buzzing in his ears grew to a pounding roar, the sound of sharp metal cutting flesh, gunshots, and the smell of smoke.

"You're out of your mind." His voice came out in a low growl. "This isn't an operation. It's an extermination. Senari isn't a Syndicate safe house or a front for other operations. It's just a town, full of regular people."

Nix finally looked up from the map and locked eyes with the Commander, daring him to disagree.

This was wrong, and they all knew it.

The Commander said nothing. His eyes drifted away from Nix as he interlaced his fingers beneath his chin. All Nix saw was Kai, like a slap in the face. He couldn't stop the next words from coming out of his mouth.

"Haven't you done enough harm by blindly following orders you know are wrong? Who else has to die because you don't care enough to do what's right?"

His words snapped the Commander out of his silence. The color rose to his face as he leapt to his feet. His reaction was faster than Nix anticipated, and before he could even take a step back, the Commander's fist connected hard with his face. Nix stumbled, then braced himself for another blow.

Mel jumped between them, gripping the Commander's arm. To his surprise, the Commander seemed to deflate, the color draining from his face as quickly as it had risen. His shoulders dropped as he let out a long exhale.

"Everyone out," he said, his voice cold and sharp as a blade. "Everyone but him."

"Commander, I think—" Mel's protest was quickly cut off by the Commander's glare. With a nod she let go of his arm and turned away. She threw Nix a look that said, "you brought this on yourself," as she shuffled out of the room with the others.

Nix scowled back at the Commander, his cheek stinging.

"I'm sorry," he mumbled. "I shouldn't have said that, but I didn't sign up for this."

"You signed up to do whatever we want you to do," the Commander snapped. "Don't forget that. And don't forget that this mission is only happening because of you."

He jabbed Nix hard in the chest with his finger and Nix braced himself, expecting another blow. Instead, the Commander turned on his heel and walked away, each of his steps like a hammer pounding his harsh assessment into Nix like nails.

"You okay?"

Mel's voice startled him. He hadn't heard her come back in.

He exhaled and shrugged.

"He doesn't like these orders any more than you do," Mel said. "It's the same for all of us, but what can we do?"

Nix thought back to their conversation from earlier.

War meant no one could choose the life they wanted for themselves. He had been a weapon for most of his life. Gram and Mel had been separated for years. The Commander had little choice but to follow orders that made no sense. The girl...

He balled his hands into fists.

There was nothing any of them could do about it. All they could do was try to protect the things they cared about in whatever ways they could. And half the time they'd probably end up failing.

It didn't mean he wasn't going to try.

I can't talk to the others about this dream. It would only make Gram worry. Ryu too. He tries not to show it, but I know he still cares for Nix. I know talking about him is something that is hard for him.

I'm worried though. I thought maybe things had gotten better for him. It's strange, but sometimes it almost feels like he belongs with the Military, in a way he never did with the Syndicate. Even with Gram, Nix always kept to himself because he felt like he didn't belong.

Sometimes I see him with the soldiers, and he seems so much more relaxed than I've ever seen him before. He still doesn't say much, but he smiles, and the others talk to him like it's a natural thing to do.

It makes me wish I had tried harder to see him for who he really is, to see his kindness and his loyalty, his desire to do the right thing.

I only hope I get the chance to make it right.

This dream makes me worry though. Nix is on the ground, curled up in a ball while another man, a soldier, is kicking him. Other soldiers run into the room. Electricity courses through Nix's body. Someone pulls the other soldier away before pulling Nix to his feet. They don't seem like they're trying to help Nix, though. They drag him away, not seeming to care that he's in pain or struggling to stay conscious.

He wakes up in a cell, alone. His side aches and his shoulder feels sore. He sits for a long time, feeling like the walls are closing in. No one comes, not even to bring him food. He starts to feel weak and nauseous with hunger.

That's when I woke up.

I wish I knew more. I wish I knew if this was the past or the future. I wish he was here and safe.

I wish I could change the past, make different choices. Maybe then, none of this would have to happen.

Chapter Twenty-eight

Mel didn't seem like her usual cheerful self in the days leading up to their departure for Senari. She was distracted and irritable. Normally she'd laugh along with Jax's jokes or show only mock frustration over his bickering with Keller, but now she was quicker to snap at them than even Barton. Nix was always surprised by her patience with Barton's rigidity, but lately it seemed like all she did was argue with him.

Whatever was bothering her wasn't his business, but her irritability set everyone else on edge, making it hard to ignore.

Jax and Keller had taken Nix to the rec room after they'd finished loading supplies. Nix sat by himself in one of the chairs, fidgeting with an old radio Jax had swiped for him, while the other two bickered over a game he didn't know how to play.

Mel stomped into the room, looking agitated.

"Get out," she snapped.

Jax's eyebrows shot up in surprise and Keller gave him a look that seemed to say, *What's her problem?*

"Don't be like that, Mel," Keller whined. "I'm in the middle of kicking Jax's ass."

Jax snorted. "Hardly. But we'd best listen to her, unless you want to get your ass kicked for real."

He stood, and Keller followed him, grumbling. Nix moved to follow them as well, but Mel stopped him by moving swiftly toward the door and locking it.

"What's going on, Mel?" he asked in confusion.

Instead of answering him, she stepped closer and began to deactivate his channeling restrictors.

"What the hell?"

"Shhh," she silenced him. Not that it mattered. Every Micro in the Garrison was about to know what she'd done.

His head buzzed as his channeling flowed through his body. He closed his eyes in concentration, willing his telepathy to return more quickly.

Finally, he felt the insistent buzz of her thoughts, a confusing jumble of warring ideas.

"*I can't do this,*" she thought. "*I can't make you do this. You're right. Attacking Senari is wrong. And Gram. You have to warn him that we're coming. I have to get you out of here.*"

"Whoa, hold on," he transmitted, trying to calm her.

He knew others could sense him. He could feel their alarm, and they knew something wasn't right. He had to do something fast, or they were both going to be in trouble. He reached out his thoughts until he found Jax.

"*You'd better get back here,*" Nix projected.

Jax let out a stream of mental swearing as he realized what Nix's telepathic communication must mean.

"Mel, you need to put the cuffs back on. You need to get out of here."

"No," she thought. "*You were right. I don't want to see anyone else get hurt because I was too afraid to do the right thing.*"

"*This isn't the right way, Mel,*" he insisted. "*I'm not going anywhere. I can't.*"

She knew that escape had never been part of his plan. If he left now, if he went to Senari or Chusan, there would have been no point to turning himself in in the first place.

"*When the time comes, I'll do whatever I can to get a message to Gram,*" he transmitted. "*But we have bigger problems right now. They know my cuffs are off. They're coming.*"

He could hear the shouts from outside. They were close.

Mel jumped as a loud pounding came from the door.

"It's me," Jax called.

Nix knew Zane and his team weren't far behind.

"*Open the door,*" he transmitted to Mel as he pulled one of the deactivated cuffs from his writs. He threw it on the floor and stomped down hard, breaking it as Jax burst through the door.

"Sorry about this," Jax said as he punched Nix hard in the face. Nix staggered back. The other man's muscles definitely weren't for show. Jax aimed a second punch to his stomach, forcing the air from his lungs. Nix dropped to his knees as Zane burst through the door with Reed and half a dozen other soldiers squeezing in behind him.

"What's going on here, Captain Gale?" Zane barked accusingly.

"That'll teach you to mess with me, you little shit!" Jax shouted as he kicked Nix in the ribs.

Nix groaned and threw an imploring look at Mel.

"*You have to use it,*" he transmitted.

"I said that's enough!" she shouted half-heartedly, her hand trembling as she pulled the transmitter for his kill node from his pocket.

"*I'm sorry,*" she thought.

Nix curled up in pain as the electricity spread through his body.

"Take him to a cell," he heard Zane order as hands gripped his arms. "Someone take Jaxon outside to cool off. Gale, you'd better let me escort you to the command center.

Nix struggled to raise his head as several soldiers dragged him from the room. The last thing he saw was Mel's worried expression as Zane gripped her by the arm and prodded her toward the door.

Nix's body ached, every muscle sore from the spasms caused by the kill node. Sharp pain accompanied every breath he took and every movement he made. The pain made it difficult to keep his breathing steady, to keep his panic in check in the small, dimly lit prison cell the soldiers had shoved him into after fixing a fresh set of channeling restrictors on his wrists.

The nausea in his stomach slowly turned to hunger with the crawling of time. He didn't know how long it had been. He only knew his body had started to feel weak. The pain in his ribs was the only thing that kept his thoughts from retreating into foggy numbness.

At last, the door screeched open. Barton stood in the doorway, frowning.

"Where's Mel?" Nix croaked, his throat dry and sore.

Barton's frown deepened, and he shook his head almost imperceptibly.

"The Commander wants to see you," he said.

Nix stood and sucked in a sharp breath as fresh pain shot through his side. Jax's acting had been a little too good. He steadied himself against the wall of his cell until the pain subsided enough for him to straighten and take a cautious step toward Barton, who showed no signs of sympathy or of offering any assistance. Nix clenched his teeth and concentrated on following behind him without stumbling.

The Commander stood on the far side of the room when they entered, his back to them, stiff and erect.

"Wait outside," he ordered Barton, without turning around.

Barton saluted and left—closing the door behind him. The Commander said nothing, but Nix could see his jaw muscles working even from across the room. At last, he let out a long sigh and rubbed his forehead as he turned around.

"I suppose I have to give you credit for thinking quickly," he said. He paused, frowning as he looked at Nix. "You look awful. Sit down."

Nix sank into one of the hard chairs, resting his pounding head in his hands. He closed his eyes, feeling exhausted.

"When did you last eat?" the Commander asked.

"The morning of the fight."

"Those idiots."

The Commander stepped to one side of the room and tossed a packaged meal into the microwave before slamming the door. As the meal heated, he opened a cupboard and pulled out two small bottles and a box of medical patches.

"What happened to Mel and Jax?" Nix finally ventured to ask.

"They're fine," the Commander said. He slid the heated meal across the table before pulling a second off the shelf. "Major Zane filed a formal complaint against Mel, stating that she was lax in her supervision of you, and that she delayed taking control of the situation after your channeling restrictor had been broken. She's been removed from the strike team and is to have minimal contact with you going forward."

"But she won't be punished?" Nix asked in surprise.

"The official record states that your channeling restrictors were broken as part of an altercation between you and Jaxon. Though Mel's response was slow, there's no evidence that she actually did anything wrong."

Nix sighed in relief. Though he was sure being removed from the team was considered a serious enough punishment, it was better than what had happened to Gram.

"What about Jax?" Nix asked as he pulled the lid off the meal in front of him.

"After the beating he gave you, I think most would rather see him rewarded than punished," the Commander said as he pulled a second meal from the microwave. "Still, you could have escaped without the channeling restrictors, so he had to receive a reprimand, even if only for show. He's been assigned extra duties."

The Commander placed the second meal next to him, along with a small tray containing a glass of water, a bottle of painkillers, a jar filled with some kind of ointment, and the box of medical patches.

Nix looked up from his meal in surprise. It wasn't like the Commander to show concern for him.

"You could have escaped," the Commander reiterated. "Or you could have done nothing and let Mel suffer the consequences of her actions. Instead, the only one who came out of this mess with any serious repercussions is you. For the second time, you've placed yourself in harm's way to protect my subordinate, and for that I'm grateful."

Nix didn't know what to say. The Commander waved at Nix dismissively with one hand before sitting down across from him and picking up his tablet.

"Eat, and then we'll talk some more."

Nix took two painkillers from the bottle and downed them along with the entire glass of water. When he'd scraped the last bit of food from the second meal, he pushed the empty containers away. The Commander continued to study his tablet for several more minutes before setting it down and interlacing his hands under his chin.

"Tell me about—" he stopped and shook his head slightly, as though changing his mind about what he wanted to ask. He cleared his throat before continuing. "Tell me about Gram. Is he well?"

"Last time I saw him he was well enough," Nix lied. The last time he'd seen Gram he'd thrown a couch at him. After that, Gram had taken the girl to Syndicate territory, which meant there was a good chance Gram was not alright.

The Commander sighed.

"You're like him, you know."

Nix scoffed. He was nothing like Gram. Gram was friendly, likable, caring, reliable. He was everything Nix wasn't and everything Nix wanted to be.

"I didn't want to see it, but after today it's clear to me," the Commander said. "Gram has always been the one to act first and worry about the consequences later. He always does whatever needs to be done, and always worries about everyone but himself. In the past, whenever we found ourselves in trouble, he was usually the one who found a way out, more often than not by putting himself in harm's way."

The Commander smiled regretfully, then cleared his throat, straightening his shoulders.

"He's cocky, reckless, and foolhardy. He never thinks things through and usually ends up getting himself hurt. That's how you're like him."

Nix chuckled, the sound coming out as a painful wheeze. As loyal, courageous, and effective as Gram was, anyone who knew him also knew that he was equally reckless, self-confident, and annoying as hell.

It was more than Nix could ever hope for, to be compared to him.

"I don't know what kind of trouble he has gotten himself into this time," the Commander said, "but I know better than you might imagine that love makes people do foolish things. I assume Mel did what she did because of him?"

Nix nodded. There was no point in hiding the truth from the Commander.

"Gram's most likely in Syndicate territory. Mel wanted me to escape so I could warn him about the Military's plans."

The Commander let out a tired sounding sigh, no doubt recognizing how similar her actions had been to Gram's reckless decision five years ago.

"That sounds like something Gram would do," was all he said. After a pause, he asked, "What do you think of the upcoming operation?"

Nix hesitated, then shrugged.

"You know what I think," he said, referring to his prior objections. "Aside from that, it seems like a big risk. We haven't dealt any significant blows to the Syndicate, and yet they pulled their operatives back? It's almost like they knew we would move on their territory and wanted to increase their manpower."

The Commander nodded, as though he had the same concerns.

"Kaori has to have a hand in all this," Nix said. "I don't know the extent of it, or what her plans are, but I do know that the last thing she would ever want is for the Military to succeed. She wants to take control of the Syndicate for herself, and that will never change."

The Commander's eyebrows pulled together as he rested his chin on his interlaced fingers.

"You think this is a trap?"

Nix nodded.

"I think she wants to use the Military to weaken her brother's position," he said. "But if she can weaken the Military in the process, that will only help her in her quest for power."

Nix's stomach tightened as the pieces finally fit into place. He should have realized it all sooner. The questions he'd been unable to answer all this time finally made sense.

"Five years ago," he said quietly, "she tried to do the same thing."

The Commander's face paled.

Nix told the Commander everything. About the coup he and Kaori had staged to overthrow her father. How the chaos of the Military's attack made it easier. How she betrayed him and left him behind after he stopped her from killing Ryu.

He'd never told the story to anyone before, not even Gram, but he was tired of seeing people get hurt for pointless reasons. He was tired of trying to guess what Kaori's schemes meant, tired of the people he cared about getting hurt because of her ambitions. He was tired of always making the wrong choice.

If the Commander was going to do anything to fix this mess, Nix had to tell him everything.

"If Gram went to Syndicate territory," the Commander said slowly, after Nix had finished, "that girl must be with him."

Nix hesitated, then gave the Commander the smallest of nods.

"The Research Division still wants her," the Commander said.

"But—"

They had him, didn't they? Wasn't that the whole point? Wasn't that why he was doing all this?

The Commander's frown deepened.

"They believe they had some success in their experiments on her," the Commander said, looking sickened by his own words. "They have you, yes, but without her they are basically starting over from scratch."

"That's what this is really about, isn't it?" Nix asked, balling his hands into fists. "That's why they want us to invade. It must have been Kaori. She knew I went to see Ryu. She must have told them that I'd sent the girl there."

The Commander shook his head.

"You aren't wrong," he said evenly, his matter-of-fact tone a contrast to his expression. "She's only part of the reason. There's a rumor that the Syndicate also did telepathy research, and that their current leader was given the ability. If that's true, then he's an even more valuable target than...than the Copelan girl."

Nix went cold. Kaori wanted her brother out of the way, and she knew just what to tell the Military in order to get them to act.

"Ryu," Nix said quietly, his voice barely louder than a whisper. He cleared his throat before continuing at normal volume. "You're right. His father was obsessed with ability research. We were always stealing from research facilities—notes, equipment, even test subjects. Reizen even experimented on his own children. And he had something the Military didn't have. He had me. It wasn't just my telepathy he wanted. All of my abilities were made stronger because of it—because of my channeling."

He stopped as another realization hit him.

"That's why the Military wanted the girl. They thought she had the potential for telepathy because of how strong her channeling is."

Because hers was the closest he'd ever seen to someone having channeling on par with his, almost like she too had an ability that needed such large amounts of energy.

That was it.

He wanted to kick himself for not realizing it sooner.

The researchers didn't know. She could never be a telepath because she already had another ability.

"They think they made a breakthrough?" he questioned out loud, half to himself. "All they did was break her."

He laughed darkly and looked at the Commander.

"I know why the Syndicate pulled out their operatives," he said. "I thought it was all Kaori, but it was her. It was the girl."

"What do you mean?"

Nix grinned. All the dreams and nightmares suddenly made sense.

"We don't need to worry about getting a message to Gram. She's going to see us coming."

Part Four

Into Light

Even though you're far away
I've never felt so close to you
Or anyone.
Your entire life has filled
My dreams and haunted
Me when I'm awake.
I know you
More than anyone
Maybe even more
Than myself,
And yet you remain
Out of reach.

Even though you're far away
I hear you in my head
Like a heartbeat,
A whisper to remind me
Of who I want to be.
And so I reach out
For your voice
Like a lifeline,
Wishing you were here
Instead of
Out of reach.

Chapter Twenty-nine

"Are you alright?" Ryu asked, stepping up beside Thea in the busy meeting room that adjoined his office.

She shook her head and said, "I'm sorry. I'm just worried."

"Why don't we take a short break," he said.

Thea followed him into his office, relieved by the quiet as he closed the door behind them.

"We've done all we can to prepare," Ryu said, motioning for her to sit while he prepared two cups of tea for them. "Now all we can do is trust in our people."

He paused, and his face flushed slightly.

"Sorry, I meant..."

"It's okay," Thea said. "I hope we've done enough, and that everyone comes back safe."

He must have felt her hesitancy because he paused and asked, "It's not the battle you're worried about, is it?"

His voice turned cold. She'd learned over the last few weeks that his coldness wasn't directed at her. It was meant to hide feelings he didn't want to deal with.

He cleared his throat. "Do you want to talk about it?"

The question made Thea feel guilty, and she shook her head.

"I'm okay. You have more important things to worry about right now."

"Thea, I appreciate all you've done. I can't tell you how much your help has meant to me these last few weeks." He handed her one of the cups as he sat down beside her on the couch. "I hope you know that you mean more to me than that, though. If something is troubling you, I'd like to help."

Thea took a tentative sip of her tea. It was better than the tea he'd given her the first day she'd met him, but still not as good as Lucan's, which she would soon run out of.

"I'm sorry," she said. "I didn't mean to imply that you don't care. You've been a good friend to me since I came here, and I appreciate that. I don't want you to have to worry about me when you have so many other things on your mind."

"It's too late," Ryu said, reaching out to squeeze her hand, "because I am worried and I'm going to stay worried until you tell me what's bothering you."

Thea smiled, but hunched her shoulders as she took another sip of her tea. The truth was, she didn't want to tell him she was worried about Nix. She knew it was hard for him to reconcile his feelings for the other man with the hurt he still felt over his betrayal.

"You're worried about Nix, aren't you," Ryu said quietly, the coldness returning to his voice.

Thea nodded.

"He's important to you," Ryu said, removing his hand from hers, his voice quiet and emotionless.

Thea felt her face warm.

"He's done a lot for me," she blurted out awkwardly. "And he's in this situation because of me."

Ryu sighed and rubbed his forehead. Before he could respond the door opened and Gram appeared in the doorway.

"There you are," he said. "The scout's back."

Ryu set down his cup and stood. Thea followed him back toward the meeting room, but Gram stopped them in the doorway, a nervous smile lighting up his face.

"He's here," he said, meeting Thea's eyes.

"What do you mean?" Ryu asked, his eyebrows pulling together.

Nobu noticed them and stepped closer, flexing his muscles warily. Though Ryu had come to trust and rely on Gram, Nobu had not.

"Nix," Gram said. "He's here. Or at least he's close."

Ryu looked to Nobu who shook his head.

"The scout reported that the Military troops have reached Jinsan. That's too far away to sense anyone, even someone with as much channeling as the Ghost. You must be mistaken."

"Oh, there's no mistake," Gram insisted with a chuckle. "I've tracked that dumbass all over the Wilds. I recognize that energy anywhere."

"We know that Nix has been part of an advance team," Thea said.

"To send an advance team this far would be foolish," Nobu insisted.

"Maybe they're foolish then," Gram countered. "Or maybe something happened, and he got away."

Thea shook her head.

"No, he wouldn't try to escape, I'm sure of it."

She'd felt it in her dreams, his resolve to protect her.

"Then it sounds like we'd better send a team of our own," Ryu said before Nobu could argue further.

"I'm going."

Ryu and Gram both turned to Thea, but she cut off their objections.

"This is why I came here," she said. "To bring him back. I'm not going to sit here and do nothing."

"You putting yourself in danger will only make it harder for him," Gram said. "If the Military takes you, then everything he did will have been for nothing."

Thea huffed but before she could argue Ryu held up a placating hand.

"Please, Thea, let me send a recon team. I promise to keep you updated on anything we learn."

"We had a deal, Ryu," she said. "Please. We have to get him away from the Military."

Ryu nodded, though she recognized the conflict in his eyes.

"It's not in our best interest to allow him to continue to help the Military," Nobu said.

Thea hardly found his words comforting, but they seemed to satisfy Ryu. He nodded.

"We'll do what we can, Thea. For now, please stay here."

"I'll keep you updated on what I can sense," Gram said quietly in her ear.

"Fine!"

It was frustrating. He was so close, but he felt as far away as he ever had.

When Zane's team was assigned to join Barton's, the Commander told them it was because their operations in the west fell under Commander Stewart's jurisdiction, but they all knew the real reason. Commander Stewart had objected to Nix's involvement in operations from the start, and the incident between Jax and Nix had only proved what a danger his presence was. She didn't trust Commander Astley to keep his team in check, and so Zane's team was meant to serve as extra security to make sure Nix stayed in line.

Nix didn't care for Zane or the other members of his team, but they were competent fighters who respected the chain of command. Barton was to remain the commanding officer in the field, which meant Nix didn't have to worry about following orders contrary to what the Commander wanted.

Their operations progressed easily into Syndicate territory. He wasn't surprised that they met little resistance. The Syndicate knew they were coming. The real fight would come when they reached Tanri. He was sure of it.

There was only one thing still gnawing at the back of his mind.

Kaori.

As they marched closer and closer to her personal agenda, she made no signs of deviating from the Military's aims. Whatever her plan was, it seemed she was in no hurry to enact it.

The only thing Nix found strange was how much time she spent with the members of Zane's team.

Zane himself seemed to loathe her as much as he did Nix. He reprimanded his team members on more than one occasion for interacting with her, and it seemed because of that, Reed mostly avoided her, too.

The short, stalky looking enhancer named Walt seemed to spend the most time with her.

Nix didn't like it.

Their two teams stopped to rest before making their final approach into Tanri.

"*Keep an eye on Kaori,*" he transmitted to Barton and Jax as Kaori sauntered past. "*If she's going to make a move, it will be here.*"

Jax gave him the smallest of nods. Barton remained stoic, as if they hadn't communicated at all, though Nix could feel his acknowledgment in his thoughts.

"Our break has been long enough," he said aloud, standing from where he'd been sitting on a large rock. "The sooner we can get information back to the Commanders, the sooner they can move out."

Zane shot Barton a look, clearly annoyed to be taking orders from his younger peer. He holstered the gun he'd been inspecting and stood as well.

"Everybody up, let's move out."

Weapons were holstered, jackets and helmets were donned, packs were closed. After a moment of noisy bustle that set Nix on edge, the group was ready to move in on their target location.

Though Tanri was technically its own village, sprawling out from the mouth of the narrow mountain valley, most in the Syndicate thought of it as merely an extension of Chusan. It was the gateway, the sentinel standing guard, the gaping mouth ready to swallow intruders into the depths of the Syndicate's strongest village.

The closer they moved toward the town the more aware he became of the growing pressure in his head, the dull, familiar throbbing that he knew had a single source.

She was close.

Not close enough to limit his telepathy or even to sense anything distinct. It was merely a growing awareness he couldn't ignore, a pulsing beacon pulling his attention forward to where she waited deeper in the mountains ahead. He tried to ignore it, tried not to think about how the closer he got, the more danger she was in.

Instead, he tried to focus on the familiar houses and narrow streets set into the steep, rocky slopes. The town seemed deserted, quiet, but Nix knew better.

Anticipation hung in the air, taut as a string about to snap. He could sense the thoughts, writhing around them, ready to pounce.

"*Stop*," he transmitted to the group before they'd reached the edge of town. "*They were ready for us. If we get any closer, we'll be dead.*"

"You aren't in charge here. We don't take orders from you," Walt whined out loud, his voice cutting through the silence like a sword.

Nix cringed.

"Shut up, you idiot," Jax hissed, his own whisper still too loud.

"He's right," Reed said, stepping forward angrily. "And you have about as much authority as he does Jaxon."

Jax tensed, ready for a fight, but before he could say or do anything impulsive Barton stepped between the two men.

Barton shot Jax a warning look then stepped closer to Reed.

"But I do give the orders here," he hissed quietly knowing that speaking out loud was foolish, but that Zane's team couldn't be pacified through telepathic communication. "The success of this mission depends on his telepathy. Communicating out loud is dangerous, and likely to get us killed. If you don't want that to happen I suggest you remain silent and assume any orders he gives, come from me."

Veins stood out in Reed's neck as the muscles in his jaw worked. Zane stood as well, his muscles tightening as he stepped up next to Reed. He glared at Barton angrily, knowing the other man was right and hating it.

"*Is that understood?*" Barton thought, wanting Nix to transmit the message.

Reed's eyes bulged in fury when he did, but Zane placed a firm hand on his arm, a silent message of his own.

"*Yes. Sir.*" Reed thought.

Barton turned to look at each person in turn. Jax nodded and stepped back in relief but stiffened again as he followed Barton's gaze.

"Where's Walt?" he blurted out loud.

Nix swore.

Kaori and Zane's Micro, a woman named Everly, were gone as well.

"We have to go after them," Nix said out loud. Telepathic communication would only slow them down, and they needed to go after Kaori.

"You just said we should fall back," Barton countered. "I have to agree. Two soldiers defecting to the Syndicate puts our whole operation in danger. We need to contact the Commander."

"That's a serious accusation," Zane snapped. "I won't allow you to question the loyalty of my soldiers."

"Look around," Keller said with a snort. "They're gone. What other explanation is there?"

"That's enough," Barton said firmly.

Before Zane could reply, both he and Barton held a hand to their ear as they received radio communication. Barton's face turned pale.

"That was Captain Gale," he said. "They're under attack. We're falling back."

"Is it the Syndicate?" Jax asked.

Barton shook his head.

"Then who?"

"It's an internal attack. That's all she could tell me."

Soldiers siding with Kaori. An internal attack among the soldiers. Jiren. It all clicked into place.

Kaori had told him the only side she was on was her own. He'd thought she'd been evading his question, like usual, but it had been the truth. She didn't care about weakening the Syndicate or helping the Military, because she didn't care which side won. She was trying to destroy them both.

The others picked up their gear and turned back the way they'd come. Nix hesitated.

If Kaori had managed to instigate an internal conflict in the Military, there was no question she could do the same in the Syndicate, where she had even more supporters.

Barton noticed his hesitation and turned to him with a frown.

"*That's an order,*" he thought.

"*Kaori caused this. I'm sure of it. She's planning to do the same thing here. I have to stop her.*"

"What's the problem?" Zane asked, noticing that the two of them had stopped. His hand itched toward his gun.

Nix took a step back and the familiar pounding thoughts in his head grew louder, clearer. She was getting closer.

"I can't go back," he whispered.

Zane was on him before he could take another step. Reed followed. They grabbed his arms, their strength rising in anticipation.

Barton didn't move.

"What are you doing?" Zane seethed. "The prisoner is trying to escape. Use the switch."

Barton's thoughts warred with each other. The Commander didn't want Kaori to be able to act freely. They were supposed to watch her, but the argument had distracted them. They'd failed. The army was under attack and the Commander needed their help, but it was a Military problem—something Nix wasn't part of.

Yet here they were on the Syndicate doorstep and the chance that Nix actually meant to betray them wasn't small.

Barton lifted his hand. Nix tensed, expecting him to reach for the kill node controller in his pocket.

Instead, Barton pulled his gun from its holster and aimed it at Zane.

"Let him go," he said.

Jax and Keller stepped behind Barton and pulled out their own guns before Zane's Manipulator could make a move.

"You think you can get away with treason just because your father is a marshal?" Zane spat.

"I'm not getting away with anything," Barton said, his voice calm. "I have orders from Commander Astley, and you're out of line."

Zane's eyes darted between Barton and the others. His breath came out in a furious huff. Nix held his breath, waiting.

Finally, slowly, Zane released his grip on Nix's arm and Reed followed. Nix sprang out of their reach.

"This isn't over," Zane hissed.

"Be grateful I'm not having you restrained," Barton said. He turned to Nix with a nod. "Find Kaori and the traitors who followed her. That's an order."

"I'm sorry," Nix started to say, but before he could finish all hell broke loose.

Fighters sprang from the trees, poured out from the nearest buildings. Shouts and the sounds of fighting filled the air from deeper in town. The girl's thoughts strummed louder and louder in his head, the chaos making it difficult for him to figure out what was going on.

"Go," Barton repeated as he turned to intercept the nearest attacker.

Nix hesitated and Barton reiterated his command.

"Tell the Commander I will come back," he said as he turned to run.

"Wait," Jax called as he dodged an attacker. His radio lifted from his pocket and floated toward Nix. "Be careful. And take care of that idiot Gram for me!"

Nix smirked as he grabbed the radio, then turned and broke into a run.

"What's happening, Gram?" Thea asked impatiently as Ryu conversed with his advisors.

Gram shook his head.

"I don't know. They're still pretty far away, and they haven't moved in a while. Maybe they're waiting for more troops to arrive."

Thea jumped as a man rushed into the room.

"Sir, several teams have already moved from their standby locations. They appear to be converging on the targets."

"What?" Ryu asked. "Has there been any contact with those teams?"

The man shook his head.

"I reiterated your orders to hold position, but received no response."

A woman entered the room before Ryu could respond.

"Sir, the recon team reports that your sister is no longer with the soldiers. We don't know where she is."

Thea spun toward Gram, her eyes wide.

"I have to go."

Gram shook his head, but it was Ryu who spoke.

"Thea, no. It's even more dangerous for you now than before. Please, I need you to stay here."

Thea shook her head and resisted the urge to shrink away, aware that all eyes in the room had turned toward her.

"I didn't come her for protection," she said, reiterating the words she had said to him when they'd first met.

He clenched his jaw with a sad look in his eyes.

"You came here to help, didn't you?" His voiced turned flat. "You can do that by not giving me something else to worry about right now."

"I'm sorry, Ryu. I can't."

She turned and was out the door before he could reply.

"Wait!" Gram stepped up behind her.

She stopped in the hall but set her shoulders back stubbornly.

"Just wait," he repeated. "There's no point in running off when you don't even know where he is."

Gram placed a hand on her elbow and led her outside.

"You know where Tanri is, right?" he asked, pointing toward the southern mouth of the narrow valley.

She nodded.

"Well, there's a thousand Syndicate between you and them and they might not all be friendly. Kaori's out there too. You sure you want to do this?"

Thea nodded.

"Then let's go," he said.

"No, Ryu needs you here."

"Ryu needs to not be thinking about you right now. It'll be better for him to know you're not alone."

"I won't be for long," she said.

Before he could stop her, she broke into a run.

"*What are you doing here?*" Nix transmitted to the girl, unable to keep his frustration from bleeding through his thoughts.

What had Gram been thinking, letting her get involved in this? Nix had done all this to keep her safe, and now she was running into the danger.

Why couldn't she just stay safe?

Her thoughts filled with relief when she heard his, but there was a hot flash of anger there as well.

"*I'm looking for you, you idiot!*"

Nix scowled. How foolish could she be?

The fighting, it seemed, hadn't reached Chusan yet, but as she left the valley and ran down the winding trail into Tanri her senses picked up the chaos. She stopped to catch her breath as she listened, trying to choose a path that would keep her away from most of the fighting.

A man jumped out from the shadows, startling her and making her heart race.

Was he an enemy or an ally?

Would he know the difference when he saw her or think she was part of the attack?

Nix ground his teeth and increased his speed, as the man lunged forward for an attack.

The girl stumbled slightly in her attempt to evade him, but quickly regained her balance and turned his momentum against him, slamming him to the ground.

She was different, Nix realized. Her adrenaline buzzed in his head, but not the usual overwhelming panic. She was calmer, more focused. Instead of simply pushing herself to move faster or be stronger, she was watching her opponent and looking for his next move. Gram's style was so evident in her movements that Nix couldn't help but smirk.

She stepped away from her opponent and broke into a run, her thoughts filled with fresh resolve. She was going to save him. It wasn't a question. It was a certainty.

"*I did this to keep you safe,*" Nix pleaded.

Even with training, she didn't know how much danger she was in. Kaori was here and he didn't even know what her full objective was.

"*I don't want to be kept safe,*" she shot back.

He ground his teeth in renewed frustration. If he couldn't reason with her, he was just going to have to protect her himself.

To do that, he was going to need a sword.

He changed his course toward the nearest thoughts, knowing it didn't matter if they were on Ryu's side or not. They were going to take one look at his uniform and attack him either way.

Fighting bare-handed always took too long, but his impatience to reach her only made it worse. After finally knocking out the three combatants he'd encountered, he picked up one of their fallen swords and turned his attention back to the girl.

"Meet me in the central square," he transmitted.

She was close and familiar with the route.

It wasn't easy to avoid fighting. Having her so close made it more difficult to pinpoint nearby thoughts, and he ran into one group of Syndicate while trying to avoid another. By the time he'd dealt with them, she'd already reached the square.

At last, he stepped into the open space, his eyes already searching for her. Almost immediately, she barreled into him. He let out a grunt of surprise as she wrapped her arms around his waist and buried her face in his shoulder as if it were the most natural thing to do, as if she'd done it a thousand times before.

A sob escaped from her throat as tears streamed down her cheeks, not tears of fear or even anger.

Only relief.

He let out his own exhale of relief. He raised his free hand up stiffly, but stopped, his arm hovering a few inches from her back. Before he could make the decision to embrace her, she pulled away and punched him hard in the chest.

"That's for being an idiot!" she snapped, smiling even though tears streaked her face.

Nix sucked in a breath and pulled his hand up to grab his still bruised ribs.

"Oh, I'm sorry!" she exclaimed, bringing her hands up to her mouth. "I didn't realize you were still hurt."

She'd had a dream about the incident with Jax but she hadn't known the context, or the timing. Fresh worry filled her thoughts, and he let out a small chuckle.

"It's okay. I'm okay," he told her, his voice gentle. "It's not what you think."

"But they hurt you." Her voice shook as she wiped her face.

He shook his head.

"It's what we had to do to protect Mel."

He transmitted the memory to show her what had happened.

Her thoughts filled with warmth, as his eyes trailed over her. She was a mess. Her pale hair clung to her face and stuck out in a halo of static. Her clothes were covered in dust and her cheeks were smeared with dirt, tears, and the fading yellow color of an old bruise.

Hesitantly, he reached out a hand to brush her hair from her face. She leaned into his touch, and he stepped closer, the hum of her thoughts in his mind a comfort he hadn't realized he'd missed.

She looked up at him, her hair shining with the last rays of the evening sun and her eyes glowing like warm pools of amber light, melting away the cold weight he'd been carrying inside him since he left.

I never understood why
No matter how I tried
I couldn't stay away
The lies and the pain
Were never enough
To erase what we had
Or what we wanted to be
Or the fact that you
Were the only one
Who really saw me.
We each had our walls
Made by wounds and scars
That we never could tear down
Not even for each other
And yet I wanted to, for you.
That's the reason why
No matter how I tried
I couldn't stay away.

Chapter Thirty

"Well, isn't this sweet?"

All the girl's warmth disappeared, like the sunlight itself had vanished, leaving only dim light and a chill.

They both whirled around as Kaori sauntered into the square, her swords in hand, already red with blood. Kuda walked beside her with the two soldiers from Zane's team following close behind.

"Brings back memories, doesn't it, Ghost?" Kaori gestured around the square.

They'd been here plenty of times, of course, but he knew which time she was referring to. This was where she'd tried to kill Ryu. This was where she'd left him to die.

"You know I've never wanted to kill you," she said with an almost affectionate smile. "You just won't stop getting in my way. So what's it going to be this time?"

"Why are you doing this?" The girl's voice shook. She wanted to be confident and brave, but when Kaori turned her cold smile toward her, she hunched her shoulders and took a step back.

"Why does anyone do anything, sweetheart?" Kaori's voice was light, but her eyes held only disdain. "For money, for power, for revenge. You could say I'm here for all three. Oh, and I guess there's the thrills, too."

The girl clenched her jaw and raised her chin, her thoughts consumed by sudden, overwhelming rage. It wasn't just that Kaori had hurt people she cared about. The way she toyed with people, manipulated them, hurt them— she hated all of it. She wanted Kaori to pay for the things she'd done. She wanted her dead.

Nix felt her anger fade just as fast as it had come. The thought of killing someone sickened her, and she rejected it as completely as she rejected Kaori. She couldn't be the source of something as horrific as what Kaori had done to her, and to Kai.

The familiar images flashed through her mind, and she started to tremble, her eyes wide with hollow fear.

Kai's life bleeding out as he pleaded with her to run. His still form as he lost consciousness. The gruesome nightmares she'd endured since his death.

"Thea."

Her name felt heavy and awkward on his tongue. Had he really never said it out loud before? Apparently not. Her surprise at hearing him say it pulled her from the waking nightmare.

He pulled the radio from his pocket and held it out as he stepped protectively in front of her. "You don't have to do this. Go find Gram. Tell him to radio Mel. I'll take care of Kaori."

She shook her head, steeling herself with fresh resolve. Instead of taking the radio, she stepped up beside him, pulling a dagger from the pouch at her hip.

"No," she said firmly. "We do this together."

He knew he couldn't argue with her, and the truth was, he didn't want to.

"Fine," he projected, "but leave Kaori to me. I know how she fights. Try to keep the others at a distance as much as you can."

Thea nodded. Before anyone could react, she leapt forward and closed the distance to Everly, knocking her to the ground before she could pull her gun. Before Walt could pull out his own gun, she jumped away and flung her dagger toward him.

She really had become stronger.

He turned his attention back to Kaori and scowled.

"I guess that's it then." She sounded disappointed. "You've chosen her. It really is such a waste, Ghost."

"Why are you actually doing this, Kaori? What do you hope to achieve?"

She stalked toward him slowly and he tensed, trying to anticipate her attack while also keeping an eye on Kuda circling to his side.

"You always think I have ulterior motives, Ghost, but I'm a simple woman. I've only ever wanted my due in life." She was close enough now he could reach out and grab her if he wanted to. She didn't attack, and neither did he. He knew better than to trust what he thought he could see.

"Are you really telling me you're doing all this, manipulating the Military and the Syndicate, starting a war all because of Ryu—all because your father chose him over you? I don't buy it."

Her expression darkened, her calm nonchalance slipping into agitation. She began to circle around him slowly. He turned with her even though it gave Kuda the opportunity to slip behind him.

"What do you know about it, Ghost?" Kaori spat. "You act like you're taking some kind of high ground, but you only know what it's like to be one of the favored, to have an ability everyone desires, to be admired because of that above everything else. You have no idea what it's like for the rest of us."

She dashed in for a testing strike. He knew better than to rush in to try and overpower her. Kaori had spent her entire life cultivating a fighting style specifically meant to lure Macros in with their speed, and use it against them. He could only fight her carefully, at her pace. He parried her first sword and jumped out of the way of the second. Her movements so far were only what they appeared to be. She wasn't fighting him seriously.

Yet.

He let out a snort and put more distance between them.

"I'd love for you to explain to me how my abilities have made my life easier. You're fooling yourself Kaori. Your father was an insane piece of shit, but you can't tear the territories apart over that, or your petty jealousy, or whatever."

Kaori laughed mirthlessly.

"That's the Ghost I remember. Harsh as ever." She let out a wistful sounding sigh. "I always thought that if anyone would come to see things my way, it would be you. We really could have been great together, Ghost. I really will be sad to kill you this time."

Her expression and stance changed. She was done playing with him.

This time, when she moved toward him, he jumped back to dodge instead of trying to parry. Hot pain bit into his shoulder from behind and he swore to himself. He'd forgotten about Kuda. He pushed his channeling into his shoulder as Kuda pressed his sword down even harder.

"Nix!" Thea called out, jumping away from her opponents to rush to his side.

"Stay back!" he shouted. He didn't want her getting involved in a fight with Kaori.

Of course, she didn't listen. She never did.

Kuda jumped away as she sent a dagger flying toward him. Kaori smiled eagerly as Thea stepped protectively between them.

The two soldiers began to circle in closer, but Kaori waved them off.

"Rendezvous with the others. Make sure things are going according to plan," she said before flicking her tongue over her teeth. "I'm going to enjoy taking care of this one myself."

Nix wanted to move between Thea and Kaori, but that would leave her back open to Kuda. Desperately, he transmitted to her, *"Be careful, she can alter your perception with her ability. Don't let her get too close."*

"I know."

Unwillingly, Nix turned his attention to Kuda. He had to deal with him quickly so he could help Thea.

"I've been waiting a long time for this, Ghost Boy," Kuda sneered.

Nix readjusted his grip on his sword. He had to end this quickly.

Thea needed him.

Kuda lunged toward him first. It was a stupid move and guaranteed Nix's victory. Nix sidestepped his attack easily and lunged with his own sword, embedding it in Kuda's abdomen. Pain shot down his left arm as he caught Kuda's sword arm with his left hand. He ground his teeth and did his best to ignore it as he sliced sideways before kicking Kuda forcefully away from him. Kuda's body flew across the square, colliding against the far wall with a sickening thud, a trail of blood pouring from his wound. He wouldn't be getting up again. If he wasn't already dead, he would be soon.

Thea let out a shocked cry at the sight. She'd been keeping Kaori at a distance with her daggers, but they clattered to the ground. She froze before turning away with a horrified cry, the memory of her brother's bleeding body overwhelming her thoughts.

Kaori smiled before rushing in for an attack.

Nix jumped between them, catching one strike with his sword. He kicked Kaori hard, causing her to fly backward. Her second sword caught his jacket but didn't pierce his skin.

"*It's okay,*" he transmitted to Thea. "*I'm here. You don't have to do this alone.*"

Her thoughts cleared and her resolve returned. She didn't want him to have to face Kaori alone, either. She wanted them to do this together.

Kaori struggled to her feet, her hair clinging to her face. Her clothes were torn and dirty and her arms had several cuts from Thea's daggers. One arm hung limp at her side, broken from Nix's kick.

"It's over, Kaori. You can't win like this."

He wanted her to give up. He had no desire to kill her. Maybe he couldn't read her mind, but he knew her. He wanted more for her than this.

Maybe that was the real reason he'd gone back to her again and again. She had been his first friend, his first family, his first lover. He'd only ever wanted her to have the same chance Gram had given him.

The chance to start over.

Seeing her now, he thought he understood for the first time how broken she really was—how broken she had always been underneath the facade of cold mockery and nonchalance.

He lowered his sword.

"Whatever you hope to accomplish with all of this, you deserve more than that." His voice was quiet, pleading. "Come back with me."

Kaori let out a cold laugh.

"You really are the sentimental one, aren't you? What? Do you think we should live happily ever after with the peacekeeper and the little girl over there? You think we should go make nice with all your new Military friends?" Her usually calm voice was growing more agitated with every word. "That's not me, Ghost. And that's not you either. People like us don't get to live happily ever after. We're tools, and we'll never be anything else. The best we can do is scrape out a little bit of respect by taking what we want by force."

Nix shook his head.

"You might be right," he said, "but I don't care anymore. You've already lost Kaori. You can try to escape, I won't stop you. After this I doubt anyone in the Syndicate or the Military will ever believe you again. You're done manipulating things. If I ever do hear about you causing trouble, I'll find you and I'll stop you again."

He turned away. "Let's go, Thea."

The next moments seemed to happen in slow motion. Through Thea's thoughts he saw Kaori run toward him, sword in hand, preparing to strike with her uninjured arm. Before he could turn around, Thea forced her remaining channeling into her legs and rushed to push him out of the way. As she collided into him, he saw the look of triumph on Kaori's face. Thea was still off balance. She wouldn't be able to avoid the attack. His body moved on instinct. He caught Kaori's arm and drove his sword into her abdomen, just as he had been trained to do, just as he had done to Kuda and so many others.

Her sword clattered to the ground as her arm went limp in his hand. He caught her as she fell against him and eased her to the ground.

"I...I'm sorry," Thea said quietly, her thoughts a mix of guilt and relief. Nix only felt numb.

Somewhere, in the back of his mind, he knew he should go to Thea and make sure she was alright, but his body didn't move. He simply sat with Kaori in his arms, blood bubbling from her wound with every ragged breath she took.

"Are you hurt?" he asked Thea without looking at her. His voice sounded strange to him, somehow too rough and too quiet at the same time.

"No."

The word hung in the air with all the unspoken things she couldn't manage to say.

He fumbled for the radio in his pocket and held it out to her, his hands slick with blood.

"Will you be okay to get back to Gram and Ryu on your own? You don't have much energy left."

"I'll be fine."

This is my fault. Of course he doesn't want me here.

"Tell Ryu, if you see him."

"I will. I'll tell him to send someone to help her."

Nix shook his head.

"She won't last."

"I'm sorry," she choked out again, and then her thoughts started to move away.

He knew it wasn't fair to her, to push her away, but right then he couldn't do anything else.

"Why did you stay?" Kaori rasped. Nix didn't answer her. He didn't know what to say. He wasn't sure he even had the answer.

"It really is such a waste, Nix."

She reached her hand up shakily and stroked his cheek before letting it drop.

As her energy slipped away along with her life and her blood, so did the mental blocks that kept him from reading her thoughts. They were as faint as her remaining life, little more than a whisper, but for the first time in a long time, he felt like he knew her.

"It wasn't all bad, was it? We had some good times, didn't we?"

He smirked.

"We definitely had some good times. Remember the first time we met? You were always sneaking into the prison and getting in trouble for it."

Now that he'd found his voice, his words poured out. He told her everything he'd kept inside since that day she'd marched up to his prison cell and told him she thought he was interesting. He didn't know how long he sat there talking or when she finally stopped breathing. His throat hurt, and the distant sound of fighting had gone silent.

He could sense Ryu's approaching thoughts before he heard his footsteps, which meant Thea had likely gone back to Chusan.

Nix didn't turn around. Neither man spoke. Like Nix, Ryu wasn't entirely sure what he was supposed to feel.

"How long?" Ryu finally asked, his voice thick and quiet.

"Not long," Nix said.

"I'm sorry."

"Me too."

"We should...take her back. Take her home. Do you need me to carry her?"

Nix shook his head and hefted her lifeless body in his arms. His ribs throbbed and his wounded shoulder burned as his clothes pulled at the drying blood. The pain helped clear his head of the numb fog he'd felt since stabbing Kaori.

The last light of the evening had long since faded, but it was still easy for Nix to recognize Gram as he stepped out of the shadows on the winding road leading into the valley.

"Why are you here?" Nix asked him, "You should be with Thea."

Gram raised his eyebrows, not missing the fact that Nix called her by name. Then he shrugged.

"Nice to see you too, dumbass." Though Gram's voice held a touch of annoyance, it lacked its usual teasing bite. He sighed before finally answering. "She wanted to be alone. She'll be alright though."

Nix frowned. Gram was worried about her, but at the moment he was more worried about Nix.

Nix followed Ryu numbly, only peripherally aware of the aftermath of the battle around him. The people working to carry away the dead and wounded stopped to stare at them. Some murmured angrily as they recognized him, but no one attempted to hinder their progress.

"Where do you plan to take her?" Gram asked quietly. "The infirmary is pretty swamped."

Ryu shook his head.

"Home."

The large room of the main house fell silent as they entered, but Nix barely noticed. Thea's thoughts had grown louder, more present in his thoughts as they neared. He could no longer ignore them. She wasn't in the house, but alone in the training arena. She was worried about him.

Nix followed Ryu down the narrow hallways of the house, though he could have found his way to Kaori's room without a second thought. Every step was heavy with the familiarity of memories that her lifeless body in his arms made all the more painful.

They entered the room, and Nix saw that though nothing had changed, the room was as much an empty shell of what it had once been as Kaori's body was now. The furnishings were the same, but the elements that made the room Kaori's were gone. There were no stacks of books by her bed, no notes or jars of herbs on the desk. Even her scent was long gone from the room, replaced by the staleness of non-use.

Nix placed her body on the bed, Thea's thoughts tugging at him like a beacon—a lifeline keeping him from sinking into the suffocating emptiness of Kaori's vacant room.

Nix didn't know how long he'd sat there in the heavy silence. He'd forgotten Gram and Ryu were even still in the room until Ryu stepped closer, clearing his throat.

"I'm glad my sister always had you," he said. "I'm glad you were with her in the end."

Nix just pursed his lips and nodded. The truth was, he'd done everything he could to distance himself from Kaori over the years. She had always been the one to seek him out. He finally understood that it was because she needed him, too. Now that she was gone, and it was too late, he wasn't sure how he was supposed to feel about that.

"I'll have clothes and food prepared for you," Ryu said.

Then he was gone, and it was just him and Gram, and Thea's thoughts in his head.

Nix stood. He'd made her wait for him long enough.

Gram stepped closer and placed a hand carefully on his uninjured shoulder.

"Let's get you cleaned up before you go see her."

Nix looked down at his hands and clothes, covered in blood, and nodded. Gram was right. Thea shouldn't see him like this.

He followed Gram from the room without looking back. There was no point. There was nothing left for him there but the past. Thea was waiting for him.

A thousand times
You've held me
In your arms
Quieted my fears
And made me
Feel like I
Was safe

A thousand times
You've held my
Hand in yours
And pressed your
Lips against
My skin

A thousand times
A thousand dreams
A thousand days
Of a life
That hasn't
Happened yet

A thousand times
You've loved me
You just don't
Know it yet.

Chapter Thirty-one

Nix had killed Kaori, and it was her fault.

Thea knew she shouldn't feel relieved, but she couldn't help it.

Kaori had caused so much pain, had haunted her nightmares for months, and now she was gone.

She didn't know what to say to him, or how to comfort him, when he was hurting and she only felt relief. All she had been able to do was stand awkwardly and watch as Kaori lay in his arms gasping for breath. When he'd told her to go find Ryu, she was hurt, but she was also relieved.

And she hated herself for it.

Hadn't she promised herself she wouldn't let him face anything alone anymore? And yet she had left him to watch the person he loved die in his arms. The person he'd killed because of her.

Tears burned her eyes as she sat alone on the low wall of the training arena, wondering if Kaori was gone and where Nix was now.

"I'm sorry I haven't come to find you yet." His mental voice entered her thoughts, startling her out of her own. *"Are you okay?"*

She felt an immediate rush of relief that was quickly replaced by shame.

"Don't worry about me," she thought. *"You should rest."*

"I'll come find you soon," he promised.

"You should rest," she reiterated.

It was odd the way his thoughts were more than just mental words. She could feel his laughter in her head and the way his heartbeat quickened with the anticipation of seeing her. She wondered if that was normal with telepathy.

Her head went silent, leaving her with only her own mix of eagerness and worry. She wanted to see him, and she didn't.

After all this time, after all this waiting and wanting, he was finally here, and she didn't know what she was supposed to do or say.

She'd dreamed of him so many times, of his past and of their future. She felt like she knew him, even though she didn't. Or at least he didn't know that she did. How was she supposed to act when she already knew that she loved him and that he would love her someday, but he didn't yet?

She couldn't think about the future right now because right now he was hurting, and it was her fault.

What was she supposed to say? What was she supposed to do? What would he think when he read her thoughts and knew what she was holding back?

She didn't know.

"*I'm coming,*" he told her, and the tears escaped her eyes. They wouldn't stop, no matter how much she tried to wipe them away.

Nix frowned as he stepped into the shower. His shoulder burned and fresh blood oozed from his wound, but the pain had nothing to do with his expression.

Thea blamed herself for what had happened to Kaori.

Of course, it wasn't her fault. Kaori had made her choice, and he had made his. It was no one's fault.

That wasn't the only reason for his frown, though.

It was the conflict building inside him.

He'd spent the last few months replaying their final moments together over and over in his head, believing he'd never see Thea again and wishing he hadn't wasted so much time.

Now he was here and so was she, but he couldn't stay, no matter how much he wanted to. He'd promised the Commander he would come back, and more than that, if he stayed, the Military would have even more reason to continue coming after her.

She had seen a future with him, a future that she wanted, but he didn't see how that future could ever become reality. Because of that, he couldn't allow himself to consider how he really felt about her or how she felt about him.

"We better take care of that shoulder," Gram said as Nix stepped out of the bathroom. "Lucan would kick my ass if he found out I let you run off with a wound like that."

Nix nodded absently and tapped his fingers against his leg impatiently as Gram applied ointment to the wound.

"You have another scar," Gram said, tapping the wound on his other shoulder. "What happened?"

Nix shrugged, then winced.

"Happened during one of our raids," he said, then frowned. "Did you contact Mel?"

Gram sighed.

"A lot's happened. They're okay, but we can talk about that later."

Nix nodded.

Gram placed a bandage on his shoulder, and Nix quickly threw on a clean shirt before reaching for the door.

"You sure you don't want to eat first?" Gram asked.

"Later," Nix said as he stepped out of the room.

Nix didn't know what he felt for Thea, but the one thing he was certain of was that he didn't want to spend another minute away from her. For so long, he'd done everything he could to avoid her. Now he couldn't get to her fast enough. He'd spent so many hours trying to tune out her thoughts. Now he clung to them like a lifeline. Tomorrow he would have to return to the Military. Tonight was all they had. He wasn't going to waste any more time.

"*I'm coming*," he transmitted.

He chuckled at her spike of nervous anticipation. Amidst all the conflict inside him, he felt the same.

He found her sitting on the low wall that circled the training arena. He had so many memories of this place and none of them were pleasant. When he saw her sitting there with her knees pulled up to her chest and her hair glowing in the moonlight he wanted to run to her, scoop her up in his arms, but instead he froze, unable to move.

Monster.

He wanted nothing more than to let go of the past, move forward, be with her—but maybe he didn't deserve that.

After all, everything that had happened to her was his fault.

The experiments.

Living in constant fear.

Her brother's death.

It would be better for her if he turned around and left right then, let her live a peaceful life here with Ryu.

Let her forget about him.

He took a step back.

She turned at the sound of his foot scraping against the ground. When he saw the fresh tears shining in her eyes, he couldn't turn away. His legs moved forward and before he'd realized what he was doing he'd pulled her down from the wall and into his arms.

"I'm sorry," a sob wrenched from her throat as she clutched the fabric of his shirt. "I'm so sorry."

For Kaori. For the way she'd treated him. For everything.

He squeezed her tighter and buried his face in her hair, wishing he didn't have to let her go.

He pushed her gently from his chest, just enough that he could cup her face in both his hands and rest his forehead against hers.

"There's nothing for you to be sorry about," he whispered as he wiped the tears from her cheeks with his thumbs.

She shook her head, and he pulled her into his chest again, holding her until her tears quieted. Once she was calmer, she pulled away from him, her eyes falling on his wounded shoulder.

"What about your injuries?" she asked, worried that holding her might be causing him pain.

"They're fine," he grumbled. "Gram insisted on bandaging my shoulder."

She laughed, her eyes searching his face in amusement.

"You know, I used to think you scowled like that all the time because you were angry, but that's just your natural look, isn't it? Turns out you aren't as scary as you let everyone believe."

His scowl deepened and she laughed again before leaning closer and kissing him on the cheek.

Nix pulled away in surprise and she brought her hands up to her mouth in shock.

"I'm sorry!" she said, her face burning red. "I'm sorry, I shouldn't have done that."

Nix didn't know how to respond. She'd done it because in her dreams she'd done it hundreds of times, and he'd kissed her just as often.

The truth was, he wanted nothing more than to pull her closer, crush his lips against hers and kiss her until he couldn't breathe, to let her fill the emptiness inside him with her love and warmth.

It took every bit of his willpower to stop himself, because it wasn't fair to her.

He was leaving. He couldn't give her the future she wanted.

But it was more than that.

He tried to tell himself that Kaori didn't deserve his grief after all she'd done, but the wound was there, nevertheless. Like the cut on his shoulder, ignoring it would only make it worse. He could use Thea like a salve or a bandage, but like any wound, only time could really heal it.

If he let her, he was sure she could ease the pain, stop the memories from bleeding out, but he didn't want to turn her into something to be used and discarded when he no longer needed her.

She deserved more than that.

Tears welled up in her eyes as his look of surprise turned to a hard scowl.

"I'm sorry," she whispered again and moved to leave.

He grabbed her hand and pulled her back toward him, crushing her against his chest. He buried one hand in her hair, his other snaking tightly around her waist as his lips brushed her neck, her ear, her cheek.

"Nix?" Her breath caught, making her voice crack.

Nix took a deep breath and pressed his cheek against her hair, stopping himself.

"*I'm sorry,*" he transmitted, not trusting his voice or his ability to say the right words. "*I'm not upset, I just...can't.*"

Sorrow filled her thoughts, sharp like another wound being ripped open.

Of course he doesn't love me yet. I knew that. I'm so stupid.

"*It isn't that,*" he transmitted.

He didn't know how to explain it to her.

"*I don't know who I am without her,*" he told her, even though he knew it wasn't the right thing to say, even though he knew it would hurt her. "*I've always ever been who she wanted me to be. I've spent most of my life just trying not to lose to her, but it was never enough.*"

Thea had accepted him, but he still didn't know if he could accept himself. He wasn't sure he even knew who he was or if he knew how to love someone else. Somehow, she seemed to understand, like the connection between them told her all the things his words alone couldn't convey.

"Thank you for taking me as I am, and as I was," he said, his voice a husky whisper.

She shook her head, and a fresh wave of regret crashed through her thoughts.

"I treated you so poorly for so long," she choked out, her shoulders trembling. "It wasn't fair. I projected all my fears onto you, and I never tried to see you."

He chuckled and squeezed her tighter.

"It's not like I made it easy. I'm sorry I ever pushed you away. I was an idiot."

"I guess we both were," she laughed through the tears wetting her cheeks again. "But we're both here now. That's enough for me."

He took a shaky breath and pressed his lips against the top of her head, not trusting himself to do anything more.

"Thank you for letting me take things at my own pace," he transmitted again.

He helped her climb back onto the wall before hopping up beside her. He wrapped one arm around her shoulders as they talked late into the night. Something inside him seemed to shift the longer he was with her—like thick, heavy shutters closed with rust and age being slowly pried open. Her thoughts poured into him like light into long vacant darkness. No matter how much he tried to resist it, he could feel her love, filling up the emptiness inside him.

Whatever else lay ahead, whether he could be with her or not, he knew one thing with certainty—he would never be the same again.

Nix had always been so quiet, so distant. They'd really only had one conversation before, and he hadn't said much. It surprised her that they could so easily talk for hours.

Nix told her about his time with the Military, about Mel, Commander Astley, and the rest of his team. She enjoyed watching his expression as he talked, the way his eyes lit up with amusement and the way a crooked half-smile would sometimes spread across his lips. She especially liked the satisfied look in his eye when she told him about her meeting with Ryu, like he was proud of her.

He told her about the time Kai figured out he had telepathy, and the way her thoughts were clearer to him. That was why he'd tried so hard to avoid her. She told him about her realization that her dreams were actually an ability. He laughed knowingly when she described her training with Gram.

"I'll have to pay him back for that," his deep voice rumbled against her ear.

She laughed. "I'm sure he'd say something like, 'I'd like to see you try.'"

When they returned to the main house, hand in hand, the night was already fading to the gray light of dawn.

"Did you eat?" she asked with a yawn as they reached Gram's room.

"Not since yesterday morning."

Thea shook her head disapprovingly and opened the door a crack. After seeing that the room was empty, she opened the door, and he followed her inside. She popped a meal into the microwave for him, then turned to leave. He grabbed her hand and pulled her back toward him, wrapping his arms around her from behind.

"Unlike you I'm still a mess from fighting," she said, unwinding his arms and looking back at him with a frown. "And you need to rest."

"Fine," he groaned.

She laughed at the scowl on his face.

"I'll make you something better in the morning," she said as the microwave beeped.

She knew she ought to go straight to sleep after her shower, but she returned to Gram's room instead. She wanted to say goodnight, at least. The room was quiet when she poked her head in. Two empty meal trays sat on the small table. She crept to the sleeping area and found Nix already asleep on Gram's bed.

She sat down quietly on the edge and reached out to brush the hair from his forehead, careful not to disturb him. She smiled. She still couldn't believe he was here. She didn't want to leave him, afraid he might disappear, but she was exhausted, and the next day was sure to be a busy one. She yawned and moved to stand up, but his hand grabbed hers and pulled her back toward him.

"Stay," he murmured sleepily before his breathing deepened again. Thinking he was asleep she tried to pull her hand from his, but his grip tightened. The truth was she didn't really want to protest. She sank down into the warmth of the bed and he wrapped his arm around her waist to pull her closer. With his body a solid comfort behind her she sank into a deep and dreamless sleep.

❖

"Good news everyone!"

Thea tried to sit up as Gram banged noisily into the room, but Nix's arm was still draped across her. She tried to disentangle herself from his hold, her face red hot with embarrassment. He groaned and held her tighter, burying his face in her hair. Gram's laugh and raised eyebrows only added to her embarrassment.

She finally managed to extract Nix's arm from her waist and hopped up from the bed without looking at Gram. She kept her face turned away from him as she busied herself with smoothing her hair and clothes in a preoccupied manner.

"Hey dumbass!" Gram bellowed, his voice unnecessarily loud. "Wake up! I said I have good news!"

Nix groaned again and closed his eyes tighter. He pulled a pillow over his head and turned his back to them.

A giggle escaped from Thea's throat at the display.

The sound got his attention. He sat up and squinted one eye open, still looking groggy and disoriented. Gram threw open the curtains and Nix's sleepy scowl turned to a tortured groan.

"What the hell are you shouting for?" he grumbled.

"I've got good news!" Gram told him, his voice still too loud.

"Good for you. Tell me about it later." Nix laid back down, his back towards them.

"Nah, you're gonna want to hear this one," Gram insisted.

Nix let out another groan and flopped onto his back with a wince. He draped one arm over his eyes, shielding them from the light.

"Fine," he said, "what is it?"

"We're prisoners!"

Nix pulled his arm from his eyes and let out a snort.

"Clever. I guess that means you didn't think it up."

Gram opened his mouth with mock hurt.

"Mel and I came up with it together, I'll have you know."

"That explains it then," Nix said, sitting up with a smirk teasing his lips. "Mel is smart."

"I'm confused," Thea interjected before their teasing could turn into an argument. "Why is being prisoners a good thing?"

"I'm technically still with the Military, and they still want this dumbass back," Gram told her, pointing to himself and Nix in turn. "Ryu took us prisoner so he can negotiate with them."

"I guess that makes sense?" She wasn't so sure. "Do you really think that will work?"

Gram shrugged.

"Dunno, but it buys us time. Otherwise, this idiot is likely to run off again."

Nix grimaced guiltily before scowling at Gram.

"You were planning to leave?" Thea asked, her hurt and surprise evident in her voice.

"I promised them I'd come back," he answered quietly, not meeting her eyes. "I figured last night was all the time I had."

"Sounds like you two need to talk," Gram said, clearing his throat. "You can thank me later!"

He left them with a wave over his shoulder.

"You should have told me," Thea said quietly, crossing her arms and not moving from where she stood.

"I was planning to tell you today." There was no defensiveness in his voice, only fact. Whatever his reasoning was, it made sense to him. He held his hand out, still not looking at her. "I'm sorry."

She sighed and crossed the room to sit next to him on the bed, her hand slipping into his. His shoulders relaxed as he interlaced his fingers with hers. He looked up at her with a frown as his eyes searched her face, and probably her thoughts.

"Why do you have to go back?" she asked him.

He was free now, wasn't he? Wasn't that the point of everything she had done?

She raised her chin stubbornly and snapped, "This had better not be about protecting me."

"It's not," he said quickly, then sighed while rubbing his forehead with his free hand. "They trusted me. I left them to find you, even though they needed me. I just feel like I have to go back. Once I do, I'm not sure I'll be able to leave again."

She was surprised. Whatever she had expected him to say, that hadn't been it. She hadn't thought there was any explanation she'd be able to understand, but with his words, all her anger melted away. She didn't want him to go, of course, but she admired his loyalty and honesty.

"Thank you for telling me that."

She resisted the urge to kiss his cheek and instead laid her head against his shoulder. He wrapped his arm around her and squeezed her tight against him as he took a deep, shaky breath.

"I don't know what the future holds for us," he said, his voice a quiet rumble that made her shiver.

She counted her heartbeats in her chest, waiting for him to continue. When he didn't, she straightened so she could see his face. To her surprise, he leaned in close, his face a breath away from hers. His eyes seemed to burn into her as he reached a hand up to cup her cheek, his fingers trembling against her skin. His breath was hot against her face, his lips nearly touching hers.

And then he pulled away.

"I don't want to hurt you," he whispered, his expression pained and conflicted. "*But I don't want to waste any more time. I don't want to push you away anymore.*"

Thea shook her head and reached up to press her hand against his.

"I trust you," she said.

He lowered his lips to hers, soft and hesitant, like he was afraid she would run away. She wrapped her arms around his neck and leaned into his kiss, a sigh of warm relief escaping her lips. He pulled her tighter against him as his lips moved to her cheek, her jaw, her neck, like he was convincing himself she was real. Then his lips found hers again, crushing, hot, and hungry. She realized then how much he'd been holding himself back. She let herself get lost in the feel of his touch, of his mouth on hers, his breath against her face, on her neck, back on her lips.

He was really here, and he wanted her.

Her head spun as he pulled away and rested his forehead against hers, his breathing heavy, and that crooked smile that she loved teasing his lips. She placed her hands on his cheeks and gave him another quick, soft kiss.

"I love you," she whispered.

His lips found hers again and determination welled up inside her. They were going to find a way. She wasn't going to lose him again.

A shot rings out and
The first body falls.

An attack,
Not from the enemy.

Battle lines fall
To disarray
As friend turns to foe,
And I know,
The only ones I can trust
Are the few by my side
Who've stayed by me
Even through my
Mistakes.

I've made so many,
And I wonder now
If it was worth it.

Will I get the chance
To make it right?

Will I meet the ones
I should have saved
In another life?

I form a wall to save
The friends at my side
And vow to tear down
The walls that have
Pushed them away,
To build a new life,
A new future,
So no one else
Will face the same choices
I had to make.

So no one else will have
To make my same mistakes.

Chapter Thirty-two

Nix stood stiffly away from the group with his arms folded tight across his chest and his eyes fixed on the flames leaping inside the furnace. He didn't react as Thea stepped close beside him, her arm brushing against his. His jaw clenched as Ryu and Nobu slid the coffin into the furnace. Thea reached up to place her hand on his arm, but he made no sign of acknowledgement.

Tears stung her eyes.

He was hurting, and she didn't know how to comfort him.

Gram stepped up on Nix's other side and clapped a hand on his back. He whispered something that she couldn't hear, and Nix's shoulders seemed to relax a little. He reached down and interlaced his fingers with hers.

"You okay?" she whispered, leaning her head on his shoulder.

He just shrugged.

No other words were spoken at Kaori's funeral. The five of them simply watched the flames consume her coffin and her body in silence, the mix of conflicting emotions almost tangible in the air.

Relief.

Guilt.

Regret.

Grief.

It seemed none of them knew quite what they were supposed to feel.

They stood silently until the hot fire inside the furnace burned itself out. Ryu stepped closer to them and gestured toward the house.

"Why don't you come into my office? We have much to discuss."

His voice came out thick, with a slight quiver, his pain evident in his inability to keep his tone flat.

"Are you okay, Ryu?" Thea asked.

Ryu gave her a small, sad smile and gestured toward the house again.

"I'm fine. Please, come inside."

Nix sat beside her on the couch in Ryu's office. Ryu sat across from them in one of the large chairs and Gram stood, leaning against the wall. Nobu hadn't joined them.

"I'm sorry we haven't been able to talk much in the last few days," Ryu said.

Thea shook her head.

"You've had a lot to do, and Gram has been filling us in."

"Then you know that the Military also faced internal conflicts similar to the fighting in Tanri."

Thea nodded.

"We still don't really know what happened," Gram said, "or how extensive the damage was. The rumors are that there was fighting in the capital, and that the Grand Marshal might have been killed, but no one knows for sure. Mel promised to send me the official report once she gets it."

Ryu pursed his lips, like he was still unsure whether he could trust Mel's information.

"The important thing is that the Military is in no position to continue their assault. They are retreating back to the Garrison to care for their wounded. I suspect they also want to be able to communicate with the capital. Their Commander, however, has agreed to a negotiation in one week."

"Commander Astley?" Nix asked.

Gram nodded.

"Commander Stewart was injured pretty bad, so Nolan's been given temporary command over the Garrison in her place, as well as authorization to negotiate with the Syndicate."

Nix nodded, rubbing absent little circles into the back of Thea's hand with his thumb.

"Do we know why both the Syndicate and the Military were attacked by their own people?" Thea asked.

Nix's thumb went still, and his body stiffened. His other hand balled into a tight fist in his lap.

"Kaori," he said quietly. "I'm sure of it."

"We don't know for sure yet," Ryu said, "but it seems likely she had something to do with it. Many of the prisoners she helped escape from here were soldiers. I'm sure her motives went beyond simply doing the Military a favor."

Gram nodded.

"Mel says the dissenters they captured all had different reasons for participating in the attack. Some thought they were helping to end the war. Some believed they were rooting out corruption. Some mentioned Kaori specifically. Said she promised them important positions in the Syndicate if they agreed to help her."

Nix ground his teeth, and Thea placed her free hand on his arm. He took a deep breath and relaxed his clenched fist.

"The Commander and the others are okay, though?" he asked.

Gram nodded.

"Jax was shot, but he'll be okay."

Ryu cleared his throat.

"Early reports suggest that many Research facilities were also attacked," he said. "If this is true, the Military may have even less reason to insist we return the two of you. If what Gram tells me about this Commander Astley is true, I'm hoping for a positive outcome at the negotiations. Maybe we can even put an end to this war."

Thea nodded absently. She felt Nix squeeze her hand as her pulse quickened. She squeezed his back, trying to sort through the ideas forming in her thoughts.

"You said the Research facilities were attacked?" she asked hesitantly.

Ryu nodded.

"I always wondered why Kaori wanted to kill me," she said quietly, her voice shaking as the inevitable memories resurfaced in her mind. Nix gripped her hand tighter. "It didn't make sense. If she was working with the Military, shouldn't she have been trying to capture me?"

"She was only pretending to work with the Military though," Gram said.

Thea shook her head.

"I know, but it still never made sense, why she wanted me dead so badly. She tried to convince me to join her, that night she came to the base. I guess she thought it wasn't worth trying to change my mind."

She saw Nix shaking his head out of the corner of her eye, already knowing what she was about to say.

"Do you think what she really wanted was to stop ability research?"

"There's no use trying to understand Kaori, or her motives," Nix growled, his voice harsher than he probably intended.

Ryu sighed.

"I believe there may be some truth to what you are saying," he said. "You wouldn't be the first research subject she's targeted over the years, for seemingly no reason. I don't believe she wanted others to suffer what our father had done to us."

"Then she went about it in the worst way possible," Nix muttered. He stood and turned toward the door. "I need some air."

Gram let out a sigh but didn't say anything to stop him. Ryu stared at the door for a long time, a conflicted expression on his face.

Finally, he cleared his throat and turned back to her.

"Gram will be going with me to the negotiation," he said, "but it will be safer for the two of you to stay here."

Thea nodded.

"We finally have a chance for peace," he continued. "It wouldn't be possible without your help. Thank you, Thea. Please know that I'll do everything I can to help you. To help both of you."

"Thank you, Ryu. Are you okay?"

This couldn't be any easier for him than it was for Nix.

"I'll be fine," he said.

His flat tone told her he wasn't fine.

He stood and left the room as well.

"That sounds like a guy who needs a drink. I'll take care of him if you go take care of that other idiot."

She shook her head.

"Do you think maybe I should let him be alone?"

"Nah, go on. We both know being alone only makes him more stupid."

Thea hesitated as she stepped out of the room. She didn't know what she was supposed to say to Nix once she did find him.

She still felt guilty every time the subject of Kaori came up. Kaori was gone, and for her that only brought a sense of relief. She couldn't hide that from him, and she worried that her feelings would only make his grief harder to process. She didn't want him to end up having to comfort her.

She shook her head and moved down the hall. He was hurting and she had promised herself that she wouldn't let him suffer alone anymore.

As she stepped outside the main house, she started making a mental list of the places he was likely to be. His voice entered her mind, along with an image of the training center.

"*I'm here.*"

She could sense a bit of resignation in his thoughts, and she bit her lip guiltily, convinced that he really did want to be alone after all, but as she neared, he reached out his hand with a smile that seemed genuinely glad to see her. She leaned her head against his shoulder with relief.

"You okay?" she asked tentatively.

He nodded. "I just needed to clear my head. I'm glad you came."

She didn't prod. If he wanted to talk, he would. If he didn't, she wasn't going to force him.

"It's just more evidence that I never really knew her," he muttered.

She turned to try to see his face, but the shadows made it hard to read his expression.

"I know you cared for her," she said finally. "That doesn't bother me. Regardless of what she did to me, and to Kai, I never want to pretend like she wasn't important to you."

Nix let out a sigh. When he spoke his voice sounded angry, though she knew that anger wasn't directed at her.

"Honestly, I don't know what she was to me, or how I'm supposed to feel. She looked out for herself and no one else. She betrayed me more times than I can count. Nothing can change that. It's just...hard."

His voice trailed off, its hard edge gone.

"I know," was all she said.

He wrapped his arms around her. She leaned into him as he buried his face in her hair and let out a shaky breath.

"*Sorry,*" his thought filled her mind. "*And thanks.*"

A shadow, a wraith, a ghost.
I've dwelt in darkness
For my whole life,
And now I wonder if
I can ever fully face the light.
Maybe I don't deserve this life
With you.
I wanted to change,
But maybe I was fooling myself,
And the only place I really belong
Is alone in a cell.
A weapon, a monster, a beast.
It's all I've ever been.
Cursed to live alone,
Even when others are near.
You broke the spell and
Made me believe I could belong,
But every day my memories
Remind me of what I've been.
Can I become someone who
Loves when I've only ever
Been someone who
Brings others pain?

Chapter Thirty-three

The rumors were mostly true. The Grand Marshal, as well as several members of the Military's ruling council had been assassinated. Marshal Barton had been voted as the next Grand Marshal. He accepted the position only as a temporary measure, stating that the attacks proved it was time for the Military and the government to change. He promoted Commander Astley to marshal and gave him full authority to act on his behalf at the negotiations with the Syndicate.

Gram and Nix were given full pardons. Nix was no longer considered a prisoner or a fugitive. Marshal Astley had even offered him an enlistment under his command, if he wanted it. Gram had not only been restored to his former rank but was given a promotion. He chose to return to the Garrison with the other soldiers, but he kept in touch and promised to visit Chusan again after things had settled down.

Nix, of course, had stayed with Thea in Chusan. Staying with the Syndicate wasn't his first choice, but staying with her was. She liked it there, and she liked helping Ryu.

That didn't make it any easier for him to be back. Though Ryu had ordered that Nix be left alone, most people weren't happy to see him walking around Chusan with Thea.

Monster.

He shouldn't be here.

Traitor.

Neither one of them belongs here.

Danger.

The clan leader is a weak-spined fool.

As the weeks passed, it became harder and harder for him to ignore the angry whispers, the threatening glares, or the resentment pounding in his head anytime Thea wasn't close enough to dampen the other thoughts around him. Every day was more difficult than the day before. There were too many memories he'd rather forget. Too many familiar faces reminding him of who he had been, of who he didn't want to be anymore.

A ghost who couldn't control his power.

A monster who didn't belong.

A weapon only good for fighting.

By the time a group cornered him on the street, it was all too easy to slip back into who he had always been, to let the anger and the adrenaline take control.

"Nix stop!"

Thea grabbed his arm and pulled him away from the man whose face was already swollen and smeared with blood.

He hadn't even heard her approach.

He leaned against the wall, breathing heavily, and turned as Nobu's heavy footsteps thundered into the alley.

"What happened?" he asked, his eyes narrowing at Nix.

"They attacked Nix," Thea said.

Though she hadn't seen it happen, she was certain. He wouldn't have done this without provocation.

Nobu didn't seem convinced.

"Is that true?" he asked.

Nix shrugged and turned to walk away.

Nobu grabbed his arm in his powerful fist and spun Nix around to face him. Thea's eyes went wide. She wanted to protest, but the truth was, she was a little afraid of Nobu.

Nix had been in this position too many times, with the large, powerful man towering over him, threatening him into obedience. Only Nix wasn't a child anymore. He grabbed Nobu by the wrist and squeezed, enhancing his strength to pry the man's hand from his arm. Nobu gripped his arm tighter, squeezing so hard Nix thought his bone might snap.

"Stop it," Thea squeaked.

"The clan leader tolerates your presence here, in spite of my objections," Nobu rumbled quietly. "I will not allow you to tarnish his name or violate his trust...the way you did to his father."

That's when Nix swung, his fist connecting with the larger man's chin, knocking him back. Nobu released his grip and reached for his sword, but Nix was faster. He pulled the larger man's sword from its sheath and held it to his throat, his teeth bared in anger.

"Stop it!"

Dust swirled around them, and a stack of nearby crates toppled over as Thea jumped forward, placing her hand gently, pleadingly on his.

Nix took a deep breath and dropped the sword.

"I'm sorry," he mumbled, then turned and ran.

Thea knew it hadn't been easy for Nix to be in Chusan, surrounded by so many painful memories and so many people who still resented him. She had hoped it would get easier as time went on, but instead she could sense him growing more distant, retreating back to the quiet, angry person he had been when they'd first met.

She didn't blame him. She only wished she knew how to help.

Now, as she climbed the steep slopes up the hillside outside of Chusan, a sinking worry settled in her stomach like she'd swallowed a stone. She was out of breath as she finally reached the top and found him sitting in the shade of the trees, as she had found him so many times over the last few weeks. He didn't look up as she approached, didn't reach out his hand or smile. He simply sat frowning at the valley below.

Thea knelt on the ground beside him. She reached out for his hand and placed it gently in her lap before wiping the blood from his knuckles with the medical kit she'd picked up.

"You saw the message from Gram?" she asked him, choosing not to talk about the fight.

Gram had sent word that he was planning to return to Chusan before leaving for the capital with Mel and the other soldiers.

Nix turned to her without meeting her eyes and the feeling in her stomach grew heavier.

"You're going with him, aren't you?" she asked before he could say anything.

Nix frowned and nodded.

"I hadn't decided until now," he murmured, "but I think it would be best."

Thea waited, expecting him to say more, hoping he would say more, but he didn't.

"Ryu wants you to stay," she ventured. He was upset because of the fight, because he felt like he didn't belong here. Maybe he just needed something to reassure him.

Nix scoffed and his face darkened.

"No, Ryu wants you to stay," he snapped. "He'd much rather I was gone, trust me."

"At least Ryu is trying."

The thought entered her mind before she could stop it. She closed her eyes with a grimace, hating that she'd thought it, and hating even more that he could hear it.

"I can't stay," he said, the pain in his voice unmistakable.

Sometimes she wished he wasn't a telepath. She hadn't meant to hurt him. She knew he was trying, and this was hard for him, but he wasn't the only one hurting.

She shook her head, trying to push her thoughts away before she hurt him even more.

Her eyes met his, and he held her gaze like he was searching for an answer to some question he hadn't asked. When he looked at her that way, it only made her feel anxious—and frustrated. It wasn't fair that he always knew what she was thinking, but half the time, she had no idea what was going on in his mind.

His eyebrows pulled together, and he frowned, a look of sad resignation on his face.

"I'm glad you'll be here to help Ryu," he said quietly. "He needs you."

His words held a certain finality to them.

He didn't want her to come with him.

Thea turned away, not wanting him to see the shock or the sadness on her face. His hand brushed hers, but she pulled away and stood.

"Thea," he said, but she didn't stop or turn back. She ran down the hill and back toward the main house, unable to stop her tears.

There was a tenseness between them after that, like all the Wilds were already separating them. Nix had never been talkative, but he spoke even less, usually only answering her with a shrug, or a few quiet words. He spent even more time alone, either in the hills or in the garage.

Thea missed the little gestures that she'd grown so comfortable with since they'd reunited. He still held her hand whenever they were together, but she missed the way he used to brush her hair behind her ear or kiss the top of her head. She missed his habit of rubbing little circles into the back of her hand when he was thinking. More than anything else, she missed his smile, the way one corner of his mouth would turn up and his blue eyes would light up like stars.

She supposed that once he was gone, she wouldn't have even his hand to hold.

Gram frowned as the three of them sat in her room.

"What's going on with you two, you back to fighting already?"

Apparently, the tension between them was that obvious.

Nix scowled, and Thea stood to leave. "I think I should let you two talk," she said quietly, trying to keep her voice from shaking. "I promised Ryu I'd help him with something."

It was a lie. She simply couldn't bear to listen to the two of them discussing a future that didn't involve her.

Gram seemed irritable after that conversation. His usual insults didn't feel like teasing. It felt like he meant them. This only put Nix in an equally foul mood. He was quick to snap at Gram's comments when he would have usually ignored them with only a roll of his eyes.

Thea knew she should feel upset that they were wasting their last few days together, but when she looked at the two of them sitting there, all she could do was laugh. Gram, sitting with his arms crossed over his chest, hunched in his chair with a pouting expression, and Nix scowling, pointedly trying to ignore him, was a sight that was too comically familiar.

"What?" Gram asked, curiosity pulling him out of his petulance.

"Please don't tell him," Nix sighed with exasperation. "It'll only make him more annoying."

This only made Thea laugh harder.

"I was just thinking about the first time I met you guys," she said as she tried to catch her breath. "You were fighting then too, weren't you?"

At the time, she hadn't known them well enough, hadn't understood their personalities or history. Now, as she thought back to that first meeting, she could see it in a new light.

Gram snorted, a trace of humor finally reaching his eyes.

"Well, this guy hasn't changed at all," he said. "He's still a dumbass."

Thea smiled and bit back another laugh. Gram's childishness hadn't changed either.

"And you still think you know what's best for everyone," Nix snapped.

He looked like he regretted the words before he'd even finished saying them. That hadn't changed either. He was still quick to lose his temper and say things he didn't mean.

The amusement faded from Gram's face and he sank back into sulking as Nix stormed out of the room.

"*Sorry*," she thought, feeling guilty for teasing them. "*I shouldn't have said anything.*"

"*Don't be.*" His thoughts were gentle. "*I just need to get out for a bit.*"

Gram tried to pull himself out of his sulking as he updated her about the ongoing negotiations and his life at the Garrison.

"Are you really okay with this?" he asked her suddenly, changing the subject. "Are you really going to let him leave?"

The question caught her off guard, cutting her like a knife. The tears came before she could think to stop them.

"Of course I don't want him to leave." Her voice shook and cracked as she spoke. "I want him to stay as much as I've ever wanted anything, but it's not fair of me to ask that of him. I know it's hard for him to be here."

"I get it," Gram said with a sigh. "I was worried about him staying here, and I think it makes sense for him to leave. The real question is why aren't you leaving with him?"

Thea looked away, wringing her hands in front of her.

"Because he doesn't want me to. I know it's hard for him to be around me because of his telepathy..."

Gram interrupted her with a long, loud laugh. It was the first real laugh she'd heard from him since he arrived.

"Ah, you two!" he exclaimed through his laughter. "You're perfect for each other, you know that? You're both a couple of dumbasses."

Thea wasn't sure whether to be offended or flattered.

"You haven't really talked about any of this have you?" he asked her with a grin.

"We talked, but..."

Gram interrupted her with a cackle and a slap on his knee.

"Oh, I'm sure. If I know Nix it was all, 'You know I can't stay,' without ever asking what you thought." Gram feigned a scowl and deepened his voice dramatically when he impersonated Nix. Then he clasped his hands in front of him and gave her a sad, wide-eyed expression. "Then I bet instead of telling him what you think you were like, 'I understand, Nix. I want you to be free.'"

Gram broke into another fit of laughter after finishing his impersonation.

Thea felt herself blush with embarrassment.

"We aren't like that," she said defensively, though the truth was their conversation had gone much the way Gram described.

"That's not a conversation!" Gram exclaimed, slapping his knee again. "The thing about Nix is...He's. A. Dumbass."

He accentuated each word as though he wanted to make sure she understood.

"If you don't tell him what you want, he's never going to get it. And I know what you're thinking," he said, holding up a hand to stop her from objecting. "He's a telepath. He already knows what you're thinking. The thing is, we're all thinking a million different things all the time. We can't control it. Thinking something doesn't mean it's what you've decided or that it's even what you want."

He eyed her as though daring her to disagree with him.

"But..." she didn't know what to tell him. She didn't even know what she wanted herself. Finally, she said, "Of course I don't want him to leave. But...I'm scared. I can't control what I think, and sometimes I think things that hurt him. I know my thoughts are clearer to him than most people's. What if he wants to leave because he's tired of it? I can't make him stay and I can't ask to go with him. It wouldn't be fair."

She had seen a future with him, but maybe this was all it was ever meant to be, a few fleeting weeks of happiness before they went their separate ways. It wasn't fair to bind him to a fate that only she wanted.

Gram shook his head.

"Those aren't the questions you should be asking me," he said. "Those are the things you should be telling him. You say you're scared? If you don't tell him what you want, then maybe the only thing he knows is that you're too afraid to take a chance on him. You're leaving him to make assumptions, and we both know he's not smart enough for that."

Thea snapped her mouth shut, her protests dying on her lips. Gram was right. She was an idiot. Why hadn't she realized it sooner?

"Well, that simplifies things for me," he said, standing and stretching his arms over his head. The grin on his face was unmistakable—his sour mood was gone, and he was planning some sort of mischief.

"What are you going to do?" she asked hesitantly.

Nix was already in a bad mood. She didn't want Gram to make things worse.

Gram's grin broadened with enthusiasm.

"I'm going to kick his dumb ass of course."

Nix groaned audibly as soon as Gram came into view, huffing from the exertion of climbing the steep trail. Nix had already known he was coming, of course. The groan was so Gram would know how annoyed he was by it.

"There's nothing to talk about," Nix said out loud.

Gram's conversation with Thea didn't change anything. He knew she liked it here. He knew her friendship with Ryu was good for her, that it helped heal some of the loss of losing her brother. He also knew she was afraid of being in a relationship with him. He couldn't expect her not to be.

He wasn't planning to leave her forever. He just wanted to give both of them some time.

"I don't want to talk," Gram said as he fingered his gun. "I seem to remember you throwing a couch at me. It hurt like hell! I don't think I've paid you back for that yet."

Nix crossed his arms over his chest and looked at Gram appraisingly. Maybe it wasn't a bad idea. He could use a way to work out some of the frustration Gram had given him over the last few days.

"You can try," he said smugly. "I doubt you'll succeed."

"You know, Luc has this whole theory that you've been holding back on me, and that I can't handle you anymore."

Nix's noncommittal shrug implied that Lucan was right.

"Guess I have to prove him wrong, don't I?"

Nix moved before Gram could draw his gun, disappearing behind a tree and shifting from trunk to trunk in an attempt to maneuver behind him. Gram fired between the gaps in the trees, the bullets ricocheting harmlessly off the trunks behind him. After a few missed shots, Gram began to circle, slowly, relying on his sensing to ensure Nix didn't surprise him from behind. Gram kept a few trees between them, making a speed attack difficult.

Nix grinned.

Yeah, Gram was good. That's what always made their fights so fun.

"Do you know what I think?" Gram called out as he lunged to the side in an attempt to get a clear shot of Nix.

"I thought you didn't want to talk?" Nix growled back, his grin fading.

He maneuvered to Gram's other side and found a clear path to close the distance between them.

"Now, what I think," Gram continued, ignoring Nix's response, "is that you're scared too. If anyone is going to mess up this relationship, we both know it isn't going to be her. I think you're afraid that one day Thea is going to wake up and realize she was actually right about you in the beginning. That she'll hate you all over again."

It was one thing to hear the thought in Gram's mind. He could ignore it more easily, shove it away. When Gram said the words out loud, he couldn't shut them out.

Gram fired.

"Shit," Nix muttered.

He tried to dodge, but it was too late. Before he could decide which way to jump, the first shot had already caught him in the shoulder. The second hit him in the chest, taking his breath away. Gram closed in. Nix tried to counter, but as usual Gram used his movement against him and Nix landed hard on his back.

"You cheated," Nix grumbled, panting as Gram stood over him with a smug grin.

"It's not cheating," Gram insisted. "It's called tactics. You should try it sometime."

Nix reached out and pulled Gram's nearest leg out from under him, knocking him onto his back. He sat up with a smirk, his elbows resting on his knees. Gram let out a groan.

"Don't think I won't remember this you little asshole," he chuckled.

Gram's face turned serious and Nix scowled.

"You love her." It wasn't a question. "You need to tell her, dumbass."

Gram sighed and ran his hand through his hair before continuing. "I've never seen you stupid happy like you are when you're with her. I'm glad for you. Whether you believe it or not, you deserve to be stupid happy. If you're afraid of screwing things up, well then, the first thing you need to do is go have a real, honest conversation with her about this. Because what you're doing right now is screwing things up. And just know, if you do screw this up, I will kick your ass for real. Because that girl deserves to be happy too, and for some reason that no one can understand, she's stupid happy when she's with you."

Gram stood up and stretched. He started to walk away but Nix made no move to follow him. He stayed sitting on the ground thinking about Gram's words.

"By the way," Gram called back. "I'm moving in with Mel. I'm not a peacekeeper anymore. Nolan's going to have to find someone else to take my job, I guess."

"*You dumbass*," he added mentally, thinking he had better not have to spell it out for Nix any more than that. Gram was giving him a solution, but it was up to him to decide what to do with it.

Nix pulled himself up and dashed past Gram, heading back to Chusan.

He hated when Gram was right. More than that, he hated letting Gram know when he was right. It would only make him that much more annoying in the future.

But the truth was, Gram was right. He was being a dumbass.

He ignored the glares and whispers as he burst into the main hall. He nearly bowled over a woman in the hallway, but he just mumbled an apology without slowing down.

Thea turned around when he entered the room, surprise and nervousness on her face. He swept her into his arms before she could speak. With relief and excitement erasing all the tension he'd felt the last few days, his mouth found hers and he pulled her tighter against him.

He released her when they were both breathless. It took her a moment to gather her thoughts, but he waited for her to speak first.

"I'm going with you," she told him firmly, as though she expected him to argue with her. She seemed surprised when instead he kissed her again.

"I want you to come with me," he said, unable to keep the smile from his lips. "I always did, but I didn't want to push you if you were having doubts. About us. I'm sorry I didn't talk things through with you."

He looked away, suddenly feeling embarrassed. She put her hand on his cheek and gently turned his face back toward her, shaking her head with a smile.

"I should have told you how I felt. I'm sorry. I..."

She paused as her eyes filled with tears. He held her tighter, not wanting her to pull away from him.

"The truth is, I am scared," she admitted, hanging her head to hide her tears, "but not because I have doubts about my own feelings. I know that I want to be with you. I love you and nothing can change that."

He pressed his lips against her forehead, wanting to kiss her again but not wanting to interrupt her.

"I know what it's like for you to be around me," she said, her voice shaking. "And I can't always control my thoughts. I don't want to hurt you. I don't want to be selfish."

"I want you to be selfish," he said quietly, his face half-buried in her hair.

"But—"

Kaori was selfish.

He shook his head.

"Kaori wasn't honest. Not with me or herself. If she had been either, things might have turned out differently."

"I'm sorry." Fresh tears slurred her words.

I hurt him again.

He pulled back from her enough to look into her eyes.

"All I want is for you to be yourself, to not hide yourself from me. Because there isn't anything about you that could turn me away."

"But I—"

He shook his head, cutting her off.

"I hurt you before. I pushed you away."

"It was my own stupid self that kept me away," he insisted. "From the beginning, I admired how sincere and genuine you were."

But I didn't see how good he was.

Didn't she know that she made him happier than anything else ever had or could? He supposed she didn't know because he had never told her. The realization made him feel self-conscious. He'd never been good with words. He cleared his throat, but his voice came out gruff anyway.

"I love everything about you, and I can't think of anyone whose thoughts I'd rather hear. I guess that's why Gram says I look stupid happy when I'm with you."

She laughed as she wiped the tears from her eyes.

"It's true," she said with mock seriousness. "Your face isn't nearly as scary as it used to be. I like that."

She rested her head against his shoulder and said, "I'm stupid happy when I'm with you too."

He tipped her chin up and lowered his lips to hers. His kiss started gentle but built along with his desire. His hands slid through her hair and down her back as her hands moved up his chest and under his jacket. He pressed her hips tighter against him before releasing her to let his jacket slide to the floor. She let out a surprised laugh as he scooped her up in his arms and carried her to the sleeping area.

As he set her down on the bed, his hand slid up her hip to her waist, his fingers finding the soft skin beneath the edge of her shirt. His lips moved slowly, brushing against her jaw and neck. He kissed her again before sliding his hands up her stomach, pulling her shirt up and over her head. Her fingers tangled in his hair as he kissed her again, a soft moan escaping her lips.

Reluctantly he pulled away, his eyes locking onto hers.

"Are you sure?" he asked. *"Are you sure you want this? With me?"*

"Yes," she thought trying to pull his face back down toward hers.

A smile spread across his lips as he bent closer.

"I'm going to have to hear you say it," he murmured against her ear. "I am a dumbass, after all."

"I want this," she whispered, her hands moving down his back and sliding under his shirt. "I want you."

His lips crashed against hers again, breaking just to let her pull his shirt over his head.

Their lips met again, then their skin, their bodies, their minds, not hiding anything or holding anything back.

It was freedom and ecstasy like he'd never felt before.

It was everything he had ever wanted, and everything he never thought he could have.

He really was a dumbass for ever thinking he could leave her.

It was a mistake he was never going to make again.

Sunlight sinks below the
Distant edge of day and the
Time we spent together
Comes to an end.

Light fades to night and
Though my heart is strong my
Hands are weak.
Too weak to hold yours.
My shoulders cannot
Share your burdens,
Neither can my legs
Carry me to walk
Beside you.

Day turns to night but the
Sun remains and
Comes again.
Life moves on
Even after sorrow.
Love turns to loss but
Joy remains and
Comes again
Whenever we seek to
Find it.

Chapter Thirty-four

"I hate Market Day," Nix said as he slid into the seat across from Gram and Ryu. He closed his eyes and pinched the bridge of his nose as the thoughts from the crowded streets and tavern hummed in his head.

Gram laughed and slapped him hard on the back, making his headache throb even more.

"Serves you right for leaving me to do all the work by myself so many times."

They sat at their usual table on the second floor of the tavern, overlooking the room below.

"How's Mel?"

As soon as Nix asked, Gram beamed enthusiastically and pulled his phone from his pocket.

"She's tired of course, but she and the baby are healthy. His name's Quin. Do you want to see a picture?"

"Not especially," Nix said, as he leaned over to look at Gram's screen. "Well that's a relief, he clearly takes after Mel. I was worried that he'd be ugly like you."

"Of course he takes after Mel!" Gram countered indignantly. "He's the cutest kid in the world!"

Nix snorted.

"Anyway, where's Thea? I want to show her."

"In the kitchen helping her father."

Thea had convinced her father, Jonah, to move to Karza so she could be close to him. She'd wanted him to live at the base, but he had insisted that he'd rather live in town. He'd been enough of a burden to her, he'd said. He wanted to work and feel useful again.

Nix owed Kay about a thousand favors for giving him a job at the tavern, and they never missed an opportunity to remind him, or to harass him for a bigger tip, even though Jonah was an excellent cook, and his food was always popular.

"I'm glad he came here," Ryu said. He'd been quiet until then, as he often still was around Nix. "It's been good for her."

Nix nodded. Thanks to continued treatments from Lucan, the physical consequences of her time in the research lab were nearly eradicated. Her traumatic memories still plagued her though, just as Nix's past would always haunt him. Kai's death remained a source of nightmares, and probably always would. Having her father close helped. So did her friendship with Ryu. He'd become like another brother to her.

Ryu had been more than a little disappointed when Thea had left with Nix. He wouldn't have tried to stop her, of course, but he had hoped she would choose to stay with him. He did his best to hide his feelings for her, but he couldn't hide them from Nix.

"How're things going with the council?" Nix asked, not wanting to dwell on something that would only put a strain on their still healing friendship.

"We've been officially sworn in," Ryu said, "but there's still a lot for us to implement and even more we need to decide. I believe things are going well, though. Public opinion toward the changes is mostly positive."

He paused and smiled at Gram. "Councilor Astley will be glad when Mel returns to work. I'm not sure he's ever going to forgive the two of you having a baby at such a busy time."

Gram laughed and said, "He'll get over it."

"I hear you've been having success rounding up insurgents?" Ryu asked Nix.

"Oh, he's been super successful," Thea said as she slid into the chair next to Nix. He took her hand with relief. Her proximity did a lot to relieve his headache. He didn't know why he ever thought it was a burden that her thoughts drowned out nearly everything else.

Still, he scowled at the mischievous look in her eyes.

"Apparently," Thea went on, "he's become something of a hero for the kids in the Western Territory, where we've been helping families from the Wilds resettle. They call him The Dark Soldier, Peacekeeper of Justice. He's the lone warrior who stood up to an entire army of Syndicate in order to protect the people of the Wilds."

Gram let out a laugh so loud, several nearby customers turned to give him disapproving glares.

"Now this I have to hear," he said.

"Do you really?" Nix grumbled.

"There was a village in the southern foothills that was attacked a while back by bandits, probably all insurgents," Thea continued. He couldn't be upset once her face lit up the way it was now, even if it was at his expense. "Fortunately, we were there, helping villagers prepare for resettlement. Nix helped with the bandits, and all the kids were really impressed. After they resettled, the story spread, growing each time it was retold. Instead of a few bandits, it became an entire army. Nix is basically a legend now. All the kids run out to see him whenever we show up. I'm pretty sure I've seen a few start to dress like him too, and this hair of his is becoming quite a trend."

"You mean this mess that he cuts himself?" Gram managed to choke out before laughing so hard he couldn't say anything else. Nix just scowled.

"It's ironic," Ryu said wistfully. "The Syndicate reduced to nothing more than villains in children's stories, when those same children belonged to Syndicate families not that long ago."

Gram cleared his throat, trying to maintain a serious face for Ryu's sake.

Those calling themselves the Syndicate were really just a group of disgruntled bandits dissatisfied with the new government. The Syndicate Ryu had been born and raised to lead, that his family had fought and died for, no longer existed. There was a part of him that felt a little lost without that aspect of his identity.

Nix understood all too well what that was like.

"Anyway," Ryu went on, clearing his throat, "Thea tells me the power station repairs are going well?"

Nix groaned.

"Thea exaggerates. Most of them aren't in good enough condition to be easily repaired. I don't have the time or the resources for that to be possible. I'm doing my best to get the ones with the least damage up and running."

Ryu nodded.

"Open trade between the Eastern and Western Territories is going to make life better for everyone, but what people here and in the West really need is communication and reliable electricity. I'll make sure this gets put on the agenda for the next council meeting. You ought to mention it to Councilor Astley as well," he said to Gram.

Ryu told them more about the recent council meeting as well as the progress Jax was making at the Garrison, training former Syndicate and Military soldiers together. Nix noticed the way his face reddened as he talked about one of the young soldiers he'd been spending time with. Nix hoped the budding relationship would lead to happiness for Ryu. He deserved it.

Thea and Ryu talked about making more improvements to the clinic in Karza, with the hope of eventually expanding it into a hospital. He'd heard Lucan mention it on more than one occasion and he smiled, wondering if he knew what an excellent advocate Thea was for him.

As they talked, Gram looked for every opportunity to refer to Nix as Dark Soldier or Peacekeeper of Justice. When Nix finally reached over and punched him hard on the arm Thea told Gram it was his own fault, even though she'd been the one to tell the story in the first place.

Thea gushed over pictures of Gram and Mel's baby. It seemed Gram had a never-ending supply even though their son wasn't even a month old. He was all too pleased by Thea's eagerness to look at each one. Nix couldn't help but smile at Gram's obvious joy, and even found himself leaning over Thea's shoulder to look at the pictures himself.

"So, when are you two going to get yourself one of these?" Gram asked as he showed off yet another picture of Mel and the baby fast asleep.

Thea's face turned red, and Nix rolled his eyes.

"You make it sound like something we can pick up at the Market."

Thea was normally in high spirits after visiting with their friends, but today she was quiet as they returned to the base.

Nix knew why.

"You're tired," he said as they unloaded the supplies they'd purchased in Karza. "You should go rest while I put these things away."

Thea shook her head. "I'm fine."

She wasn't fine.

Nix reached for her and pulled her close to him, taking the package from her hands before wrapping his arms around her.

"You overdid it today," he insisted. "I know you helped Gram and Ryu unload the supplies at the clinic before helping your father with the lunch rush."

Thea smiled and tried to push him away.

"Okay fine, you're right. I'll go rest after we put this stuff away, I promise."

Nix didn't release her. Instead, he tilted her chin up, forcing her to look at him.

"What Gram said is bothering you, isn't it?"

She tried to look away, but he placed his hand on her cheek gently, holding her gaze as he said, "We should talk about it."

Tears filled her eyes, and she pulled his hand from her face.

"What's there to talk about?" she said. "It's not what's right for us."

"What makes you so sure?" he asked.

She buried her face in his chest, and he placed one hand gently on the back of her head.

"I don't want to leave you."

Ever since hearing about Mel's pregnancy, Thea had been having the same dream. Though she'd gained more control over the ability, one aspect of the dreams remained the same—it wasn't always easy to tell the future from the past. Was it her mother who grew more weak and pale every day? Or was it her? Was it her father that she saw, sitting by her mother's bedside, worry and grief turning him into a shell of who he'd been? Or was it Nix?

Yes. She wanted a baby. She wanted a family with him. But not at the cost of losing what they had, of leaving him alone.

It's not like he even wants a baby.

He let out a soft chuckle, and she pulled away to look at him.

It was true that he'd never thought about having a family. He'd lived his whole life in the past. He'd never once thought he could have a future like this.

Family was something he'd never really had.

Sure, Gram and Lucan and Ryu were his family. Thea was his family.

He'd never realized he wanted more until she'd thought about it herself. But he did want it.

He wanted a family that was theirs and theirs alone.

He brought his lips down to hers, kissed her soft and gentle, then pulled away and met her searching eyes.

"You're enough for me," she said. "I'm happy just being with you, and with the others too. Our family is fine the way it is."

Nix shook his head, a smile on his lips.

"I think we should talk to Lucan about it," he said, his voice thick.

"Really?" she squeaked, a flash of excitement in her thoughts. She cleared her throat and shook her head. "I don't know. I—"

"I want a family with you," he said, "but only if that's what you want. If Lucan thinks it's safe, then I think we should try."

Thea threw her arms around his neck and kissed him. He squeezed her tighter then scooped her up in his arms and carried her from the kitchen toward the bedroom.

"We have to finish putting our things away," she protested. "And I have to make dinner."

He chuckled as he set her down on their bed and leaned over her. He kissed her forehead, her cheek, her lips. One hand trailed down her arm, slid over her waist and rested on her hip. She wrapped her arms around his neck again, pulling him closer. When he pulled back, her thoughts did not match her protests. He laughed and stood up with a smug smile.

"Right now, you have to rest, and I have to put our things away. Then I have to make dinner."

She threw a pillow at him as he left the room.

"There's something wrong with me, isn't there?"

She knew it. After the experiments and all the drugs that had affected her body, of course there would be something wrong with her.

Tears filled her eyes. As she stared down at the paper in front of her. Another negative pregnancy test.

She couldn't have children. She was sure of it.

She tried to tell herself it was okay. Their family was enough the way it was.

A sob escaped her throat, and Nix pulled her head into his shoulder.

"Sometimes these things just take time," Lucan said in his gentle, reassuring voice. "It's normal for a lot of people to not get pregnant right away."

"Is there anything that can help?" Nix asked.

"I can run some tests if you'd like, but the most important thing you can do is get lots of rest and try not to push yourself too hard. I can mix up some herbs for you that might help."

"Thanks," Nix said as he rubbed Thea's back comfortingly.

"Thank you, Lucan," Thea said quietly, still feeling too devastated to hope that anything would work.

Nix kissed the top of her head before holding out his hand to help her stand.

Thea appreciated that he never tried to comfort her by telling her that everything would be okay. He never tried to placate her with empty promises or reassurances. He was simply there, sharing in her pain.

"Lucan said you need to rest," Nix said later as she made dinner.

Thea shook her head with a smile.

"Of course you would like that bit of advice, wouldn't you?"

She turned around and planted a quick kiss on his frowning lips. He caught her hands before she could turn away.

"It's not my fault you're always pushing yourself too hard. Now I just have a good reason to get you to stop."

Thea laughed and pried her hands from his.

"That doesn't mean I should lie in bed all day."

He kissed the back of her head and moved beside her.

"Will you at least let me help?"

She handed him the knife in her hands and slid the vegetables she was cutting toward him.

"Always. Here, you can cut these for me."

Nix had always eaten prepackaged meals, because they were easy, and that was what Gram had done. With only a little bit of instruction from her, he'd picked up quite a skill for cooking. He even enjoyed it, and was always eager to help her in the kitchen.

"Cooking relaxes me," she said as she pulled more ingredients from the fridge. "Lucan also said I should try not to be stressed, right? If I sit still and do nothing, I'll lose my mind. So don't baby me too much, okay."

Nix laughed quietly.

"I get it," he said. "I'll try not to baby you if you try not to overdo it."

"Deal," she said as she bumped his shoulder lightly.

She knew neither one of them were likely to keep that promise.

She didn't mind too much, though. Even though she'd never liked being someone who needed to be cared for, she thought it was cute when Nix fretted over her. If she was ever going to let anyone baby her, it was going to be him.

She didn't know if Lucan had simply been right about her needing more time, or if his treatments had made the difference, but she finally did get pregnant.

Her pregnancy was difficult, just as she had feared it would be.

Constant nausea made it hard to eat, and she suffered from painful headaches. She could hardly walk without feeling dizzy, and her body felt weaker than it ever had, even after the experiments.

When she saw the frantic worry in Nix's eyes, she knew her worst fears had come true. She didn't argue when he suggested they rent an apartment in the city so they could be close to Lucan and the hospital there.

Gram teased Nix for being overprotective, but he fretted almost as much. Being doted on, worried about, and stuck in bed made Thea feel smothered. If she didn't lose her mind first, she was definitely going to lose her temper.

Every time she thought that Mel swooped in to rescue her. It seemed she had an endless list of tasks for the two men to do outside of Thea and Nix's apartment.

"Thank you," Thea told her one day as Mel quietly made her a cup a tea. "I love them, but sometimes I can't stand them."

Mel laughed.

"Don't worry, I felt the exact same way when I was pregnant, and I only had Gram to deal with. Here, this will help."

She handed Thea a tablet opened to an online shop for baby clothes and supplies. They spent the afternoon purchasing items Thea couldn't imagine herself ever using, even though Mel insisted they were essential. It was a nice respite and kept her mind off her anxiety and frustrations.

Their son Kai was finally born almost two years after that day in Karza when Gram had shown them pictures of his own son.

"Well, that's a relief," Gram said during his first visit to their apartment after Thea was released from the hospital. "He looks like Thea. I was worried he'd be scary like you."

"Hey, Nix isn't scary," Thea protested as Kai slept peacefully against her chest. "He's cute when he's all grouchy and scowling.

Nix scowled, as if to prove her point, which only made her and Gram both laugh. His face softened as he placed one finger against Kai's sleeping palm. Kai's tiny hand curled reflexively around his father's finger. Thea smiled, feeling happy warmth at the sight.

"I wouldn't want him to look like me," Nix said, his voice gentle when their teasing would normally make him gruff and irritated. "It would be a waste when his mom is so beautiful."

"Now that's a good response," Mel said, smacking Gram half-heartedly on the chest with the back of her hand.

"Hey, I basically told him the same thing when he said it."

"How childish do you have to be to wait two years to throw that line back at him. It's embarrassing!"

After Gram and Mel went home, Nix wrapped his arm around her shoulders. She leaned her head against him sleepily.

"*I love your grumpy, scowling face,*" she thought with a yawn, reaching her free hand up to his cheek.

"I love you, and our son," he whispered before kissing her gently on the forehead as he stroked Kai's soft, white hair.

"I think he looks like him," she said, thinking of her brother who shared her child's name.

She had lost her home, her parents, even her health. When she'd lost Kai she'd thought she had lost everything. Gram, Mel, Lucan, and Ryu had become her new family. She had a new home with Nix and their son. She had made mistakes, and she had regrets, but she hoped when she looked at Kai and said his name, when she told him the stories her mother had told her, she would remember the good things. She would teach him the lessons her losses had taught her: to forgive, to be brave, to love and let himself be loved, that change is always a choice and it's never too late to make it. She was sure she would never stop grieving for what she had lost, but with everything she had gained she knew she could keep moving forward.

Acknowledgements

First of all, thank you for reading! Your interest and support mean so much to me. This story is so close to my heart, and I'm thrilled to be able to share it with you.

This book wouldn't exist without a few special people. First of all, I'm so grateful to my brother for encouraging me to start writing in the first place. You told me to write something just for me, and so I did. This journey has been life changing and it all started because of you. Thank you!

Second, I want to thank my dear friend and fellow author, Emel Kae. Your encouragement has meant the world to me. Thank you for holding my hand through every existential crisis and for giving me so much helpful feedback. I would have given up on this story if it weren't for you. I appreciate you so much.

Finally, thank you to my husband for supporting me and being patient with me as I slowly descended into writing madness. Thank you for always asking me about my characters and my story, and for letting me ramble about it when I needed to.

I'm so grateful to the writing communities I've joined and the many friends I've made there. So many people have given me encouragement, advice, and support, I can't possibly list them all. Just know that if we've ever interacted on social media, I appreciate you.

Want more?

Visit my website

avrablake.com

Follow me on Social Media

@avrablake on Instagram

If you enjoyed this book please consider leaving a review.

www.ingramcontent.com/pod-product-compliance
Lightning Source LLC
Chambersburg PA
CBHW020007120726
47903CB00004B/1181